STEVE HEUZINKVELD

CUTTHROATS OF THE FALL

THE FALL SERIES BOOK FIVE

First published by Steve Heuzinkveld 2024

This novel is entirely a work of fiction. The names, characters and incidents portrayed in it are the work of the author's imagination. Any resemblance to actual persons, living or dead, events or localities is entirely coincidental.

Steve Heuzinkveld asserts the moral right to be identified as the author of this work.

First edition

ISBN: 978-0-6452886-6-7

This book was professionally typeset on Reedsy. Find out more at reedsy.com

Dedicated to my parents, Bernard and Claire Heuzinkveld, who were both sleeping when I called them in the middle of the night to say that the book was finished.

Thank you for supporting my dream of being an author.

Foreword

While this story is based on real locations throughout the United States, I have used fictitious names for some towns and neighborhoods, so that I can change certain aspects of these locations for the sake of the story.

Thank you, and enjoy!

CHAPTER 1

"Come on, we can take these guys," Taylor Seabrook whispered as she lay flat on her stomach, peering over the edge of the red rock ridge, staring down at a crowd of people working beside a bend in the river.

"There's too many of them," Riley Armstrong gave her a hushed reply as they hugged the barren hilltop. She narrowed her eyes at the group of men and women kicking up clouds of dust down below. "There's no way we'd be able to pull this off peacefully."

"Who said anything about doing this peacefully?" the freckled red-haired girl scowled sidelong at her. "If we're really gonna leave these guys alive after we steal their shit, then I can guarantee at least one of them is gonna nail us in the back as soon as we try to leave. Why should we leave it to chance? We've got enough ammo to kill them all twice – and we'd still have plenty of bullets leftover for the road."

"These people haven't done anything wrong," Heather reminded her little sister with an icy glare, despite her own grip on the late Everett Lawson's assault rifle. "We don't need their gas bad enough to kill them for it. And besides..." she

1

nodded towards Riley, "That's not her style."

"Fuck style," Taylor seethed, saliva spitting from between her braces and sizzling in the arid dirt. "We're gonna have to leave this river sooner or later. And I'd rather be driving across the desert in a car with some air-con – not pedaling on a fucking bicycle in the middle of a Nevada summer."

Riley found herself agreeing with the girl.

There was an end point to the river that they had been traveling along.

And even if they loaded themselves up with as much water as they could carry, she knew that they would stand a far better chance of crossing the desert to California if they had a car.

But finding a vehicle wasn't the issue.

The problem was finding the fuel.

Until now.

Riley watched as the small crowd of ragged survivors hurried to and fro down below, hauling red diesel drums from the back of a truck and rolling them down to the riverbank, where the waterway took a sharp turn.

A pair of panic-stricken men feverishly loaded up the barrels onto an idling motorboat before jumping back aboard, ferrying their precious cargo across the river's bend, towards another big rig waiting for them on the other side.

"Hustle, y'all!" one heavyset woman yelled as she clambered down from the closest truck's cabin, waving her arms at the others. "I just heard them over the radio. They're coming up fast. We don't have much time left!"

"Just a couple more trips and we're outta here!" another woman hollered above the ensuing shouts of alarm. "We can hold them off for a while, but we need to take as much fuel as we can carry. We've only got one shot at this – let's make it count!!"

Riley bit her bottom lip.

Whoever these people were, they were expecting company.

Hostile company.

If the startled crowd was to abandon the rest of their cargo now, then a brief window of time would open up for Riley's group to pick through whatever had been left behind.

But if the three women made their move too early, or if they lingered for too long down below, finding themselves cornered along the river's elbow, then it would only take a few bullets fired from either side to launch the whole payload sky high.

"No, this is too risky," Riley finally decided, slowly retreating from the ridgeline. Safely out of sight, she rose to her feet and dusted off her black singlet and shorts – the only clothes that she could find to combat the heat. "If there's another group out here that's already coming after these people, then I don't want us getting caught in the crossfire."

The two Seabrook sisters shared a conflicted glance, but they followed her lead back down the slope all the same.

Only a short distance upstream was a small cove – hidden from view on both sides of the river bend – where they had parked their pontoon and all of their gear.

"We're gonna wait it out though, right?" Heather asked, leaning her weight on Taylor as she hobbled back down towards the boat. "We can just sit back, wait for this other group to come through and take what's theirs, and then we'll grab whatever they leave behind."

"You wanna loot their corpses?" Taylor frowned sidelong at her sister. "We need *fuel*, not whatever shit they've got in

3

their pockets."

"We'll have to see how this plays out first," Heather replied as she sat down on a rock. "Let's say these guys manage to get outta here alive. They've got the keys to the truck. And whoever's chasing them just want the fuel, right? Maybe they can't carry it all in one load, and they'll have to make a second trip. Or, maybe they can, so we siphon fuel from the truck's engine instead. Failing that, we can still stick to Plan A and just float on by."

"That's if these guys can even escape," Riley began as she climbed aboard the pontoon. "What if it's not just about the fuel? What if whoever's chasing them searches the area for survivors? And what happens if some trigger-happy nut-job hits one of those diesel drums when the bullets start flying?" she shook her head before tossing their heavy backpacks over the side of the boat into the dirt, "Too many *ifs* for me. So gear up – we're going cross-country now."

"It's way too soon though," Taylor argued as she picked up her pack, dusting it off hotly. "We're still at least a couple days out from the Hoover Dam. If we leave the river now – and we're not stupid enough to go off-road across the desert – then we're gonna have to take the highway. We'll be going straight through Vegas."

Riley paused with her backpack in hand.

The girl was right.

Over the past three months that it had taken for Heather's wounded leg to heal enough for travel, they'd had plenty of time to plan out their route.

But while discussing their possible pathways from Utah to California, they had always agreed that Las Vegas was the one place that they wanted to avoid.

4

After one year in the post-apocalypse, the City of Sin was certain to have become a breeding ground for all sorts of deviants and desperadoes – no doubt far worse than it already once was – making it a veritable hellscape for three young women.

"We don't have a choice," Riley's gaze flicked between the two sisters as she shouldered her backpack. She turned towards their three mountain bikes stacked in a pile on the other end of the boat. "There's at least a dozen people down there, and they're running scared from somebody. I'd say that's a good enough reason for us to leave while we still can."

"We could always hit one of those diesel drums ourselves," Heather smirked as she limped over to her backpack in the dirt. She shrugged with indifference, "Who cares if they come after us next, Riley? It's not like we can't hold our own."

The pair of women locked eyes, with the fiery redhead drumming her fingers against the side of the assault rifle hanging from a strap around her neck.

"Look, these guys are probably gonna kill each other anyway," Taylor chimed in, hoping to hurry them towards a decision. "Whoever's left standing after the fight is gonna be down on both bullets and people. If we hold them at gunpoint while they're still counting their corpses, and we tell them that all we want is one barrel of fuel, do you really think they're gonna argue?"

Riley flexed the slender muscles of her jaw.

Her gaze slid sideways towards the barren hilltop.

Nobody would see them watching from the ridgeline – the two groups would be too busy fighting with each other.

And even if somebody did notice them, at least they'd be

holding the high ground.

"Fine, we'll watch and wait for an opportunity," Riley conceded as she picked up one of the mountain bikes anyway, lifting it over the side of the boat and passing it down to Taylor. "But if I say we need to move, then the two of you better be ready to haul ass."

CHAPTER 2

Riley Armstrong and the Seabrook sisters lay side by side behind the red rock ridge, backpacks strapped and mountain bikes standing only a few yards away – just in case.

They watched as a cloud of dust rose up on the horizon, looming larger as it closed the distance to the river's elbow, like the angry thunderhead of an oncoming storm.

Riley's shoulders shivered as a sudden chill ran up her spine, despite the dry summer heat of the midday sun bearing down on the three women.

But it wasn't the sight of the surging dust cloud that was setting her nerves on edge.

It was the music.

Long before they could even hear the engines rumbling in the distance, a cacophony of discordant war drums pervaded their ears, clashing with the sounds of blaring horns and guttural chanting, almost as if a legion of otherworldly creatures were tearing across the desert, intent on claiming the souls of the fleeing fugitives.

Riley pitied the people down below.

Not because they looked like a group of innocents who had

never wronged anybody in their entire lives.

She highly doubted that was the case.

In fact, they had probably crossed the very same people who were now pursuing them.

But still, Riley pitied them, because of how poorly they had prepared themselves for the incoming attack.

There were no sentries – only frequent glances over their shoulders.

None of them had their weapons in hand – they were more preoccupied with rolling all of the diesel drums down to the riverbank.

And there was nothing to hide behind – they hadn't even thought about moving their truck lengthways across the dirt road to obstruct the approaching vehicles.

It seemed that the apparent leaders of the small band of fugitives were more focused on ferrying the last of the barrels across the river, rather than the people themselves.

"Maybe we should give these guys a hand," Riley muttered as she drew her pistol from the holster on her hip.

"I was thinking the same thing," Heather agreed, the barrel of her assault rifle already pointing towards the encroaching cloud of dust.

"But what happens when we shoot," Taylor voiced her doubts, just as they began to feel the culminating *thrum* of engines shaking the ground underneath them, "And the people we're trying to protect start fucking friendly-firing at us instead?"

But there was no time left for them to second-guess their resolve.

The infernal music had already reached its horrible crescendo.

The column of vehicles crested a rise in the dirt road, their windshields flashing in the midday sun.

A semi-trailer led the charge, the bass-filled boom of its horn filling the air as it thundered towards the group of survivors down below.

Next came four pickup trucks, each one bearing a mounted turret in its cargo bed, the long barrel of a heavy machine gun jutting out over each truck's cabin like a scorpion's tail.

And bringing up the rear of the mobile artillery was a long bus with its top sawed off, carrying a post-apocalyptic war party of beefy brutes brandishing an array of shotguns, assault rifles and sub-machine guns.

"Oh shit, y'all, that's me out!!" one heavyset woman panicked, shouldering past another survivor as she hurtled towards the motorboat idling on the riverbank. "Fuck out the way, bitch! I ain't dying today!!"

The small crowd descended into chaos as they scrambled for safety.

"We can't all fit on the boat!"

"Weapons up, let's buy us some time!"

"Fuck that – I'm swimming!"

Cracks of gunfire rang out as a few of the fugitives rushed to form a defensive line.

The driver of the oncoming semi-trailer threw open his door, climbing out halfway as he held the steering wheel steady, even as his windshield shattered in the hail of bullets.

The madman grinned in the wind – as if he was daring death to take him – before leaping down from the driver's cabin and rolling in the dirt.

The empty semi-trailer plowed into the back of the parked truck, the two heavy vehicles tearing each other to shreds as the big engine bulldozed its way through rending metal.

BADOOM!!

The ground trembled in the thunderous explosion.

Riley hugged the hilltop, turning away from the blazing flash of light.

A wave of angry heat washed over her back as debris from the blast rained down from above, flaming fragments landing all around them.

"Oh, fuck!" Taylor flinched backwards as she stared up at a jagged shard of metal, half-buried only a few inches away from her face.

The barrel of Heather's assault rifle shook as she tried to blink out flecks of dirt from her eyes.

Heart hammering in her throat, Riley squinted against the black cloud of smoke as it billowed up towards them from the wreckage. Keeping a firm grip on her pistol, she traced the silhouette of one of the pickup trucks roaring through the haze.

KAK-KAK-KAK-KAK-KAK!!

Before she could even line up her shot, the heavy machine guns opened fire, spraying the dazed and disoriented fugitives with overlapping streams of hot lead, tearing their torsos in half before their knees could even hit the ground.

Riley's eyes went wide, her gaze fixating on the scattered bodies as the smoke cleared, rivulets of blood forming to flow down into the river, tainting the water with the foaming flood of crimson.

The truck idling on the far side of the river turned its wheels, the other fugitives cutting their losses and kicking up a cloud of dust, even as some of the survivors still swimming across the water screamed in their wake.

Only the four mounted turrets answered their calls.

Riley stared along the top of her pistol, holding one of the gunners in her sights.

But even with her finger on the trigger, there was no point in firing.

The massacre was already over.

The bus at the back of the cold-blooded convoy rumbled to a stop behind the smoking ruin of the semi-trailer, the troop carrier's engine muffled only by the infernal discord of trumpeting horns, war drums and guttural chanting still emanating from the bowels of its cargo hold.

"Riley?" Heather's husky voice drew her back to the red rock ridge, her striking green eyes clear and ready for combat. "Are we still doing this?"

"It's a little late for that now," Taylor stared hard at the carnage down below. "We might still be able to get some of that fuel though."

Riley followed the freckled girl's gaze towards a few of the red diesel drums bobbing up and down along the river, floating among a cluster of dead bodies as the current carried the bullet-riddled corpses downstream.

"No, we don't stand a fucking chance against these guys," Riley breathed, admitting defeat. She flipped on her pistol's safety lever and holstered the weapon, before glancing pointedly at the dozens of brutes shuffling off the bus, scouring the area for any lingering action. "If they catch the three of us up here, we're dead."

CHAPTER 3

"What the hell did we just walk into?" Taylor finally broke the silence as soon as they were at a safe distance away from the bloodbath, riding their mountain bikes across a barren plateau.

"I guess they stole from the wrong people," Heather's voice vibrated as they pedaled along a rugged dirt trail.

"They didn't look like people to me," Riley called back over her shoulder, keeping her eyes trained on the narrow path ahead as they neared the edge of the plateau. "More like animals, if anything."

The three gear-laden women followed the bike trail down the side of the mountain, taking their time around the sharp twists and turns, and squeezing the handbrakes for every sudden drop, knowing that even just one slip-up along the steeply sloped track could lead to their deaths.

The craggy landscape from Utah to Nevada was packed with perilous playgrounds destined for thrill seekers and adrenaline junkies, but with the amount of food that they had left, it was the only route that Riley and the Seabrook sisters could afford to take.

After months of being unable to find any fuel for a vehicle, they had been forced to rely on river currents to carry them west instead, passing by a plethora of long-abandoned recreational areas along the way.

Stopping to shelter in ransacked boat houses and maintenance sheds, they had managed to scavenge some useful supplies along the river, upgrading their watercraft and picking up new equipment all the while.

But now that they were down to whatever they could carry on their backs, Riley hoped that it would be enough to see them safely to California.

"How's that leg holding up?" she asked, glancing back as they reached the bottom of the slope, where the dirt trail turned into a rough gravel road.

"Better than it's ever been," Heather smiled sarcastically, wincing slightly as she bounced in her seat. "If it was bad, you'd know about it. Let's keep going. It's not like we have much of a choice out here anyway, right?"

"Not really, no," Riley admitted as she surveyed the arid terrain.

Scattered shrubs of sagebrush, greasewood and cacti dotted the sparse landscape, but besides a dumped sun-bleached couch way off in the distance, there was nowhere for them to stop and rest among the desert scrub.

"I'll bet there's a bunch of unmarked graves around here," Taylor ventured as they passed by a set of tire tracks leading off into nowhere.

"Yeah, back when people actually bothered to bury their kills," Riley stifled a cough as she sucked in another lungful of dust.

Still working her bike's pedals, she reached down to grab

13

some water from the bottle cage, biting it open and taking a swig as she tried to remember the last person she had buried.

It can't have been that long, her eyebrows furrowed as she cycled through all of the dead faces she had seen over the past year.

Riley clicked the water bottle's lid shut as she realized – the only person she had ever buried was her father, Nolan Armstrong.

Every other corpse had either been cleaned up by somebody else, burned to ashes, or simply left behind to rot.

Just like the people who had been massacred back at the river.

"We're gonna have to find somewhere to hole up for a while," Riley decided at the end of her thoughts, squinting into the desert's shimmering distance for a good location.

It was still early in the afternoon, and they had plenty of daylight left before they would have to set up camp for the night, but she didn't want to take any chances.

"Well, you're the one carrying the tent," Taylor prompted, as if she needed reminding.

Riley's shoulders were already chafing underneath the weight of her heavy backpack, tent bag and sleeping bag, the collective burden rubbing her skin raw around the straps of her black tank top.

"Just look for somewhere that isn't out in the open," she ignored the touch of mockery in Taylor's tone. "I don't want us getting spotted by those fucking war wagons back there. We're gonna have to hold off on hitting the freeway for a day or two as well, just to be safe."

"A day or two," Heather echoed skeptically. "Are you sure we can afford to waste that much water on waiting around in the middle of nowhere?"

"We'll be fine," Riley reassured her, having learned how to study the local maps in order to track their journey's progress. "There's another river west of here that feeds into Lake Mead. It runs underneath a bridge on the freeway – we're not gonna miss it. We'll ration the water we have, and when we're ready to move again, we'll make a stop by the river to refill."

"As long as you're sure," Heather huffed as the gravel road gave over to cracked asphalt. She breathed a sigh of relief, "Finally back on solid ground."

"Hey, looks like we might not even have to set up the tent," Taylor grunted as she caught up to ride side by side with Riley. "You wanted somewhere outta the open. Check that out."

Away on the left, a group of tin roofs glinted in the afternoon sun, and whitewashed concrete walls soon materialized, emerging from the blur of the shimmering heat.

"I'll take concrete over canvas any day," Riley replied, easing up on her bike's pedals with a glad smile.

They had ridden farther than she thought, having reached the outskirts of a small town. And from the local maps, she knew that all of the towns in the area were situated along the same river that she had been hoping to find.

She was about to say something else, when her words caught in her throat.

Because blending in with the buildings in the distance, a big white van was driving parallel to the three women, matching the speed of their mountain bikes.

CHAPTER 4

"It's gaining on us!" Taylor shouted into the wind as they rode their bikes into the outskirts of town.

Hurtling towards a street corner lined with overgrown hopbush shrubs, Riley chanced a glance over her shoulder.

The bulky white van was rapidly closing the distance between them, rumbling along a dirt road and sending up a cloud of dust in its wake.

Riley tore her gaze from the vehicle just in time to take the turn, leaning her entire body to one side as she hit the corner at full speed, still pumping the pedals as the wall of yellow hopbush streaked past her peripheral vision.

"I can't keep this up!" Heather panted from the rear, lagging behind. "We're gonna have to make a stand soon, or my fucking leg's gonna give out on me!"

"We can't stop here!" Riley called back as she scanned their surroundings.

On their left was the row of overgrown shrubs.

And on their right was a barbed wire fence, with half a dozen hangars along the side of a small airfield in the distance.

They didn't have a choice – they had to keep going.

The sound of wheels screeching reached their ears as the big white van mounted the road, burning rubber across the asphalt, the voracious vehicle vaulting after the three young women.

"In here – quick!!" Taylor yelled, squeezing both of her handbrakes simultaneously.

She swerved into a gravel driveway at the end of the hop-bush shrubs, the sudden loss of traction sending her bike's tires skidding out of control, launching her sideways into the dirt.

"What the fuck, Taylor!?" Riley spat as she clamped down on her own brakes, her rear wheel grinding to a halt.

They had stopped at the entrance of a cemetery, with its double gates standing wide open, as if it was waiting to wrap them up in its cold embrace.

Forced to linger while Taylor recovered from the crash, Riley planted both feet on the ground and drew her pistol, flipping off the safety lever and turning at the torso to take aim at their pursuers.

"WATCH IT!!" Heather shouted as she turned into the gravel driveway, peeling straight past Riley's line of sight.

Jerking up her barrel for a fleeting moment, Riley took aim at the oncoming van again.

Lurching around the corner, the vehicle was already in firing range.

Cracks of gunfire smacked Riley's eardrums as the pistol barked in her hands.

A series of small spider webs exploded across the black windshield with each bullet.

But the glass didn't shatter.

Instead, the van's engine revved even harder, its driver

gunning straight towards her.

Riley's pupils dilated as the roaring vehicle loomed larger, unbothered by her bullets.

An icy bolt of adrenaline surged through her veins, and she threw herself off the bike, leaping for the gravel driveway just as the van tore past, mangling both her bicycle and Taylor's behind it.

"Move your fucking legs, bitch!" Heather yelled, hugging the stock of her assault rifle to her shoulder.

Riley rushed headlong through the cemetery's entrance as the fiery redhead let off a burst of bullets, three rifle rounds ripping through the air.

"Oh, shit," Taylor's voice cracked, cradling her grazed arm as she stood staring beside her sister.

Despite Riley's skin glistening with sweat, a rash of goose-flesh budded up her arms as she spun around to see the big bulky vehicle slowly turning in a wide circle.

Her mouth went dry as she realized that they weren't being chased down by a van at all.

It was an armored truck – the type that a bank would have used to transport cash.

And nothing short of an explosion was going to breach its bulletproof shell.

"Aim for the tires!" Riley shouted as the truck bulldozed through the barbed wire fence on the other side of the road.

"What do you think I was aiming at?" Heather hissed sidelong at her, firing off another burst of rifle rounds all the same.

Riley whipped up her pistol as the truck came around, squeezing off a few shots of her own at the front wheel, but with little effect.

The reinforced tires just kept on turning, perfectly capable of driving on punctured treads by design.

Rusty metal hinges whined above the rumbling of the vehicle's engine as Taylor swung one of the graveyard's gates shut.

"That's not gonna make a difference," Riley seized the girl by the arm before she could cross over to the other gate. She locked eyes with Heather, "Get moving!!"

Stowing away their weapons, the three women took off up the gravel driveway towards the cemetery's burial plots, their cumbersome gear still weighing heavily on their backs.

The armored truck revved its engine menacingly in their wake, ramming through the entrance with ease, the flattened gate barely even leaving a scratch on the grille.

"You think they're with the same guys we saw earlier?" Heather huffed as she pedaled, gearing down on her mountain bike to build up speed along the rocky road.

"I don't hear that weird-ass music," Taylor glanced down at her grazed arm as she ran, the wound from her bike crash scored with a grid of bloody grit.

"I don't care who they are," Riley fumed between breaths. "If they wanna steal our shit, then they're gonna have to get outta that truck and fight us for it."

"Yeah, that's if they don't run us down first," Heather replied as the truck tore up the gravel road behind them. "What's the plan here, Riley?"

There was no way that they could outrun a vehicle.

Especially not with all the extra weight they were carrying.

And with the armored truck bearing down on them, she had to decide quickly.

"Stay off the road!" Riley set their first priority, shoving

19

Taylor sideways.

Not wasting any time, Heather turned to follow her little sister towards the burial plots, steering her bike in between the headstones.

Wanting to throw off their pursuers, Riley split off in the other direction, pumping her legs past rows of bronze plaques and wooden crosses.

Gravel crunched underneath the truck's tires as it slowed to a steady roll, skulking through the cemetery like a prowling predator, searching for the weakest link among the three targets.

Panting slightly, Riley switched her pace to a brisk walk, wary of expending too much energy without knowing where she was headed. She dropped one hand to the holster on her hip as well – just in case one of their pursuers decided to crack open a door for a pot-shot.

Shading her eyes against the harsh glare of the afternoon sun, she scoured the far reaches of the graveyard for somewhere to make a stand, hoping to find something with solid walls, like a storage shed or a mausoleum.

But between the untended plots and the hopbush shrubs lining the edges of the cemetery, there was nothing but tombstones.

"We found another way out!" Taylor called from across the graveyard, as if on cue. "Come on, Riley!"

The armored truck's engine growled in response, daring her to make a move.

Riley swallowed.

Slipping out through an exit was the next best thing to making a stand.

But only if she could manage to get past the bulletproof

behemoth.

Flexing the slender muscles of her jaw, Riley set her sights on a T-intersection up ahead, and she began jogging towards a smaller gravel road perpendicular to the main driveway.

The truck rumbled with renewed vigor, its wheels kicking up clouds of dust as it gave chase to the lone woman.

Riley slowed to readjust the straps of her backpack and camping gear as she neared the side road, the collective burden chafing against her raw shoulders.

The armored truck seized advantage of her momentary distraction, speeding around the corner of the intersection to catch her off guard.

Hey, I think we've got a bite, Riley snorted in between breaths, before veering back towards the main driveway, running straight past the rear of the truck as the big bulky vehicle lost her within its own turning circle.

"Let's go, Riley!" Heather yelled from an opening in between the hopbush shrubs.

The two Seabrook sisters had found the pedestrian access for the caretaker's shack.

Riley was only a few dozen yards away, when her ears pricked up at a series of *clacks* behind her, with each one louder than the last, the sounds somehow more sinister than the angry revs of the truck's engine.

Don't tell me there's a hole in my bag, she dreaded the thought of losing a third of their supplies through a hole in the bottom of her bulging backpack.

Chancing a glance over her shoulder, Riley's heart leapt up into her throat.

The white armored truck was gaining on her, knocking over tombstones and grave markers in its relentless pursuit, already mere inches from devouring her shadow streaking across the ground.

Ducking her head down into her chest, Riley sprinted towards the opening in the wall of overgrown shrubs, despite the growing ache of her own gear bouncing hard against her lower back.

With the truck's engine roaring in her ears, and the heat of its grille breathing down the back of her neck, Riley bolted in between the hopbush shrubs without a second to spare.

The hulking vehicle slammed hard on its brakes, but not fast enough, crashing into the natural barrier and showering the three women with an explosion of yellow flowers and leaves.

"Eat shit and die, motherfucker!!" Taylor shouted, flipping the bird at the black windshield as the truck shifted into reverse.

"Close call," Heather remarked, with a slight smile playing at her lips. "Maybe you should've stayed on your bike."

"Forget the bikes," Riley breathed hard, narrowing her eyes at the path of destruction that their pursuers had left behind. "I want that truck."

CHAPTER 5

"You're kidding," Taylor frowned and smiled at the same time as they crossed the street towards a double-story brick-lined building.

"You got a better idea?" Riley asked, pointedly glancing around at their limited options.

Situated in the outskirts of town, the area surrounding the cemetery was largely empty, with the exception of the tin-walled caretaker's shack, and a paint-peeled motorhome parked in the neighboring dirt lot.

The nearest housing estate was at least a mile across open ground, and with the white armored truck patrolling the surrounding streets, there was no way that the overburdened trio would be able to scramble to safety in time.

"No, I just mean the name," Taylor nodded towards the racy billboard towering above the building. "*Lap Doll Lounge* – they may as well have just called it *The Sleazy Strip Club*."

"I've never known a strip club to be anything other than sleazy," Heather snorted with a twitch of her eyebrows. Winking sidelong at Riley, she added, "Come on, let's go see if they're still doing afternoon specials one year into the apocalypse."

"That's if your sister can even get in," Riley joined in on the joke, shooting half a smirk at Taylor. "The bouncers are gonna reject you for sure."

"Fuck both of you," Taylor rolled her eyes in annoyance, even as she struggled not to succumb to a smile.

The cheer in the air died the moment they found the front entrance slightly ajar.

Glancing back over her shoulder, Riley scanned the street for any signs of the armored truck, or anybody else in the area, before drawing her pistol and fishing a small flashlight from her backpack's side pocket.

Heather climbed off her mountain bike, silently passing the handlebars over to her sister, before clicking on the weapon light attached to the end of her assault rifle.

The two women shared a terse nod on either side of the strip club's entrance, and Riley shouldered her way inside, cautiously venturing into the shadowy foyer.

Quietly padding over a windswept pile of sand, she kept her pistol trained on the window of the coat room, waiting for Heather to limp past and check around the corner before sweeping her handgun over the wooden counter.

Satisfied, Riley turned towards the club's main lounge, while Taylor wheeled Heather's mountain bike inside and shut the door behind her, the latch's soft *click* deafening in the silence.

The air was thick with the dormant reek of cigarette ash, overpriced beer, cheap perfume and sweaty regret, the fetid fumes having permanently permeated themselves into the zebra-striped couch cushions long before the world had ended.

Riley and Heather stood on one side of the lounge, tracing the beams of their flashlights across graffitied velvet walls, dust-caked mirrors and cobweb-covered booths.

Glass crystals twinkled around the bullet-riddled bar, a row of broken bottles having been used for target practice, while the remains of a leather swing set dangled over the main stage, suspended on a single chain hanging down from the second-story ceiling.

"Heather, you take the back, I'll check upstairs," Riley whispered as she unshouldered her camping gear, dropping the tent bag and her sleeping bag at Taylor's feet. She locked eyes with the freckled red-haired girl, "Call out if you see anything."

Taylor nodded, pulling out a flashlight of her own as Riley navigated her way towards the stairs, taking care not to step on any of the broken glass.

Checking the spaces behind the bar and the DJ booth as she climbed, Riley turned her attention towards the VIP room next.

The beam of her flashlight bounced off a disco ball as she entered the room, illuminating a pink padded leather sofa that encircled a small stage, where the decomposing corpse of a woman lay shackled to a stripper pole, surrounded by empty cans of food, a pet's water dish and a waste bucket.

Riley stifled a gag as she backed out of the room, slamming the door behind her.

"What the fuck, Riley!?" Taylor whispered a shout from the ground level.

"I guess we're not doing the whole stealth thing anymore," Heather supposed as she emerged from the back. "All clear so far – I've just got the bathrooms left."

"One more up here," Riley croaked as soon as she found her voice again, turning towards the open door at the end of the walkway.

The afternoon sunlight filtered in through the partially-closed blinds of an office, outlining the silhouette of a man sitting behind a desk, his workspace strewn with promotional flyers of scantily-dressed women.

Riley lowered her pistol.

The man wasn't a threat.

He was slumped in his chair with his head lolling to one side.

Ruddy brown splotches stained the wall and the carpet – but he hadn't died alone.

Behind the desk – kneeling in between the dead man's legs – was the rotting corpse of another woman, with a bullet-sized hole in the top of her skull.

She probably hadn't even known it was coming.

"I hope you blew your own dick off when you shot her," Riley spat in disgust. "No wonder you brained yourself, you sick son of a bitch."

Lifting up her hiking boot, she kicked over the office chair, sending both bodies sprawling across the floor, and sparing the dead woman the indignity of having her face forever buried in the vile degenerate's crotch.

Riley fingered open the blinds, squinting against the harsh glare of the summer sun as she peered out at the empty street and the cemetery beyond.

She could see the armored truck making another pass along the road between the graveyard and the small airfield in the distance.

Whoever was in the vehicle, they weren't planning on

leaving without a prize.

And that's exactly what Riley was banking on.

Stepping away from the window, she clenched her flashlight in between her teeth, gathering up a handful of promotional flyers from the desk before heading back downstairs.

"All clear," Heather reported as the three women rendezvoused beside the main stage. "We've got another exit out back. I'll cover it. What did you find?"

"Just a couple of bodies upstairs," Riley replied, flicking on the safety lever of her pistol and setting it down on the stage beside her flashlight. She began dividing the flyers into two piles before turning to Taylor, "There's a good view of the road from the office. You keep watch while we're setting up."

"Alright," she nodded, starting towards the stairs, but she faltered on the first step. "Is there anything else I can do to help though?"

"Yeah, actually, there is," Heather huffed before turning to face her little sister. "You could go upstairs and keep watch while we're setting up. And put your fucking vest on. What's the point of even having it if you're just gonna leave it in your backpack?"

"That vest didn't do shit for Everett," Taylor grumbled to herself as she stormed up the steps.

"And don't go into the VIP room either," Riley called after her. Ignoring the girl's curses, she lowered her voice and leaned closer to Heather, "You're too hard on her. Taylor's smarter than you give her credit for. She could really help us out if you gave her the chance, especially while your leg's still healing."

"I know, but I don't think she's —"

"Okay, that's creepy," Taylor's voice came down from

27

above as she shone her flashlight into the VIP room. "Do you think this chick starved to death or dehydrated first?"

"You were saying?" Heather locked eyes with Riley, shaking her head with a cynical smile. "If she wasn't my little sister, I'd say we should use her for bait."

"I've already got the bait covered," Riley replied as she picked up her pistol and flashlight again. "I'm gonna wheel your bike back outside. Let's see how long it takes for them to notice."

"You better be sure about this," Heather warned, grabbing Riley's arm before she could turn to leave. "Because if we don't get that truck, and they fuck up my bike the same way they did yours, then I'm as good as dead if we need to start running again."

CHAPTER 6

Riley stood in the shadows of the strip club's foyer, waiting behind the wooden counter of the dusty coat room as the silence stretched on, keeping her gaze fixed on the crack of afternoon sunlight streaming in through the front entrance.

She didn't want her eyes to fully adjust to the darkness, so that when their pursuers barged in and flooded the foyer with sunlight, at least she wouldn't go completely blind in the sudden burst of brightness.

Having salvaged Heather's water bottle before wheeling the woman's bike outside, Riley took another swig, surveying her trap for the umpteenth time.

It was a simple one – but sometimes simple was best.

Taking the idea straight from the Lawson Family's play-book, she had scattered the stack of racy promotional flyers, littering the pictures of lingerie-clad women across the floor.

And just like the pin-up posters of bikini models plastering Stan's bedroom wall had drawn Zack's last few moments of attention, Riley figured that her prey would be equally as distracted when they walked in.

Even if the flyers only served to pull away their focus for

half a second – any advantage was still an advantage.

"Heads up, they're on their way!" Taylor called out from the second-story office. "I think they saw the bike. They're slowing down!"

Riley clicked the water bottle's lid shut and stashed it behind the counter.

Sure enough, she could hear the *thrum* of the approaching armored truck's engine changing as it shifted gears.

The vehicle's tires chewed up the gravel of the parking lot as it slowly rumbled to a stop.

Riley strained her ears to hear above the pounding of her own heartbeat.

"Jake, I'm telling you," one man's voice came muffled through the club's entrance, "That bike wasn't there the last time we passed."

"Still doesn't make any sense, Clay," a second man replied over the sound of the truck's doors slamming. "If they've been running and hiding from us this whole time, then why leave it out in the open like that?"

"I really don't give a shit," Clay shot back as their footsteps crunched across the gravel. "I'm tired, hungry, and I've been itching to fuck something since I woke up this morning. Probably same as them – that's why they made a mistake."

"I guess it wouldn't be the first time somebody did," Jake supposed as one set of footsteps stopped just outside the entrance.

"Exactly," Clay replied as he walked around the side of the building, his voice fading. "Now, let's bag these bitches and have ourselves a party."

We've already got one planned for you, bitch, Riley smiled to herself as she held her handgun steady.

The front door creaked open, widening the crack of sunlight streaming across the floor, casting a triangular spotlight over the scattered stack of sultry promotional flyers.

Come on, come on... Riley silently urged her prey to step inside the kill zone.

She was starting to think that maybe her trap's distraction was working a little too well, when she heard Heather bursting into the lounge area, hacking and wheezing as she slammed a door shut behind her.

Eyebrows furrowing in confusion, Riley's gaze slid sideways just as a strange *hiss* sounded from outside.

Before she could react, a small metal canister rolled across the floor of the foyer, spraying out a cloud of smoke, the fog rapidly spreading around the strip club's entrance.

Still holding the doorway at gunpoint, Riley quickly yanked the front of her tank top up over her face, covering her nose and mouth with one hand.

"I can't see shit!" Heather spluttered in between wheezes, bumping into furniture as she stumbled through the lounge, the beam of her flashlight waving frantically around the room. "Taylor, you stay upstairs! I'll come to you!"

"What the hell's going on down there?" Taylor shouted from the office. "Why aren't you watching the back!?"

Riley's eyes were starting to sting.

The longer she held her gun aimed at the entrance, the blurrier her vision became.

She blinked hard through the haze, but the searing pain only worsened, her eyes watering themselves into a soupy blindness.

"Fuck this fucking leg!" Heather's garbled yell came from around the corner as she knocked over a table. "Taylor, is that you? I said don't fucking move!!"

"It's not me – I swear!" Taylor shouted back. "Nail that son of a bitch!"

"Riley, say something or I'll shoot!" Heather choked out a threat.

Trying to form a reply, Riley felt a tickle scratching at the back of her throat.

She fought the urge to cough – as inevitable as it seemed.

Their trap had failed.

They were getting smoked out.

But Riley wasn't going down without a fight.

She bounced on the balls of her feet, hyping herself up for an all-out assault.

"Count to five and start spraying!!" Riley roared on her last clean breath, leaping over the wooden counter and plunging through the burning cloud of mist.

Staggering outside into the glaring sunlight, she swept her pistol across the parking lot, blindly blasting bullets at the shimmering silhouettes swimming across her dazzled vision.

With the powdery cloud's fine particles lodged in her lungs, Riley doubled over, reeling and hacking, but still squeezing off lead slugs until her gun *clicked* empty.

Falling to her hands and knees, she reached for the combat knife strapped to her thigh, when a sharp pair of prongs stabbed her in the back, shooting excruciating jolts of electricity throughout her entire body, teeth chattering and brain rattling around her skull as she fell face first onto the ground, foaming at the mouth until she blacked out.

CHAPTER 7

Riley shivered herself back into consciousness, her eyelids feebly fluttering open as she tried to make sense of her surroundings.

She was lying face down on a cold concrete floor, her hair and clothes soaking wet, with the coppery taste of blood in her mouth.

The instant she tried to move, her stiff muscles locked up, convulsing in the lingering aftermath of the electrical shock, her aching body tightening in knots before her stomach seized the opportunity to dry heave.

"Look who's finally decided to join us," a gravelly voice observed as Riley slowly stirred back to her senses. "I thought for sure you would've woken up when we hosed you girls down."

Caught in an unfamiliar setting, Riley's fight or flight response kicked in, flooding her fatigued system with newfound adrenaline.

Surging through the pain in her body, she shoved herself upright, only to bang the back of her shoulder against the underside of a long metal bench.

"Keep it together," Heather whispered, sitting only a few feet away, her hair and clothes similarly saturated. "Wait for an opportunity. There's nothing else we can do now."

Riley and the Seabrook sisters were stuck inside a holding cell, surrounded by three brick walls, with a grid of rolled steel bars separating them from the rest of the one-room sheriff's office.

Lounging with her feet up on a desk was a woman who looked to be in her late fifties, with the drawn leathery face of somebody who had spent her entire adult life working outside.

"Oh, there's plenty else you can do," the gravelly-voiced woman picked up on Heather's muttering. "For starters – you could tell me exactly where it is you three girls were planning on running off to?"

"We already told you, lady," Taylor seethed, throwing up her arms in frustration. "How many more times do you have to hear our story before you actually fucking believe us!?"

"Just one more time," the woman shrugged lazily, as if she had all the time in the world. She nodded towards Riley. "But I wanna hear it from her now. Let's see if your stories match up."

Riley glanced from left to right between her two cellmates, wondering what they had said while she had been unconscious.

Heather returned her gaze, lips tightening as she shook her head slightly, the expression on her face silently hoping that Riley had been listening in all along.

Maybe they had told the woman the truth – they were just passing through on their way to California.

But that would have been a rookie mistake – because if they could somehow manage to escape, then their captors would

34

know which way they were headed.

Looks like we're fucked, was the only logical thought that came to mind.

Stretching her sore muscles with an exaggerated yawn, Riley rubbed the back of her clammy neck before rising up to sit on the long metal bench, her eyes searching the floor as she stalled for more time.

"Where are my boots?" she furrowed her eyebrows, looking around the holding cell.

Both Heather and Taylor were barefoot too.

"They took all of our gear," Heather replied, patiently waiting for her to catch up. "Weapons, backpacks, sleeping bags... All we have left is right here in this cell."

"So we're down to just the clothes on our backs?" Riley's shoulders slumped, her tongue pressing against the inside of her cheek.

After all of the months that they had spent stockpiling supplies for the trip.

After all of the equipment that they had picked up along the way.

In just a mere matter of hours, they had lost everything.

"Doesn't have to be that way," the leathery-skinned woman offered from behind the desk. "I'm giving you the chance to earn back at least some of what you lost. And all you have to do is tell me where you were headed."

"Cut the shit," Taylor called her out on the lie. "Do you really expect us to believe that you're just gonna hand back *anything* of what you stole from us? We already know that's not gonna happen. So you can take your questions, turn them sideways, and shove them all the way up your fucking – "

"Taylor," Riley cut her off before the impetuous girl could

35

finish her sentence, subtly cautioning her against insulting their only lifeline to the outside world. "Remember what you saw back in that VIP room? Let's try not to die like that."

"You don't wanna answer my questions," the gravelly-voiced woman concluded, swinging her feet off the table and pacing out from behind the desk. "Fine by me. I still get paid either way. Let's just hope you three girls can keep your stories straight when Radek's people start asking the questions."

"Who the fuck is Radek?" Taylor's voice cracked as her anger gave over to spiteful curiosity.

The woman answered her with more respect than the level she had been given – blatantly ignoring the question as she strolled over to the front door.

"Hey, are you gonna let us out?" Riley rose to her feet, grabbing the bars of their cage.

"You're free to go," the woman replied casually, glancing pointedly at their cell door. Her leathery face cracked into a smile as they pushed open the rusty hinges with a high-pitched whine, savoring their surprise. "Never gets old. Don't bother stealing anything on your way out. None of it's gonna get you very far anyway."

With that, she opened up the front door and stepped outside, leaning against the wall with her back turned to the three newly-released captives.

Suspicious, but not taking the chance to escape for granted, Riley and the Seabrook sisters edged their way towards the exit, with Heather snatching up a coffee mug from the desk – just in case.

The woman didn't even flinch as they drew up behind her – she only moved to strike a match, lighting up a cigarette as she stared out at the twilight creeping over the desert's horizon.

Down the building's wide front stairs and across the parking lot, three men stood milling around the white armored truck.

"What'd you get, Barbs?" a lean keen-eyed young man with dirty blonde hair was the first among them to notice the woman smoking at the top of the stairs.

"Not a damn thing, Jake," she reported, taking a long draw of her cigarette. "Nothing I'd trust to be true, at least."

"So you had us waiting out here this whole time for nothing?" a dark-skinned man asked next, his eyebrows raised in resentment. He elbowed Jake in the ribs, "I told you this was a waste of time. We would've gotten paid hours ago if we just drove straight to the drop-off point. Instead, she's had us standing around with our dicks in our hands."

"Do you know how much the bounty is on those thieves, Clay?" the woman said in a shroud of smoke. "Let me tell you – it's enough money to make even Lincoln crack a smile."

"I doubt that," the third man voiced his skepticism. Lincoln was built imposingly tall, bald, and with a dour face of stone. "But if it's enough to settle my debt in full, then throw them back in the holding cell and give me five minutes alone. You know I'll get the truth outta them, Barbara."

"You're talking about those people who stole the fuel, right?" Riley interjected, before their captors could consider conducting a less-than-civil interrogation. She figured that trying to hide the information they had would only draw more doubt. "We had nothing to do with that. We just saw them moving barrels across the river. Most of them got slaughtered, but the ones who survived had a truck waiting for them on the other side. I don't know where they were headed, but I'd say east of the river is a good place to start."

"And what were you three doing there?" Jake asked, narrowing his eyes suspiciously.

"Passing through," Heather replied bluntly, still gripping the coffee mug behind her back.

"Let her answer," Barbara flicked ash from her cigarette as she nodded towards Riley.

"Passing through," she echoed in solidarity. "You don't need to know where we were coming from or where we were heading, but we wanted to avoid going through Vegas, so we figured taking the river was our best option. Our only involvement in what went down was being witnesses to a massacre."

"You're gonna have to give us more than that," Clay cocked his head to one side with a smug grin. "I mean, it's kinda convenient that you three just happened to be at the exact same place, at the exact same time, don't you think?"

"I agree," Lincoln nodded, folding his arms across his chest, "Too much of a coincidence."

"What else do you want us to tell you?" Taylor fumed, glaring back at them. She whirled on Barbara, "Fuck this. I thought you said we were free to go."

Clay chuckled at the idea.

They weren't going anywhere.

Riley could have guessed as much.

All three men were carrying a taser holstered on their hip.

We'd never make it across the parking lot, Riley knew, locking eyes with Heather, the two women sharing the same train of thought.

They could take Barbara as a hostage, but that wouldn't make much of a difference.

They'd still be surrounded and held at gunpoint before they could even finish reeling off a demand.

One step out of line, and they were going straight back into the holding cell.

But Riley's brow creased in a moment of clarity as she saw another option.

"Think about it," she began, casually walking down the building's front stairs, singeing her bare feet across the sunbaked concrete as she tried to close the distance between her and the three men. "If we were with those thieves, then why wouldn't we have just swum across the river with the rest of them? Why would we ride our bikes *back* this way – especially if we were afraid of getting caught?"

"Because you didn't wanna get mowed down along with the others," Lincoln surmised, giving her a deadpan stare. He turned to Barbara, "I'm with Clay on this one. I doubt these girls just happened to be drifting down the river in the middle of a diesel heist. Like I said, give me five – HEY, BACK UP!!"

He whipped out his taser at lightning speed, catching Riley mid-step, aiming directly at her wet tank top.

"Put your dicks away, boys," Barbara sighed as Jake and Clay were still fumbling for their weapons. "Her story matches up with the one these two girls told me inside. Who knows though? Maybe it was all an act and she was awake the whole time. But tell me this – if you were about to knock over a whole shipment of diesel, and you knew Radek's convoy would be gunning for you straight after, then why the hell would your backup plan be a couple of mountain bikes? If I had a shit-ton of fuel, then I'd want something that could really haul ass."

Clay and Lincoln glanced sidelong at each other, both of

them failing to come up with a logical explanation.

"I guess that settles it then," Jake shrugged, holstering his taser again.

"If you already thought that we weren't with those thieves," Taylor bristled, frowning at Barbara, "Then why were you being so anal with all those fucking questions?"

"Doesn't hurt to be sure, especially with the bounty they're offering," Barbara replied as she dropped the butt of her cigarette, grinding it underneath her heel. She turned to Heather next, holding out her hand, "As for you, I'll take that mug back now. *Wait for an opportunity.* Come on. Everybody always goes for the mug."

Snorting with a guilty smirk, Heather glanced over at the three armed men on the other side of the parking lot before begrudgingly handing over the makeshift weapon.

"So what happens now?" Riley turned sideways, her gaze shifting left and right as she kept all four of their captors in her peripheral vision. "I don't believe you're just gonna let us go."

"No, I meant what I said," Barbara spoke over her shoulder as she set the coffee mug down inside the building's doorway. "But you girls aren't gonna get very far. You've got nothing but desert for miles around, and you'll be walking barefoot with just the clothes on your back."

"There's been a few people who were crazy enough to try," Lincoln admitted with a strange sense of reverence. "But now the highway's littered with their corpses."

"You'd be lucky to die that way though," Clay snorted, tilting his head with a pragmatic cluck of his tongue. "Three unarmed girls walking down the side of the road in the middle of nowhere – you don't need me to fill in the blanks."

"And what's the other option?" Riley knew that they were just trying to funnel her towards the most reasonable choice – but it all depended on what that choice was.

"You ride with us," Jake answered, jerking his head towards the back of the armored truck. "Get in."

CHAPTER 8

"Welcome to fabulous Las Vegas," Barbara grunted sarcastically as the armored truck slowed down. "City of fake tits, small dicks, and stiff shit."

"This isn't how I imagined my first trip to Vegas," Heather remarked in the back of the truck, hugging her bad leg to her chest.

Riley and the Seabrook sisters were on the floor with their backs up against the wall, sitting opposite Barbara and Lincoln. And – with the exception of their one surviving mountain bike – all of their gear, weapons and supplies were riding up front with Jake and Clay on the other side of the locked cabin door.

Lincoln had his incessant stare fixated on Riley.

He had caught her eyeing the taser holstered on his hip one too many times.

But even so, she couldn't help but smile to herself.

Because he had no idea that Heather and Taylor were thinking the exact same thing.

They all lurched to one side as the truck rumbled to a stop.

"Like I said – you girls are free to go," Barbara insisted, her knees popping as she clambered to her feet. Unbolting the rear hatch, she looked back over her shoulder, "There's just one thing you need to do for us first."

Riley and Heather exchanged a wary glance as the woman swung open the back doors.

Dusk had already settled in across the sky.

They were parked just beyond the vast expanse of an intersection in between a wide avenue and a six-lane boulevard lined with palm trees.

Across the avenue, a replica of the Statue of Liberty stood tall against a backdrop of skyscrapers, while a colossal bronze lion on the far side of the intersection seemed to stare directly into Riley's soul.

"How many you got?" a gruff voice called from the roadside.

"Only three this time," Barbara answered, sitting on the truck's rear lip before jumping down. "Come on, girls, this'll only take a minute."

Lincoln raised his eyebrows expectantly, waiting for them to comply, with one hand on his taser.

Riley supposed that they could rush him, since he only had one shot against the three of them, but along with Jake and Clay, she had no idea who else was waiting for them outside.

She rose to her feet, determined to either wait until an opportunity presented itself, or however long it would take to see whether Barbara was actually telling the truth.

Riley climbed off the back of the truck, the asphalt still warm against her bare feet as she stared around to get her bearings.

Of all the times that she and her parents had passed through Las Vegas on their way to visit Grandma Eleanor in Nebraska, she had never seen The Strip so empty.

There wasn't another vehicle in sight.

The sandy sidewalks and pedestrian walkways were empty.

And all of the once-bright neon lights were wreathed in mere shadows of their former glory.

It seemed that the only place with any power now was the Norse-themed Valhalla Hotel, a three-towered resort and casino with a gigantic Viking warship bridging the roofs of its penthouses. A long snaking walkway led up to the main building, with the fierce gargantuan head of a roaring warrior at its forefront, threatening to devour any wayward visitors within the massive maw of his open jaws.

Tempting their fates at the mouth of the grisly entrance, a group of heavily-armed security guards flanked a registration table, where a clerk sat behind a laptop, with a tablet and ledger by his side.

"Slim pickin' these days, huh?" the gruff-voiced guard spoke from behind a concrete barrier lining the corner of the intersection. He motioned for the new arrivals to climb over. "Let's hurry it up then."

With Lincoln behind them, Riley, Heather and Taylor hopped over the concrete barrier in Barbara's wake, stepping onto the weathered red carpet protruding from the monstrous Viking's mouth like an outstretched tongue.

"Right thumb on the tablet, please," the clerk didn't even bother to make eye contact.

Riley stared down at the device, its electronic screen almost alien to her after spending a year in the post-apocalypse. Flexing her scarred fingers, she pressed her thumb against the tablet until it lit up with a green checkmark.

She stood to one side as the Seabrook sisters reluctantly

registered their thumbprints as well, while Riley's gaze traced over the shotguns and assault rifles borne by the guards.

"All three are fresh meat for the grinder," the clerk declared in a monotone voice, his fingers tapping away at the keyboard of his laptop. His eyes lingered on the screen for a few moments, suppressing a smirk before reaching down for a lockbox at his feet. He lifted the small safe up onto the table and popped it open to reveal a bunch of plastic tokens. "Only one of these girls is worth full price. The other two are half each."

"What the fuck?" Barbara stared down at the stack of casino chips as the clerk pressed them into her hand. "This is two thirds of what we should be getting."

"We've reached Culling Point," a sharp-faced brunette woman stepped out from behind the security guards, staring back at Barbara with a cocksure grin. "Too many people. Not enough resources to go around. You know the deal."

What people? Riley furrowed her eyebrows, glancing around at the bleak emptiness of the surrounding streets.

Barbara clenched the casino chips in her fist, glancing sidelong at the three women with a speculative gaze, probably wondering how much they would be worth if she voiced a suspicion of them having a connection to the diesel thieves.

"So are we done here?" Taylor asked, her grudge-filled glare flitting from Barbara to the brunette woman. "This is the only thing we had to do, right? We're free to go now."

"You're getting ready to put up another tournament," Lincoln broke his silence, ignoring the girl's questions as he stared down at the back of the laptop.

"That's right," the clerk nodded, flipping through the pages of his ledger before glancing up again. "And you still

45

have your debt. Even the total for these three isn't gonna cut it."

"It'll get paid," Lincoln promised with a no-nonsense tone, before turning on his heel and marching back towards the armored truck where Jake and Clay were busy unloading the stolen gear.

Just as Lincoln was climbing back over the concrete barrier, the familiar sound of a sinister symphony reached their ears, with guttural voices growling and wailing infernal incantations over blaring horns and thunderous war drums.

An icy shiver ran up Riley's spine, and she began edging towards the armored truck as the cold-blooded convoy came roaring down the boulevard.

Both Heather and Taylor followed her lead as the four pickup trucks with mounted machine guns screeched to a halt in the middle of the intersection.

The long bus with its top sawed off rumbled to a stop in between the trucks, and the post-apocalyptic war party of barbarian brutes filed down onto the asphalt, while their fiendish Viking music boomed from the bowels of the bus's cargo hold.

Despite the discordant Scandinavian soundtrack, the sinewy savages were a mongrel mix of races – with whites, blacks, Latinos, Native Americans and Pacific Islanders – all united by their mutual capacity for violence.

Their feral faces were striped with differing patterns of blue, black and red paint, but all of them wore the same necklace, each with an identical upside down hammer pendant.

Riley glanced back at the group of security guards gathered around the registration table, each of them wearing the same symbol as well.

"What's our move here?" Heather whispered as the music died down, the fiery redhead's gaze laser-focused on Lincoln tossing her mountain bike out from the back of the armored truck.

Riley glanced around at their options.

Putting up a fight would be futile – they were unarmed, caught in between their captors, the guards, and the bloodthirsty brutes from the bus.

Going for the high ground was out too – the staircase to the nearest pedestrian walkway was in full view of the mounted machine guns.

And Jake and Clay had already swung the armored truck's back doors shut, with Lincoln locking up the rear hatch from the inside.

"Our move is – we don't move," Riley replied, realizing that they didn't have any other choice.

The group of goons from the bus approached the concrete barrier, leering lustfully at the three young women as they stopped a few yards away, forming a lazy line in front of the red carpet.

Riley's pupils dilated as her gaze dropped down to what was in each of their hands.

"Don't look away," Heather spoke softly, before taking on her usual tone of nonchalance again. "We've seen worse."

"Yum yum yum," Taylor pretended to be unfazed by what they were carrying, glaring back at the gore-spattered grunts in defiance.

"Blood tribute to The Valkyrie," the first brute growled, dropping a cleaved hand over the side of the concrete barrier.

"Blood tribute to The Valkyrie," the next one echoed, tossing a severed ear onto the red carpet.

One by one, they threw their morbid offerings of mangled limbs, torn appendages and other gruesome trophies into a pile, locking eyes with the sharp-faced brunette woman standing behind the registration table.

"Dagur, it looks like you've brought some good news," the woman surmised, venturing forth from her security guards until the small mound of human remains were at her feet.

"We caught the thieves trying to cross a river," a thickset onyx ogre of a man reported. A red lightning bolt had been painted across the dome of his skull, zigzagging over one eyelid and running down to his jaw. "Some of them got away. These ones weren't so lucky."

"And the shipment?" she raised her eyebrows, flicking her gaze towards the convoy in the middle of the intersection. "I don't see the truck they stole."

"We got some of it back," Dagur turned, watching as half a dozen diesel drums were hauled out from the bus's cargo hold. "They had another truck waiting for them on the other side of the river. By the time we –"

"Save it," she cut him off, folding her arms at his failure. "Get your crew back on the bus. Take two barrels and don't come back until you find the rest. And Dagur – if you're not here in time for the tournament, then Radek will know why."

Eyes burning at the threat, he whipped out a long knife in response.

"Blood tribute to The Valkyrie," the big silverback gorilla turned the blade on himself, slicing open his palm and drizzling fresh crimson over the macabre mess at her feet.

"They're really taking this whole Viking thing to heart," Riley gave a small snort as she and the Seabrook sisters watched Dagur march back towards his men, roaring orders and shoving the sadistic savages back aboard the bus.

"Like a bunch of deranged Vlads and Vanyas," Heather agreed, reminding her of the Russian twins they had met back in Colorado.

"Those two weren't exactly sane either," Riley remembered with a touch of fondness as the hellish Viking music started playing again. "But at least they weren't complete fucking psychos like these guys."

The callous convoy wheeled around the intersection, turning back the way they came, whooping and howling into the night.

"So I take it we're not at Culling Point anymore?" Barbara remarked as she drew up alongside the so-called Valkyrie, pointedly glancing down at the bloody heap on the red carpet. "Give us full price for the other two, and we'll be on our way."

"You've already been paid," the brunette woman shot back as she turned on her heel. Leaning closer, she added, "You want more money – find more people."

Barbara held her scornful stare for a long moment, but her gaze soon turned downcast, choosing to quietly divide the casino chips in her hand instead.

"No, that's bullshit!" Clay called from the other side of the concrete barrier.

"Calm down, calm down," Jake held him back as the guards fanned out, their shotguns and assault rifles raised, every last one of them yearning for action.

"Let's get the fuck outta here," Barbara murmured as she held up a hand of submission. She climbed back onto the road before turning to Riley, Heather and Taylor. "Come on, you too. Before we all end up being blood tributes to The Valkyrie."

CHAPTER 9

"We've done what you asked," Riley argued as she stood barefoot beside the front wheel of the armored truck, "Why the hell should we go anywhere with you now?"

Other than to kill you all and take back our gear, she already knew the answer to her own question, but she was curious to hear what the woman would have to say.

"You're welcome to find your own way," Barbara shrugged as she handed Lincoln his share of the casino chips through the truck's driver's side window. "Or you could come with me. I can help get you girls set up in town. Either way, the offer's there. So if you try to murder me on the streets one day, you'll be the ones with the guilty conscience – not me."

Riley's gaze slid sideways to meet Heather's, who returned half a smirk.

It seemed that Barbara had captured enough survivors over the past year to know exactly what was on their minds.

"I dunno why you bother, Barbs," Clay grunted as he swung Riley's heavy backpack over his shoulders. "Just seems like a waste of time and money to me."

"At least it's not coming outta our shares," Jake reasoned

as he tied up the rest of the stolen supplies on either side of the last surviving mountain bike. He left Heather's backpack on the ground with a nod of respect aimed at Barbara, "Except for this, that is."

"You won't find any of your weapons or tools inside," Barbara said as she invited the three former captives to take the backpack. "But we've left you with half the food."

"Wouldn't be the first time we've had half our shit stolen," Taylor scowled sidelong at Riley, bitterly reminding her exactly how they had met.

"Hey, Lincoln," Barbara called for his attention as he started up the truck. "Can we get a lift on your way back over to the impound?"

"No time to waste," he shook his head as he stared up at the lights of the Valhalla Hotel. Shifting the engine into gear, he explained, "I've gotta square the rest of my debt before this next tournament starts. I'm gonna gas up and head back out there while the trail's still fresh. See if I can find any stragglers."

With that, he swung the truck around and sped back down the boulevard.

"I guess we're walking," Heather supposed, draping her arm around Taylor's shoulders.

"Watch the graze," the freckled girl hissed, the scrape down her arm still tender from crashing her bike outside the graveyard. "Riley, you wanna get that bag?"

"No, I thought we might leave it here," Riley replied sarcastically, stooping to pick up the light backpack, its contents shifting inside.

She shot a glance over her shoulder at the guards standing around the hotel's entrance, locking eyes with the brunette woman for a brief moment.

"Who was that back there?" Riley asked as they crossed the avenue.

"Yeah, what was all that *Valkyrie* bullshit about?" Taylor's curiosity kicked in.

"Hey, Barbs, we're gonna go on ahead," Jake decided, having already heard the story.

"We're losing the light," Clay agreed eagerly, growing impatient with Heather's slow progress as they cleared the intersection. He adjusted the straps around his shoulders as he picked up the pace, "And this shit isn't gonna sell itself."

"Well, thanks so much for the escort," Barbara narrowed her eyes before sending them off with a wink. She paused to light up a cigarette, settling into an easy stroll down the sandy sidewalk. "That was Miranda back there – Queen Bitch of Valhalla, ever since she won one of the tournaments."

"Okay, you're gonna have to explain that part too," Heather joined in as she limped along beside her little sister.

Now it was their turn to ask the questions.

"Tournaments are Radek's way of weeding out the herd," Barbara replied with a puff of smoke. "There aren't enough supplies coming in from outside to keep up with the growing population, so they announce a new competition whenever we reach Culling Point."

"Hold on a second," Riley frowned at the fault in their logic. "You wouldn't be at this *Culling Point* right now if you'd just left us the hell alone. Why go to the trouble of kidnapping people and bringing them back here if you're worried about overpopulation?"

"People still need to be entertained," Barbara shrugged with the patience of a woman who had evidently had this conversation a countless number of times. "Plus, it helps keep everybody in line. You try to steal something – anything except for diesel, that is – you go to the tournament. You kill without cause, you go to the tournament. You owe Radek's people money, like our boy Lincoln does, and guess what? You go to the tournament."

"That doesn't really sound like much of a punishment," Heather cocked an eyebrow as they passed underneath a pedestrian walkway. "What's the big deal?"

"Because after all of the tournaments they've run," Barbara leveled her gaze with them, her drawn face grim in the deepening moonlight, "Only two people have ever walked out alive. Miranda was one of them. And the other one is some adrenaline junkie dickhead with a death wish who keeps signing up."

"So it's possible to win then," Riley supposed, running her thumb along the scars of her fingers in thought. "I mean, if this one guy can keep on surviving, then there's gotta be some kinda trick to it, right?"

"Honey," Barbara began, flicking ash from her cigarette, "If you saw how many people die during those tournaments, you'd be just as shit-scared about it as Lincoln is."

"You still haven't told us about *The Valkyrie*," Taylor brought up her question again. "I mean, those psychos were literally dropping body parts at her feet."

Riley gave the girl a curious sidelong glance, remembering that Taylor had praised Demi for slicing off Stan Lawson's nose – and that was taken from him while he was still alive.

"That's just some Viking barbarian bullshit they've all bought into," Barbara shook her head with a derisive scowl. "They're a bunch of airhead ex-bouncers and corrupt cops who used to be on the casino's payroll. Radek's managed to mind-fuck them all into embracing the whole messed-up medieval mythology. Then after Miranda won the tournament, people took to calling her The Valkyrie, and now they pay pointless tributes for her *guidance* and *protection* in battle. Makes you wonder – how the fuck did we even last this long as a species?"

"If you think that's bad," Heather snorted with a twitch of her eyebrows, "You should hear Riley's story about the man-raping cult in Nebraska."

"Nothing surprises me anymore these days," Barbara replied with a world-weary sigh.

They crossed over to the other side of the boulevard at the next intersection, passing by a row of ransacked restaurants and bars.

The sidewalk was beginning to grow cold underneath Riley's bare feet, and the night's cool breeze cut through the thin fabric of her tank top.

"How much farther is it to wherever we're headed?" she finally asked the question that had somehow been at the bottom of their list.

"Not long now," Barbara jerked her head towards a gigantic billboard towering over a small strip mall.

Riley cocked an eyebrow at the unlikely row of ruined storefronts, doubting that this could be their destination, when the jumbled sounds of a clamoring crowd soon reached her ears.

Beyond the big billboard, the orange glow of flickering flames spilled out across the sidewalk, dancing with the shifting silhouettes of people walking to and fro, their shadows stretching out from a jam-packed plaza surrounded by food stalls and old souvenir kiosks. Trashcan fires illuminated the square, wreathing the underbelly of an immense overhead canopy in a shroud of smoke.

"Mrs Greene!" a chubby kid with a big smile called from beside the plaza's entrance, standing behind a wall that he could barely see over. "Jake and Clay said you'd be coming."

"Hey, Manny," Barbara finished the rest of her cigarette before approaching the boy. "What happened to the lights?"

"We didn't get a delivery today," Manny shrugged. He nodded his head towards the Valhalla Hotel, a distant beacon along the boulevard. "That's the only place with any power now."

"Probably keeping the rest of the diesel to themselves after the heist," Barbara mused bitterly. She turned her attention back to the boy, "You got everything?"

"I've *always* got everything," he shot her an exaggerated wink before turning to Riley, Heather and Taylor. "And don't you forget it. If you ever need anything, make sure you come on down to Manny's Mega Emporium!"

He disappeared for a moment, rummaging through stacks of boxes behind the wall before producing three pairs of green hotel slippers.

"Thanks, but I'd prefer my boots," Riley soured at the sight of the slippers.

"I've got boots too!" Manny exclaimed, standing on his tiptoes to squint down at her bare feet. "You'd want something around a size eight, right?"

"Only if you're selling the boots for the same price," Barbara replied, already knowing the answer. She placed a single plastic token on the wall, before staring sidelong at Riley, "My charity only goes so far, honey."

55

"Charity!?" Taylor echoed incredulously, shrugging Heather's arm from around her shoulders. "You're the one who stole our fucking –"

"These are perfect," Heather cut her off, limping over to grab a pair of slippers.

"Beats being barefoot," Riley supposed with a begrudging breath, "But not by much."

Sliding the makeshift shoes on, she glanced over the wall to take a look at Manny's Mega Emporium, which was just a chaotic cluster of cardboard boxes and black trash bags.

Lying in the middle of the clutter, a muscular brindle pitbull stared back up at her, its long tongue lolling lazily over a small lockbox that hung from its collar.

Manny stooped beside his dog, stashing the single casino chip into the staunchly-guarded safe.

"Don't bother about the change," Barbara called him back to his feet. She transferred her last cigarette into her breast pocket and laid an empty box on the wall. "Just give me some more death sticks and tell your brother he owes me a bottle."

"Yes, ma'am," he nodded, happily switching over the empty box for a full pack.

"Isn't your brother worried you might get robbed?" Taylor wondered as she took Heather's arm around her shoulders again.

"He's with the water crew," Manny replied, the welcoming smile fading from his face. He jerked a thumb over his shoulder at his pitbull, "Besides, Boomer's bitten off more fingers than I've sold shoes."

"I've seen a lot of three-fingered thieves in the tournaments," Barbara backed him up, reminding them about the punishment for theft. "Everybody does their part around here, one way or another."

With that, she turned away from Manny and the entrance to the square, leading the three women down a dark laneway that ran in between the plaza and the strip mall, their hotel slippers scraping along the asphalt in the shadows.

A rash of gooseflesh flowered down Riley's arms as she remembered the alley back in Utah, where Heather had impaled her leg behind a row of townhouses.

"Alright, this is far enough," she decided, glancing uncertainly at the back entrances of the buildings lining the square. "We'll find our own way from here."

On the surface, Barbara Greene sounded civil enough.

But Riley had been burnt too many times in the past to trust anyone now.

Braxton Shepherd.

Calvin Fisher.

Rose Lawson.

Each of them had lulled her into a false sense of security.

And each of them had turned out to be a snake in the grass.

For all Riley knew, Barbara was planning on selling her and the Seabrook sisters to the highest bidder.

And three fresh young women were sure to fetch a good price.

She flexed her scarred fingers, anticipating an ambush from the shadows.

"Fine by me," Barbara finally shrugged, studying the confused resolve on Riley's face before pointing towards a tall building rising up at the end of the laneway. "The hotel rooms start on the fifth floor, but don't stop until you get up to at least the fourteenth. Trust me. They get a whole lot cleaner the higher up you go."

"I'll bet they do," Heather huffed, glancing down at her bad leg with a dismal twist of her lips.

Riley peered up at the hotel, reading its name – *Jade Mantis* – the bold letters prominent even in the darkness of the night.

"So that's it?" Taylor's scowl dropped a hint of alarm at the thought of losing their guide. "What are we supposed to do now?"

"That's up to you," Barbara turned on her heel, starting back towards the plaza's entrance. Feeling the weight of their stares though, her shoes scraped to a stop, and she sighed up at the night sky. "Make sure you've all got work before your food runs out. You can forget about *going pro* though – you're too skinny to compete with any of the Vegas girls. With the three of you working together, you might make enough money to buy your way outta here in a couple years. But you try taking any shortcuts, and this town will eat you up alive."

CHAPTER 10

"Stop," Heather cautioned as she hobbled up the dimly-lit stairwell, clinging to the inner railing. "What are you doing?"

"I can barely see the steps," Taylor complained in the fluorescent gloom, her hand reaching for the glow stick lying on the next landing. "You really wanna risk breaking your other leg? Let's just take one of these for some light until we can find a room."

"Pretty sure that counts as stealing," Riley countered as she drew up behind Heather. "Let's try not to piss off the locals on our first day here."

"You're one to talk," Taylor grumbled, scowling in the darkness as she led the way up the stairs, feeling every step with her feet.

"Can you cut the shit?" Heather scolded her little sister. "What's gotten into you? Kansas was six months ago now. Drop it already."

"We had everything we needed," Taylor's resentful voice echoed in the stairwell. "Weapons, gear, food, water, meds... and somehow we managed to lose it all to a bunch of assholes who didn't even have to fire a single shot – *again*."

"They had tear gas and tasers," Riley reminded her, still feeling the dull ache in her lower back from where the pair of prongs had injected jolts of electricity surging throughout her entire body.

"Yeah, and you had me sitting upstairs the whole time," Taylor shot back, pausing at the next landing to glare down at their silhouettes as she waited for her sister to catch up. "I could've stabbed one of them while they were still reloading."

"Or you could've stabbed one of us," Heather huffed, remembering the blinding confusion brought on by the tear gas. Dragging her bad leg up onto the landing, she limped over to the hotel floor's access door and pulled it open. "I counted five levels. I'm done."

They left the stairwell, entering the elevator hall and following the sparse trail of glow sticks around to the south side of the building. Moonlight streamed into the hallway from a row of open doors, striping the corridor's shadowy green carpet with eerie pale streaks.

Taylor stood at the entrance of the closest room with a grim expression.

Glancing sidelong at her sister, she checked the next room. And the next. And the next. And the next.

She walked back from the last south-facing room in the corridor, still wearing the same somber face.

"I'm not going up any more stairs," Heather's husky voice was absolute, wincing with every step towards the first room.

Riley caught her from behind and brought her over to the doorway, and they stared around at their bleak accommodation for the night.

The doors from the entrance, the bathroom and the closet had been torn off the hinges.

There was no furniture in the room either.

Rectangular outlines marred the walls where picture frames had once hung.

Even the lampshades and light bulbs had been removed, their empty fixtures dangling down from the ceiling on defunct lengths of electrical cable.

"Let's take this one for the night," Riley set down their last backpack of supplies in a corner of the room. "We'll rest up here and see if we can find a better one tomorrow."

"Tomorrow sounds good," Heather agreed, limping over to the bare floor-to-ceiling window and gazing out into the night, the Valhalla Hotel's grid of lights blazing brightly in the distance. "Kinda makes you appreciate what we had back in Colorado. I'd trade my good leg even for that shitty room they stuck us in towards the end."

"And then I'd say you need to work on your bartering skills," Taylor muttered as she crossed the room towards their backpack. "What should we have for dinner tonight?"

Riley was about to answer, when her ears pricked up.

For a moment, she could have sworn that she had heard somebody else moving around outside.

She held a finger to her lips, frowning at the open doorway.

Sure enough, she could hear the ragged breaths of another person on the seemingly abandoned floor, their bare feet padding across the corridor's carpet.

"You know," a creaky voice came in from the hallway, harsh and scratching, like nails on a chalkboard. "I was just asking myself the same damn thing."

CHAPTER 11

"Been a while since I had any visitors," the man's grating voice continued, his face wreathed in a veil of darkness just beyond the doorway. "It must be my birthday."

The sniggering stranger stood at the entrance, waiting for one of them to make a move.

The three women had nowhere to run.

There was nothing for them to hide behind.

And the only weapons to hand were their bare fists.

"Fuck off, creep!" Taylor shouted as she stormed towards the room's small corridor, stopping just short of the ransacked closet.

Heather slid sideways with her back against the wall, shuffling into position behind the front corner of the room, standing as still and silent as a shadow.

"So much for all those tournaments keeping everybody in line," Riley gave a small snort as she kicked off her slippers, joining the Seabrook sisters at the room's choke-point.

She squared her shoulders, ready to take another man's life.

"This is *my* floor," the stranger snarled menacingly, craning his neck into the doorway. "And you three are gonna have to play nice if you wanna stay here."

His silhouette materialized in the moonlight, revealing the emaciated rake of a man with hollow cheeks and protruding ribs.

He reeked of rotting sweat and stomach bile.

His entire body was smeared with grease and grime.

And he was almost completely naked, besides the soiled scrap of a curtain girding his waist, the defiled fabric folded up into a makeshift loincloth.

"How do you girls wanna pay for the room?" he grinned lewdly, his ravenous gaze dragging across Riley and Taylor indiscriminately, smacking his cracked lips with a deranged yearning.

Riley stifled a gag, her skin crawling at the thought of even breathing the same air.

"We'll let you leave while you still can," Taylor glared back at him, clenching her fists. "That's how we'll pay."

The living zombie tilted his head to one side until his neck cracked, his look of longing giving over to one of outright lunacy, and he shrank back into the shadows of the hallway.

"What the fuck?" Riley gave herself permission to breathe again.

"That guy was a freak show," Taylor glowered into the darkness in his wake before glancing sidelong at her sister. "You're lucky you didn't have to see him."

"I think I'm good to go up a few more floors now," Heather decided with a welcome change of heart.

"Yeah, let's get the fuck outta here," Riley agreed, relaxing her shoulders as she turned around to fetch their backpack.

But she froze in place as her ears pricked up again.

There were footsteps running through the corridor outside.

She whipped her head around just in time to see the emaciated man sprinting in through the doorway.

He plowed into Riley and Taylor at full speed, knocking them both off their feet.

Without a moment's pause, the gnarled intruder spun on his heel, double-backing to bury his bony fist into Heather's navel.

She folded over at the waist, clutching her stomach as she fell to the floor.

"YOU MOTHERF–"

Taylor's outrage was cut short as he kicked her full in the face with his bare foot.

Riley was still clambering upright when he pounced on top of her next, pinning her to the floor and snapping his slimy teeth at her neck.

Raw adrenaline surging through her veins, Riley thrust her elbow up into his throat, keeping his clacking jaws at bay.

Wild-eyed and slavering, the skeletal savage grabbed her wrist, twisting and jerking her arm out of his way with a burst of unprecedented strength.

Lying on her back without a weapon, the only thing that Riley had to her advantage over the man was her own weight.

Writhing with the momentum of her twisting arm, she turned her body underneath him, shoving with her shoulder until she was on top of the scrawny stranger.

Straddling his starved hips, she aimed a devastating knee thrust into the folds of his loincloth before stamping his nose, chin and forehead with the heel of her free hand, breaking his grip on her other wrist.

But rather than being knocked into the depths of a punch-drunk stupor, he simply shuddered with excitement, both hands clawing at her face for more.

Pupils dilating in the moonlight, Riley caught one of his reaching forearms with both hands and flung herself off to the side, stretching his elbow across her thigh as she planted her feet onto his bony cheek and protruding ribcage.

"I'm gonna have some fun with you now, bitch!" the grimy ghoul spat an idle threat underneath her heel, grunting and bucking like a feral beast as he struggled to break free of the arm bar.

"Ugh, my fucking head," Taylor groaned groggily, pushing herself upright and cradling her temples.

"What are you doing!?" Heather shouted in between wheezes for breath, "Help Riley!!"

"I've got him," Riley replied with a strained voice, rolling her torso forward before throwing all of her weight backwards, yanking the emaciated man's elbow down hard against her thigh.

She was listening for the satisfying *snap* of tendons tearing from his bones, when she felt the sickening sensation of the repulsive wretch's sandpapery tongue snaking across her bare foot.

He started sucking on her toes, groaning with depraved delight, before trying to turn his head underneath her heel to take a bite.

Riley jerked back her foot with a shuddering wave of disgust.

Seizing his opportunity to escape, he squirmed his skinny chest out from underneath her other leg and sprang to his feet.

Growling like a rabid dog as blood gushed from his broken nose, he twisted and turned his forearm out of Riley's grip. Grabbing her arm in turn, he hauled her upright and shoved her into the wall, before knocking her flat again and scrambling on top of her chest.

"Stop struggling, you little slut," the wild animal snarled as he planted his knobbly knees along the ridges of her collarbones. Locking up each of her arms with a swift twist of his lanky legs and ankles, he added, "You might even enjoy yourself."

Grunting and thrashing underneath the reeking rake of a man, Riley tried to throw him off her chest, but this time he wouldn't budge.

His limbs were entwined with hers.

Flailing in anxiety, she swung her fists up at his lower back, aiming for his kidneys, but with her elbows pinned to her sides, her panicked punches had little effect.

The gaunt grin on his malnourished face said it all.

Blood was streaming from his nose into his mouth, staining his slimy teeth crimson red as he loomed over her, frothing eagerly at the hate in her eyes.

He waggled his gnarled fingers in the air, staring down at his trapped prey with a speculative smile.

"GET OFF HER!!" Taylor's yell filled the room as she tackled him from the side.

But the grimy ghoul caught the girl's weight with ease, only rocking sideways for a moment as he seized a handful of her hair. Yanking down hard, he gave her another brutish blow to the face before throwing her senseless body back across the room.

"You're gonna pay for that, you son of a bitch!" Heather panted, still clutching her stomach as she staggered to her feet. She took one step towards him before her bad leg gave way, and she dropped to her knees. Grimacing in pain, she called over her shoulder, "Taylor, get up!"

"You ginger whores are gonna have to wait your turn," the loathsome lowlife licked his cracked lips at the pair of Seabrook sisters before turning his attention back to Riley. "Now, where were we?"

Riley's heart leapt up into her throat as his fingers began fumbling with the folds of his loincloth.

In a crazed fit of desperation, she tried hitting him in the back again.

But she couldn't reach him with her knees.

And she couldn't wrap her feet around his neck either – not at the angle he was sitting.

The depraved deviant pulled the scrap of defiled fabric free from his groin, still grinning down at Riley as a new nauseating wave of noxious fumes pervaded her senses.

He held his soiled loincloth above her in the moonlight, taunting her with it, the vile dreadful moment stretching on for an eternity.

And then he dropped it on her face.

CHAPTER 12

Blind with her face buried in the folds of the feral man's makeshift loincloth, Riley frantically flailed her head from side to side, desperately trying to shake off the revolting rag before she could succumb to its sickening stench.

Still straddling her shoulders, with his lanky legs and ankles locked around her arms, the ghastly ghoul sniggered as he planted one of his gnarled hands on top of the stinking scrap of fabric, intent on suffocating her in the insufferable snare.

Heightening waves of nausea hit Riley with every involuntary gasp and splutter for air, her shuddering stomach flipping in somersaults as she thrashed wildly with her arms and legs.

And then she went limp.

She was on the verge of passing out.

Riley knew that if she struggled for any longer, she would only launch herself into a full-blown panic attack, soon followed by hyperventilating into unconsciousness.

And she wasn't about to let this perverted predator win that easily.

Hardening her resolve, Riley willed herself to regain control of her breathing, numbing her senses to the loincloth's pervading stench as she retreated into the recesses of her mind.

Memories of her father's lessons in self defense flashed across her mind's eye, but she already knew that they had never covered this position.

All of the techniques that Nolan Armstrong had taught her were designed to ensure that she would never end up on the floor.

She couldn't rely on her training this time.

She had to think of something on her own.

Only a few feet away, Heather's shouts to rouse her sister kept falling on deaf ears.

Riley clenched her jaw.

It was all up to her now.

I'm pinned to the floor, she ran through her options again, before her brow creased in a moment of clarity. *But my hands aren't.*

Without hesitation, she turned her wrists, jabbing her thumbs into the man's emaciated hips.

He snarled savagely in response, shifting his weight in an attempt to escape the pain.

Failing that, he gripped her throat with his other hand, trying to rush her towards a blackout instead.

But Riley only dug her thumbs in deeper, gouging the malnourished muscles of his torso, reaching for a non-existent button hidden in the shallow core of his starved stomach to switch him off permanently.

She could feel her lips turning blue as the rangy wretch throttled her throat.

Her ears filled with the pounding rush of deoxygenated

blood pooling up inside her skull.

And then everything went still.

Her hands fell back to the floor as the pressure on her throat disappeared.

She felt completely weightless, the bony burden lifting from her shoulders.

Riley Armstrong lay motionless in the depths of darkness, fading off into oblivion.

And then the reeking rag was ripped from her face.

She sucked in a lungful of clean air and rolled over to one side, dry heaving from the filth, the guttural gag burning through her raw throat.

Involuntary tears stung her eyes as she looked up to see Heather limping away towards the bathroom, stripping off her shirt as she went.

Furrowing her eyebrows in confusion, Riley scrubbed the grime off her face before following the sounds of struggle nearby.

Taylor was riding the gaunt ghoul's backside as he staggered around the room, trying to throw her off.

But her legs were tied in a knot around his starved stomach as she choked him with the discarded drawstring of a missing curtain wrapped around his neck.

Clawing at the cord, the skeletal savage rammed her back against the floor-to-ceiling window, the glass shuddering as blood-tinged bubbles blew from his broken nose.

Riley surged to her feet, her entire body boiling with rage after being defiled.

The man froze at her approach, his eyes filling with the furious vengeance scrawled across her moonlit face as she rushed across the room.

Anchoring her left foot on the carpet as she turned her hips, Riley lifted her right leg chest-high, before stomping her heel down hard on one of his knobbly kneecaps, snapping his scrawny leg backwards like a toothpick.

The sound of glass shattering in the bathroom was soon muffled by his scream of agony as he went down, his mangled stump hitting the floor, with Taylor's extra weight on his back only adding to his anguish.

The battered girl tightened the curtain's cord around his neck again, his screech turning into a high-pitched whistle as she cut off his windpipe.

"Stop struggling, you little slut," Riley's voice dripped with venom as she clasped her hands around the back of his skull.

Tremors of impact shook her arms as she drove her knee into his face again and again and again.

He began choking on his own teeth as she knocked them down the back of his throat, and what had once been his busted nose soon became a stove-in flap of flesh and cartilage.

"My turn," Heather declared as she drew up behind them in the window's reflection.

She was clutching a broken shard from the bathroom mirror, handling the jagged piece of glass with the bundle of her shirt.

He stared up at them both with the eyes of somebody who had long been blinded by the haze of perverted depravity, only just now realizing the depths of his wrongdoings.

But his regret wouldn't save him now.

With one final knee to the revolting wretch's skull, Riley stepped back from the ruins of his face, watching with grim satisfaction as Heather slashed open his throat from ear to ear.

71

"Fucker," Taylor panted, letting go of the curtain's draw-string around his neck.

She grabbed a handful of his greasy hair and wrenched his head backwards, savoring the sounds of his gurgling death throes until his bony body flopped to the floor.

"That's one down," Riley breathed, souring at the sight of his blood spattered across her leg. She glanced over her shoulder at the open doorway, "But we're gonna need some proper weapons if we wanna make it through the rest of the night."

CHAPTER 13

"Are you sure you're gonna be okay while we're gone?" Taylor asked as she lingered outside the bathroom's doorway.

Heather was sitting on the edge of the bathtub opposite the broken mirror, wearing only her sports bra and shorts, but still clutching her makeshift knife.

"I'll be fine," her voice echoed slightly in the darkness, reassuring her younger sister for the umpteenth time. "I didn't climb up all those stairs only to head back down again just because of a little fight with the neighbor. Plus, you two already know that if I come with you, I won't be able to make another trip back up the stairs later on – we'd be sleeping out on the streets tonight instead. No. This is the way it's gotta be."

Riley and Taylor weren't about to leave Heather completely high and dry though.

Using the few glow sticks that had been scattered around the entrance to the stairwell, the three women had already cleared the rest of the fifth floor room by room, checking for any other unwanted guests who might have been occupying the hotel.

But even though their search had thankfully proven fruitless, Riley couldn't help but harbor a sneaking suspicion that somebody who had lived up here for long enough would have known exactly where to hide.

And that's why they had littered the bathroom's entire floor with glass crystals from the shattered mirror.

Then, using Taylor's impromptu strangling device, they had pulled the curtain's drawstring taut across the bathroom's entrance, looping the length of cord through the open doorway's bottom hinges, and tying off the other end behind the base of the toilet bowl.

Everett Lawson probably wouldn't have approved of using a tripwire in the literal sense, but it was still an effective defense regardless.

If there was anybody else still hanging around with a mind to mount another assault, they'd snag their foot on the line and fall flat on their face across the broken glass shards, giving Heather plenty of time to shank her next victim.

"Maybe Taylor should stay up here with you," Riley suggested, already beginning to have her doubts about the trap.

She had just realized that if multiple attackers were to come in through the doorway, one at a time, then they'd have no trouble overwhelming the woman – especially if she was all by herself.

"You're gonna need Taylor watching your back out there," Heather immediately knocked back the offer, the fiery redhead's green eyes piercing through the veil of darkness as something else passed unsaid between the pair of women.

Taylor's better off out there with you than in here with me.

Firm in her decision, Heather sniffed dismissively, her silhouette turning away in the shadows.

"We'll be back with the gear as soon as we can," Riley promised before turning to Taylor, "You ready to go?"

The girl swallowed sullenly as she stared into the bathroom, the silence stretching between the two Seabrook sisters.

Finally, she adjusted the straps of her backpack and headed out into the corridor, scanning the length of the moonlit hall one last time before turning the corner.

"I think that creep might've broken some of my braces," Taylor drew in a sharp breath as she touched her swollen cheek. "Could you take a look at them for me when we find some decent light?"

"Sure," Riley answered stiffly as they reached the stairwell's access door.

She gripped the handle before pausing, looking sidelong at the girl in the dimly-lit elevator hall.

"What?" Taylor bristled for a moment, her defensive scowl dropping a hint of alarm as she remembered to listen to their surroundings for any sounds of movement.

"Not here," Riley replied, glancing back over her shoulder before shoving open the door.

Entering the fluorescent gloom of the hotel's stairwell, Riley stepped towards the inner railing, craning her neck up and down as she surveyed the spiraling flights of stairs both above and below.

Taylor shuffled in behind her, the access door slamming shut with a reverberating boom.

"Here, then?" her impatient curiosity echoed in the stairwell.

"No," Riley shook her head as she started down the first step. "Just call out if you see anything."

With her palms raised like a pair of coiled vipers, she took her time going down the somber stairs, pausing at every landing and keeping her ears open as she peered into the darkness of the shadowy corners.

They were making slow progress, but they couldn't rush their descent.

If there was somebody else lurking in the shadows, waiting for the opportunity to strike, then they would only have a split second to defend themselves.

"It feels like there's even less light than before," Taylor whispered from behind after a few floors, the contents of her backpack rustling as she checked over her shoulder. "Do you think some of the glow sticks died out?"

"Either that," Riley's mouth dried as her mind turned towards the sinister alternative, "Or they've been moved."

Now that she thought about it, they hadn't passed another one of the fluorescent rods since entering the stairwell.

Dead or missing – some of the glow sticks were definitely gone.

But they couldn't head back upstairs to retrieve the solitary light now – they had already passed the halfway point to the ground floor, and there was no guarantee that the single glow stick was even up there anymore.

The darkness seemed to be closing in on them.

Riley couldn't even see her hands in front of her own face as they reached the next landing.

"I don't like this," she muttered over her shoulder as an icy chill ran up her spine. "See if there's an exit here. We'll find another way down."

"Sounds good to me," Taylor whispered back as she searched the walls with her hands. Her sweaty palms streaked across a wooden surface, and she latched on to a door handle.

"Fuck. I think it's locked."

She gave the handle another twist and shake.

Nothing.

"Let's keep moving," Riley decided grimly, taking the next flight of stairs.

Breathing shallow as they relied on their other senses, the pair of women dragged their hotel slippers down every unseen step, blindly trying to feel their way through the gloom.

The unspoken certainty that they were walking into a trap grew with every inch forward.

But it was too late for them to turn back now.

If they were being stalked in the stairwell, then they had already given away their position a long time ago with all the noise.

It wouldn't matter whether they went up or down at this point.

Riley knew that they were still safer heading downstairs though – they would either be holding the high ground against any assailants waiting below, or if the attack came from behind, then there would be nothing in their way to block them from reaching the exit.

Unless they were hit from both sides.

Riley's heart hammered in her chest, dreading the thought of a hundred phantom fingers reaching out from the well of inky blackness, intent on dragging them both into the baleful bowels of the abyss.

Just as she was trying to ward off her own horrible mental image, she stumbled at the top of the next flight of stairs.

Instinctively, her hand shot out, reaching for the stairwell's inner railing.

But she couldn't find anything to grab hold of.

Her fingers floated in the darkness, clutching at the empty air as she lost her balance, blindly toppling over into the void.

CHAPTER 14

"Shit!!" Riley shouted as she fell sideways in the pitch black stairwell, her heart flying up into her throat.

"Oh, fuck, oh, fuck..." Taylor's panicked murmuring bounced off the walls.

Riley thrust her arms out to break her fall, stopping herself short of a head-over-heels tumble, only to sprawl out spread-eagled, with the cold kiss of concrete on her cheek.

Her eyebrows furrowed until she realized – they had already reached the ground floor.

She felt a giddy wave of gratitude wash over her, breathing out the tension in her muscles as she clambered to her feet.

"I can't see anything!" Taylor yelled as she shrank into a corner, "Talk to me – what the hell's going on!?"

Riley felt around for the door handle, taking a moment to recompose herself before cracking open the exit.

Taylor shielded her eyes as a sudden burst of light from the lobby flooded the stairwell.

"Got you," Riley winked, as if she had been playing a prank all along.

"That wasn't funny," Taylor fumed, waiting for her eyes

to adjust to the dazzling light before shouldering past.

Riley couldn't have agreed more, glancing up at the empty flight of stairs behind them before following Taylor.

They stepped out into the hotel lobby, both women breathing a sigh of relief.

Rows of flaming torches set inside dirt-filled planters had been arrayed around the edges of the entrance hall, illuminating the Jade Mantis Hotel's opulent foyer.

Long spiral streamers of golden dragons and bulbous red Chinese lanterns hung down from the cavernous ceiling, but dominating the center of the room was a gigantic jade-colored praying mantis – the hotel's namesake – its big bug eyes seeming to stare into every nook and cranny around the lobby, and even into the shadows beyond.

Riley and Taylor passed underneath its watchful gaze as they made their way towards the exit with their heads on a swivel, just as vigilant as the praying mantis.

"I'll bet that creep who attacked us stole the rest of the glow sticks," Taylor mused as they retraced their steps back towards the dark laneway in between the plaza and the strip mall. "Just in case one of us escaped and ran for the stairs."

"Yeah, probably," Riley agreed absent-mindedly, her thoughts already preoccupied with another matter – the one that she had carried all the way down from the fifth floor. Her hotel slippers scraped to a stop in the middle of the laneway, and she turned to Taylor, "Hey, I want you to know something. You're not gonna like it, but it's something that you need to hear anyway."

"Okay," she raised her eyebrows with a shrug, her attention already shifting towards the discordant sounds of the crowd still clustered in the plaza.

"You're not down here because I need you to back me up," Riley began, patiently waiting for her to make eye contact again. "You're down here because Heather wants me to watch over you."

"I don't need you to watch over me," she frowned and smiled at the same time, taking offense at the very idea that she needed any level of supervision.

Riley reached out and flicked the girl on the forehead.

"Ow!" Taylor retreated a few steps, but she wasn't as hurt as she was confused. "What the fuck was that for?"

"That's why your sister doesn't trust you," she explained, trying her best to teach Taylor the same way that Nolan Armstrong had taught Riley, back when her mother had always stopped her from going out with her friends. "You can't defend yourself. Every single time we get into a fight, you're the first one to go down."

"Yeah, but at least I get back up," Taylor argued indignantly. She jerked a thumb over her shoulder at the hotel, "Let's not forget who just saved your asses back there. *And* it was me who killed that fucking Green Beret back in Utah. You two would've been dead a long time ago if it wasn't for –"

Riley flicked her on the forehead again.

"Are you done?" Riley raised her eyebrows. Without waiting for an answer, she continued, "Good. Because one day, you're gonna wake up, and you won't have anybody left to save. Me and Heather will both be dead because you don't know how to protect your face. That guy back there knocked you out *twice*. Don't think for a second that you won that fight by yourself. You need to keep your guard up – or you're gonna be stuck out here on your own."

"Fuck you," Taylor ripped the backpack from her shoulders

and threw it on the ground. "If you don't need me down here, then I'm going back up to my sister. You can sell the food, buy back our gear and bring everything upstairs all by yourself."

Riley rubbed the back of her neck.

She knew that she couldn't let Taylor go alone.

But if they both went upstairs, then Heather would just send them straight back down again.

And every minute that they wasted was another minute that their gear was on sale to everybody else in the plaza.

"I'm not stopping you," Riley shrugged, hoping that a touch of reverse psychology would work. She waved her off back towards the hotel, "Go ahead."

"I don't need your permission," Taylor shot back, turning resolutely on her heel.

"And after you're gone," Riley glanced down at the back-pack next, stirring the girl's suspicions, "Maybe I'll just keep all this to myself."

"You wouldn't," Taylor called her bluff, but her footsteps faltered all the same.

"Wouldn't you?" Riley tested, already knowing the answer.

She knew how much the girl resented her for raiding their stash back in Kansas.

"After everything we've been through," Taylor huffed, holding her gaze, "Do you really think that I'd just leave you to fend for yourself – alone and unarmed, without anything to eat?"

Riley's head cocked slightly.

The rebellious redhead had never taken the high road before.

"If I left you like that," Taylor continued, her eyes narrowing as she closed the distance between them, "You'd just come after us anyway. And we both know I'd hunt you down if you did that to us. But I'd prefer not having to waste my time looking for you."

Without another word, she begrudgingly bent down to sling the backpack over her shoulders again.

Self-preservation over moral standards, Riley stifled a smirk. *At least she's honest.*

Together, they turned back towards the boulevard, heading for the plaza's entrance on the corner of the laneway.

The orange glow of flickering firelight spilling across the sidewalk grew more menacing with each step, as mental images still fresh in Riley's memory flashed across her mind's eye.

The river running red with blood after the massacre they had witnessed.

The decomposing body of a woman starved and shackled to a stripper pole.

And the emaciated man's ghoulish grin, his slimy teeth gleaming in the moonlight.

Shutting out her thoughts, Riley drew a galvanizing breath, hardening her resolve to face whatever was waiting for them next.

CHAPTER 15

An orange aura hung over the public square, the glow of flickering flames emanating from a series of trashcan fires, casting light and shadows across the bustling crowd.

Riley had half-expected the post-apocalyptic Las Vegas to be filled with a bunch of destitute and deranged degenerates – just like the one that they had met in their room – but instead, there seemed to be a sense of community throughout the vibrant marketplace.

Smoking barbecue grills stood along one side of the plaza, where a line of cooks flipped and turned cuts of sizzling snake and lizard meat. Cashiers catered to a row of customers seated at each food stall, swapping stories and trading jokes like they were old friends.

Elsewhere in the square, a team of vendors wheeled around a shopping cart full of water bottles, crews of dust-laden scavengers haggled with merchants over the day's haul, and survivors strolled in between the stalls trying to decide whether to buy tools or toiletries.

Riley hadn't seen a group of people this large since Colorado.

And for Taylor, it had been much longer.

Even now, the freckled girl's eyes were trained on a graying Asian man sitting on the edge of the plaza's center stage, his voice deep and resonant as he brought a story to life for a group of children gathered with their families.

"Hey, are you with me?" Riley prompted, studying the swollen welts on Taylor's face in the glimmering firelight.

"Huh?" she asked distractedly before snapping back to the entrance of the plaza. She nodded towards the graying man's waving hands and animated gestures, "It looks like he's missing a finger. I was just trying to – "

"Keep your guard up," Riley reminded her, aiming another flick at her forehead.

"Can you stop with that shit already?" Taylor snapped irritatedly, searing her with a scathing glare as they entered the square.

Riley had hoped that Manny's Mega Emporium would still be open for business, but the young entrepreneur was sitting in the crowd with the other children, too busy watching the show after the day's work.

Boomer – the boy's brindle pitbull – was on full alert now though, growling at the pair of newcomers as they passed by the jumble of cardboard boxes and garbage bags stacked up beside the wall.

His bared fangs were a stern confirmation that the store was closed for the night.

"Let's try one of these guys," Riley decided instead, heading towards the row of smoking barbecue grills. Trying her best to ignore the sweet wafting aromas filling the air, she caught the attention of the nearest cashier, "Hey, would you be interested in buying some food?"

"*Me?*" he laughed incredulously, along with his customers, "I *sell* food, lady."

"We've got jerky, peanuts, canned goods…" Taylor's voice trailed off as the man held up a silencing hand.

"And we've got a steady supply of fresh meat," he countered, jerking his head back towards the barbecue grills. "So unless you're here to eat something, I'd suggest trying to sell your supplies to one of the merchants instead."

A busty blonde woman with a year's worth of regrowth sat down at the food stall, and the cashier quickly turned away from the conversation to take her order.

"I guess these people can afford to be picky," Taylor scoffed as they turned towards the rows of market stalls.

"Yeah, now you know how it feels," Riley gave her a small snort, reminding the girl of all the times that she had knocked back any particularly chewy or crunchy foods due to her braces. Riley paused beside one of the trashcan fires, studying the crowd before beckoning Taylor to come closer, "Stop here for a second. Let me take a look at the damage."

"Thanks," she replied before hooking her mouth open with a finger, wincing at the pain of her swollen cheek.

"It's hard to tell," Riley murmured, turning the girl's face to one side for a better look at her braces. "Oh yeah – you've definitely got some snapped wires in there."

"I hate these fucking things," Taylor hissed under her breath. She ran her hands through her hair with a heavy sigh. "What are we gonna do now?"

"We could cut out the broken ones with a pair of pliers and a flashlight," Riley shrugged, giving her the only practical answer that she could come up with. After all, they couldn't exactly make an appointment with an orthodontist nowadays.

She clucked her tongue as she added, "See, you wouldn't have this problem if you knew how to protect your face."

"I swear, if you try to flick me again, I'll break your fucking fing–"

"Pardon the interruption," a clean-shaven man approached from behind, setting both women on edge. He spread his hands in a gesture of peace, only holding a bottle of water in the crook of his thumb. "Sorry, I didn't mean to scare you. I just heard you back there while I was having dinner. I'm in the business of buying and selling – were you two ladies looking to offload some food?"

"That's right," Riley answered as she sized him up in the light from the trashcan fire.

The man was tall and well-groomed, wearing a black business suit.

With his easy grin projecting confidence to the pair of newcomers, he reminded her of a traveling salesman – and she imagined that setting himself up as a merchant in the marketplace would have been a natural transition for him.

"I'm Eddie, by the way," he introduced himself before nodding towards Taylor's backpack. "Would you mind if I take a look?"

Riley gave Taylor a nod, and she shrugged the bag from her shoulders.

"Alright, let's see what we've got in here," he said speculatively, rolling up the sleeve of his suit jacket before fishing around inside the backpack's main compartment. Taylor kept a firm grip on the bag's straps while he held each item up to the light. "Canned soup... peanuts... couple bags of rice... oh, I haven't seen these in a while..."

Riley scanned their surroundings as the prospective buyer

browsed through the backpack, wary of anybody else approaching.

But aside from a few other merchants enviously eyeing off the exchange from behind their market stalls, it seemed that everybody else in the plaza was perfectly content with minding their own business.

"You've got quite the haul here," Eddie remarked, showing them that his hand was empty as he stepped away from the backpack. "How much do you want for it?"

Riley ran her thumb along the scars of her fingers.

She had no idea how much the food was worth.

And she didn't know how much it would cost to buy back their gear either.

"Can we come back to you with a price?" she asked, wanting to gauge the market first.

"You can," he began, scratching his cheek with mild annoyance. "Or, I could just give you the best offer you're gonna hear. I'll give you eight hundred right now, for everything. Including the backpack."

"Eight hundred..." Taylor echoed in disbelief, exchanging a sidelong glance with Riley.

"I know – crazy right?" Eddie chuckled as he unscrewed the cap of his water bottle. "You'd think that the end of the world would've curbed inflation a little bit. Nope. Just made it a whole lot worse."

"I think we're still gonna shop around," Riley insisted, hesitant to take the first offer.

People were still entering the plaza in twos and threes, while merchants eagerly awaited new customers freshly-fed from the food stalls.

From the looks of the marketplace, Riley and Taylor would

still have plenty of time to compare prices before making a final decision.

"I'll level with you," Eddie lowered his voice, sidling closer to Riley. "I'm running outta things to sell. Which isn't a bad thing – it just means that my customers love me. But if my inventory dries up, then they'll start buying from somewhere else, and I'd prefer to keep my business running smoothly."

"That sounds like your problem, not ours," Taylor frowned, her voice void of any sympathy as she swung the backpack over her shoulders again.

"I don't wanna miss out on any sales," he ignored the insult, his eyes flitting towards the new wave of customers browsing the stalls. "And I'm sure you ladies would've heard this phrase before – *time is money.* So, I'm willing to throw in an extra hundred if that'll make you happy. Of course, I understand if you'd prefer to shop around first. Honestly, I'd probably do the exact same thing if I was in your position. But if we're just gonna procrastinate on making this deal, then I'd have to lower my offer accordingly. It wouldn't be eight hundred anymore, and certainly not nine."

With that, Eddie turned away, but he didn't stray too far, taking a sip of his water bottle as he gave them a moment to decide.

"What if we ask him for a grand?" Taylor whispered in Riley's ear.

She bit her bottom lip in contemplation.

If a merchant was hounding them for new supplies, then this was a seller's market.

They had the power to dictate the price.

She just didn't know whether they could trust his valuation.

If he was ripping them off, then they wouldn't have anything else left to sell.

But if his offer was genuinely above the market price, then they would have a lot more money available to buy back their gear.

"What'll it be, ladies?" Eddie faced them again, his eye-brows raised expectantly at Riley, sensing that she was the decision maker of the two.

Supposing that they could always haggle with another merchant, she was about to turn down his offer, when she noticed somebody else marching directly towards them from across the square.

"Eddie, I see you're taking advantage of new people again," an athletic woman with long black braids and a nightstick holstered in her belt called out above the noise of the plaza, louder than she needed to.

"I'll tell you what – let's make it a grand," Eddie's easy grin fell from his face as he turned towards Taylor instead, producing a stack of casino chips from his suit jacket's inner pocket.

"Get the fuck away from her," Riley growled with ice in her tone. She glanced back at the approaching woman, "How much is a backpack of food worth around here? This guy just offered us a grand."

"*A grand!?*" she exclaimed incredulously, stopping within inches of the man's face as she dauntlessly stared up at him. "What the hell do you two have in that backpack – caviar? And where'd a scumbag like you get that kinda money from, Eddie?"

"Dakota, please," he took a step backwards to win back some personal space. "We're in the middle of a business transaction here."

"In the middle of another *scam*, more like it," the woman chastised him.

Swift as a whip, she seized his wrist, digging her thumbnail into his skin as she used her other hand to pry one of the casino chips out of his clenched fist.

Riley glanced warily left and right as a small crowd of onlookers began to form around the trashcan fire, watching the altercation with keen interest.

"Ah, no wonder you're so rich all of a sudden," Dakota remarked as she shoved him off balance, before holding up the plastic token for everybody to see. "He's trying to pay with chips from another casino." She locked eyes with Riley, "We only use the chips that come from Valhalla around here. If it doesn't have a picture of a Viking's helmet, it's worthless."

"You fucked up this time, Eddie!" one of the onlookers shouted.

"We gave you so many chances," another bystander shook her head in disgust.

"It's off to Valhalla for you now, bitch," a third voice rang above the noise as Eddie was manhandled out of the marketplace. "We'll see you in the next tournament!"

"No," Dakota held up a hand to silence the frenzied mob. "Take him over to the Tiger's Den first. Maybe he can serve another purpose. It's too dark to drag him all the way to Valhalla now anyway."

Despite the new destination sounding just as foreboding, Eddie's shoulders appeared to relax as he breathed a sigh of relief.

The crowd grumbled among themselves before turning away.

"That piece of shit just tried to scam us," Taylor protested, glancing around indignantly as the onlookers dispersed. She whirled on Dakota, "Don't we get a say in what happens to him?"

"You're new around here," Dakota observed, pointedly looking down at their hotel slippers. She flipped the worthless casino chip at Taylor, "The only thing you get to say is *thank you.*"

"Hey – before you go," Riley stopped the woman as she turned to leave. "We came here to sell our food and buy back the gear that was stolen from us. I don't wanna run the risk of getting scammed by anybody else, so where would you recommend?"

"There's a couple of good places, if you know how to haggle," Dakota began, before directing their attention towards the group of families gathered around the plaza's center stage. "But if you just want a fair price without any headaches, then Manny's the kid you wanna talk to. Catch him after the show, and he'll get you whatever you need. If you want my advice though – keep the food. That's about all anybody works for around here anyway. You'd just be offloading your supplies only to buy them back at a premium."

She studied the faces of the two women, sensing that they had no intention of heeding her advice. With a smirk of amusement, she shook her head as she returned to patrolling the plaza.

Just as they were watching Dakota leave, Riley's focus zeroed in on a familiar mountain bike going up for sale in one corner of the marketplace.

Leaving the warmth of the trashcan fire, she ventured from stall to stall, ignoring the merchants trying to ply their wares in her wake as she scanned each face in the crowd.

And that's when she saw them.

Two of the people responsible for why Riley and the Seabrook sisters were stuck in this mess in the first place.

Jake and Clay were laying out plastic tokens on the counter of an old souvenir kiosk, splitting up the profits between themselves after having sold the last of the stolen supplies and equipment from their former captives.

"What's the plan?" Taylor murmured beside Riley, the rebellious redhead raring for another fight, despite the swollen welts on her face.

"The plan is – you stay here," Riley fixed her with a stern sidelong glare, leaving no room for an argument. "Go sit with Manny, but don't make any deals with him until I get back. And wear the backpack on your chest – just in case somebody else tries stealing from us."

"What about you?" Taylor asked as she switched around her bag's shoulder straps, hugging the backpack instead.

"I'm gonna take back what's ours," Riley replied, narrowing her eyes at the pair of thieving bounty hunters.

CHAPTER 16

Riley pretended to warm her hands over one of the plaza's trashcan fires as she watched Jake and Clay parting ways.

She was still working on her plan of attack, but now that the two men had split up, her window of opportunity was only growing larger with each passing moment.

Her inconspicuous gaze followed Jake as he approached one of the market stalls, engaging the hooded merchant manning the booth in a terse conversation.

Clay wasn't wasting any time either, having already found his purchase for the night, taking a scantily-dressed woman by the hand and twirling her around with a lust-filled grin.

Riley knew that if she wanted her attack to go smoothly, then she was better off with picking the target that wouldn't leave a witness.

She turned her attention back to the other bounty hunter.

"That's bullshit!" Jake suddenly exploded, lunging across the stall's table to seize the merchant by the front of his jacket. "That's more than double what you charged last time. You can't just jack up the price overnight."

"Supply and demand, brother," the man wearing the hoodie

shrugged with a sheepish grin, even as one hand reached behind his back to grip the handle of a screwdriver tucked into his belt. "We got a deal or not?"

"Is there a problem here?" Dakota asked as she drew up alongside the booth, flanked by a pair of wiry watchmen, intent on keeping the peace.

"No, we're good," Jake grumbled out of the side of his mouth, snatching something small from the stall's table.

Angrily pocketing the package, he flung a fistful of casino chips at the merchant's face before storming off.

"Let him go, he'll be back," the man laughed off the insult as he stooped to pick up the scattered plastic tokens. "They always come back."

Keeping her eyes trained on Jake moving through the crowd, Riley waited for the trio of peacekeepers to move along before sidling closer to the stall, glancing over what was on sale.

"I'll be with you in a second," the hooded merchant called from underneath the counter, searching the ground for any more casino chips that he might have missed.

Behind him was a glass display cabinet, its shelves lined with an array of pharmaceutical drugs. Bottles and boxes with long complicated names stood side by side with unmarked blister packs of pills and plastic baggies of crystallized chemicals.

Those assholes sold all of our gear just to buy sex and drugs, Riley's tongue bitterly pressed against the inside of her cheek as she turned around, leaving the stall before the dealer could pitch his poisons.

She scanned the crowd again, her sharp eyes soon locking on to the back of Jake's head, recognizing his dirty blonde hair as he strode out of the square.

Putting on an easy stroll to avoid attracting any unwanted attention, Riley passed by the group of children gathered around the storytelling entertainer on the plaza's center stage. Taylor was among them now, sitting cross-legged beside Manny as they watched the show, with the backpack of food in her lap and a rare smile on her swollen face.

Having seen the marketplace's apparent security force in action, Riley was confident that Taylor would be safe in the crowd, and after everything that the girl had been through over the past year, she of all people deserved a break from what the world had become.

For Riley though, there was still work to be done.

Keeping her distance behind Jake as she followed him out of the plaza, Riley hugged her arms to her chest against the cool breeze, the night's moderate temperature still a stark contrast to the arid desert's daytime heat.

Only a handful of people were out on the moonlit streets, either on their way to the bustling marketplace or heading back to their shelter – whether they were staying at the Jade Mantis Hotel at the end of the laneway, or at some other appropriated accommodation along the six-lane boulevard lined with palm trees.

Trailing behind the drug addict with the length of a small strip mall in between them, Riley's hotel slippers scraped over a slight bump in the sidewalk, the noise prompting Jake to glance back over his shoulder.

Heart jolting in her chest, she leapt for cover behind a bus stop, earning herself a puzzled expression from a pair of survivors crossing the boulevard.

Pretending to have dropped something, Riley probed around on the pavement in a feigned search, mindful of staying behind cover as she listened for Jake's footsteps with bated breath.

This is a new low, she gave herself a small snort, staring down at the sandy sidewalk beside the bus stop, weighed down by the words of her own inner voice.

Riley could picture what she must have looked like, crawling around on her hands and knees, putting on an act for a pair of rubberneckers, just to hide the fact that she was about to kill some lowlife junkie and loot his corpse.

But it wasn't like she hadn't done that before – the latter part at least.

With an icy shiver, she remembered her first kill – Bobby – and rifling through his pockets in the ruins of a rusty caravan parked behind the nightmarish shed of his meth lab.

Everything had changed so much over the course of the past year, and yet she couldn't help but smile to herself at the irony of how some things had managed to stay the same.

But if she could grab Jake's next fix before he shot himself up with it, along with whatever casino chips he had left, then she and Taylor wouldn't need to sell the last of their food in order to buy back their gear.

Riley flexed the slender muscles of her jaw, steeling her resolve.

Her ears pricked up as Jake resumed his steady stride down the sidewalk, still heading in the same direction, his footfalls fading into the distance.

Kicking off her hotel slippers and sliding them into the waistband of her shorts at the small of her back, she rose to her feet again, eyeing the other people in the street before padding out from behind the bus stop.

Still wary of seeming suspicious, Riley pulled the hem of

her black tank top down over the bulge of her protruding slippers, but even if anybody took notice of the barefoot woman stalking Jake down the sidewalk, she doubted that there would be any consequences for whatever might happen next.

Not after the would-be conman, Eddie, had been spared from the purported punishment of being sent to participate in Valhalla's next violent tournament.

And certainly not after Riley and the Seabrook sisters had slain the repulsive wretch who had attacked them back in their hotel room.

If those deeds could slip by without drawing any significant penalties, then she supposed that it was open season on a drug addict who had just stolen and sold what was rightfully theirs.

You kill without cause, you go to the tournament, Barbara's words of caution rang in Riley's ears, only providing affirmation to her thoughts.

Because she had plenty of cause.

Clearing the strip mall's row of ruined storefronts, Riley glanced back over her shoulder to check if anybody else was still strolling across the boulevard.

They were alone now.

She still had Jake's taser to contend with though.

The paralyzing weapon was holstered on his hip, but from what she had seen outside the sheriff's office only a few hours ago, the guy was slow on the draw.

Picking up her pace to close the distance between them, Riley's pupils dilated as her prey slowed down, and she quickly ducked out of sight again, stealing behind a dumpster-sized power box.

Peering around the side of the box, she watched as Jake turned to enter his drug den of choice – an upmarket Italian restaurant that had been ransacked a long time ago.

Crawling out from behind cover, Riley stayed low as she skirted around the artificial hedgerow lining the restaurant's outdoor terrace, tailing Jake into the building.

The once-dignified establishment was completely ravaged inside.

Scavengers had taken all of the tables and chairs, probably salvaging them for firewood. But they hadn't stopped there. Dusty wine racks and wait station cabinets had been stripped down to their bare bones, display boards had been torn from the walls, and somebody had pried off the wooden paneling surrounding the bar.

The only things that they had left intact were the building's windows and a row of defunct refrigerators behind the bar – everything else had been taken.

Flitting from one moonlit shadow to the next, Riley followed the lean junkie up a wide set of stairs and down a bathroom corridor in the back corner, her bare feet silently padding across the tiled floor of the gloomy passage wreathed in darkness.

Jake's footsteps stopped at the far end of the stale-aired hallway, and a set of keys jangled as he stood in front of a door, its rectangular frame outlined by a ribbon of light shining through from a room on the other side.

Pulse pounding in her ears, Riley edged forward on the balls of her feet as she made her stealthy approach in the darkness, closing in on his silhouette like a nocturnal predator.

He had his key in the door, utterly unaware that she was rearing up behind him like a python poising to attack.

And with one sharp breath, her arms wrapped around his neck in a rear naked choke.

"Who the fuck –" he managed to splutter, before she forced his head against the crook of her elbow, cutting off his windpipe.

Clawing at her throttling arm, the drug addict desperately tried to wrench himself free.

Riley leaned backwards in response, using gravity to add pressure to the squeeze on his throat, smelling the scent of fear muddying the man's musk.

Gagging as he fought for breath, Jake fell to the floor on one knee, dragging her down with him.

Thrown off balance with her weight now on top of him, Riley could already feel her chokehold beginning to break, and she slipped her other hand out from behind his head, blindly searching for the taser holstered on his hip instead.

Sensing the shift in her arms, Jake grunted with exertion as he powered himself upright again, lifting Riley's feet up off the floor and slamming her backwards against the wall.

Riley snarled in pain, but she held on, tying her legs in a knot around his waist as she ripped the weapon free from his holster.

"You junkie piece of shit," she hissed in his ear, still riding his back as she jammed the taser's barrel into the nape of his neck. "Give me one good reason why I shouldn't scramble your fucking brains right now."

"Well, first off – I don't even know who the fuck you are," he croaked, tugging at her arm still wrapped around his throat.

"You sold almost everything we had just to buy some drugs," Riley's forefinger toyed with the trigger, yearning to jolt the junkie's memory. "You better hope your dope dealer does refunds."

"And secondly," Jake continued, despite being only a finger's twitch away from thousands of volts rattling up his cervical spine. "You've still got the safety on."

"Bullshit," Riley called him on his bluff.

She squeezed the stiff trigger impotently.

Icy panic clawed at her face, and she fumbled for the safety lever with her thumb.

Feeling the shift of her hand, Jake twisted around and rammed her into the wall on the other side of the corridor, knocking her grip loose.

The taser fell to the floor with a clatter.

Riley slid off his back and shoved him away.

Dropping to all fours in the darkness, her fingers scrabbled across the tiles, blindly searching for the weapon.

And then the door creaked open.

CHAPTER 17

"Jake, is that you?" a middle-aged woman dressed in a nightgown stood in the doorway, curiously peering down at the breathless pair groping around on the tiled floor. "Who's this you've brought?"

"Mom, you shouldn't be on your feet," Jake's face filled with concern as he scrambled to the woman's side, draping her arm around his shoulders. He glanced back at Riley in the light emanating from the room, recognizing her as one of the captives from earlier that day. "This is uhh..."

"Riley," she growled as she clambered upright, her sharp gaze dropping to Jake's hand clutching his taser.

He wasn't pointing the weapon at her, but he wasn't putting it away either.

Riley hadn't come up empty-handed though.

In all the confusion in the darkness of the corridor, she had managed to pick up his precious package – a small plastic bottle – with pills rattling around inside.

"Well, you can call me Mrs Roscoe," the woman smiled in introduction before turning sidelong to her son. "What on earth were you two doing on the floor?"

"I thought I dropped my keys," Jake lied with a shrug, his keen eyes trained on the bottle in Riley's hand.

"They're still here in the door, you goose," Mrs Roscoe reached for the keys hanging from the door handle, her hand trembling in the air for a moment before her arm flopped to her side. She leaned her weight on her son, "I think you'd better set me down. Come on in, Riley. Don't be a stranger."

But Riley's feet were firmly rooted to the spot.

The last time that she had accepted a sketchy invitation, she had been strung up in the Lawson Family's front yard for it.

And besides, she already had the drugs in her hand.

She could pretend to follow them inside, and then slam the door shut in their wake. Turning on a dime, she'd be able to bolt back down the corridor before Jake could even think to swing his taser up at her heels.

By the time he caught up to her, she would have already been back under the protection of the marketplace's peace-keepers, selling his next fix to the highest bidder and using the proceeds to buy back the gear that he had stolen.

But judging by the way that Jake was hauling the middle-aged woman back inside the restaurant's office, leaving Riley in limbo at the door, she held a sneaking suspicion that the drugs weren't for him at all.

She lingered in the doorway, still clutching the bottle of pills as she peered into the candlelit backroom.

The office space had been split up into two sections, with a thin wall of plywood partially separating the front half of the room from the rear. A candle burning on a nightstand stood in the walkway between the two halves, its dancing flame casting light on dusty bedroom furniture that had once belonged in a hotel room.

"She seems like a nice girl," Mrs Roscoe remarked with a weary sigh as Jake sat her down in an armchair beside the nightstand. She moved to pick up a book, when a thought struck her, "Oh, where are my manners? I'll go put on the kettle. Would you like coffee or tea, Riley?"

"Neither, Mom," Jake answered on her behalf with a strained voice. "We don't have a kettle anymore, remember?"

"Ah, that's right," Mrs Roscoe settled back into her seat with a cloudy look in her eyes. With a slightly embarrassed expression, she explained, "We couldn't keep up with the electricity bills, so we had to sell off whatever we weren't using anymore." She looked over at Jake, "How was work today, son?"

"Another slow day," he reported, with a sidelong glance at Riley. "We only made three sales."

"Well, tomorrow's another day," Mrs Roscoe gave him an encouraging smile. "We'll be back on our feet in no time. You'll see."

With that, she picked up her book, reading in the candlelight for a few moments before frowning down at the page and flipping back to the start.

Riley furrowed her eyebrows at the woman.

It seemed that Mrs Roscoe wasn't even aware that the world had ended.

Or maybe she had known about it, and her apparent short-term memory had spared her the anguish.

"Dementia?" Riley guessed with a whisper, looking over at Jake.

Exhaling heavily, he ran a hand through his hair as he stared around the room.

Finally meeting her gaze, he sniffed before deciding to holster his taser, either supposing or hoping that Riley was no longer a threat.

"She's got CNS – central nervous system – vasculitis," Jake answered in a somber voice, wheeling out an office chair and offering her a seat as he sat down on his desk.

Riley remained standing in the doorway though, politely refusing the invitation.

She had learned too many hard lessons when it came to trusting strangers – appearances weren't always what they seemed.

"That slows it down some," Jake continued unfazed, nodding towards the bottle of pills in her hand. "It's supposed to keep the seizures at bay and stop her from having a stroke, but it's not a cure."

"So this is why you sold all of our gear," Riley surmised, holding up the medicine to inspect the label in the candlelight, "*Prednisone?*"

"That, and a bunch of immunosuppressants," Jake replied, jerking a thumb over his shoulder at a cluster of more plastic bottles and boxes on the table behind him. His breath hitched, and he blinked rapidly at the floor, unable to meet her gaze anymore. "We came real close this time. We've only got two of those prednisone pills left... You gotta understand, I don't enjoy doing what I have to do, but –"

"You should take pride in your work, son," Mrs Roscoe chimed in as she turned a page in her book, only half-listening in on the conversation as she gave him an oblivious kernel of wisdom. "Find fulfillment in everything that you do, and you'll never have a dull day in your life."

Riley watched a single tear roll down Jake's cheek.

He has to take care of his mom, she finished his sentence in her head.

Her tightly-wound shoulders slackened with sympathy, having borne the burden of being a breadwinner herself. In order to keep her own mother well-fed during her pregnancy, Riley had stolen from Heather and Taylor's group back in Kansas.

But that hadn't come without consequences.

"You realize that you're gonna have to pay us back for this, right?" Riley prompted, shaking the bottle of pills to get his attention again.

"With what?" Jake groaned, roughly pawing at his cheeks before looking back up at her. He swept his hand around the room. "We've already sold off everything we had. You want the furniture too? You'd just be wasting time and effort. It's cheaper than food nowadays. We don't have anything else to give."

"That armored truck you picked us up in," the words came out of her mouth before she even had a chance to think of anything else. Raising her eyebrows at him, she doubled down on her demand. "You give us that, and a full tank of fuel, and we're square."

"It's not mine to give," he shook his head. "Otherwise I would've already sold it. We hire the truck from Radek's people. And all of the vehicles go back to the impound if they're not being used. Stops anybody from trying to siphon out the diesel."

"Then rent it out again," Riley shrugged, glancing over at Mrs Roscoe before lowering her voice. "Drive us out to the edge of town and we'll take it from there. If anybody asks, just say that you had engine trouble and you had to ditch it.

And if they try to come back and tow it, then by the time they get there, it'll be gone. And with all the scavengers hanging around here, nobody's gonna question a missing truck."

"No, they'll just hold Lincoln responsible instead," Jake shut down the idea, "If not him, then Barbs, Clay and me. And I'm not about to let my friends take the fall – especially not over selling some supplies to the people who need them."

"Then I guess I'll just have to sell this," Riley supposed with a half-bluff, holding up the bottle of pills before clenching it in her fist.

"Don't," Jake warned, sliding off the desk with one hand resting on his holstered taser.

Riley's bloodstream spiked with an icy bolt of adrenaline at the threat.

She knew that in an instant, she could lunge into the room, twist his wrist behind his back and disarm him, taking both the weapon and the medicine for herself.

But a movement flashed in her peripheral vision.

The fragile Mrs Roscoe flipped back to the first page of her book, starting over again.

All the fight left Riley then.

She rubbed the back of her neck, caught in a deadlock.

No matter which way she tried to claim back compensation for what had been stolen, it seemed that somebody else would have to suffer.

And although Riley had done some pretty nasty things over the past year, she wasn't about to deprive a disabled woman of her medicine.

"You owe me," she growled, tossing Jake the bottle of pills, "Big time. You piece of sh–"

She caught herself mid-sentence as Mrs Roscoe glanced up

at the curse, and Riley spun on her heel, storming barefoot back down the shadowy corridor.

"Who was that?" Mrs Roscoe wondered, her faint and confused voice following Riley into the gloom of the ransacked restaurant.

It wasn't until she had stepped back out onto the sidewalk that she let out what she had really wanted to say – something that she had been holding back ever since she and the Seabrook sisters had lost all of their gear.

"FUUUUUCK!!"

CHAPTER 18

Riley's bare feet were cold against the pavement as she padded down the dark sidewalk, preferring the stealth of her soft footsteps over the scrape of her hotel slippers that were still bulging from the back of her waistband.

It was getting late now, and she was walking alone through the city's unlit no-man's-land – a black bridge of darkness in between the fading glow of the plaza ahead, and the blazing lights of the Valhalla Hotel far away in the distance behind her.

The Las Vegas Strip's sea of concrete and asphalt was otherwise lifeless, but she still kept her eyes peeled for any potential predators prowling the barren boulevard.

Because she knew that letting her guard down in the deepening darkness would be an open invitation for a deranged degenerate.

Or a whole gang of them.

Shadows shifted behind the ruins of ravaged storefronts as shrouds of silhouettes seemed to scamper from one inky black well to the next, melting away in the same moment that they had materialized.

Whether the fleeting figures were born from imagination or intuition, the lurking lunatics mocked the lone woman's progress along the sidewalk, their slimy coal-like teeth grinning in the void as they yearned for an opportunity to surround her.

And acting in tandem with the slinking shadows, a sinister silence stalked the streets.

Riley could no longer hear the noise of the clamoring crowd in the distance – there was no garbled chatter of the marketplace, no metallic rasp of barbecue tongs scraping the grills, nor the resonant voice of the spirited storyteller entertaining families from the center stage.

It was as if all of the night's sound had been sucked out of the air, and she was alone in the world.

"Oh fuck," Riley whispered under her breath, the hushed curse deafening in her own ears. "Taylor."

If the crowd was already gone, then the girl who had no idea how to protect her face would be on her own – vulnerable and out in the open – waiting alone with the last of their food.

An icy shiver ran up Riley's spine, her thoughts filling with dread as she considered what a pack of desperate lowlifes would do to get their grubby paws on such a prize.

Veins spiking with adrenaline, she arched her back and broke into a headlong sprint.

We never should've split up, the young redhead's regrets rang around Riley's head as she pounded the pavement. In her mind's eye, she could still remember the girl mourning her dead friends back in Utah. *All I wanted to do was get our shit back.*

The grim memory scarred Riley's retinas as she hurtled towards the plaza, and just as she was forcing her focus to snap back on track – for a split second – she caught a glimpse of her own face grieving in Taylor's place.

A rash of gooseflesh flooded her arms and legs as she bolted through the entrance to the square.

"Taylor!?" Riley shouted, the area surrounding the plaza's center stage completely abandoned. "Shit, shit, shit..."

CHAPTER 19

Heart hammering in her chest, Riley spun in circles, staring around in disbelief.

The entire marketplace had died in her absence.

Embers burned low in the trashcan fires arrayed across the square.

The rows of merchant stalls had been buried underneath a patchwork of canvas.

And the only person standing beside the barbecue grills now was a feeble old man, hunched over with his gnarled fingers foraging for scraps of burnt meat buried among the ashes.

"Taylor!!" Riley yelled, her panicked gaze scanning the faces of the few stragglers still winding down for the night.

But aside from a few curious glances, nobody seemed to care.

She was about to call out to the old man, when something hairy brushed past her leg, and a wave of hot air blanketed her heels.

Nerves jolting into overdrive, Riley whirled around and backpedaled for distance, thinking that some silent stalker from the street had followed her into the square.

Instinctively, she whipped up her palms in a combat stance, ready to defend herself.

But she was only staring out into the night – nobody was there.

Glancing down, she locked eyes with Boomer, the pitbull cocking his head up at her with mild curiosity, before he trotted off with a bored half-bark.

Catching her breath, Riley watched as the muscle-bound dog headed back towards Manny's lean-to tent shelter beside the entrance.

Hoping that the kid would have some answers, she took a few steps towards his makeshift shelter, when she heard somebody calling out her name.

"Are you gonna help me with these bags or not?" Taylor's voice carried across the empty square.

The brazen girl stepped out from the shadowy entrance of a former karaoke bar along the rear wall of the plaza, with a bundle of all too familiar backpacks and bags of camping gear arrayed at her feet.

Heaving a grateful sigh of relief, Riley crossed the square towards the surprisingly intact row of small businesses. The unscathed karaoke lounge was flanked by souvenir stalls and specialty stores that had somehow survived the squads of scavengers that had swept through the city.

"I thought I told you not to make any deals until –"

Riley faltered as she caught sight of a pair of dark figures standing in the open doorway underneath the bar's unlit neon sign.

Slowing her stride, she gave her eyes some time to adjust as she peered at the two men watching her approach.

One guy had thick eyebrows and the beginnings of a sparse

goatee, while the other had tousled black hair and a small hoop in one of his earlobes, the gold earring glinting in the dying light of the plaza's trashcan fires.

"Somebody gave me an offer and you weren't around," Taylor grunted as she shouldered her backpack. "You're welcome."

"We were supposed to be making a deal with Manny," Riley reminded her, before jerking her head towards the two men standing in the shadowy entrance. "Who the hell are these guys?"

The man with the earring snorted in amusement, smirking sidelong at his friend.

Neither one of them bothered to give her an answer though.

"They're cool," Taylor vouched for them, turning to offer her grazed arm as proof. She had scraped off some skin after crashing her bike outside the graveyard earlier, but now the wound was bandaged. "They gave me some instant cold packs for my face too, and they even cut out the broken wires from my braces."

Riley studied her face for a moment.

The girl's welts had visibly improved – there was no longer any swelling.

And fixing her damaged braces was one less thing to worry about.

Taking a deep breath, Riley calmed her nerves.

The pair of shady mutes weren't a threat.

Not after treating Taylor's wounds and returning all of their gear.

And yet, something still wasn't adding up.

"Everything's here, right?" Riley glanced down at their bags, toying with the idea of conducting a full inventory check right there in front of the karaoke bar.

"Most of it," the guy with the goatee finally broke his silence. "We're keeping all of the meds though. And somebody else already bought your bike – that's between you and them now. But if you're staying over at the Jade Mantis, then going up and down those stairs every day carrying a bike over your shoulder would've been a bitch anyway."

"We don't plan on staying long," she replied, although now the truth of that statement hinged on how far Heather would be able to move on foot. Riley knew that they would have to cut a separate deal to buy back the bike. Shelving the problem for later, she continued, "What about our guns?"

"What guns?" the other man was quick to play dumb, failing to stifle a grin.

"Don't fuck with me," her tone turned icy, staring daggers at him. "I've had a long day and I'm not in the mood for games right now. Which one of these bags has the guns?"

"You're better off forgetting that they ever existed," a woman's voice floated up from the depths of the karaoke bar. The orange glow of a flaming torch illuminated a downward flight of stairs just beyond the entrance, and Dakota soon emerged from the lower level. "Nobody around here is allowed to carry any firearms. Radek's rules. You're not getting them back."

"I don't give a shit about this Radek guy or his rules," Riley shot back, turning her ire on the woman instead. "We've already given you all the food we had left. Now give us our weapons – and all of the bullets – and then we're outta here."

Taylor shifted her weight uncomfortably.

The two men in the doorway parted, and Dakota stepped out into the plaza.

"Even if I *could* give you back everything," she began, turning her gaze between the pair of women, "You still wouldn't be able to leave."

"We'll find our own way," the determination in Riley's voice made up for the doubt in her mind.

The arduous journey from Las Vegas to Redhurst was still a daunting prospect – no food, no transport, and with only the water that they could carry on their backs – crossing the desert on foot in the middle of summer was dancing dangerously close to the edge of a slow death.

"What I mean is – you're obligated to stay here now," Dakota nodded towards Taylor. "Just ask your friend what kinda deal she made."

"That backpack of food was the only thing we had to offer," Riley said slowly, before turning her gaze on the girl.

"The food wouldn't have been enough," Taylor's voice cracked, shrinking underneath the weight of her stare. "Manny gave me three choices – we could trade for the things that we had in our backpacks; take the bike and the camping gear; or I could get myself patched up. But I could only pick one. And that was the *best* he could do."

"So what was the fourth option?" Riley raised her eyebrows, already knowing which choice she had made.

"We get everything – including the food, but only after... " Taylor stopped herself short, swallowing the rest of her sentence. "Look, can we just talk about this later? If you and Heather are gonna chew me out over the best possible deal we could've gotten, I'd rather you both did it at the same time so that I only have to listen to all the bullshit once."

"What the hell did you sign us up for?" Riley seethed as she glared at the girl, demanding to know what she had promised to these people.

The man with the earring sniggered at something that only he seemed to find funny.

"Shut it, Hanzo," Dakota warned, waving her flaming torch at his face as she locked eyes with Riley. "Come back tomorrow, and you can go over all the details with the man in charge. We're gonna keep the rest of your food here though – think of it as an insurance policy until you can hold up your end of the deal." Then, reaching into her back pocket with her other hand, she produced a can of spiced ham, tossing it towards Riley before adding, "This is just so you don't show up hungry tomorrow... I did tell you to keep the food."

Taylor's gaze was all over the darkening plaza, taking a sudden interest in everything except for Riley as she knelt down beside the rest of their gear.

Silently fuming, she opened up her backpack and shoved the canned ham inside.

"You girls sure didn't waste any time," the gravelly-voiced Barbara Greene remarked as she strolled along the rear wall of the plaza, stopping in front of the karaoke bar. She pointedly glanced down at their reclaimed gear, "How much did all that cost you?"

"I guess we'll find out," Riley gave her a terse reply as she zipped up her backpack and rose to her feet, shooting a scathing sidelong stare at Taylor.

"Jin, go ahead and take Barbs downstairs," Dakota instructed, passing her torch to the guy with the goatee.

"Hey, thanks for the heads-up about the hotel by the way," Taylor smiled sarcastically before Barbara could turn to leave, seizing the opportunity to shift some of the heat off herself. "Some crazy guy attacked us the minute we stepped into a room."

"And which floor did you girls stop at?" Barbara wondered in a knowing voice, slouching with one hand on her hip.

"My sister couldn't make it past level five," she bristled at the woman's leisurely tone.

"Hold on, I thought we blocked off that floor months ago," Dakota frowned, looking at Jin and Hanzo for confirmation.

"Well, it was open when we got up there," Riley shrugged, before turning her mind towards how she and Taylor were going to split the burden of carrying all of their gear up the stairs.

"Either way, I did say don't stop until you get to at least the fourteenth," Barbara reminded them both, as if climbing the stairwell for over a dozen stories wouldn't have crippled Heather's leg into another three months of recovery. "I also remember saying – you try taking any shortcuts, and this town will eat you up alive."

"Yeah, we just didn't think you meant that in the literal sense," Riley countered as she swung her backpack over her shoulders.

"It's Vegas, honey – anything goes," Barbara sighed, turning to follow Jin down the stairs into the karaoke bar. She paused at the threshold though, glancing back to scan the plaza. "I don't see your peg-leg friend limping around out here. Where is she?"

"Heather's still up on level five," Riley cocked her head slightly at the woman's concern.

"Dakota, you better go with them," Barbara's voice suddenly tightened. Wide-eyed dread filled her gaze as she dropped her laid-back demeanor, and she stared gravely at Riley and Taylor. "There's a hell of a lot more than just one guy in there."

CHAPTER 20

"HURRY THE FUCK UP!!" Taylor screamed in panic, kicking off her hotel slippers as she sprinted headlong out of the square, both she and Riley abandoning the rest of their gear in front of the karaoke bar.

Boomer's startled barks echoed behind them as they dashed down the dark laneway back towards the Jade Mantis Hotel.

With her bare feet pounding the asphalt in the girl's wake, Riley unslung her backpack and opened it up on the fly, rummaging through the contents as they bounced around.

Boots, gloves, clothes, canned ham...

"Don't tell me you took my fucking knife too!?" she yelled over her shoulder as they swerved around the corner towards the front of the hotel.

"Hanzo!?" Dakota shouted in turn, gripping the handle of the nightstick holstered in her belt as she shadowed their heels.

"I'm pretty sure it's in there – keep looking!" he yelled back, bringing up the rear. "Oh shit, which bag did you take?"

Riley shot him a withering glare.

But it was too late to turn back now.

There was no time to lose.

The four runners raced up the front steps, with Taylor crashing through the entrance, the shuddering glass door threatening to shatter from the impact.

Surging across the lobby, they skirted around the gigantic statue of the praying mantis dominating the center of the room, only to stop dead in their tracks outside the elevator hall.

A group of people were gathered around the entrance to the shadowy stairwell, with at least a dozen of them sporting smears of blood on their faces, hands and clothes.

"Dakota!" one of the cashiers from the food stalls cried out, tottering towards the four newcomers.

"What's going on!?" Dakota's gaze flitted from his ashen face to the injured survivors lying on the floor, moaning in pain as they staunched their wounds.

Riley's pupils dilated as she peered at some of the victims nursing bite marks.

"It's a fucking bloodbath up there," the cashier's voice trembled with trauma. "We were on our way back up to our rooms, and... and..."

His breath hitched, and his words failed him.

The rest of the group were quick to fill in the silence.

"Those sons of bitches attacked us all at once!"

"Upstairs – downstairs – it didn't matter where we ran!"

"I thought all those floors were supposed to be sealed off!"

Just as their cries clamored to a crescendo, a bone-chilling shriek reverberated from the stairwell, and the lobby fell to fearful murmurs.

"Go straight to the Tiger's Den," Hanzo growled at the first person to head for the exit. "Tell them to send everybody."

Riley's hand was still digging around in the depths of her backpack as the panicked group of people shuffled past.

Finally catching hold of her combat knife, she ripped the blade from its sheath, clenching the handle in between her teeth as she zipped up her backpack.

"What are you doing?" Dakota frowned, eyes on Taylor grabbing a flaming torch from the nearest dirt-filled planter, the brazen girl pushing past the fleeing survivors as she made a beeline for the stairwell. "We should wait for backup before we go upstairs."

"Fuck that – my sister's up there," Taylor marched into the gaping maw of the stairwell, only glancing back for a moment. "Riley, are you coming?"

"As if you have to ask," she shouldered her backpack again as she followed the girl inside. "You follow my lead though. And make sure you protect your face this time, or you're gonna get yourself killed before we even reach Heather."

With a spiteful scowl, Taylor nodded in agreement, before jerking her head towards the first flight of steps.

A pair of dead bodies lay broken at the bottom of the stairwell, both having hurled themselves over the inner railing in a desperate bid to escape the brutality that had befallen them.

"We're not letting you go up there by yourselves," Dakota called from behind, pulling the nightstick from her belt as Riley mounted the steps. "Just go slow. It sounds like they're organized this time – I don't want us taking any chances."

"Ah shit," Hanzo muttered to himself, pulling a set of brass knuckles from his trouser pocket and slipping them on. He grabbed another torch before joining the climb, "Here we go again."

With the light from the flickering flames at her back, Riley's shadow leapt across the walls, flying from corner to corner as they crested each landing.

Despite knowing that Heather was in danger, Riley willed herself to maintain her steady pace up the stairs to avoid rushing into a trap.

She had learned that lesson one too many times back in Utah.

They were creeping past the next access door, when another blood-curdling scream from one of the floors above sent shivers down her spine.

"Why the hell would you let anybody stay here if it's not safe!?" Taylor's whispered shout filled the stairwell as the anguished echoes faded.

"We thought they'd all be dead by now," Dakota replied, keeping her voice low.

"Who are *they*?" Riley's curiosity got the better of her as she led the way up the stairs.

"Just regular people who ran outta food," Dakota answered grimly, dredging up a dreadful memory that she had hoped to have kept hidden. "Back when Radek first started offering bounties for new people to populate the city and fill his tournaments, anybody hunting for fresh survivors would strip them of everything they had before dumping them here to fend for themselves."

"Some decided to join our community, but most went their own way," Hanzo added, walking backwards up the stairs to make sure that they wouldn't be caught by surprise from behind. "After living on rats and roaches for months on end though, I guess it wasn't much of a leap to human flesh next."

Riley flexed the slender muscles of her jaw, realizing the

reason why she and the Seabrook sisters had been sent away with enough food to last them for a while.

Their captors hadn't wanted to bolster the ranks of the cannibals.

"No matter how many times we tried to flush them out," Dakota continued as they cleared the next landing, "They kept on coming back. So we lured as many as we could down to the lower levels, barricaded the doors, and hoped that they would all just starve to death."

"My question is – how the fuck did they get out?" Hanzo wondered as he peered over the stairwell's inner railing at the steps below, still watching their rear.

"Maybe through the vents," Riley ventured a guess, remembering the emaciated rake of a man who had attacked them.

His skeletal frame could have easily fit through an air duct.

"But then they could've done this ages ago," Taylor chimed in from behind, passing by wet splotches of blood smeared across the wall. "Why wait until today?"

"Because the power went out today," Riley knew, recalling the conversation that they had heard between Barbara and Manny. Radek's people hadn't made a delivery of diesel following the heist, hoarding the remaining fuel for their own generators. "These guys could've been waiting for the lights to shut off before they made their move – so that nobody else would notice that all the barricades were gone until it was too late."

That's what I would've done, she neglected to add.

They mounted the fifth floor's landing, shuffling over torn scraps of clothing as they passed by a pair of bloody handprints that had been torn from the inner railing.

Riley pressed her ear to the wooden surface of the access door, furrowing her eyebrows at the sound of faint groans coming through from the other side – but whether they were moans of pleasure or pain, she couldn't tell.

"Ready?" she whispered, clutching the door handle as the others drew up behind her.

"Hold on," Taylor glanced back at Dakota and Hanzo, both of them taking a galvanizing breath before giving her a nod. The girl swallowed her nerves as she stared back at Riley. "Let's go."

CHAPTER 21

Riley yanked open the access door and burst out into the gloom of the fifth floor's elevator hall, clenching the combat knife in her fist – tip pointed downwards – as she glanced left and right.

Taylor shuffled through the doorway next, the flickering flames of her torch casting light over a trail of fresh blood. The crimson streak cut a slippery swathe through the glow sticks scattered across the floor, staining the hotel corridor's green carpet red as the grisly track disappeared around the corner.

Pulse pounding in her ears, Riley edged along the far side of the elevator hall, her sharp gaze tracing the bend of the bloody trail into the hallway beyond.

Her stomach lurched at the sight of three skeletal figures hunched over on the floor, only half a dozen yards down the corridor.

Their backs were turned to her, with a pair of legs snaking out from underneath the horrendous huddle, their victim's shoes lifelessly jerking and twitching with every violent *snap* of tendons and ligaments.

Taylor stifled a gag as she, Dakota and Hanzo furtively formed up behind Riley, the orange glow of their torches painting the sickening scene in a hellish hue.

The trio of feasting cannibals obliviously smacked their lips as they slurped on steaming entrails, gnashing and grinding their slimy teeth on ragged chunks of human flesh torn from the bone, occasionally rearing back their heads in muffled moans of malnourished ecstasy.

Swallowing the bile burbling in her gullet, Riley kept the cluster of living zombies in the corner of her eye as she motioned for Dakota and Hanzo to move up.

Dakota gripped the side handle of her nightstick, ready to do some damage with the short end of the baton, while Hanzo squared his shoulders, his brass knuckles gleaming in the light of his torch.

"Stay back," Riley silently mouthed at Taylor, waiting for the girl's reluctant nod.

With the combat knife a serrated extension of her fist, and the pair of peacekeepers by her side, Riley's bare feet padded out onto the corridor's carpet, her eyes laser-focused as they crept towards the three gorging ghouls from behind.

Lost in the euphoria of devouring their fresh kill, the revolting wretches were blind to the flickering flames of Hanzo's torch lighting up the corridor, ravenously wolfing down their unlucky prey without a care in the world.

Gladly taking advantage of their distraction, Riley stepped within striking distance, raising her blade for a swift execution, when an ear-piercing shriek filled the hallway behind them.

A cold spike of adrenaline laced with icy dread bolted through her veins.

They had been spotted.

"Shit," was the first thing that came to Riley's mind as the trio of man-eating monsters turned away from their meal.

Not wasting any time, she aimed a downward stab at the closest cannibal.

But the blade narrowly missed its mark as her target jerked forward, all three of them clambering over the half-eaten corpse and surging to their feet in a flash, as if they had been anticipating a surprise attack the entire time.

The callous creatures whirled around, their feral faces gleaming with mottled sheens of grime and blood in the flames of Hanzo's torch, savagely snarling with long strips of flesh caught in between their teeth.

"BEHIND YOU!!" Taylor's shout came from the elevator hall.

Retreating a step from the trio of cannibals, Riley and the others whipped their heads around just in time to catch a glimpse of a crazed woman charging down the corridor, arching her back as she barreled towards them at full speed, spear-tackling Riley's torso with a blade-thin shoulder.

The momentum was enough to knock Riley off her feet, and she landed in a heap beside the mauled victim, wedged sideways in between the dead body and her own backpack as she grappled with the wild woman screaming on top of her.

Without a moment's pause, the other three bony blood-stained beasts bent over Riley. Quickly gauging that she was wielding the most lethal weapon, they were intent on disabling her as soon as possible.

Pinned to the floor, heart hammering in her chest, Riley twisted around to awkwardly jam her elbow up into the starved woman's ribcage, staving off the most immediate threat while she swung her blade past the grasping hands reaching for her wrist, frantically stabbing and slashing at the six lanky legs surrounding her.

Impossible to miss with so many targets, the combat knife's serrated teeth sawed through scrawny flesh and plunged through an ankle before Dakota and Hanzo sprang into action, beating the bony brutes backwards with their baton and torch.

With Hanzo's firebrand arcing from side to side across the width of the corridor, Riley stared up at the emaciated woman's grimy face, gleaming and dimming above her in the shifting flames. The woman's blood-tinged teeth glistened as she slavered over her next meal, snapping her jaws while scratching and clawing at Riley with her brittle fingernails.

Grunting and rasping in exertion, Riley used one arm to wrestle with the wild-eyed woman while working to flip the blade in her other hand.

But her palm was slick with sweat, and the knife slipped out of her grasp.

"TAYLOR!!" she roared in a fit of panic, before balling up a fist and throwing a rushed punch at the woman's forehead.

A jolt of pain shot through Riley's wrist at the impact, and her hand went back to scrabbling across the carpet, searching for her lost weapon.

The hideous harpy shook herself out of the momentary punch-drunk stupor, and she raked her fingernails across Riley's cheek, one splintery claw snapping off in the slash.

Snarling at the sting of her gouged face, Riley's fumbling fingertips finally brushed over the knife's hilt again, and she snatched it up with a white-knuckled grip, thrusting the crimson edge up at the cannibal's throat.

But the vile woman blocked the blow, and seizing her knife

hand with two gaunt fists, she yanked up Riley's forearm, jaws opening to take a bite out of her flesh.

Trying to jerk away from her clacking teeth, Riley growled as she struggled to rip her arm free, but it was no use – the woman's frenzied grip was like being caught in a vise.

Out of options, Riley dropped her defensive arm from the madwoman's ribcage, and she reached around to grab a greasy lock of the harpy's hair instead, wrenching her cadaverous skull to one side.

But the malnourished tangle only sloughed away from the skeletal savage's scalp.

Holding the handful of shorn hair in disbelief, Riley watched with wide-eyed horror as the fiend's fangs closed around her forearm.

And then a sudden explosion of flames forced her eyes shut.

"Yeah – protect your face, bitch!" Taylor yelled triumphantly, standing over Riley with her blazing torch.

Immediately dropping the attack, the would-be assailant rolled over to one side of the corridor, shrieking in agony as she gingerly held her smoldering cheek.

Catching her breath, Riley extracted herself from the wedge in between her own backpack and the half-eaten body.

Clambering upright, she crossed the corridor to put a swift end to the deranged banshee's warbling wail – one ruthless knee to the face, and a deep slash across her windpipe for good measure.

The victory was short-lived though.

There were still three more cannibals in the corridor to contend with.

And emerging from the far end of the hallway, drawn by all the noise, another menacing figure bathed in blood began limping rapidly towards them, eager to join the fight.

CHAPTER 22

The pair of peacekeepers from the plaza had their backs up against the wall in the hotel corridor, with Dakota's nightstick wedged firmly underneath the chin of one hollow-eyed cannibal as he tried to wrestle for control of the baton.

Staring dauntlessly back at the bloodstained savage, she growled as she swung the weightless wretch around, slamming the back of his skull into the wall before forcing the length of her baton across his throat, cutting off the air to his windpipe.

Hanzo, on the other hand, was struggling with the other two deranged deviants.

One malnourished monster had his lanky legs splayed out on the floor, blood gushing from his wounded ankle, but still managing to keep Hanzo's fist with the brass knuckles out of the fight, holding on to his wrist with unnatural strength.

But it was the third grimy ghoul who was keeping him occupied, darting in and out of range as the wiry watchman frantically swung his firebrand from side to side, the madman flirting with the dying flames of the torch as he eagerly searched for an opening.

"Make sure there's nobody else coming up behind us," Riley spoke over her shoulder as blood dripped from the gashes across her cheek.

"Call out if you need me," Taylor didn't argue, knowing how vulnerable they were in the middle of the hallway.

She cast the light of her torch over the remains of the half-eaten body before peering into the darkness behind them – each open doorway lining the corridor housing a potential rat nest of former humans just waiting to pour out and overwhelm them.

Riley set her sights on the lone figure limping towards them from the far end of the hallway. Based on the shadowy straggler's shambling gait, she still had enough time to help Hanzo and tip the odds back in their favor before the blood-covered beast would descend on them.

The wounded creature sitting at Hanzo's feet bleated a warning cry at Riley's approach, but her primitive prey was too fixated on getting past the peacekeeper's flashing fire-brand.

Raising her combat knife, Riley silently coiled up behind the cannibal dancing in and out of reach of Hanzo's flaming torch.

Her pounding heart raced to the rhythm of the emaciated man's erratic steps, waiting until she could perfectly predict his movement patterns before deftly plunging her blade into the side of his neck.

Standing as stiff as a board, a shocked gurgle escaped the man's blackened lips as Riley ripped the knife free, with a fountain of his tainted blood spraying out across the carpet.

Desperately trying to staunch his pulsing wound with one gnarled hand, the repulsive wretch staggered away in retreat, tottering towards Taylor, the girl standing in the middle of the corridor with her back turned.

Riley was on him in a flash, kicking out the backs of his knees before opening his throat from ear to ear, drawing grim satisfaction from the swiftness of the execution.

"About fucking time," Hanzo grunted behind her, finally free to thrust the dying flames of his firebrand into the face of the cannibal at his feet, breaking the grip around his wrist like he was burning off a leech, before stooping to finish off the deranged deviant with his brass knuckles.

Riley was turning to deal with the last lunatic limping towards them, when her pupils dilated in alarm.

"DAKOTA, WATCH OUT!!" she yelled as the encroaching blood-spattered figure loomed alongside the lithe woman, lifting up an improvised blade for a death blow.

Still choking out the gaunt ghoul with her nightstick, Dakota broke off the attack, hurling her spluttering foe into the sinister newcomer.

But to their surprise, the lone menace shoved the blade into the back of the reeling cannibal's neck, the sound of glass popping as the bag of bones flopped onto the floor.

"We probably should've stayed together," Heather's husky-voiced hindsight filled the silence that followed. She shielded her eyes from a sudden blaze of light as Taylor whirled around with her torch to gaze at her sister. "Come on. Let's get the fuck outta here before any more show up."

CHAPTER 23

"Thanks," Riley managed to hold back a hiss of pain, but she couldn't help grimacing.

She was sitting on the edge of the plaza's center stage as Barbara swabbed disinfectant at the bloody gashes across her cheek – three-and-a-half jagged souvenirs from the cannibal woman's grubby fingernails.

"Don't mention it," Barbara winked, pointedly glancing around at the marketplace, where the other survivors of the stairwell's carnage were still being stitched and bandaged. "Jin tells me all these new medical supplies came outta your gear."

"I figured we wouldn't get it all back," Heather reflected nearby with a sour tone, scrubbing off splotches of dried blood from her legs and torso with a wet wipe.

"Small price to pay, considering the amount of people it helped save," Barbara shrugged before standing upright again, stretching out her back as she studied Riley's face. "Let that air out a while – I'll go see if I can rustle up a bandage."

Riley nodded wearily, hunching over as she cradled an instant cold pack against her swollen wrist – a sore reminder of Nolan Armstrong's self defense lessons – her father had always told her to use palm strikes instead of fists.

She gazed up at the stark silhouette of the Jade Mantis standing tall behind the plaza. The windows of the hotel's lower levels were streaked with the orange glow of flaming torches lighting up the rooms and corridors from within.

Dakota and Hanzo had stayed behind with a swarm of reinforcements, conducting a search-and-destroy sweep for any other cannibals still hiding in the building.

Word of the attack had already been sent to the upper floors, with more survivors being escorted down in droves, preferring to seek safety in numbers with everybody else in the public square, rather than risk falling victim to a second slaughter later on in the night.

To lift their spirits, Manny was trundling a shopping cart around the plaza with his older brother, freely handing out bottled water to the displaced refugees, and refusing any forms of payment in the wake of the crisis.

Their eyes lit up with gratitude at the gesture of kindness, and for a moment, Riley yearned to be a part of the community, contributing her skills towards something bigger than her own survival.

And with the world the way that it was now, she supposed that it certainly wouldn't hurt to surround herself with a bunch of hard-working people who looked out for each other when times were tough.

"You look like you could use a bath," Heather's voice broke the spell, her green eyes staring sidelong with a wry smile.

She slid the pack of wet wipes along the apron of the stage.

"Been a long day," Riley exhaled in agreement.

Balancing the cold pack on top of her swollen wrist, she

pulled out a towelette with her good hand and began wiping away the layer of sweat and grime that had built up across her face and neck, wincing slightly as she scrubbed near the gouges on her cheek.

"You could say that again," Heather snorted with a twitch of her eyebrows.

She hugged her bad leg to her chest, chuckling slightly even as she recounted the horror that she'd had to face by herself while the other two were gone.

Not even one minute after she'd heard the fifth floor's stairwell door slam shut behind Riley and Taylor, a pair of cannibals had found Heather hiding alone in the bathroom.

But in spite of her leg still being in recovery, the fiery redhead had single-handedly slain both of the ravenous wretches, before smearing her body with their blood as a baleful warning against all of the other lurking lunatics stalking the halls.

Riley had to admit – the woman was a fighter.

Just like her.

"We shouldn't have left you alone up there," she shook her head in hindsight, her eyes turning downcast.

"I'm actually glad that you did," Heather replied with a strange sense of relief. "Did you hear how many people were in that stairwell when they got ambushed? It was a hell of a lot more than three. Just think – if you had me hobbling along with you two, slowing you down, I can almost guarantee that we would've been the first ones to die." She waited for Riley to make eye contact before adding, "You can't expect to save everyone, Riley. Sometimes, we've gotta save ourselves."

Riley blew a long breath before giving her a nod.

"I think that should do it," Taylor declared proudly behind

them, dusting off her hands as she stepped back to admire their freshly-assembled tent in the middle of the plaza's stage. "Riley, can I get some of that spiced ham? I'm starving."

"I don't think any of us really know what it feels like to be starving," Riley replied in a hollow voice, unable to imagine the level of hunger that it would take before another human being looked even remotely appetizing. Putting the thought out of her mind, she shrugged off her backpack and set it down at her feet, inviting the girl over with a jerk of her head, "Come on then, before you turn feral."

"So let me get this straight," Heather began, glancing back over her shoulder at the tent as she worked through the math. "You guys left with that one backpack of food, and that was enough to buy us back everything that we lost…"

"Everything but the guns, meds, and your bike," Riley nodded as she watched Taylor rummaging through the contents of her backpack.

"And yet we still have a can of spiced ham left over," Heather concluded with feigned curiosity, before leveling a skeptical frown at them both. "Either your bartering skills are better than everyone else's in this whole fucked up colony, or there's something else that you two aren't telling me."

"I'd tell you if I knew," Riley replied, before raising her eyebrows expectantly at Taylor, waiting for the girl to reveal what she had promised in exchange for the return of their gear.

"Can't we just drop it until tomorrow?" Taylor bristled as she pulled out the canned ham from the backpack and withdrew a few steps, trying to further delay telling the inevitable truth. "I'm hungry. I'm tired. Right now, I just wanna eat something and go to bed."

"Taylor," Heather spoke her little sister's name like it was a warning, a command, and the bane of her existence all rolled up into one.

"You're gonna get all the details tomorrow anyway," Taylor's voice cracked under the weight of her stare. She nodded towards the former karaoke bar along the rear wall of the plaza, "Dakota said that you'd be able to go over everything with the man in charge. There's no point in me giving you half an answer now."

"Yes, there is," Riley's head cocked with irritation at the girl's reluctance to give them even the slightest idea of what she had signed them up for. "And who the hell is this *man in charge* anyway? Is it that Radek guy – why would he be coming over here from Valhalla?"

"No, not Radek," Taylor exhaled, chewing a slice of ham thoughtfully before deciding to shift some of the heat off herself. She flipped the focus on Riley, "You'd know who it was if you'd just stayed here in the plaza with me. But instead, you left me behind so that you could go off on your own and chase after those guys who sold all of our shit... and you still came back empty-handed anyway, so what was the fucking point of that?"

Riley rubbed the back of her neck, and she shot a guilty sidelong glance at Heather, anticipating an earful over abandoning Taylor in the middle of a crowd of strangers while she had gone after Jake.

"I don't need to hear all the details," Heather shrugged indifferently, to their mutual surprise. Her gaze flicked over to her sister, "Whatever Taylor-level dumb shit you've managed to pull off this time – it worked. We've got our gear back now. We'll make one more trade for my bike tomorrow.

And then..." her voice dropped to a whisper, checking to make sure that nobody else was in earshot, "We'll leave town before anybody can force us to hold up our end of the deal."

"Are you sure that's a good idea?" Riley furrowed her eyebrows.

As opposed as she was to whatever hare-brained bargain Taylor had made on their behalf, she couldn't help but feel like a greater reprisal would be waiting for them if they tried to run away without settling the debt.

"It's not," Taylor said stiffly, her eyes tracing over the sentries covering the entrances to the plaza. "I don't think they're gonna let us go that easily."

Riley and Heather exchanged a puzzled expression as the girl finally deflated, sitting down on the stage's apron in between them, evidently having lost her appetite.

"That deal I made..." she continued, her gaze turning downcast so that she wouldn't have to look either of them in the eye. "I promised that we'd help them kill Radek."

CHAPTER 24

Riley had woken up to the dissonant chorus of power drills whirring and hammers banging outside, blanketing the plaza in a layer of sound that she had eventually been able to tune out over the course of the day.

But now, standing at the entrance of the square in the midday sun, staring out at the organized chaos of grandstands and a series of arenas that were being set up along the length of The Strip's six-lane boulevard, all of the commotion was impossible to ignore.

Despite the massacre of the diesel thieves along the river-bank yesterday afternoon, coupled with last night's carnage in the stairwell, it seemed that Radek's people were still intent on culling the city's dwindling population with the next deadly tournament.

"These guys aren't even stopping to take a break," Heather observed, shading her eyes against the harsh glare of the summer sun bouncing up off the sea of asphalt and concrete in shimmering waves. "They'll start dropping from heatstroke if they don't let up soon."

"Must have a deadline they need to hit," Riley supposed,

watching the workers as they feverishly assembled seats and barricades.

"*You don't hit the deadline, you go to the tournament,*" Heather mocked Barbara's gravelly-voiced warnings about Radek's way of keeping everybody in line.

The entire labor force was comprised of people who had come from the plaza and its surrounding streets – anybody from the Valhalla Hotel was merely there to monitor the construction progress.

Even now, a bunch of beefy barbarian brutes – each wearing an identical upside down hammer pendant – were patrolling the boulevard, needlessly shoving the overburdened laborers as they lumbered towards their next task.

No wonder this Radek guy's at the top of somebody's shit-list, Riley thought to herself, her boots scraping the concrete as she turned away from the noise.

"Come on," she jerked her head towards the former karaoke bar at the rear of the square. "Let's go see if we can talk our way outta this mess."

The two women had decided to leave Taylor in the tent, giving her the responsibility of watching over their gear. All three of them knew the real reason why she was staying behind though – the girl had already thrown them into a pit full of shit with her reckless deal, and they didn't need her tagging along to dig them any deeper.

A dozen rugged Asian men stood loitering around the entrance to the karaoke bar, eyeing the pair of women as they approached.

Riley cocked her head in disdain at their blatant ogling, one hand magnetically drawn towards the combat knife strapped to her thigh.

"Who rolled out the virgin brigade?" Heather snorted, loud enough for all of them to hear. "Are you guys gonna move, or just stand there and gawk all day while you're waiting for your balls to drop?"

One man emerged from the jeering crowd with harsh words on the tip of his tongue, when the guard named Jin stepped out behind him, grabbing the guy's shoulder with a brief whisper in his ear.

The thug's jaw clenched, his hostile demeanor shifting, and he swallowed his spite.

"Clear a path – they're here for business," Jin instructed the others, waiting for them to stand aside before beckoning Riley and Heather to follow him inside. "Welcome to the Tiger's Den."

With her hand still on the hilt of her blade, Riley glanced back over her shoulder as Jin led them down the flight of stairs just beyond the doorway's threshold. The group of men remained outside, shuffling back together to block the entrance again.

"*The Tiger's Den*," Heather echoed with a huff as she held on to the handrail, trying to keep her weight off her bad leg. "Weird name for a karaoke bar."

"It's not the name – it's the reputation," Jin replied as he reached the foyer at the bottom of the stairs. He rested an elbow on the coat room's counter, giving a nod of greeting to the woman behind the booth. "Back before the world ended, this was the local watering hole for the Red Tigers."

"The *who*?" Riley's brow creased at the name.

It sounded familiar, but she couldn't quite place where she had heard it from.

"One of the many gangs who used to own a slice of this

143

city," Jin answered patiently, aware that organized criminal empires weren't at the forefront of everybody's knowledge – and especially not for newcomers. "Now we're the only ones left."

"Guess that explains why this place hasn't been picked clean yet," Heather supposed, peering through a tinted glass door at the bar's unsullied furnishings beyond the foyer.

Candle-lit lanterns lined ledges and tables where half-empty drinks might have once stood, bathing the bar's main lounge in dim pools of light. Padded leather sofas stood on one side of the room underneath a gigantic wall-length mirror, facing a surprisingly well-stocked bar, while a corridor opposite the entrance led towards the private karaoke rooms.

Riley ran her thumb along the scars of her fingers.

For a moment, it seemed as though the empty venue was simply suffering from a temporary power outage, and the desolation of the apocalypse had never quite managed to reach this place – an underground oasis unspoiled by the scourges of scavenging.

"We're gonna need you to hand over your weapons," Jin's voice brought her back to the foyer, jerking his thumb towards the clerk standing behind the coat room's counter. "You'll get them back after we're done."

"Fuck that," Riley snorted at the request, remembering the last time she had voluntarily given up her knife to somebody who had seemed civil on the surface.

That lapse of judgment had gotten her stuck in a snare in the Lawson Family's front yard.

She wasn't going to make that same mistake again.

"Seriously though, you can't be armed in here," Jin insisted, before glancing up at the group of men standing around at the top of the staircase, who were evidently listening in.

"Well, if you want our weapons that bad," Heather dropped a hand to the hilt of her own combat knife, backing up Riley, "Then come and take them."

Three of the thugs began sauntering down the steps, boldly taking her up on the dare.

"Last chance to do this the easy way," the clerk behind the booth warned, slowly reaching for something hidden underneath the counter.

"So much for talking our way out," Heather muttered at the irony as the pair of women stood back to back in the narrow foyer.

Riley gripped the handle of her sheathed blade, quickly weighing up their options.

They were glaringly outnumbered – even if they didn't have Jin and the clerk to contend with, they'd still be fighting an uphill battle against the dozen men who they had already managed to piss off outside, plus any other peacekeepers patrolling the plaza.

Riley wasn't going to kid herself.

If it came to a fight, their chances of survival were slim to none.

And yet she still loathed the idea of surrendering her weapon.

"If you want this meeting to happen," Riley chose the only reasonable option, eyeing the trio of thugs coming down the stairs before glancing back at Jin, "Then you'll have to tell your boss he can come to us instead. We're not giving up our knives."

"You don't get to make demands around here," the woman

behind the booth sneered, followed by a metallic rattle underneath the counter.

"Wait," Jin quickly held up a pacifying hand, steadying the clerk behind the counter and the men on the stairs. "Everybody, just relax for a second," he stalled for time as he thought of a compromise. His gaze flicked between Riley and Heather as he stroked the scattered bristles of his sparse goatee, deep in contemplation. Exhaling heavily, he finally relented, "Fuck. Okay. Here's what we'll do."

Both women breathed an inaudible sigh of relief, their tense grips easing off their knives as they turned to hear him out.

But instead, without another word, Jin slapped Heather's hand aside, deftly plucking the blade from her sheath and tossing it over the counter.

Riley's dilated pupils barely had enough time to register the flurry of movement before he lunged towards her next.

Reacting purely on instinct, she whipped out her combat knife, but before she could even think to point the blade at him, he caught hold of her wrist and spun her around, twisting her arm behind her back.

"Something's gonna snap if you don't let go," Jin muttered the menacing promise in Riley's ear as he threw her chest up against the counter.

He gave her contorted hand a firm squeeze, and a hiss of pain escaped her lips, the tendons in her wrist stretching to their absolute limit.

"Riley," Heather's voice sounded hollow. "Maybe we should play along."

"What the fuck are you talking ab–" Riley's strained outrage caught in her throat as she glanced up to stare into the barrel of the clerk's pistol, pointed directly in between her eyes.

Faced with the specter of certain death, Riley felt as though all of the air in the foyer had been sucked out into the plaza, leaving behind only the sound of her own pulse pounding in her ears.

Her gaze turned downcast with the bitter pang of defeat, and her fingers slowly unfurled from the hilt of her blade.

"Dunno why you had to be so difficult about it," Jin said resentfully, taking the knife before releasing his grip on her wrist. "I said you'd get them back."

Riley didn't want to admit that she had drawn her weapon without thinking.

But she knew better than to apologize for it.

It was better for them to believe that she would rather fight against overwhelming odds, than acknowledge that her hostility had simply been a nervous twitch of muscle memory.

"What people say and what they do are two very different things," Riley grunted as she massaged her wrist, blaming her knee-jerk reaction on all of the silver-tongued snakes who had betrayed her trust in the past.

Braxton Shepherd.

Sergeant Turnbull.

Calvin Fisher.

The Lawson Family.

Their names were burnt into her mind like scars on her memory.

"We've had too many bad run-ins with other survivors," Heather agreed, watching warily as Jin slid Riley's knife across the counter. "Like the shit you pulled on us just now – can't take anybody at their word these days."

"If you can't trust a bunch of gang members in a post-

147

apocalyptic Las Vegas," the clerk lowered her pistol with a derisive smile, "Who can you trust?"

Taking a deep breath, Jin opened the tinted glass door leading towards the bar's main lounge, silently gesturing for the pair of women to follow him inside. Whatever warmth that had been on his face when he had greeted them earlier was gone now.

But trust requires a choice, Riley belatedly answered the clerk's taunting question in her own thoughts, locking eyes with the trio of thugs staring back at her from halfway up the staircase. She flexed the slender muscles of her jaw. *And right now, we don't have one.*

CHAPTER 25

Two rows of tinted glass doors lined the dimly-lit corridor on the far side of the karaoke bar's main lounge area. But whatever purpose the private function rooms had served for the Red Tigers in the past, they certainly weren't being used for singing anymore.

All of the former furniture had been thrown out of each room, clearing as much space as possible to make way for a twisted mass of bunk beds and storage racks, arranged meticulously to make use of every cubic inch of real estate available.

"Way to turn a perfectly good bar into a barracks," Heather broke the uneasy silence that had fallen between them. "Guess it beats being eaten by a bunch of cannibals though."

"We're closer to the plaza here," Jin explained over his shoulder without breaking his stride. "If anything happens in the marketplace, we're only one set of stairs away."

"Just don't forget to pick up your weapon on your way out," Riley glanced back at the foyer, briefly locking eyes with the woman behind the coat room's counter before they turned a corner. "I thought nobody around here was allowed to carry any firearms."

"And nobody is," Jin lied, as if the clerk hadn't been holding a pistol to Riley's head only moments ago, "At least as far as Radek's people are concerned."

"So what happens if they find o–"

Riley's question died on her lips when she caught a glimpse of a man locked up in one of the former karaoke rooms, handcuffed to the frame of a bunk bed.

An unbidden memory flashed across her mind's eye – the shirtless black man who had been held prisoner by the cultist community in Lake Springworth, sobbing in silence as he stared catatonically up at the ceiling after Lorraine had finished with him.

Riley clenched her fists to ward off a shiver of disgust, and her boots scraped to a stop in the hallway as she stared through the tinted glass door into the room.

But to her relief, the sleeping man shackled to the bed frame wasn't a victim.

In fact, he was quite the opposite.

It was Eddie – the glib-tongued scam artist from last night who had tried to cheat her and Taylor out of their backpack of food.

"Why isn't this asshole on his way to the tournament?" Riley called ahead before Jin could disappear around the next corner.

At the idea of watching Eddie meet some horrible form of justice in whatever twisted competition that Radek's people were planning, she now found herself looking forward to the next tournament.

"None of us want him hanging around down here either," Jin replied, pausing at the end of the corridor. "But he might still be useful. So we're keeping him for now." He jerked his head towards the next stretch of hallway, "Come on – it's just up ahead."

Riley shot one final glance of contempt into the makeshift holding cell before she and Heather followed Jin around the corner.

A single candle-lit lantern occupied a niche in the wall at their backs, its light throwing their shadows down the corridor, until their shrinking silhouettes framed the outlines of their own reflections in a floor-to-ceiling mirror facing them at the end of the hallway.

"Wow," Heather stifled a smirk as she turned her head between the doors on either side of the mirror – even in the relative darkness, there was no mistaking the signs clearly marked as *male* and *female*. "You guys must really be struggling for space if your boss had to move his office into one of the bathrooms."

Jin gulped audibly at the end of the hallway, his throat bobbing up and down before glancing up at their reflections, eyeing each of them in turn with a blank stare.

Either he had chosen to ignore the insult, or he was too preoccupied to have heard it.

Then, without a word, he rapped his knuckles against the mirror.

Riley and Heather exchanged a wary glance in the eerie silence that followed.

Somewhere within the walls of the hallway, a rasping bolt slid free of its latch with a heavy *clank.*

Next, an almost imperceptible *click* reached their ears.

The two women were looking over their shoulders, when the mirror swung inwards on a well-oiled hinge, and their reflections were whisked away out of sight.

CHAPTER 26

Standing tall in the hidden doorway at the end of the corridor was a rigid man with a rough-hewn face and a gray pinstripe suit.

He looked over each of them with a dead gaze in his eyes, surveying Riley and Heather with the same measure of detached diligence that he showed Jin – a thousand-yard stare that was only worn by those who had seen too much and spoke too little.

Judging by the shadows shrouding his eyes, the man seemed like a veteran of several brutal gangland wars that the average person had never even heard about.

Oddly enough, Riley found herself remembering Keith Bowman – the uncle she'd never had – haunted by the ghost of the five-year-old boy from the worst night of his career. And yet for the most part, Keith had still been the exact same person who she had known from back when she was a kid.

But as she stared back at the rigid man with the dead gaze in his eyes, she wondered how much innocent blood had to be spilled before a person could become lost beyond redemption.

The impassive man stepped aside, seemingly satisfied with

his deadpan inspection, allowing them entrance into the former karaoke bar's commercial kitchen space.

More candle-lit lanterns illuminated the hidden room, casting light on stainless steel bench tops and workstations, spotless stoves and range hoods, scrubbed grills and ovens, and empty steamers and fryers.

Most of the cooking equipment was defunct without any electricity, but that didn't stop the handful of chefs scattered around the kitchen from preparing new meals – kneading and rolling dough, skinning and filleting freshly-caught reptiles – all of them working to the beat of a rhythmic *thock-thock-thock* of chopping knives on cutting boards.

"Kentaro will see you now," the man in the pinstriped suit gestured towards an open doorway along the rear wall of the kitchen beside the walk-in fridge.

"Kentaro..." Heather echoed dubiously, her gaze tracing the path from his extended arm to the doorway, before frowning back at him. "Wait, so you're not the guy we're here to see?"

Staring straight through her gaze, he neglected to give her an answer.

And in the strained stretch of silence, a *swish* and a *thud* sounded from behind.

Riley whipped her head around to see that Jin had already left the kitchen.

She watched through the disguised door's two-way mirror as he walked back up the corridor, leaving the pair of women to whatever fate was awaiting them.

A rash of gooseflesh crept up Riley's arms as the metronomic *thock-thock-thock* of chopping knives suddenly died down, and in its place, the chefs' gleaming blades began scraping harshly against honing rods, sharpening their knives in sinister unison.

"What the hell's going on?" Heather demanded an answer from nobody in particular.

But the kitchen's crew simply continued with their idle display of intimidation, eyeing the pair of newcomers with the same air of begrudging impatience as the pinstriped guard.

Realizing that they were only being hurried along, Riley drew a deep breath to exhale her nerves and summon her resolve.

"This is what we came here for," she muttered, more to herself than to Heather.

The pair of women took a wide berth around the grating gauntlet of grim-faced chefs, their boots squeaking over the rubber floor mats as they edgily ventured across the kitchen, stopping just short of the backroom's open doorway to peer inside.

"Glad you girls finally decided to join us," Barbara Greene winked up at them from the floor.

She was lazing on a padded cushion behind a knee-high wooden table, sitting beside a well-groomed Asian man with graying black hair and a shrewd gaze.

Even as the rasping chorus of sharpening knives continued behind them, Riley could feel her tightly-wound shoulders beginning to ease as she stepped inside, gazing around at the small backroom.

She had expected to meet the leader of the Red Tigers in some palatial office, surrounded by lavish status symbols and bodyguards to laud his power and influence over his underlings and business associates.

But Kentaro seemed to be a simple man.

His base of operations was a spartanesque stock room

that looked exactly like a stock room – the walls were lined with half-empty storage racks, the floor consisted of plain unpolished tiles, and with the exception of the cushions arranged around the low wooden table in the center, there was nothing else inside to clutter the room.

And then Riley's eyebrows creased in realization as she recognized Kentaro – the graying Asian man was the same spirited storyteller who had been entertaining the crowd of children and their families from the plaza's center stage last night.

"Please, join us for lunch," Kentaro's deep and resonant rumble cut across the racket of rasping blades, the ominous noise from the kitchen promptly ceasing as he gestured towards a pair of cushions on the other side of the table. "My talented chefs have prepared a meal from the food you left with us."

Riley's gaze went from the man's missing left little finger to the array of bamboo bowls, chopsticks, green bottles and shot glasses laid out before them.

"That looks a little too fancy to be anything we brought," Heather confessed as she accepted the invitation. With a slight wince, she eased herself down onto one of the cushions, stretching her bad leg out to the side.

"Well, you had all the ingredients," Barbara replied as she lifted the lid from one of the bamboo bowls. Waving away the cloud of wafting steam, her leathery face cracked into a smile, savoring their surprise. "When's the last time you girls had some freshly-made dumplings?"

Salivating at the sight of the succulent bite-sized pillows, Riley could barely form a coherent response, so her rumbling stomach answered on her behalf as she sank to her knees on the cushion beside Heather.

"We haven't had a decent cooked meal in a long time," Riley managed to say around her watering mouth. She hesitated despite her hunger though, unable to swallow a sudden suspicion, "What's in them?"

"Poison," Barbara scoffed sarcastically, before reaching across the table to spin the bamboo bowl around a few times. Using her chopsticks to pluck out one of the dumplings at random, she popped it into her mouth and began chewing before giving them the real answer, "Tuna and mushrooms."

Riley recalled the countless number of times that she had passed over both of the canned foods while rummaging through their supplies. Neither she nor the Seabrook sisters had any idea on how to make either of the ready-to-eat meals seem appealing, but they had brought the cans with them all the same, because food was food, and the three women knew better than to let sustenance go to waste over something as trivial as taste.

And yet ironically, the tuna and mushrooms were now the main ingredients in the best meal they'd seen in months.

"Goes down a treat with some soju," Barbara eased their doubts further by cracking open one of the green bottles, filling up her shot glass first before pouring for the table. "Korean rice wine – tastes just like vodka, but without the burn."

"I think I'll pass," Riley knocked back the offer, wanting to stay sharp. She glanced down at her pair of chopsticks uncertainly, never having learned how to use them. "Can I get a fork though?"

"You uncultured swine," Heather whispered in her ear. With a wry smile, she picked up a single chopstick and stabbed

157

at one of the tender dumplings, threading her makeshift skewer through the doughy pouch before devouring it whole. Taking a shot to wash it down, she glanced around at the sparse stock room's surrounding shelves, "Would it be too much to ask for some soy sauce to go with this?"

"If only we had any left," Kentaro answered with a somber tone of reminiscence. "Back when the food supplies first ran out, the city was filled with people who were desperate enough to eat and drink all of the condiments to ease their hunger."

Riley's stomach growled at the mention of *hunger*, but she waited for him to start eating before she descended on the dumplings herself.

She grimaced slightly though – not over the lack of sauce for the fluffy pockets of tuna and diced mushrooms, but because the gouges on her cheek kept tugging at her wound's bandage every time she chewed.

"I'm sure it tasted a hell of a lot better than a bag of cat biscuits," Heather supposed, glancing sidelong at Riley as they remembered the road to Utah.

"Even pet food – and the pets themselves – weren't beneath some people," Kentaro soured at the dismal reflection, shaking his head in disgust before sitting up straight again. "And now those same people who subsisted on the fringes of our fledgling community have stooped to cannibalism instead. Please allow me to offer my sincere regrets and deepest sympathies for the horrors you faced last night. We hadn't anticipated an attack, but we should've remained vigilant from the moment that our generators ran dry."

"And I should've told you about the cannibals," Barbara added solemnly, sharing the burden of responsibility. "I've stopped telling any of our new arrivals for a while now. I just didn't think it was worth mentioning – we haven't had an incident like that in months. We thought they'd already starved to death by now."

"How could you let those people get that bad in the first place?" Riley posed the question that she had been pondering since last night. After seeing the amount of reptile meat grilling on the row of barbecues in the plaza, it seemed that the colony of survivors certainly weren't facing a food crisis anymore. "Why not just feed them? I know they didn't wanna join your community, but even if they didn't have anything to offer in exchange for the food, at least you could've avoided an attack."

"Feeding them wouldn't have prevented last night's slaughter," Kentaro replied as he lifted the lid from another bowl of dumplings. "They despise us, and rightly so. Many of them were brought to Vegas against their will, stripped of everything they had, and left to fend for themselves. We've done what we can to try and minimize any bad blood from newcomers since then, but as long as Radek keeps offering bounties for fresh survivors to fill his twisted tournaments, the problem will continue to perpetuate... unless we stop him."

"That's what we came here to talk to you about," Heather set down her makeshift skewer, eager to discuss their supposed role in the uprising against Radek and his people. "That girl you spoke with yesterday – she's not in a position to make any kind of promises on our behalf. She's the most inexperienced member of our group, and she made a rushed decision without thinking to clear it with one of us first. Whatever's going on in this city – whatever plans you've made – we don't want any part of it."

Kentaro regarded Barbara with a stern gaze, as if somehow she had been the one to disappoint him.

"Honey, you're a part of this thing whether you like it or not," Barbara downed a shot of soju before leaning back with one hand on the tiled floor, brushing off Heather's refusal. "You've already heard too much to back out now."

"No, they have a right to choose," Kentaro shut down the idea of forcing them to fight for his cause against their own will. Despite his discontent, he swelled with a sense of pride. "That's the difference between me and Radek. He won't give you a choice."

"So that's it then – we're off the hook?" Riley asked to confirm her understanding, before popping another dumpling into her mouth.

She had hoped that the conversation would have lasted longer than the meal, but she was determined to make the most of it.

"Of course," Kentaro tapped the table twice with his fingertips, making eye contact with one of the chefs in the kitchen. He pointedly glanced down at the scattered bamboo bowls before continuing, "If that's what you wish, then we can declare that the deal is invalid, owing to your friend's lack of authority in making agreements."

"Well, thanks for lunch," Heather shrugged indifferently as a pair of chefs shuffled into the room to clear the table. She shifted on her cushion, hissing under her breath as she tried to get up, before turning to Riley, "You mind giving me a hand?"

"Not so fast," Kentaro interrupted their hasty retreat, apparently not finished with them yet. "Now that we've declared that the deal is invalid, all of the supplies and equipment that formed our end of the agreement no longer belongs to you." He studied the pair of women with his shrewd gaze, giving them a few moments for the ruinous realization to sink in, before adding, "The rest of your food will remain here as well – consider it as a cancellation fee."

"So much for giving us a fucking choice," Riley gave him a snort of contempt.

He wasn't explicitly coercing them to go against Radek and the brutes of Valhalla.

But he was certainly making it clear what would happen to them if they didn't.

Riley rubbed the back of her neck, forced to choose between danger and destitution – which was another danger in itself.

No weapons.

No gear.

No food.

And a city full of degenerate assholes who would love to take the little they had left.

"I think I'm gonna hang on to these," Heather snatched up two unopened bottles of soju before the chefs could clear them off the table as well. She narrowed her eyes at Kentaro, "I like to be wined and dined first before you fuck me – and I haven't had nearly enough."

"I never said you'd like the alternative," Kentaro replied truthfully, clasping his hands on the table as his gaze flicked between the two. "But the choice is still yours to make. In fact, there's a third option that you might not have even considered – you can keep everything as promised, and the girl who made the agreement yesterday can carry out your end of the deal by herself."

"I'm almost tempted to say yes," Heather remarked with

a bitter smile playing at her lips. "Because she will single-handedly find a way to fuck up your grand plan, and we'll still get to hold on to all of our gear just for the attempt."

"And let's not forget the fourth option," Riley added, introducing a bluff that Kentaro hadn't accounted for. "We could tell Radek's people about the gun you're hiding in the foyer. Maybe they'll turn this whole place over and find some other firearms you're not supposed to have. Like the pistol and the assault rifle we lost when we were captured." She turned her icy glare on Barbara next, "I don't remember you handing over anything to Miranda yesterday. They must be around here somewhere."

"Hey, maybe they'll give us rooms at the Valhalla for our cooperation," Heather backed her up, adding weight to the charade by providing an extra incentive for their betrayal. "I bet they've still got beds with clean sheets over there, plus lights, air-con, and the best amenity of all – no fucking cannibals."

"The two of you can cut the shit now," Barbara could see through their spiteful facade, although her gravelly voice held a hint of apprehension. "I've met a whole lot of different people in my life – and I like to think that I can tell the good from the bad. You girls just don't have it in you to eat at the same table – sharing the same food – with somebody you're about to stab in the back."

Riley bit her bottom lip for a moment, overcome with a sudden pang of guilt.

And then she remembered that all of the food had been theirs to begin with.

"Could you blame us after everything you've put us through?" Riley's bluff became a tangible threat as she decided to double down. "You tried to run us down with your truck yesterday. Then you hit us with tear gas and tasers. You captured us, threw us into a cell, and then you turned us in to collect a bounty. You stole all of our gear and then you dropped us off outside a fucking cannibal nest. And now you're using our own supplies as bargaining tools to help you kill somebody that we've never even met. You keep saying that Radek's the enemy – but in the space of a single day, you've fucked us over a hell of a lot more than what he has."

Barbara flinched at the accusations, no longer able to look her in the eye. Fingers trembling slightly, she reached for the box of cigarettes in her breast pocket.

In the silence that followed, a shadow fell across the table, and Riley turned to see the pinstriped guard standing in the doorway behind them, holding a sub-machine gun at his waist.

His dead gaze stared at the pair of women on the floor, patiently waiting for the kill order to ensure that their threat to switch sides would never see the light of day.

"Let's hope it doesn't come to that, Batu," Kentaro held up a steadying hand. He tapped Barbara on the shoulder before she could light up a smoke. "Not in here. You'll spoil the food." Then, he clasped his hands on the table again as he turned back to Riley and Heather. "Okay. We can make a new deal."

"You still haven't even told us what you want us to do," Heather pointed out.

She shared a sidelong glance with Riley, supposing that they could at least listen to whatever half-cocked plan the man had in mind.

"All we need from you is a fucking distraction," Barbara

growled in annoyance as she reluctantly stowed away her cigarette.

"My men and I will take care of the rest," Kentaro nodded in confirmation.

"That's it?" Riley's head cocked slightly, waiting for the catch. "You don't want us to kill anybody?"

"We're the ones with the guns," Batu answered somberly from behind.

"It would be a dishonor to allow outsiders to kill on our behalf," Kentaro elaborated, placing the reputation of the Red Tigers at the forefront of his priorities. He studied the pair of women before continuing, "We have a prisoner here – Eddie. The two of you will escort him to Valhalla. Tell the guards at the entrance that you're there to collect the bounty on a new arrival. Once they take his thumbprint and realize that he's already in their system, the guards will split their numbers to drag the three of you inside as last-minute entries into the tournament. And that's when we'll strike."

"Why us though?" Riley narrowed her eyes, trying to figure out why they had been chosen for the job. She jerked a thumb over her shoulder at Batu, "I mean, you're the ones with the guns, right? You've got all these people working for you, and you're asking *us* to be the distraction? That doesn't make much sense to me."

"Is this a suicide mission?" Heather caught on to her concern. Then, realizing the answer to her own question, she leaned back with a cynical smile, "The second you start shooting, they'll know we were in on the attack. We'll be executed before we can even make it inside. And even if they don't make the connection, we'll still be caught in the crossfire. We're not making it outta there alive."

"We'll wait until you're clear," Kentaro promised, spreading his hands across the table in earnest. "Granted, there are plenty of others who I could send, but it wouldn't be as clean. They know who my people are. And they know that my people know better."

"And that's where I fit into all this," Barbara chimed in again, her gaze settling on Riley. "Miranda watched us bring you in yesterday. You girls are new in town. She wouldn't expect you to know how things work around here – which is exactly why they won't suspect a thing when you show up with a two-bit conman like Eddie, trying to double-dip on a bounty that's already been paid."

"Sounds like we're pretty valuable then," Riley supposed, before revealing the real reason behind her line of questioning, "I guess we're in a good position to negotiate a better deal."

Heather snorted, hugging her bad leg to her chest with a speculative grin.

Barbara tightened her lips and turned her chin, as if she had swallowed something sour.

"Clever," Kentaro admitted with an odd mixture of animosity and admiration. "Very well. Make your demands. Just bear in mind that I have many other options. You – not so much. So in order for a new deal to exist, your terms should be agreeable."

If we ask for too much, we'll end up with nothing, Riley silently filled in the blanks.

"Everything that was included in the previous deal," Heather safeguarded their supplies from an obvious omission. "Plus the meds, our guns, and all of the ammo we had. And I want my fucking bike back."

Kentaro raised his eyebrows in consideration before his

165

gaze flicked over to Riley.

The weight of everyone's stares made her palms slick with sweat.

Heather's requests covered almost everything that they had lost.

And yet it was nothing compared to what Riley had in mind.

She flexed the slender muscles of her jaw.

It was all or nothing now.

"This next part's non-negotiable," Riley began, daring to ask for more, even with Batu's sub-machine gun at her back. She turned to Barbara, "And if Radek's gone, I know that it won't be a problem. I want an armored truck – just like the one you picked us up in yesterday – and a full tank of diesel. If you can guarantee us that, then we're in."

"Graduated from mountain bikes, huh?" Barbara held her gaze for a moment before looking to Kentaro in deference.

He folded his arms and stared up at the ceiling in contemplation.

Riley bit her bottom lip, waiting for his answer.

"Yes to the previous deal's terms," Kentaro told the ceiling, addressing Heather's demands first, with long pensive pauses in between. "Yes to the bike. No to the meds. Yes to the guns, the ammo, and the truck, but only after Radek's gone." His eyes slid downwards then, falling on Riley. "As for the diesel – that's not something that I can agree to, because we don't know how much is left. We don't use much around here, but after the heist yesterday, a full tank of diesel might be more than we can spare."

"For fuck's sake," Heather bristled, shaking her head even as Batu's sub-machine gun rattled behind her. "What's the point of even asking for a truck if it doesn't have any fuel?"

"*After the heist*..." Riley mused, ignoring her friend's outburst. Her brow creased with clarity as she turned to Barbara again, "Last night, when Manny mentioned that there hadn't been a fuel delivery, you said that Radek's people were probably keeping the rest of the diesel to themselves after the heist."

"Well, yeah, of course," Barbara shrugged with a frown, as if the answer wasn't obvious enough. "They don't actually give a shit about whether we have electricity or not – the fuel deliveries have always been their way of displaying their power over us. They give us just enough for our generators to last until the next day, so that we're always depending on them for more."

"Would they give a shit about the impound though?" Riley wondered, remembering last night's conversation with Jake when she had tried to make a different kind of trade – his sick mother's ill-gotten medicine in exchange for their armored truck.

But while her attempt at trading with him had failed miserably, at least she hadn't walked away empty-handed.

All of the vehicles go back to the impound, Jake's words rang loud and clear in her ears. *Stops anybody from trying to siphon out the diesel.*

If Riley could fuel up one of the trucks before the fighting broke out between Valhalla and the Red Tigers, then she and the Seabrook sisters would be out of Las Vegas before Kentaro's men could even guess at how much was left of the diesel.

"Batu," Kentaro leaned forward with curiosity. "What's the latest update from our lookouts posted at the impound?"

"No lights last night," the impassive man reported. "Security's down to a skeleton crew."

"Then that's where we hit them," Riley decided quickly, pouncing on the opportunity. "We'll still give you a distraction – just not the one you were planning. We'll steal a truck and make plenty of noise on our way out. As soon as the guards at the impound get word back to Valhalla, Radek's people will come hounding after us." Her eyes were laser-focused on Kentaro as she sold the proposal, "Then, instead of you trying to storm the hotel, you can gun them down in the street."

"Nice," Heather muttered in her ear as Kentaro and Barbara held a whispered conversation. "And here I was thinking me getting my bike back was a win."

"Told you these girls would be perfect for the job," Barbara's murmured praise pierced through her hushed discussion with Kentaro. The pair of women listened in as she continued, "They'll need some help if they're gonna pull this off though. I know you'll have your hands full, but I've got some people I can call on."

"Congratulations," Kentaro smiled as he turned back to Riley and Heather. "You have yourselves a deal. Now get up and grab whatever you need. This goes down tonight."

CHAPTER 27

"You were never gonna get those meds back," Dakota chuckled to herself as she and Riley strolled down the sandy
sidewalk of The Strip's six-lane boulevard. "Think about
it – if you were injured badly enough to need all of it, you'd
die from your wounds long before you even had the chance to
open up a first aid kit."

"Doesn't hurt to ask," Heather shrugged from the seat of
her recently returned mountain bike, resting her bad leg on
the pedal while she used her other foot to kick her wheels
along the pavement.

They were making slow progress on purpose – even with
the harsh afternoon sun beating down on their faces – wary of
drawing any suspicion from Radek's people still monitoring
the crew of fatigued laborers.

Most of the construction work had already been completed,
with a row of grandstands overlooking three barricaded
arenas built along the length of the boulevard, with the last
rectangular enclosure standing just outside the plaza.

Two of the arenas were completely empty, but the third
contained a series of raised platforms that stretched from end

to end like a long bridge, the surrounding scaffolding crowded with workers whirring power drills.

Riley's desire to be discreet gave over to plain-faced curiosity, her gaze lingering on the strange structure as they passed by, but she was unable to guess its purpose.

Deciding that it was probably for the best that she didn't know, her focus snapped back to the path ahead.

Farther down the sidewalk and out of earshot of the three young women, Jin and Hanzo flanked Eddie on either side, escorting the handcuffed prisoner while ignoring the would-be conman's constant attempts at begging and bribery.

In the end, Kentaro had decided that staging two distractions would work even better than one, and so he had chosen to maintain his original strategy, while still entertaining Riley's plan to draw Radek's guards away from the Valhalla Hotel.

His reasoning had been that if one plan failed, the other one was bound to succeed.

As an additional measure of caution though, Kentaro had also ordered that Taylor was to be confined to the plaza until Riley and Heather carried out their end of the deal – just in case they decided to follow through on their bluff at the last minute and switch sides over to Radek.

The added stipulation hadn't bothered Taylor in the slightest though – her face was so bruised and swollen after their encounter with the first cannibal in the hotel last night, she didn't even want to leave the tent.

Riley blew a long breath as they walked past an abandoned strip mall's row of ruined storefronts.

"It would've been nice to at least get our guns back *before* this went down," she grumbled, venting her frustration underneath the fading noise of the construction work behind them.

"We want Radek's men to think they've got the upper hand until we open fire," Dakota explained with a glance back over her shoulder, double-checking to make sure that nobody else was around. "But from what I saw last night, you girls should be just fine without guns."

"Yeah, but last night we were only up against a bunch of bone-bags," Heather countered with a dismal twist of her lips. It was the bitter truth. The starving cannibals had been on their last legs, driven by desperation. "These wannabe Viking warriors though... they're heavy hitters. Even if they're unarmed – and I'm betting they won't be – all it'll take is one good punch and we'll be on the ground, lights out and game over."

"Just don't get punched then," Dakota shrugged with a smirk of amusement. "Seriously though – if it was me, I'd be going in quiet too. Less chance of getting caught. Besides, you've got your knives. Use them. Fill the place up with silence and violence. Guns won't even make a difference after you get into one of those armored trucks anyway. You'll be untouchable."

"We've done knives against guns before," Riley admitted, flashing back to when she, Heather and five others had carried out an attack on Leadthorne High in the middle of winter – although only four members of the original seven had survived that night. "Our chances of walking outta there alive go *way* down. But in a pinch, it's possible."

"Are you two sure you're up for this?" Dakota's shoes scraped to a stop on the sidewalk, questioning their resolve. With both hands on her hips, she turned her head between them, "Because if you're thinking about backing out on your own plan, I'm more than happy for you to bring Eddie over to Valhalla for us instead. I'd rather be part of the ambush anyway and leave the distracting up to you two."

Riley bit her bottom lip, considering the idea.

It would be simple enough – drop off the prisoner and wait for Radek's people to realize that they were trying to double-dip on a bounty.

Far less dangerous too.

In the worst case scenario, the pair of women would be thrown together with Eddie, bound for the tournament that would be canceled the moment Radek was overthrown.

But on the other hand, they needed a vehicle and enough fuel to get them out of the desert – and merely hoping that Kentaro would give them the diesel wasn't an option.

"No, we're good," Riley turned down the easy way out, standing firm in her decision. Her gaze slid sideways to Heather, extracting a slow nod of affirmation from the fiery redhead. "We're gonna get that truck."

"Good, because we've only got one shot at this," Dakota studied them both one last time before resuming her steady walk along the pavement. "Most of Radek's soldiers are still out there hunting down the rest of the diesel thieves from yesterday. Between that and preparing for the next tournament, they've got their hands full. If we don't do this tonight, I doubt we'll ever get another chance."

"Unless somebody else steals fuel just before another tournament," Heather supposed with a skeptical smile. She stared around at the other hotels towering across the street and in the distance. "Where'd they get all the diesel from anyway? I mean, I guess some of these places might've had a decent emergency stockpile for backup generators... but it's been a year now since everything fell apart. Most of those stashes would've dried up a long time ago, right?"

"That's how Radek took control of the city in the first place," Dakota hissed through gritted teeth, reliving the loathsome memory. "We used to have a good thing going for us here – most of the big bosses and head honchos of the major hotels and casinos were working together, keeping people safe and fed so that they wouldn't break down into a mass panic. They were more concerned about their properties and businesses being looted and destroyed in all the riots, but for a while, it worked. Then this one guy showed up and started telling everybody that there wouldn't be enough supplies to go around forever."

"There wouldn't have been enough though," Riley cocked her head slightly, unable to see the flaw in his logic. "If Radek hadn't been the first person to say it, then somebody else would've figured it out sooner or later."

"No, he was doing it to push an agenda," Dakota replied before stopping to call ahead, "Jin, Hanzo! Hold up."

They watched as the pair of peacekeepers yanked their prisoner to a halt, wrangling Eddie over to a dumpster-sized power box and leaning him up against the side.

"After Radek stirred up enough chaos," Dakota continued her story, turning back to face Riley and Heather, "He told the people in charge that he knew about an oil field somewhere down south that was still in operation. He volunteered to bring back enough fuel to keep the generators running for a good while longer – or evacuate the city en masse if it came to that. They agreed, and they gave him a shit-ton of firepower to help him hold the payload on the highway. Somewhere on the road though, he managed to get into the entire convoy's heads, convincing them all to follow him instead. So when they got back to Vegas, they killed everybody in charge and declared Radek as the new leader."

"*Bunch of airhead ex-bouncers and corrupt cops*," Heather recalled Barbara's version of how Radek and Miranda had risen to power. "So where's this oil field?"

"No idea," Dakota turned her chin with a begrudging sigh. "Once a week, he sends out a convoy to go on a supply run. Sometimes they head north. Sometimes they head south. They alternate routes every week just to throw off our scent. Back in the early days, a few people tried following the convoy to find out where he gets it from – they never came back though."

Riley ran her thumb along the scars of her fingers, wondering about Kentaro's long term plan. If he and the Red Tigers succeeded in killing Radek and all of his followers, then they'd be losing their lifeline to the oil field, with only a limited amount of time before the remaining diesel ran out.

Unless...

"That shipment of fuel that got stolen yesterday..." she gave voice to her suspicions with half a smirk, "That was you guys, wasn't it?"

"I wouldn't be able to tell you," Dakota shrugged, understandably unaware of all the details surrounding Kentaro's broader strategy. "We're just taking advantage of all the chaos they've left behind." She jerked her head towards the wall of buildings bordering the pavement. "Come on, it's still a few hours to sunset. Let's get outta this heat."

Her shoes scraped the sidewalk again as she marched over to Jin, Hanzo and Eddie standing beside the power box.

Riley's feet were frozen in place though.

"What's wrong?" Heather leaned over to mutter in her ear.

"Don't tell me..." Riley's tongue pressed against the inside of her cheek, watching as Dakota led the three men towards the ruins of an upmarket Italian restaurant. "I know who Barbara's giving us for backup."

CHAPTER 28

"Tell me you're not serious, Barbs," Clay scoffed with his arms crossed, lips curling into a scornful smile as he sat beside Jake, both bounty hunters kitted out with their tear gas and tasers. "We have to work with these two?"

"I almost said the exact same thing," Heather snorted at the coincidence, leaning her bike up against the wall of the ransacked restaurant's former function room. A shadow crossed her face as her smile darkened, "But I just didn't wanna sound like a whiny little bitch."

"Well, at least I can walk without a limp," he sneered back at her with a mocking tone, her insult going straight over his head. "This peg-leg chick's gonna slow us down and get us all killed. Come on, Barbs – give us *literally* anybody else, and we can make this work."

"Keep your voice down," Barbara hushed him from beside the window, shooting a wary glance at Eddie as he was being handcuffed to the outdoor terrace's railing. "That guy out there already knows we're up to something. If he hears even the slightest detail of what we're planning, he'll use it as a bargaining chip with Radek's people. Then we're all fucked."

They fell to silence then, but that didn't stop Heather and Clay from staring daggers at each other across the length of the room.

The plan was to wait until sunset before making their move.

Kentaro's men still needed some time to get into position without raising any suspicion.

The restaurant's former function room offered a view of the six-lane boulevard outside, but there was nobody else in sight.

Only people with a purpose – innocent or otherwise – would have been caught out on the street at this time of day.

But Riley knew that Kentaro's men wouldn't be taking a head-on approach anyway.

Even now, she could picture small groups of the Red Tigers disguised as drifters and vagrants, skulking through the shadows of the city as they made their way towards various vantage points overlooking the Valhalla Hotel.

"Looks like we're gonna be stuck in here for a while," Riley muttered, rubbing the back of her neck as she sat against a wall. She pulled her hand away with a sheen of sweat on her palm, before glancing sidelong at Heather, "Did you bring any water?"

"I'm starting to wish I did," she grunted as she lowered herself to the floor. "It didn't even cross my mind while we were gearing up in the tent. Blame it on the soju."

"No, I forgot too, and I was sober," Riley reflected on their lavish lunch with a rueful grin.

She wiped off her sweaty palm on her shorts, before looking up again to see Jake staring directly at her from across the room.

His mouth was half-open, as if he had been waiting for a

177

while to make eye contact.

"Was that from me?" he asked, tapping at his cheek with a hint of concern in his keen eyes.

"Was *what* from you?" she furrowed her eyebrows, looking back at him like he was some kind of idiot, before she remembered the bandage on her cheek.

"Sounds like you were busy last night," Heather arched an eyebrow with a slight smile playing at her lips.

"Weren't we all?" Riley sighed up at the ceiling in a bid to play off her sudden self-consciousness, not even wanting to touch on the implication.

"I was *definitely* getting busy last night," Clay sniggered as he elbowed Jake in the ribs, still basking in the aftermath of his lust-filled purchase. He clucked his tongue as he remembered their present company, and he frowned across the room, "Hey, I thought we caught three girls yesterday. What happened to the other one?"

"The other one's useless when it comes to doing things quietly," Heather quickly replied, before flipping the focus back on them. "Besides, somebody needs to watch our gear while we're gone. There's a couple of assholes around here who seem to think that taking whatever they want and selling it off is something that they won't have to answer for later."

"I've noticed you don't refer to your sister by name," Barbara interceded before the tension in the room could rise any further. "Any reason why?"

Heather's pupils dilated at the sudden change of topic.

She tightened her lips as she tried to think of a response.

Riley knew the reason behind her unease – family was a weakness that people could exploit.

"Relax, you're among friends here," Barbara reached her

own conclusion, sensing their apprehension. "We're good people. You don't have to keep the whole *sister thing* a secret. Besides, Taylor already let it slip outside the bar last night."

"Taylor-level dumb..." Heather shook her head at the girl's naivety, hugging her bad leg to her chest. "Well, my sister's on house arrest now anyway. She's not involved in whatever we're about to do."

"No, she isn't," Riley agreed, before leveling her gaze at Jake and Clay. "But what I wanna know is why the two of you are? I mean, I know what's in it for us. But I thought you guys kidnapped people for a living – why would you risk such a promising career over something like this?"

"For the hero status, of course," Clay flashed a broad smile, holding his arms out wide. "Free food, free booze and free boobs always go to the underdogs who put it all on the line to bring down a tyrant."

Both Riley and Heather bit the insides of their cheeks, fighting the urge to laugh out loud at his flawed view of what the victory would actually look like – especially considering their relatively insignificant role as a mere distraction.

"Last night got me thinking," Jake cut through the mirth in their stifled smirks, exhaling heavily before looking up at Riley. "I *hate* what we have to do to strangers just so that I can afford to scrape by. Plus, the price for my mom's meds doubled yesterday – there's no way I'll be able to support her for much longer. I knew something had to change. So when Barbs got here and told us there was another way – it just clicked for me."

"Kentaro's gonna be in our debt after we do this," Barbara glanced around the room before her gaze settled on Jake. "He'll make sure that your mom gets the meds she needs

179

– no matter the cost. And if he doesn't, you know I will."

"I know," he replied in a hollow voice. Sniffing, he climbed to his feet and went over to the window, staring out at the empty street. "Still no word on Lincoln?"

"If he isn't back by now, then he's definitely skipped town," Barbara shrugged with a world-weary sigh. "I had a feeling that he would from the moment Miranda said we're at Culling Point... I don't blame him for leaving, but I wish he would've stayed one more night."

"What the fuck?" Heather cocked an eyebrow at them. "So this whole time, you've been kidnapping people and stealing their supplies to make a living for yourselves, when you could've just gassed up a truck and left?"

"Who said any of us wanna leave?" Dakota posed a question of her own as she entered the room. "We've all got people here. This is our home. And we're about to take it back."

"Is it go time already?" Clay was on his feet in a flash, peering out the window.

The sun hadn't set just yet, but it was on its way down.

"I just got the signal," Dakota reported as she pulled the nightstick from her belt. "Everybody's in place. You guys should start moving soon. Our lookouts will send us another signal the moment you breach the impound, and then Jin, Hanzo and I will bring Eddie to Valhalla." She tossed her baton over to Barbara, "Hold on to this just in case something goes wrong. I want it back after we're done."

"Just in case," Jake echoed, turning away from the window. His set of keys jangled as he pressed them into Barbara's hand. Jerking his head towards the bathroom corridor in the back corner of the restaurant, he relayed his mother's prescription, "One pill of prednisone twice a day. Give it to her just before a meal. She gets a bad stomach otherwise..."

Their muttered contingencies faded into the background as Riley rose to her feet.

She stooped to give Heather a hand, pulling her upright.

"If anything happens to me," the fiery redhead's usual tone of nonchalance took a turn towards concern as she fed off the energy in the room, "I need you to promise me that you'll take care of Taylor."

"It's not gonna come to that," Riley shook her head, not even daring to think about the possibility of something bad happening, as if having a shred of doubt would jinx the plan. She gave Heather a reassuring smile, strained as it was. "Now let's go get that truck."

CHAPTER 29

Riley's boots scraped over cracked concrete as she and Heather crossed a sprawling lot bordered by construction fencing.

Looming hulks of heavy-duty machinery were scattered across the derelict yard, with defunct forklifts, excavators and bucket trucks parked haphazardly around the long-abandoned square.

Squinting into the westering sun hanging low over the horizon, the pair of women passed underneath the long shadow of a crane before spotting Jake and Clay, both men huddled in between a lone bulldozer and a warehouse.

"I only counted two," Riley reported in a low voice as they rendezvoused.

"Same as us," Jake whispered back, fidgeting with a pair of fencing pliers.

The latest update from Kentaro's lookouts had been correct.

The impound lot was down to a skeleton crew for security.

Only two guards had been assigned to keeping watch over the entire collection of vehicles in the adjacent yard, and they weren't even patrolling the perimeter.

Not only that, the early evening air was dead silent – there was no rumbling generator to power the impound lot's alarm system, its network of security cameras, or even the surrounding floodlights.

"This is gonna be easier than I thought," Clay suppressed a snigger as he craned his neck around the corner of the warehouse, sizing up the chain-linked fence topped with razor wire that stood in between the two concrete yards. "So what's the plan?"

"We're gonna wait until it gets dark before we make a move," Heather replied, sitting on her bike as she leaned her shoulder up against the side of the bulldozer, settling in for a long stretch.

"Do either of you two know where they keep the keys?" Riley cocked an eyebrow at the pair of bounty hunters, belatedly realizing that she probably should have asked Barbara before the four of them left the restaurant.

"Yeah – they're all on a rack inside the office," Jake answered, to her relief. He glanced sidelong at Clay, as if in explanation, "I've only been inside a couple times, back when Lincoln got sick for a while."

"Thank fuck for that," Heather muttered under her breath. She pinched the bridge of her nose in thought, before looking over at Riley, "Well, I think we need to split up. Somebody needs to find the keys, and somebody else needs to go around the yard siphoning fuel from any of the other vehicles that Radek's people might use. We don't want them coming after us, and it'll be handy to have some spare gas on the road."

"Good idea," Riley nodded, as if the two women hadn't already worked out the plan between themselves during their inconspicuous stroll past the impound lot. "Jake and Clay, you guys know which vehicles they usually drive. Me and Heather will get the keys."

"So, we're the bait," Clay supposed, shaking his head in disdain.

"Where the hell did you get that idea?" Heather arched an eyebrow, although the slight tightening of her lips suggested that she already knew the answer to his suspicions.

"You're gonna have to draw the guards outta the office somehow," Clay explained, crossing his arms over his chest as he nodded towards Jake. "And what better way than to wait until we start making noise – jimmying open fuel doors and sloshing around stolen diesel? Then when we get caught, you'll have the keys, and there'll be nothing to stop you girls from jumping into a truck and leaving us high and dry... And even if they don't catch us, you'd probably leave us behind anyway just to spite us for bringing you back to Vegas in the first place. Forget that. *We'll* get the keys."

Riley and Heather exchanged a glance, both women sharing the same thought.

We can't trust that they wouldn't do the exact same thing to us.

Riley was reaching for a reply to shut him down, when Jake spoke up next.

"And when you *do* get to the rack with the keys," he poked another hole in their plan, "Do either of you two even know which set of keys belongs to which truck? Or are you just gonna grab them all and hope that one of them fits? Even if the guards don't hear me and Clay sneaking around the yard, they'll hear all that shrapnel jangling in the office before you even get a chance to set foot out the door."

Riley rubbed the back of her neck.

As much as she didn't want to admit it – he had a point.

"Okay," Riley sighed reluctantly, meeting Heather's gaze before offering a compromise. "Me and Jake will get the keys then. That's the only way we'll all be sure that everybody's doing their jobs properly, and that nobody's getting left behind. Are we all good with that?"

After a few moments of strained silence, both Jake and Clay gave a resigned nod.

"Great, so I get stuck with the whiny one," Heather huffed in annoyance, begrudgingly twitching her eyebrows in agreement.

"Great, so I get stuck with the peg-leg one," Clay shot back with equal enthusiasm.

Riley stepped in between them, silently cutting through their pointless bickering.

She peered around the corner of the warehouse at the rear of the impound lot.

Shadows stretched across the cracked concrete as the sun kissed the horizon, the throng of derelict vehicles casting their combined curtain of silhouettes over the chain-linked fence.

"Won't be long now," Riley predicted, pulling her gloves from the front pocket of her shorts and tugging them on.

She hadn't worn them since the start of summer, but they still fit like a second skin over her scarred fingers as she flexed their familiar feel.

Casting one final gaze at the neighboring yard, she shrank back behind cover, when the *thrum* of an engine reached her ears.

"Shit," Heather breathed, pupils dilating at the noise. "I thought they weren't gonna be running a generator?"

Riley's gaze darted up at one of the floodlights towering

over the impound lot.

They wouldn't be able to use the cover of darkness once those gigantic lamps kicked in.

And the security cameras would pick them up long before they even reached the fence.

"That's not a generator," Jake's mouth went dry despite delivering the good news, frowning as he recognized the distant rumble. "That sounds more like a truck." He stared up at each of them in turn with a mix of terror and defeat in his eyes. "Radek's convoy is back in town."

CHAPTER 30

"That's it – we're not going through with this," Jake was the first to give voice to what they were all thinking. He stared around at the neighboring rooftops, "Where's that Red Tiger lookout? We need to let them know that we're not going inside. Kentaro's people have either gotta stand down or kick off the attack before it's too late."

"Just wait a minute," Riley held up a hand for silence, not wanting to act on impulse.

"You wanna *wait?* For what!?" Clay's panicked confusion carried volume around the concrete yard, the echoes of his cry promptly shutting him up.

"What are you – a fucking idiot?" Riley hissed at his sudden outburst.

The question didn't need an answer.

"We need to leave," Heather agreed, siding with the skittish pair of bounty hunters. She took on a tactful tone, "Riley, this is the same group of psychos we saw outside the Valhalla yesterday. They were crazy enough to cut off trophies from those people they massacred back at that river just to make some *blood tributes to The Valkyrie.* What the fuck do you think they'll do to us if we try to steal one of their trucks?"

Riley's lips tightened as her gaze flicked over each of their faces, seeing the fear in their eyes spreading like an infection.

But she wasn't planning on giving up that easily.

Silently brushing stray strands of hair over her ear, she took another long gaze around the corner of the warehouse. Straining her eyes, she peered into the twilit darkness of the adjacent impound lot, searching the shadows for the source of the thrumming engine's sound.

"We're as good as dead if they catch us hiding back here," Jake whispered behind her, already backpedaling with Clay in tow. "You girls can either stay here or come with us, but we're not sticking –"

"Calm down," Riley stood abruptly, cutting across their hasty retreat. "There's only one truck out there. It's not the whole convoy."

With a jerk of her head, she invited them all to take a look for themselves.

Sure enough, only a single vehicle was idling outside the front gate of the impound lot, waiting for the pair of guards stationed inside to open up.

"Hold on a second," Clay frowned, squinting into the distance. "That's... that's *our* truck. I guess Lincoln didn't end up skipping town after all. But that doesn't make any sense."

"Why the hell would he come back?" Jake shared his confusion. "He knows that he's meant to go into the next tournament, unless..."

"He's already settled his debt," Heather concluded, supposing that the dour man had single-handedly tracked down enough new survivors to clear his name.

"Doesn't matter – we need to do this now," Riley interrupted their speculation, bringing their focus back on track. She glanced pointedly at the two guards greeting the truck at the yard's entrance, "While they're still opening the gate."

"I thought we were gonna wait until it got dark?" Jake gazed up at the purpling sky as he fumbled with his fencing pliers.

We don't have time to waste, Riley's mind shot back.

She didn't even want to spare a second to utter the thought.

Instead, with an impatient snarl, she snatched the tool out of his hesitant hand.

Cold adrenaline flooding her veins, Riley ducked around the corner of the warehouse, stealing towards the chain-linked fence.

She kept her head down low, using the impound lot's jumbled cluster of vehicles for cover.

Crouching beside the fence, she was forced to work the unwieldy pliers with both hands to cut through the wire.

But the first *snip* made the entire length of steel mesh shudder and jingle.

Breath freezing in her chest at the ringing noise, Riley rammed her shoulder into the fence, bracing it against the next cut, and the next, and the next.

Furtive footsteps crept up behind her while she worked, and in the corner of her eye, she saw that Jake and Clay had finally found their nerve to commit to the plan, with Heather bringing up the rear, crawling on her hands and knees.

"You want me to take over?" Jake offered, already reaching for the pliers.

"I got it," Riley shrugged him off. "Just hold the fence so that it doesn't shake – and keep an eye on the guards."

She pulled back to attack the chain-linked mesh head-on

again.

With her shoulder unencumbered, she made short work of the remaining links, splitting the fence down to the ground.

Clay stooped beside her to pull back one side of the severed fence, holding it open like a tent flap while they all squeezed through one by one.

The four intruders stealthily weaved their way through the impound lot's tangle of sedans, station wagons and minivans, stepping over windswept piles of trash and ducking underneath cobwebs hanging in between the long-abandoned sun-bleached vehicles.

Riley drew up alongside a dust-covered caravan, with the other three shadowing her in single file lockstep. She took a look around the rear end of the mobile home, peering at the pair of guards across the yard.

One was a rangy bearded balding man, with tattooed tear streaks running down both cheeks and a pistol holstered on his hip, directing the armored truck into a suitable parking spot.

The other was a brawny Latino with a horseshoe mustache and a shotgun slung across his chest, his scarred sinewy muscles catching the last rays of dying daylight as he hauled the front gate shut.

Riley was scanning the short distance to the impound lot's office, when she heard a subtle rattle sound from behind.

She whipped her head around to see that Clay had drawn his taser.

"What the hell are you doing?" Heather's hiss was muffled by the handle of her combat knife clenched in between her teeth. Carefully plucking the hilt from her mouth, she glared down at his weapon, "We're on diesel duty, dickhead. If you wanna fuck around and light yourself on fire, you can do that in your own time."

"I don't think diesel burns that easily," Jake spoke up on his behalf.

"I just thought... for protection..." Clay stammered all the same, belatedly rethinking the consequences of sparking up a taser around gas fumes. Sheepishly holstering his weapon, he asked, "Maybe I could hold the knife instead then?"

"No – I need it to jimmy open the fuel doors," Heather huffed before biting her blade's handle again. Lifting the hem of her shirt, she pulled out a pair of rubber hoses and a rag from the waistband of her shorts. Speaking around her mouthful, she added, "Here's an idea – go find us some jerry cans. And save your annoying fucking breath for blowing into the gas tanks, because you're siphoning the shit."

Riley locked eyes with the fiery redhead, both women reading each other's thoughts.

Good luck. Be safe.

The moment passed, and two pairs took off in opposite directions, staying low as they crept through the impound lot.

Riley and Jake approached the office building from the rear, reaching the back door undetected.

With bated breath, Riley gripped the door handle and gave it a hopeful turn.

The locked door shook stubbornly.

"Figures," she muttered, before glancing back over her shoulder, "Looks like we're going in through the front."

Jake swallowed edgily, but nodded.

Shuffling along with their backs scraping against the structure's stucco wall, Riley led the way around the side of the building, ducking underneath an overhanging air-conditioning unit as she peered around the corner.

"Kuba!" the rangy balding man called from beside the armored truck across the yard. "Why'd you close the gate the whole way? This guy's not hanging around."

"Then who the fuck's taking over the watch tonight?" the big Latino erupted, angrily throwing up his sinewy arms beside the entrance.

"Says he doesn't know," the first man shrugged.

"Bullshit, Aksel!" Kuba yelled back, leaving the gate shut as he strode towards the truck. "Let me talk to that little bitch – because I'm *not* putting in overtime at this dump again."

Riley flexed the slender muscles of her jaw as the two guards broke out into a heated argument with Lincoln, who neglected to climb out of the truck.

With the pair of sentries distracted, she stuck her head out from behind the building, eyeing the path around the corner.

There was nothing in front of the office to screen their approach.

She and Jake would be in plain sight from the moment they crept out from behind cover.

Gonna have to roll the dice, Riley told herself, knowing that their window of opportunity was closing fast.

Heart hammering in her throat, she crawled around the corner with Jake on her heels.

They pawed over the cracked concrete like a pair of wildcats stalking their prey, keenly aware that their entire flank was completely exposed, and with every passing moment, they were only a stray glance away from being caught.

After crawling for what felt like an eternity, Riley finally gained the shadow of the entrance.

Cracking open the office's glass front door, she flung herself inside, with Jake scrambling in behind her.

They threw their backs up against the wall on either side of the doorway, sharing a breathless smile, panting hard with relief to be out of the open again.

But before they could catch their breath, the door's hinges squealed aloud as it swung back towards the frame.

Icy fingers of terror surged up Riley's spine.

Reacting purely on instinct, her hand shot out to catch the door's handle before it could hit the latch, and she gently guided it home.

But the damage had already been done.

The whining hinges were still ringing in her ears.

Lying flat on her stomach, she dragged herself over the carpet towards one of the windows, sneaking a furtive glance over the sill.

Her pupils dilated as she stared out into the yard.

The trio of men – Aksel, Kuba, and a third who looked nothing like Lincoln – were on their way back to the office to investigate the noise.

CHAPTER 31

"Hurry up and get the keys," Riley urged quietly from her crouch below the sill of the front window. She watched as the rangy guard named Aksel loped ahead of the other two men marching across the impound lot. "We can still make it out through the back door."

"Fuck, fuck, fuck..." Jake's panicked whisper jerked her gaze away from the yard as he stared frantically around at the darkness of the office. He scanned the shadows one last time before looking back at her in defeat, shaking his head in horrible realization, "They've moved the keys."

"I thought you said y–"

The rest of her sentence died on her lips as the front door swung open, and Aksel's slim silhouette stood stark in the doorway, like a sinister specter storming in from the night.

"KUBA – INTRUDERS!!" he roared over his shoulder, backing out of the building for distance as he drew the pistol holstered on his hip.

Jake froze like a deer caught in the headlights.

Raw adrenaline surged through Riley's veins.

"GET DOWN!!" she shouted, charging across the room to

tackle Jake to the floor.

They went sprawling behind a desk just as the bullets started flying.

Cracks of gunfire bullwhipped around the impound lot, shattering the office's front door and windows, with broken glass crystals showering across the carpet.

Snapping out of his momentary stupor, Jake wrapped his arms around Riley's torso and rolled over to one side, shielding her with his body.

Almost instantly, she drew up her elbows against his chest, breaking herself free of his protective embrace.

"What the hell are you doing!?" he spluttered as her gloved fingers scrabbled at his belt, even as lead slugs zipped by overhead and punched into the drywall behind them.

"Getting your fucking taser," she growled through gritted teeth, wrenching the weapon free from his holster. "My knife's not gonna do shit to them at this distance."

"Could've said something first," Jake grunted before putting one arm behind his back, reaching for a canister of tear gas instead. "Just make sure you remember to switch off the safety this time."

Riley narrowed her eyes at him as she flipped off the safety lever, harder than necessary.

Wrapping both hands around the taser's grip, she stared up at the office's dark ceiling, waiting for a break in the gunfire.

The echoing reports were still ringing in her ears, when she heard the clatter of an empty magazine hitting the ground outside.

Heart hammering in her chest, Riley reared up on one knee behind the desk, and she lined up her sights on Aksel while the man was still reloading.

195

BADOOM!!

The desk erupted with wood chips just as the taser's cables shot out.

Before Riley could even register where the deafening blast had come from, Jake yanked her back down to the floor, checking her over as he grabbed her arm.

"You're good – keep squeezing!" he urged, grasping her fist with both hands, locking her trigger finger in place as the taser's volts surged through the cables.

Aksel's body thumped hard on the concrete outside, the man writhing and gurgling involuntarily, his garbled yells distorted by the amount of electricity crackling along the wires.

"One down, two to go," Riley stared up at the newly-formed gaping hole in the side of the desk, the taser rattling slightly in her fist. "How many shots does this thing have?"

"Not enough to take out these guys," Jake swallowed grimly, slowly releasing his grip around her trigger hand. He gazed up at the electrified cables drawn taut over the top of the desk, "As soon as the taser runs outta juice, get ready to move."

Snatching up his canister of tear gas again, he tore the pull ring free, shakily holding the striker lever against the can with bated breath.

"Looks like we got a couple of low-rank bounty hunters on our hands!" Kuba taunted them from outside as he cocked another shell into his shotgun's breech. "Let me guess – you're struggling to find new people out there, so now you wanna try your luck at ripping us off instead."

"Just remember," the third man yelled next, his distinctly high-pitched voice trying hard to match Kuba's brassy tone,

"We're the ones who gave you those tasers, you ingrate inbred sons of bitches!"

"You stupid motherfuckers might've lucked out after all though," Kuba continued, his boots scraping across the concrete as he shuffled over to a better vantage point. "Neither one of you have to die tonight, because you fucked up just in time for the next tournament. Now come on out and we'll talk this through. If you're smart, you'll know it's the only way you're getting outta here alive."

Silence hung in the cool evening air as he waited for their reply.

In the lull, the taser's crackling volts died, despite Riley still squeezing the trigger.

Aksel heaved and hacked with relief, gasping for air in between lingering convulsions.

Jake eased the spent taser out of Riley's grip, setting it down gently.

"Three..." he mouthed quietly, jerking his head towards the open doorway leading towards the office's shadowy backroom.

"Two..." she nodded as she counted with him, placing both hands on the carpet and coiling herself into a sprinter's pose.

"One!" they cried in unison.

Jake tossed the tear gas over the desk.

"G-GRENADE!!" Aksel spluttered as the canister *hissed* out a cloud of smoke, the chemical mist rapidly enshrouding the front of the building.

Launching into a run, Riley hurtled towards the backroom.
BADOOM!!

Another hail of buckshot blasted blindly into the spreading fog, the lead pellets shredding through the rear drywall and peppering the back door.

Riley felt her way through the darkness of the former staff break room, clumsily stumbling towards the tiny wisps of moonlight emanating from the fresh pellet-punctures in the exit.

"I'll get Aksel – you head around back and cut them off!" Kuba coughed out a command to the third man before calling for reinforcements. "Valhalla – impound. We got intruders. Send backup!!"

His choked shouts faded as Riley wrestled with the back exit, the door handle shaking stubbornly.

"Fuck," she muttered, her gloved fingertips fruitlessly scrabbling for the lock.

"I got it," Jake shouldered her aside, flicking open the deadbolt and throwing the door out wide.

They sprinted out into the impound lot, taking shelter behind a long-forgotten black panel van, breathlessly scanning their surroundings for the truck driver who had supposedly been sent to prevent their escape.

A pitter-patter of stilted footsteps heralded his approach, and he came scrambling around the corner of the building with a hatchet in his hand.

"What the fuck? That's not Lincoln," Jake belatedly realized, staring at their dwarf pursuer in disbelief.

"No, but he's got his keys," Riley replied softly, her combat knife whispering out of its sheath from the strap on her thigh.

"Kuba, they're already gone!" the short man shouted over his shoulder the moment he noticed that the back door had been left open.

His whole upper body swung as he scanned left and right, peering into the dark depths of the impound lot, his hatchet shaking nervously in his grip.

You should've brought a gun, Riley silently chided the man as she crouched beside the van's front quarter panel.

Deciding against blundering into the shadows after the pair of intruders, the dwarf turned back towards the front of the building, heaving a sigh of pained exasperation as he went.

Seizing the opportunity, Riley rushed out from behind cover.

The man whirled around at the sound of her running footsteps, his eyes going wide with fear as he scurried off, screaming for help.

Riley was less than two strides away from her shuffling target, when he stopped and spun around with a devious grin, his feigned retreat having lured her within striking distance.

Hefting his hatchet, he aimed a savage sideways swing at her stomach.

Pupils dilating, Riley skidded on her heels, narrowly stopping short of his axe's arcing blade, the weapon's wind whistling within half an inch of her waist.

But the sprint's lagging inertia caught up to her like a sharp shove from behind, throwing her off balance as she lurched forward, and the man quickly turned his blade for a second sweep down at her knees.

Too late to catch her balance, Riley turned her involuntary lean into a lunge, flailing her free hand at his striking forearm, before plunging her knife into the side of his neck.

Not wasting any time, she slashed his throat and ripped the hatchet free from his slackened grasp, tossing the weapon out of reach as he went down with a gurgle of surprise.

Kuba and Aksel were still choking from the tear gas at the front of the building, but Riley could hear their footsteps clumsily coming around the corner.

Frantically patting down the dying dwarf, she found a pair of keys on a ring in one of his front pockets, and she bolted back towards the black panel van, ducking out of sight mere moments before the guards reached the back of the building.

"FUCKING *PUTA MADRES!!*" Kuba roared at the sight of their fallen comrade.

"Split up... we'll find them..." Aksel managed to wheeze out between hoarse coughs.

Riley dropped to her hands and knees behind the van, peering underneath the vehicle to watch as the men's boots took off in different directions.

"Damn," Jake whispered open-mouthed as she straightened up again, staring at her blood-spattered arm glistening in the moonlight. "I'm glad you didn't have your knife on you when you snuck up on me last night."

"And look how useful you've been since then," she sassed him with half a smirk, grabbing a handful of his shirt to wipe off the blood on her arm. Before he could protest to being used as a towel, she added, "Come on – let's go find the others."

They shuffled silently through the shadows of the impound lot, flitting from one derelict vehicle to the next, wary of making any noise.

Riley was constantly checking over her shoulder, keeping an eye out for the guards, while an icy feeling of dread needled its way into the back of her skull.

Remembering how easily Heather had been brought down by one of Everett Lawson's spike traps back in Utah, Riley knew that a single blast from Kuba's shotgun – no matter where it hit – would be akin to a death sentence out here.

Aksel's trigger-happy pistol was no less of a threat either, given that her own father had succumbed to a stray shot to his spleen back in Redhurst, on the day that her entire world had been turned upside down.

And if those thoughts weren't enough to churn Riley's stomach – reinforcements from Valhalla were already on their way, and neither Aksel nor Kuba were coughing from the cloud of tear gas anymore.

CHAPTER 32

"Hey, over here!" Clay's whispered shout rose up from behind the empty cargo bed of a rusty pickup truck. "Is Lincoln with you?"

"That wasn't Lincoln," Riley replied, flashing the fresh blood on her blade. "We got the keys to his truck though. You guys ready to move?"

"We've still got three more tanks to drain," Heather huffed as she knelt beside a jerry can, watching their current score of diesel siphoning out through a long rubber tube, impatiently waiting for the fuel inside to dry up.

"We'd have been a lot faster if you weren't slowing us down," Clay muttered with a sullen glance at her bad leg.

"For fuck's sake," Heather sighed, exhaling slowly with her eyes closed, evidently having endured as much of his presence as she could handle. She looked up at Riley, jerking a thumb over her shoulder at Clay, "Genius over here just realized that the armored trucks that we're *not* taking probably have some kinda special anti-theft valves to stop us from siphoning. And that's if we can even get those fuel doors to open."

"Never mind – we don't have the time anymore anyway,"

Riley replied as she eyed the rubber tendril dangling from the pickup truck's fuel tank, fighting the sudden urge to rip the hose out of the hole. She knew that every drop of diesel would count on their way to California. "The guards are looking for us now. They've already called for backup."

"Well, that's good news for us then," Clay shrugged, before cocking an eyebrow at their confusion. "Wasn't that the plan in the first place? All we had to do was draw some of the guards away from Valhalla, so that Kentaro's people could hit the hotel. Even if we do get caught here, we can just surrender. I mean, it's not like this next tournament's gonna happen now anyway. What's the problem?"

"Yeah, that's true – if Kentaro's in charge, then..." Jake ran a hand through his hair before shaking his head. "No, we could still end up being held hostage. That's if Radek's men even take us alive at this point. We've already killed one of them. *And* we're stealing diesel – that alone is an instant death sentence."

"So what's the plan then?" Clay crossed his arms, jerking his head towards three hulking vehicles dominating the center of the impound lot. "We still haven't hit up those two semis or the spare bus yet. The armored trucks are probably all built the same, so we'd be fine with a head start, but those three could run us off the road for sure. Are we supposed to just stand around with our dicks in our hands while we're waiting for all that diesel to drain too? Because you said they've got backup coming, right?"

"I'll handle it," Jake reassured him, before turning to Riley. "Let me borrow your knife. I'll slash some of the tires while you guys finish up here, and then we'll go."

A rash of gooseflesh instantly flowered up her forearms.

In a knee-jerk reaction to his request, she tightened her grip around her blade's hilt.

"No, I'm not giving up my knife," Riley's tone turned ice cold.

The trauma of disarming herself for the Lawson Family was still fresh in her memory – despite how deep she thought she had buried it.

It didn't matter that they had broken into the impound lot together.

It didn't matter that their lives were also on the line.

She wasn't going to willingly hand over her weapon again – not for anybody.

And especially not to a pair of bounty hunters who had captured and sold Riley and her friends just yesterday.

"Here, take mine," Heather offered up her combat knife instead, cutting through the confused tension that had fallen between them. "Sounds like I'm not gonna need it to jimmy open any more fuel doors anyway. I want it back though."

Jake accepted the compromise with a puzzled frown, eyeing Riley curiously before shrinking back into the shadows.

"Look, I get it," Heather whispered her understanding, wincing slightly as she clambered to her feet. She shot a glance over at Clay before leaning towards Riley's ear, "It's tough trying to tell who we can trust nowadays. New people need to prove themselves to us."

"Yep," Riley said quietly, her gaze turning downcast in the wake of her sudden outburst.

"But we still need to give them the opportunity to prove themselves," Heather continued, stooping slightly to look into her eyes. "Let this be that moment for these guys."

Blinking, Riley flexed the slender muscles of her jaw.

As much as she didn't want to admit it to herself – she knew that she couldn't stay suspicious of every single person they came across.

They had to find new allies some time – and trust worked both ways.

"Fine," her face finally softened as she eased the grip on her combat knife. "I'll meet you guys at the truck when you're done."

"Shouldn't we be sticking together?" Clay asked uncertainly, before ducking his head at the sight of the pair of guards prowling in between the parked vehicles in the distance.

"We can't risk them catching us all in the same spot," Heather knew, giving Riley a nod. "We split up for now until we know for sure it's safe."

"I'll make sure you guys have a clear run to the truck," Riley promised, before turning to Clay. "But if you try to show up without Heather – fuck the fuel – you can find your own way outta here."

"Yes ma'am," he threw up a mock salute in her wake.

Riley ignored his insolence, silently making her way towards the row of armored trucks parked at the front of the yard.

Choosing a direct route towards their prize, she used her knife to cut through the moonlit cobwebs hanging in between the long-abandoned sedans, station wagons and minivans.

She was making good progress, with the truck just up ahead, when the sound of glass tinkling over cracked concrete reached her ears.

Riley froze, heart pounding in her throat as she listened for footsteps.

Just one squeeze, and it's all over, she reminded herself, and an unbidden vision flashed across her mind's eye – the cold abyss of a gun barrel staring back at her.

CHAPTER 33

The tinkling glass noise – a clumsily-kicked piece of trash – grew louder in the stillness, honing in on Riley's position, and she crouched for cover beside the passenger door of an old hatchback.

Clenching the hilt of her blade in her gloved fist, she coiled her muscles, preparing to pounce on whoever was approaching before he could squeeze off a shot in her direction.

She knew that she would only have a split second to register whether she was up against Aksel's pistol or Kuba's shotgun, and that would make all the difference in the amount of distance she'd have to lunge.

Either way, Riley was ready to wreak havoc on her prey.

Her hammering pulse reached its crescendo in her ears, when an empty liquor bottle rolled across her path, nestling itself against a cluster of crushed cans.

Riley's sharp gaze flicked over at the windswept pile of debris, immediately dismissing the distraction.

She strained her ears, listening for anything else, only to hear the night's cool breeze whistling through the derelict yard.

Watching and waiting for what felt like an eternity, she finally let go of the breath that she had been holding, relaxing her tightly-wound shoulders.

BANG!!

The deafening noise reverberated around the impound lot, rattling Riley back into rigid vigilance.

Sensing that the sound was too far off to be an immediate threat, she glanced back at the rusty pickup truck where she had left Heather and Clay.

Through the darkness, the whites of Clay's eyes were hovering above the empty cargo bed, his focus fixed on something in the distance.

Rising up on one knee, Riley peered over the hood of the hatchback to see a lone silhouette darting around the three giant vehicles dominating the center of the yard.

More *pops* and *hisses* filled the impound lot as Jake went to work shredding treads, slashing one big tire after the other, before dashing off in another direction to puncture the next, and the next, and the next.

Drawn by the sudden commotion, the guards called out to each other across the yard, their boots scraping the ground as they ran towards the source of the sound.

Riley's grip on her combat knife tightened as she watched Aksel and Kuba swiftly closing in on the two trucks and the bus being violently immobilized.

Hearing the pair of encroaching guards though, Jake's banging airbursts ceased as suddenly as they had begun, their lingering echoes fading into the night.

"You think a couple of punctured tires are gonna save you?" Kuba's brassy laughter rang through the yard as he stalked in a slow circle around the three hulking vehicles.

"We'll try not to fuck you up too badly before the big day tomorrow," Aksel lied, his lanky limbs still jerking in the aftermath of the taser's electrical shock. "There's still a chance you might make it outta the tournament alive."

"Might make it *into* the tournament alive, you mean," Kuba corrected him with a grin.

The pair of guards sniggered derisively, not even trying to hide their true intentions.

Riley's sharp gaze caught Jake's silhouette scrambling underneath the bus for cover.

His clothes scuffed the concrete as he crawled behind one of the big wheels, even as the four slashed tires hissed out air pressure, the entire vehicle inching closer to the ground with every passing second.

He'll be crushed before he gets caught, Riley knew, biting her bottom lip as she watched with dread.

Aksel and Kuba continued to circle around the pair of trucks and the bus, knowing that they had at least one of the intruders boxed in. There was no need for them to rush in after him either – backup was already on its way.

Riley rubbed the back of her neck, glancing sidelong at their chosen armored truck standing only a few car-lengths away.

She, Heather and Clay could still make it out of the impound lot alive and unscathed.

But that would mean sacrificing Jake Roscoe to a grisly end.

And Riley didn't want that weighing on her conscience.

"Shit..." she muttered under her breath, before stooping to snatch up the empty liquor bottle. "You owe me for this."

A cockroach fell from the rim of the bottle as she tested its weight, the bug scurrying towards the cluster of crushed cans instead.

Riley picked her target – the back of Aksel's head as the rangy guard sauntered around the side of the bus again.

Hurling the empty bottle across the yard, she watched as her glass projectile fell short of its mark, exploding at the man's feet instead, sending him into a spontaneous jig.

"What the – where the fuck did that come from!?" Aksel exclaimed in a burst of anger, whirling around as he peered into the moonlit shadows of the impound lot.

"Hey, you good?" Kuba called from the other side of their impromptu perimeter.

"Get back on the radio and tell them to move their asses!" Aksel shouted back as he examined the spread of broken glass on the ground. "I hate this fucking place!!"

Straightening up again, he abandoned the bus in his rage, heading in Riley's direction instead.

Ducking her head below the windows of the surrounding cars, she padded and pawed her way towards the armored truck, skittering across the distance in between one vehicle's hood to the next vehicle's trunk.

The fuming guard's footsteps slowed somewhere in the throng of derelict cars behind Riley, and she drew herself into a crouch beside the hood of a sun-bleached suburban.

Only a few yards of open ground lay in between her and the armored truck now.

She peered past the suburban's dusty grille before glancing back over her shoulder.

The coast was clear.

It was now or never.

Clenching her combat knife in one hand and the keys to the truck in the other, Riley took two galvanizing breaths, before making a mad dash for the truck.

She rounded the front of the truck in a split second, reaching the driver's side door before she even had the chance to consider which one of the two keys would unlock the door.

Heart hammering in her ears, she fumbled with the first key as she glanced left and right, uncomfortably aware that either one of the guards could drop her from a distance at a moment's notice.

Fingers trembling with nervous tension, she was about to give the second key a try, when the first one finally slid into place, and she thankfully twisted the lock open.

Ripping the key from the hole, Riley launched herself up into the truck's cabin and closed the door behind her as gently as possible, the door's deadbolt automatically clanking shut in the latch.

Her wide eyes zeroed in on a secondary locking mechanism – a bulky steel handle designed to catch on the cabin's center column – and she spun the locking lever into place.

"Safe," she panted gratefully, fighting hard to catch her breath.

Just as she was glancing around the cabin, her elbow hit the steering wheel, half an inch from sounding the horn, and she carefully reached down for the handle to slide the driver's seat backwards.

Exhaling slowly, Riley worked the second key into the ignition, leaving the engine off as she sat back in silence, staring at the small spider-web cracks across the windshield – souvenirs from her own pistol when the bounty hunters had been chasing her down.

All she could do now was sit and wait for the others.

She had already done the best that she could do to shift some of the heat off Jake – now it was up to him to reach the rendezvous point.

A metallic rattle sounded from outside.

But whatever it was, nothing short of an explosion could hurt her now.

Curious though, she peered out into the moonlit darkness of the impound lot.

The slim silhouette of Aksel and his pistol stalked along a nearby aisle of cars, but his back was turned to the row of armored trucks.

Riley narrowed her eyes at the pile of debris in his wake – a cluster of crushed cans.

Her mouth went dry.

The guard was slowly making his way towards the rusty pickup truck at the end of the aisle – the same spot where she had last seen Heather and Clay.

Riley couldn't see either one of them now, but for all she knew, they were both hiding on the other side, still siphoning out the rest of the fuel.

That alone is an instant death sentence, Jake's voice echoed in her head.

Even if Heather and Clay had already finished draining the truck's tank – if Aksel caught them carrying the jerry can – Riley knew that Heather didn't stand a chance of escaping with her bad leg.

Riley didn't even have to think twice about it.

Leaning over the steering wheel, she switched on the ignition and blared the horn, making as much noise as possible.

It had the intended effect.

Aksel whirled around, swearing his head off in a fit of fury as he double-backed towards the truck.

I'll meet you guys back at the fence, Riley promised, hoping that the others would somehow hear her thoughts and head back to the improvised fallback point.

Flicking on the headlights, she was about to punch the truck into gear, when her heart sank to the pit of her stomach.

Jake had already made it back to the truck.

He was down on his knees in front of the rumbling grille, shading his eyes against the blazing headlights, with Kuba's shotgun to the back of his head.

"FUCK!!" Riley slammed her fist on the steering wheel.

"Party's over, bitch!" the Latino guard barked, his brassy laughter grinding in her ears.

Safe from the pair of brutes outside, Riley cradled her head in her hands.

She had *just* secured their ticket out of Las Vegas, and only now did it become apparent that there was a price that she would have to pay.

"Ten seconds to surrender," Kuba warned, his scarred face grinning up at the truck's tinted windshield, "Before I blow your boyfriend's brains out and skull-fuck the hole while he's still warm!"

"ONE!!"

"TWO!!"

Jake lowered his arms from his face to stare up at the windshield.

"Go," he mouthed, forcing a smile against the glare of the headlights. "Just go."

"THREE!!"

"FOUR!!"

"Look who's finally decided to join us!" Aksel shouted contemptuously from somewhere nearby.

213

Riley craned her neck, peering through the side window to see that the reinforcements from Valhalla had reached the front gate of the impound lot.

There were only a handful of them, but each one was armed to the teeth.

"SIX!!"

"SEVEN!!"

A sudden thought struck Riley.

Clay had been right after all.

Kentaro's plan to overthrow Radek had probably already happened by now.

"EIGHT, BITCH!!"

Their capture wouldn't mean anything by the time they reached the Valhalla Hotel.

But if Jake died now, his death would have been pointless.

"NINE!! You really wanna watch this fucker die, huh!?"

"WAIT!!" Riley shouted. She spun the door's locking lever and slid open the deadbolt. "Stop, I'm coming out!"

She cracked open the door, and almost instantly, a rough hand grabbed her by the ankle and violently hauled her out of the truck's cabin, the back of her skull hitting the top step on her way down.

The last thing Riley saw was Aksel's tattooed tear streaks looming over her, before he pistol-whipped her into unconsciousness.

CHAPTER 34

DING!

Riley stirred awake with the coppery taste of blood in her mouth, and her eyelids feebly fluttered open, her vision blurring with the unfamiliar blaze of ceiling lights.

She was lying on her back, her arms raised above her head and in handcuffs, with Aksel's fist gripping the chain links in between as he dragged her out of an elevator into a carpeted hallway.

Jake was still unconscious, his limp body slung over one of Kuba's brawny shoulders as the pair of captors walked side by side along the well-lit corridor.

At least Heather and Clay got away, Riley supposed, watching as the empty elevator's doors closed in their wake. *But where the fuck are Kentaro and his people?*

"Holding cells for the tournament are downstairs," a man's voice spoke through a tinny speaker somewhere up ahead. "Why are you bringing your trash up here?"

"We caught these two trying to steal a truck from the impound," Aksel reported, coming to an abrupt stop. "They slashed the tires on some of the convoy's backup vehicles too."

"So?" the tinny voice came again.

Keeping her movements small to avoid attracting any attention, Riley turned her head to one side, peering past the backs of Aksel's rangy legs. In the corner of her eye, she could see that a security checkpoint had been set up in the middle of the hotel's hallway.

"So!?" Aksel slammed his palm against the security window, the reinforced glass shuddering violently. "We want a fucking reward!"

"Well, Radek's not in right now, so you'll just have to –"

"You'll just have to shut the fuck up," Kuba derailed the man's sentence with a menacing growl. "Let us through. We'll wait for him inside." He prodded the thick window with the barrel of his shotgun, "Or we can find out how tough this glass really is."

"Miranda – I mean, The Valkyrie – she's here," a jittery woman's voice came next. "You can talk to her instead. Hand over your weapons first, and we'll buzz you through."

"Fucking desk jockeys," the scarred Latino snorted in amusement as he and Aksel disarmed themselves, dropping their guns into the counter's security tray. Kuba rapped his knuckles on the glass, pointedly glancing down at his shotgun, "I want it reloaded by the time we're done. *Somebody* around here's gotta keep the thugs outside from getting in."

An electrical whirring sounded in the hallway, and a door without a handle popped open beside the checkpoint, granting them access to the rest of the corridor.

Riley kept one eye half-open as Aksel resumed dragging her along the floor, watching as the pair of security guards shifted uneasily in their seats before radioing ahead.

With her hands cuffed, her combat knife missing, and outnumbered by Radek's people, there was little else that she could do but listen and wait for an opportunity to escape.

But in the back of her mind, Riley was unable to ignore the growing feeling of regret that had taken root, muddying her preference between reckless heroism and survivor's guilt – the nagging thought that she had already lost her last opportunity to escape from the moment she left the armored truck.

Her rueful rumination was cut short as a door swung open at the end of the hallway.

"Don't just stand there," Miranda's unmistakably authoritative voice bade the pair of captors a cold welcome. "Show me what you've brought."

With a strained grunt, Aksel hauled Riley upright and shoved her through the doorway.

Riley's first instinct was to flop onto the floor and feign sleep for a while longer, but her legs acted with a will of their own, clumsily driving her forward as she stared around at the large dimly-lit room.

The penthouse suite of the Valhalla Hotel had been gutted and transformed into a medieval Viking's lair. Every surface of the room had been refurbished with rough-hewn layers of recycled timber. Thick animal furs stretched across the floor, ornate wooden shields lined the walls, and an array of Scandinavian flags hung from the rafters of an artificial cathedral ceiling.

A shallow fire pit had been dug into the center of the room, its dying flames casting dusky light over a large dining table, bordered on both sides by sideboards and display racks that showcased a wide selection of primitive melee weapons.

Momentarily lost in another era, a heavy thud at Riley's feet snapped her out of stasis, and she glanced down to see Jake groaning on the ground.

Her pupils dilated as she spotted flecks of dark crimson across the floorboards.

Most of the bloodstains had already dried up, but some of them were still fresh, the wet splotches giving off a sinister sheen in the dull glow of the fire pit.

"Where the hell are we?" Jake grunted, drawing himself up on his knees to groggily gaze around at their surroundings.

"The last place you two wanna be – I'd imagine," Miranda replied, the sharp-faced brunette woman stalking in a slow semicircle around the pair of captives. Her scornful stare lingered on Riley for a few moments, recognizing her as one of the new arrivals in the city, "I see that Vegas has already left its mark on you."

Riley cocked her head slightly, before remembering the bandage on her cheek, owing to a wild woman's raking fingernails during the cannibals' attack at the Jade Mantis.

"You should see the other girl," Riley shot her half a smirk, adopting a facade of defiance despite her mounting feeling of dread.

"And you should see *you* right now, bitch!" Aksel shouted from behind, kicking out the backs of Riley's knees and sending her to the floor, kneeling beside Jake.

"Valkyrie," Kuba's brassy rumble took on a jarring tone of reverence as he began to offer the woman an explanation, "We caught these two tr–"

"Save it," Miranda cut him off, gesturing towards a walkie clipped to the belt on her hip. "I've already heard enough. You want a reward? Fine. You're both on Dagur's crew now.

But interrupt my conversation one more time, and I'll have the two of you fighting to the death for the position instead."

Not daring to press their luck, the pair of brutes celebrated in silence, knocking their elbows together as they grinned broadly at their new assignment.

Riley and Jake exchanged a glance of uncertainty as Miranda skirted around the edge of the fire pit.

"A low-rank bounty hunter and one of his most recent catches," she mused as she sat down on the end of the dining table, measuring their worth with a cold cocksure gaze. "There's no way that the two of you acted alone. Who were you working with?"

Again, Riley found herself wondering where the hell Kentaro and his people were.

The Red Tigers should have mounted their attack on the hotel long before she and Jake had been captured.

They had been expecting a hostage negotiation, not an interrogation.

"Nobody else was involved," Jake was the first to tell the lie. "I heard the rumors going around the colony that you guys were down on manpower, with the convoy busy chasing after those diesel thieves. I figured that your lack of troops might have extended to the guard roster watching the impound as well. And I was right. I saw an opportunity to leave this cesspool of a city, and I took it."

"And you chose to work with *her* over any of your associates," Miranda nodded towards Riley, smiling skeptically at the unlikelihood.

"Nobody else was stupid enough to go up against Radek," Jake reasoned, hoping that the off-hand excuse would be enough to support his claim. "So I had to find somebody else. Somebody who was still new to the colony," he stared sidelong at Riley, failing to hide the fear in his eyes. "She was the only one who was willing to try and leave this shithole with me."

"That's more plausible," Miranda admitted, although the severity of her expression only worsened. "Now we'll see if you're lying." Locking eyes with Kuba, she snapped her fingers before pointing off to the side, "Ladle."

Riley furrowed her eyebrows as Kuba obediently marched over to the nearest sideboard.

Out of all of the macabre medieval weapons arrayed around the room that the woman could have threatened them with, she had opted for a single wooden spoon.

It didn't make any sense.

But another thought struck Riley as her gaze lingered on one of the weapon racks.

If she leapt to her feet and made a mad dash across the room, she could be armed within seconds, albeit in handcuffs, but still catching their captors off guard. All she needed was something with an edge – a sword, an axe, or even a spear – and she could hold Miranda at her mercy, forcing Aksel and Kuba to surrender.

But that plan hinged on whether the weapons on display actually held an edge.

For all Riley knew, they were just blunt decorative pieces purely for show.

Kuba returned with the ladle, and the moment was gone.

"Can't take anybody at their word these days," Miranda shrugged with an insincere tone of apology. She studied the pair of prisoners kneeling on the floor, before tilting her head curiously, "Have either of you ever heard of a *blood eagle*?"

Aksel drew in a sharp breath.

Jake shook his head slowly, frowning at the phrase.

"I'm guessing it's not some kinda dessert," Riley gave a small snort at the serving spoon clutched in Kuba's hand.

It was trembling slightly.

The man was visibly shaking, his somber gaze fixated on the floor.

Riley swallowed as she remembered the fresh bloodstains on the floorboards.

An icy shiver bolted up her spine then, as if some unseen terror lurking in a dark corner of the dimly-lit room had turned its nightmarish eyes towards her, greedily devouring what was left of her defiance.

"Let me tell you about the blood eagle," Miranda leaned forward from her perch on the dining table, the glow of the fire pit's dying flames wreathing her angular face in a hellish hue. "Viking warriors saved this particular ritual only for their most hated enemies, because even they themselves dreaded the act... But those who had the stomach for it would begin by laying their victim face down. Then, with a knife, they'd flay the flesh from his upper torso – muscles, tendons and ligaments – right down to the bone. Once the ribcage was exposed, they'd crack it open, severing each bone from the spine, slowly and painfully, one at a time. And if the victim was still alive by that point, their lungs would be ripped out through the gaping holes and laid to rest over their shoulders – just like a pair of wings..."

Her eyes closed for a moment as she traced a fingertip down her neck, as if she was envisioning some unlucky soul suffering the scourge and torment of an archaic cruelty.

A hush fell over the room as the grisly image lingered in

their heads.

Jake gulped audibly in the silence.

"You," Miranda snapped her fingers at Aksel, before her gaze flicked over to Jake, "Lay him down."

"Hold on – what for?" Riley protested, her eyes going wide with horror as Jake was shoved face down on the floor, with Aksel straddling his torso. "He already told you everything!"

"And now he'll have a chance to prove it," Miranda countered, sadistically savoring the sounds of Jake's struggle. "If he was lying, his body will betray him. He'll call out. He'll beg. He'll scream. But the pain will only end when he gives up the names of the other traitors that you two were working with."

"And when he doesn't?" Riley shot a glance at Jake, wordlessly warning him not to incriminate himself too early.

"Then he'll have been a worthy blood tribute to The Valkyrie," Miranda simply replied as she held out her hand for the wooden ladle. "It was said that if the blood-eagled didn't scream throughout the entire ritual, then they would still be welcome in Valhalla." She gave Aksel a terse nod, "Rip open his shirt."

Riley's breathing turned shallow as Aksel tore the back of Jake's shirt down the middle.

It wouldn't make a difference if he broke and told them the truth now.

They were going to torture him to death regardless.

Riley scanned the distance to the nearest weapon rack.

It didn't matter whether the displays were decorative or not.

She had to do something.

"Hold her down," Miranda's voice pierced through Riley's resolve.

Aksel obliged immediately, throwing himself off Jake and tackling her to the floor before she even had the chance to plant one foot on the ground.

Snarling against the floorboards with the rangy man's weight on top of her back, Riley twisted and writhed, frothing at the mouth as she fought to break free, until he leaned his forearm against the back of her neck, using his other hand to pin her head to the ground.

Trapped like a wild animal caught in a snare, all she could do was stare back at Jake, his head caught in a similar vise – wedged in between Kuba's knee and the floorboards.

"You thought the blood eagle was a dessert?" Miranda slid off the edge of the dining table with a cold smile at Riley's fuming glare. "Why don't we make it a three-course meal? Let's start with the entree, and save the best for last."

The callous woman maintained eye contact as she stooped to thrust her wooden ladle into the edge of the fire pit, flames leaping onto the end of the serving spoon.

Riley's heart pounded in her ears as she locked eyes with Jake.

His pupils were wide with panic as their shallow breaths mingled over the floorboards.

"That's it – I want you to watch him," Miranda continued, still staring at Riley as she scooped out a mound of burnt embers and hot ash. She straightened up again, looming over the pair of captives with the blazing firebrand. "I want you to see him suffer, knowing that you can spare him a whole world of pain... and all you have to do is tell me the truth."

With that, she poured the scalding hot ash across Jake's bare back.

His bellows of agony reverberated around the room.

Angry red blisters instantly formed and burst as the searing embers sank into his flesh.

Jake thrashed his legs wildly, desperately trying to turn his torso, but with Kuba firmly holding him in place, he had no hope of shaking off the smoldering ashes scorching through his skin.

"FUCK YOU!!" Riley roared at their tormentors, her eyes filling with the excruciating anguish scrawled across Jake's contorted face.

"You can yell all you want," Miranda spoke calmly as she bent down in between them, idly stirring the smoking embers with her ladle, listening to Jake's hollers reach new heights. "This isn't gonna stop until you give me some names – and I haven't even gotten started yet. I'm just warming him up before the main event."

Riley screwed her eyes shut, but there was no way to block out the screams.

She didn't know what was worse – listening to the sound of his skin sizzling or smelling the scent of his flesh on fire.

She wished that the people they were protecting would just come bursting in through the door, guns blazing, saving them from this nightmare.

But it was just her and Jake now.

She couldn't even imagine the pain he was going through.

Nor the pain that was yet to come.

She just wanted it to stop.

"You want some fucking names, bitch!?" Riley yelled, if only to drown out the sounds of Jake's torture. She was desperate. She had to try something. Her eyelids snapped open again as she glared up at Miranda. "Bobby, Sheila, Merle, Stuart, Elroy, Alyssa!!"

"There's a start – now slow down for me," Miranda smiled victoriously. True to her word, she used the burning ladle to scrape off the hot coals from Jake's back, before thumbing the switch on the walkie clipped to her belt. "Valkyrie here – I need somebody to write this down."

"Bree, Charlee, Trask, Calvin," Riley continued, breathing a shuddering sigh of relief as Jake's anguished shouts subsided into strained sobs. "Rose, Stan, Everett."

Miranda narrowed her eyes in suspicion, and she took her thumb off the radio.

"Fake names," she surmised, her triumphant grin turning sour. "I thought that simply bearing witness would be enough to inspire the truth from you. But maybe you'll have to experience it for yourself instead."

"None of those names were fake," Riley shot back, allowing herself a chuckle even as she sealed her own fate. "Those are all the people I've killed so far. And now I've got a few more names to add on to my list – Aksel, Kuba, Miranda, Radek."

"You think you're cute, huh?" Aksel growled in her ear. "Saying our fucking names!?"

Miranda silenced him with a cold stare.

Kuba kept his knee planted on Jake's skull, grimly surveying the human barbecue.

"Thanks, Riley," Jake panted meekly in the stillness, his gaze empty as his burnt body plunged him into a state of shock. "You could've saved yourself and left me to die. But instead, you surrendered and got outta the truck. I'm sorry for bringing y–"

His eyes rolled upwards as he slipped into unconsciousness.

Their tormentors couldn't hurt him anymore.

But they could still hurt her.

Riley was all alone now.

She bit her bottom lip to keep it from trembling.

"A killer with a conscience," Miranda sneered at the contradiction, toying with her scorched ladle as she eyed Jake's limp body with a mixture of boredom and disappointment. She sized up Riley instead, before reluctantly conceding, "I suppose you'll be one to watch tomorrow." Summarily tossing the serving spoon into the fire pit, she turned to Aksel and Kuba, "Take them downstairs. Let's see how far they get."

CHAPTER 35

"We got some fresh meat!" Kuba barked as they stepped out of the elevator, his brassy voice reverberating around the underground parking level. "One's still raw and wriggling, and the other one's been cooked well done!"

Aksel shoved Riley forward, her hands still cuffed at her waist.

A small slice of the Valhalla Hotel's parking garage had been converted into a makeshift cell house, with somber-faced survivors crammed into two rows of cages, each enclosure roughly following the striped outlines of a single parking space.

Flickering fluorescent bulbs cast intermittent light over the mournful gazes peering out from behind chain-linked fences, disappointed to see that the *fresh meat* wasn't actually a meal, but just another pair of contenders bound for the tournament.

Half a dozen of Radek's men had been assigned to monitor the prisoners, the guards jeering and mocking the new arrivals as they were hauled off towards different cages.

Jake was still passed out from the trauma of his second-degree burns – immune to the guards' insults – but that didn't stop them from trying to get a rise out of him.

"I doubt Pretty Boy's even gonna last the night!"

"I bet that skinny bitch could go a couple rounds though!"

"A couple rounds with *you*, maybe – I'd snap that little snack in half!"

Riley decided to keep her head down, fighting the urge to trade slurs, actively ignoring the crude jibes of the deriding degenerates.

Having witnessed the depths of depravity that the wannabe Viking warriors were capable of, she knew that her best course of action was to keep her mouth shut, biting her tongue until they ran out of things to say.

Aksel yanked Riley to a stop beside the last cage on the left.

One of the guards broke off the verbal abuse to draw up alongside them.

"Back the fuck up or I'll paint the floor red with your blood!" he yelled at the cell's occupants, holding a set of keys in one hand and a sub-machine gun in the other.

The huddled handful of survivors retreated to the rear as the guard unlocked the cage, and Aksel shoved Riley inside, the door swinging shut before she could even spin around, followed by the heavy *clank* of a deadbolt sliding back into place.

"You got lucky with The Valkyrie tonight," Aksel growled as he tested the lock on the door, making the cage's chain-linked fence shudder and jingle. His tattooed tear streaks stretched wide as he gave her a sinister smile behind the steel mesh, "I can't *wait* to see what happens to you tomorrow when that luck runs out."

Riley simply stared over his shoulder, determined not to give the rangy man a reason to drag her back out of the cage.

Keeping her cool, she watched as Kuba entered one of the cells across the way, unceremoniously dumping Jake onto his stomach like an old roll of threadbare carpet.

Aksel followed her gaze for a moment before loping off with a scornful snigger.

Riley gripped the fence with her gloved fingers as Jake's cellmates crowded around his burnt body, each of them wincing at his wounds before bundling up scraps of their own clothing, giving him a makeshift pillow.

"And here I was hoping that at least one of our plans had worked out," a familiar voice sighed from behind.

Riley turned to see Dakota, along with three more prisoners at the back of the cage – two were on their feet, but the third was lying in a crumpled heap on the floor.

"Ooh la la," a skinny shirtless man with a thick afro exclaimed, "Check out the badass with the bandage on her cheek."

"She looks like a fighter," a busty blonde woman with a year's worth of regrowth smiled with relief. "I think our chances of survival just went up again."

"Felix, Georgia – this is Riley," Dakota made the brief introductions before nodding towards their bloody cellmate lying motionless in the back corner. "Now, I need you guys to keep on patching him up as best as you can. We've gotta be in top condition before tomorrow starts, otherwise we're all gonna end up looking a whole lot worse than he does right now."

"Well, I'm gonna need another shirt then, Dakota," Felix sassed her with one hand on his bare hip, the other out-stretched and demanding payment. "Unless you want me to patch him up with my panties?"

"Here – it may as well be mine," Georgia let out a reluctant groan before she began lifting the hem of her shirt. "Just when I thought I wouldn't have to do this shit anymore. I signed up for the tournament so I could get away from str–"

"Stop," Riley cautioned, jerking her head towards the guards patrolling the cell house. She locked eyes with the startled woman, "If they see you putting on a free show, they'll come barging in here thirsting for all three of us." She rattled her handcuffs as she exchanged a knowing glance with Dakota. "I might be a fighter, but I'm not *that* good."

"We wouldn't stand a chance," Dakota agreed, before gazing back at their unconscious cellmate on the floor, her brow creasing with clarity as her eyes traced over his cargo shorts. "Tear out his pockets and brush off the lint – they should be clean enough. Let us know if you need any more."

"Hold on – is that Lincoln!?" Riley's eyes widened as she recognized the dour man's battered face, his stony features hidden underneath a score of swollen welts, while the rest of his body was covered in cuts. She glanced sidelong at Dakota, "What the hell happened to him? Actually – tell me later – what happened to *you*? I thought this place would've be–"

"Lower your voice," Dakota clapped a hand over Riley's mouth for a moment, before bringing her over to the farthest corner of the cage, wary of their own cellmates listening in. She answered with a whisper, "They had to call off the attack at the last second. Dagur pulled up in a pickup truck outside the hotel just as we were turning over Eddie. It was too late for us, but the rest of our guys would've been slaughtered if they didn't pull out – the truck had a machine gun mounted on the back."

"So they just abandoned you?" Riley furrowed her eyebrows, having been under the impression that the Red Tigers were above sacrificing their own people to run from a fight.

"It was the smart play," Dakota wholeheartedly supported their decision. "Dagur came back without the rest of the convoy. And with all the focus being on the tournament tomorrow, the rest of my people might still get another shot at following through on the original plan. We just have to survive long enough for them to make a move."

Riley was about to press for details, when she caught Dakota's gaze sliding sideways, conscious of Felix's growing interest in their hushed conversation.

"Anyway, we all knew the risk involved," Dakota's voice returned to normal, acting as though she was simply continuing a story. "After we got caught out trying to double-dip on a bounty, the guards dragged us down here and shoved us all into different cells. Jin and Hanzo are somewhere around here too. Same as Eddie."

She threw a contemptuous glare across the parking garage, where the clean-shaven conman was busy buttering up another pair of prisoners in his cell, no doubt priming the conversation to strike up a bargain for their protection tomorrow.

One of the men looked like a former athlete, his dark muscles glistening in the flickering fluorescent light as he smashed out a set of push-ups with ease.

The other prisoner was crunching his lean stomach, his long braided hair swinging wildly like a stallion's mane as beads of sweat trickled into his stubble beard.

The sound of fabric tearing behind Riley brought her attention back to their own cell.

"And what about Lincoln?" she asked, shooting a glance over at the back corner as Felix turned out another pocket

231

from the man's cargo shorts, ripping it from the seams.

"He didn't look that bad the last time I saw him," Dakota cast a sympathetic gaze at Lincoln's swollen face, watching as Georgia gingerly tried to blot the blood from his broken nose. "He came outta the same truck as Dagur, and they followed us to the elevators. But we were going down, and they were going up."

"I saw bloodstains up in the penthouse," Riley remembered the fresh flecks of crimson spattered across the floorboards, and she quickly came to a conclusion, "They must've been interrogating him. Before Lincoln left the city, he said he was gonna go after the diesel thieves and search for any stragglers. Maybe Dagur and Miranda thought he was working with them."

"Did you see him?" Dakota grabbed Riley by the forearm, staring into her eyes. "Radek – was he up in the penthouse too?"

"No," she shook her head curiously, "It was just Miranda in there. Why?"

"Because nobody's actually seen him since the first tournament ended," Dakota turned her chin, frowning as a sneaking suspicion dawned on her. "We thought he was just hiding out in his penthouse this whole time, but if he's not up there... then he's already dead. He's gotta be."

"What makes you say that?" Georgia looked up from beside Lincoln.

The prisoners in the neighboring cell also turned to listen to the theory.

"Come on – this is Radek we're talking about," Dakota lowered her voice again, increasingly aware of her growing audience. "Not long after he took over the city, he started roaming the streets – day or night, it didn't matter – he was always drunk and looking for somebody to fight. Then as soon as Miranda won the tournament, he just disappeared."

"You think she had something to do with it?" Riley cocked an eyebrow, although she wouldn't have put the trifling matter of murder past the sadistic woman.

"She's the only one who's been passing on *his* orders," Dakota reasoned with a skeptical tone. She gazed out at the guards in the cell house, "And none of his followers would even dare to question her. It's perfect. He killed the people in power to take control of the city – but nobody else can do the same thing to him, because they don't even know where he is. And all Miranda has to do is use his name to keep everybody else in line."

"*Yass!* Down with the patriarchy, girlfriend!" Felix seemed to be the only one celebrating the news, even going so far as to cup Lincoln's bloody chin, making his mouth move like a puppet, "It's a woman's world now, baby. Y'all better recognize."

Lincoln groaned in pain, and Georgia smacked Felix's hand away.

"Good for her," Riley supposed as she narrowed her eyes at their squabbling cellmates. "But where does that leave us? Whether Radek or Miranda's in charge, we're still bound for the tournament tomorrow. What are we even up against?"

"We won't know for sure until it starts," Dakota shrugged as she sank to the floor, leaning her back against the cage's chain-linked fence. "The challenges are different every time. I've seen people being forced to play dodgeball with throwing knives, and tug of war over a pit of flames."

"One time," Georgia chimed in, gulping audibly, "They laid

233

out a path of hot coals. And whoever couldn't make it all the way across were beaten to death by those who could."

"I just hope they don't make us fight against each other," Felix dreaded the thought. He looked at each of them in turn, before rethinking his eagerness to tend to Lincoln's injuries. "I was just starting to like you guys."

"We can't rule out that possibility," Dakota gave them the hard truth. She gazed up at Riley from her seat on the floor, "Sometimes it's a free-for-all. Sometimes it's decimation. But in the past few tournaments, they've had teams of five going up against each other – and I'm pretty sure this is our five."

"Great," Riley's handcuffs clinked as she rubbed the back of her neck, not even trying to hide her lack of optimism.

Apart from Dakota, there was nobody else that Riley could rely on to watch her back.

She didn't have much faith in Felix and Georgia to hold their own.

And Lincoln would be lucky if he didn't slip into a coma overnight.

A five-on-five fight was more likely to be two-on-five.

"Whatever we're facing tomorrow," Georgia blew a long breath in the silence, "All I know is that it's possible to survive. I mean, if Foley's been doing it for this long, and he keeps on coming back for more – then why can't the rest of us?"

"Which one's Foley?" Riley wondered, staring out across the cell house.

She remembered Barbara had mentioned that Miranda wasn't the only person to walk out of a tournament alive.

"He's in the same cell as Eddie," Dakota answered, not even bothering to turn her head. "Tyson's the black guy. Foley's the one with the beard."

Riley's eyes zeroed in on Eddie's cage again.

The glib-tongued scam artist was shaking hands with two of his cellmates – Tyson, the former athlete, and Foley, the adrenaline junkie with a death wish – apparently having struck a deal.

She flexed the slender muscles of her jaw.

That was the caliber of their competition.

"What I wouldn't give to be in that cell with them," Felix sighed, leaning his shoulder against the fence with a longing gaze. He soon realized that he wasn't just talking to himself, and he quickly perked up again, "But I would never leave my bitches. We got this, queens. Am I right?"

Riley left him hanging as she sat down beside Dakota.

"We need a Plan B," Riley whispered in her ear. "Because if your people don't come through for us again, then we're all gonna be dead by this time tomorrow."

CHAPTER 36

Finally free of her handcuffs, Riley rubbed the red rings around her wrists for the umpteenth time that morning as the group of prisoners were marched down The Strip.

A heavily-armed semi-circle of sinewy savages – each wearing an identical upside down hammer pendant – were trailing along behind the tournament's contenders, shepherding the crowd towards the series of arenas in the distance.

"Watch your step," Riley warned, her hand shooting out to grab hold of Jake's, before he could trip over a broken palm tree branch lying in the middle of the road.

"Thanks," he mumbled with a pained grimace, checking over his shoulder as he carefully treaded backwards over the top of the fallen frond.

He was backpedaling down the boulevard with the glare of the morning sun on his face, with the intention of keeping the UV rays off his scorched back. They'd had no choice but to leave his second-degree burns exposed to the elements, still too tender to be covered up by anything but proper bandages.

"We're almost there," Riley eased her gloved fingers out of his grip as they passed by a row of ransacked restaurants and bars. "How are you holding up?"

"It hurts every time the wind blows, and the itch is..." Jake's groan said enough, and he let out a long breath, trying to keep his mind from lingering on the wound for too long.

"That's a good sign," Lincoln croaked as he limped along beside them, clutching at one side of his ribcage. His facial features were broken, bruised and bulging beyond recognition, but there was still fire blazing in his eyes, the resilient bounty hunter relentlessly soldiering on. "I'd be more worried if you couldn't feel a thing. Pain means that the burns didn't go deep enough to fry your nerve endings – if they did, you would've been dead by dawn to sepsis. So be grateful for whatever suffering you're going through right now. It means you're gonna live."

"Sounds like I had that meltdown just in time," Riley supposed, her outburst last night having spared Jake from his burns becoming life-threatening.

"I don't remember anything past the pain, but thanks," Jake replied before trembling with an involuntary shiver, as if his body could remember the events of last night all too well. His keen gaze latched on to something in the corner of his eye – the ransacked Italian restaurant where he and his mother had made their home. "I just hope my mom doesn't have to see me like this."

Riley swallowed a pang of pity as an unbidden vision flashed across her mind's eye – the fragile Mrs Roscoe doddering out onto the terrace of the restaurant, confused and distressed by the sight of her son's scorched skin.

She spared a thought for her own mother, wondering what Susan Armstrong would have said if she could see her daughter right now – being marched down the boulevard by a bunch of beefy barbarian brutes, forced to participate in a macabre game of life and death.

"Stop," Riley's voice was hollow with the memory of her mother's face. "We're here."

She caught Jake's wrist, jerking him to a halt before he could collide with the person slowing in front of them.

Three barricaded arenas stretched down the boulevard, flanked by a set of grandstands on the left and a row of raised platforms on the right. A bustling crowd of somber-faced survivors were searching for the best seats to watch the event, their expressions filled with a strange mixture of dread, wonder and guilt-laden excitement.

Although there were hundreds of people gathered, there was no mistaking Taylor's bruised face among the crowd, the girl still recovering from their violent clash with the cannibals in the Jade Mantis Hotel. Barbara was lounging on a seat beside her, while Manny, his older brother and the rest of the water crew were dealing out freshly-filled bottles from their laden shopping carts.

"I don't see Heather up there," Riley frowned as her sharp eyes scanned over the sea of strangers surrounding Taylor and Barbara. By her little sister's side was the only place that Riley could imagine where Heather would rather be. "Clay's missing too."

"You think they got caught after last night?" Jake wondered as he glanced left and right at the other contenders. He ran a hand through his hair, bewildered by his own question, "No, they would've been down here with the rest of us. So where the f–"

"None of the Red Tigers have shown up to watch either," Hanzo observed as he drew up alongside Riley, with Dakota and Jin in tow.

"Would *you* wanna show your face after leaving your own people behind?" Jin asked rhetorically, evidently bitter about being abandoned outside the Valhalla Hotel last night.

"Keep it down," Dakota hissed, glancing over her shoulder as Felix and Georgia pushed through the crowd towards them. Her voice returned to normal as she gave them a shrug, "Some people just don't like watching the tournaments – for obvious reasons."

The whistling feedback of a bullhorn cut across their speculation, and they all turned to see Miranda standing on top of one of the raised platforms overlooking the first arena, with Aksel, Kuba, Dagur and a handful of other guards gathered around the platform's base.

Miranda held the bullhorn low at her hip, her finger still squeezing the trigger, purposely prolonging the speaker's jarring frequency. She waited for the murmuring crowd to fall to silence, before finally raising the mouthpiece to her lips.

"Gathered before you are the worst among you," she addressed the audience, her cold cocksure gaze sweeping over the tournament's contenders, "This is the latest collection of thieves, traitors and cutthroats. People who thought that they could take whatever they wanted without consequence – just as the Vikings once did."

Dagur led the cheer among the guards, roaring in revelry over the glorification of their adopted false identities.

"But not all of them are worthy of being called *true* Vikings," Miranda continued, gripping the platform's railing with her other hand, her scornful stare seeming to zero in on Riley. "So today, we witness who among them will be worthy of entering

Valhalla – in this life, or the next."

CHAPTER 37

The crowd cheered from the grandstands, roaring their encouragement to the tournament's unwilling participants.

At a signal from Miranda, a pair of guards leapt over the barricade into the first arena.

Two long tables stood at opposite ends of the otherwise empty rectangular enclosure, each one covered up by a sheet of blue tarp, with stacks of hidden objects bulging underneath the canvas.

"What are we up against?" Jake asked, his body still turned towards the sun as he stole glances over his shoulder.

"I don't know," Dakota replied, craning her neck. "I've never seen this one before."

"Whatever it is – we've got this," Riley looked left and right, extracting nods of resolve from Lincoln, Jin, Hanzo and Georgia. "As long as we work together, we can survive anything they throw at us."

"Unless they decide to throw us at each other," Felix scoffed with his snarky skepticism.

Riley's tongue pressed against the inside of her cheek, choosing to ignore the comment as the first tarp was removed.

The crowd of spectators and contenders alike drew in a sharp breath.

On the table at the rear of the arena lay six crossbows, and beside each weapon was a large box brimming with bolts.

"Does anybody know how to fire those?" Georgia wondered as she tied her hair back into a ponytail.

"I don't think those are for us," Lincoln croaked, his deadpan stare fixated on the other guard approaching the front of the arena.

The second tarp billowed out as the table just beyond the entrance was revealed.

Dozens of circular wooden shields were stacked in a long pile across the table, with each buckler bearing a unique combination of colors and patterns – some decorated with ornate Nordic symbols, and others painted with simple stripes and spirals.

"The Shield Wall is the first challenge of the tournament," Miranda announced over the bullhorn. "This battle formation was used by our Viking forebears to gain ground on the battlefield, while also providing shelter from enemy archers. Its success hinged on each individual warrior's ability to protect the person fighting beside them. Fail to hold the formation, and the whole wall crumbles, with each of you along with it."

Half a dozen men filed into the rear of the arena, and Riley recognized them as the six guards from the makeshift cell house in the parking garage. They snatched up the crossbows with eager grins, cocking back the strings with the ease of practiced precision before loading the bolt arrows.

The other pair of guards still in the arena folded up the blue tarps into strips, before laying them across the long stretch of asphalt in between the two tables, marking the start and finish lines for the challenge.

Riley was eyeing the grandstands, wondering if she and her friends could make a mad dash towards the crowd and lose themselves within the sea of spectators, when a lone thought convinced her otherwise – Radek's men would have no problem with firing on the crowd.

A rough shove from behind sent her staggering forward as all of the contenders were corralled into the arena, and she and her former cellmates – along with Jin and Hanzo – formed a protective ring around Jake as he backpedaled towards the table of shields.

"Looks like your boy's gonna have to turn around if he wants to live," Eddie sidled up next to Riley, the self-satisfied scam artist giving her a flash of his easy grin. He spread his hands as he shrugged at Jake, "I'm just saying – we're all in this round together. We're gonna need your head in the game and your eyes on the prize, buddy."

"Yeah, we are in this round together," Riley admitted as she picked up one of the wooden bucklers. She offered it to Eddie with a smile of feigned courtesy, before thrusting the rim of the shield into his sternum, shoving him backwards so that he tripped over his own feet. "So how about you fuck off to the other end of the line – unless you wanna die before this round even starts, *buddy?*"

Eddie clambered upright with a scathing retort on his lips, but he had no air left in his lungs to breathe it into life. Dusting off his suit jacket and gathering up what was left of his dwindling dignity, he slunk over to where Foley and Tyson were gearing up.

"Thanks," Jake mumbled as he slid his forearm through

the straps of a shield. "He's got a point though. I can't walk backwards anymore. Even if I can somehow make it through this round, I doubt I'll be able to survive the rest of the tournament without letting the sun hit my back."

Jutting his chin and screwing his eyes shut, he spun around, gritting his teeth in defiant agony as the unforgiving Nevada summer sun's rays washed over his angrily-glistening burns.

"What the hell are you doing!?" Lincoln seized Jake's shoulder almost instantly, twisting him back around before he could do any more damage to himself. "You have *zero* protection from the sun right now. Was I not being clear when I said you'd be dead to sepsis if your burns got any worse?"

"I'm gonna die from a crossbow bolt to the back if I don't," Jake wrenched his elbow out of the man's grip, although he hesitated to turn his scorched back to the sun again.

"You'd only be guaranteeing your death," Riley sided with Lincoln, easing the buckler from Jake's forearm. She held up the shield behind him instead, and he reluctantly gripped it over the back of his neck with both hands. "You can walk backwards for this round. We'll be your eyes. Don't think about the rest of the tournament right now."

Staring him down into a nod of agreement, Riley turned to pick up a shield for herself, sliding her forearm through the straps.

She was testing its weight, small but sturdy, when the other contenders fell to a hush.

Striding around to the front of the table, Foley – the thrill-seeking veteran of past tournaments – stood waiting for their attention.

Even the crowd of spectators in the grandstands were listening with bated breath, all of them eager to hear the man's proposed strategy for the challenge.

"These shitty shields they've given us are too small," his voice rang out loud and baritone, as if he belonged on a battlefield. He hunched over behind his own buckler, demonstrating that while his head and torso were protected, the shield's bottom edge barely covered the tops of his thighs. "We're gonna need two rows of people – one on the ground and the other holding their shields up at chest height – otherwise these assholes are just gonna take us out at the knees. So pick somebody you trust and form a line."

Eddie was the first to throw himself at Foley's feet.

The rest of the contestants broke out into disarray, shoving and elbowing as they all scrambled to find a suitable partner.

Felix shimmied in between the swinging shields as he made his way towards Dakota, while Georgia found herself pushed up against Lincoln in the press.

"I guess it's just you and me," Jake supposed, directing Riley's attention with a jerk of his head towards Jin and Hanzo as they formed a pair. "Sorry."

"Don't be," she locked eyes with him as she flexed the slender muscles of her jaw. "We can do this."

Riley glanced over at the other survivors still finding their positions along the shield wall, when her gaze latched on to the six crossbowmen standing at the far end of the arena.

Her heart leapt up into her throat.

The firing squad was already taking aim.

CHAPTER 38

"WAIT!! WE'RE NOT RE−" one man's shout was cut short as a bolt skewered his neck, and he dropped to his knees in gurgling shock.

Five more fell in the confusion, and the trigger-happy crossbowmen cocked back their strings for another shot.

"Quick! While they're still reloading," another contestant seized the opportunity, ducking behind her shield as she charged across the arena towards the finish line, before the next volley of spikes impaled her thighs and kneecaps.

"STAND TOGETHER!!" Foley roared over the chaos, standing with Tyson and Eddie as a pillar of strength for the others to rally around.

Only half of the panicked crowd had appeared to have heard him though, with many of the poor souls curling up into pitiful balls behind their undersized wooden bucklers, cowering in fear as flesh-hungry bolts whistled by overhead.

Riley watched as another pair of scampering survivors fell short of the rapidly-deteriorating shield wall, and she caught Hanzo by the elbow before he and Jin could rush headlong into making the same mistake.

"Get down!!" Jake yelled, upending the table beside the entrance and stooping for cover, still facing backwards, holding up his shield over the back of his neck.

In half a heartbeat, Riley and the former pair of peacekeepers flung themselves down alongside him, just as another bolt crunched into the timbers of the overturned tabletop with an angry *thock*.

"We're getting fucking slaughtered out there!" Hanzo shouted as he chanced a glance over the top of their makeshift barricade.

"And we haven't even stepped over the starting line yet," Jin panted wide-eyed, shaking his head in disbelief.

Keeping her head low to the ground, Riley crawled over to one side of the upended table, angling her shield towards the row of crossbowmen as she surveyed the arena.

Those who were still on their feet had splintered off into two separate groups, each line of shields steadily inching their way forward.

Foley stood at the center of the larger group, counting out their steps to the nervous cheers of the rapt audience, while Dakota and Lincoln led a handful of survivors along the side, using the arena's wall to compensate for their lack of numbers.

"I have an idea," Riley breathed as she crawled back to the others. She jerked her head towards the overturned table, "Forget about these shields – we can just push this thing all the way to the end."

"Yeah, that'll work," Jin nodded, before locking eyes with Hanzo, "We'll take the sides. Riley and Jake – you guys stay in the middle."

Working together, they braced their shoulders against the

wooden wall, gently nudging the table forward, taking care not to flip it over completely. Meanwhile, Jake shuffled backwards with every new inch of ground, one hand pawing over the asphalt as he diligently kept his burn wounds out of the sun.

Another volley of bolts stabbed into the tabletop, angrily drawn to their progress, but the row of crossbowmen standing at the other end of the arena could do nothing to prevent the makeshift barricade's steady advance.

The jarring noise of timber scraping along the ground was like music to Riley's ears, and just as they were beginning to pick up speed, the table hit a snag, its bottom edge caught on an obstacle in front.

Her pupils dilated in horror as the top of the table tilted towards tipping point, and the sound of the hollering crowd of spectators drowned her eardrums.

With lightning speed, Jin caught the table's teetering legs as they floated in midair, and a crossbow bolt whistled past his cheek as he wrestled their wooden wall back upright again.

"Hold on – I'll take a look," Hanzo offered as they all shared a sigh of relief. Using his shield for cover, he stole a glance around the side of the table. His face darkened. "There's a body in the way."

"Can't we just go around it?" Jake suggested, looking left and right for an alternate path.

"*Bodies*," Hanzo corrected himself, before shaking his head. "Wouldn't matter which way we went. We're still gonna bump into someone."

"We'll have to lift the table over," Riley swallowed, furrowing her eyebrows as she tried to think of a way that wouldn't end up leaving their hands and knees exposed in the act.

But before she could reach a solution, the whistle of Miranda's bullhorn cut through her thoughts.

"Warriors didn't bring tables onto the battlefield," the scornful woman berated them from her perch on the raised platform overlooking the arena. "Move it one more inch, and none of you will live to cross the finish line."

At a nod from Miranda, Dagur barked orders at his crew of brutes stationed along the sidelines. Both Aksel and Kuba stood grinning among the guards, eagerly training their guns on the four contestants crouched behind the table.

"Shit," Jake muttered as he and Riley shared a sidelong grimace.

They knew that their wooden shields wouldn't stand a chance against a lead shower.

Still staying low behind cover, they reluctantly backed away from the table.

Looking around, they had only managed to cross one third of the arena.

"Foley's the obvious choice," Jin was quick to say what none of them wanted to admit.

Despite their losses, the larger group's shield wall was still holding strong, almost eclipsing the row of crossbowmen as the united contenders shambled forward in near-lockstep, all of them keeping time with Foley's count.

The medieval firing line had set their sights on the smaller cluster of shields skirting along the side instead, pinning Dakota, Lincoln, Felix, Georgia and a few others to the wall.

"Okay," Riley rubbed the back of her neck as her gaze darted between the two groups. The crossbowmen were completely out of sight behind Foley's shield wall now. "Jin, you take Jake across the finish line. Me and Hanzo will −"

She frowned as Hanzo screwed up his face.

"You misunderstood me," Jin offered an explanation. "I meant to say – Foley's the obvious choice *for you*." He tapped Hanzo on the shoulder, who nodded in agreement, "*We're* gonna go after Dakota. We'll see you guys on the other side."

Riley and Jake exchanged a hesitant glance.

Foley's shield wall would be sure to provide ample protection.

At this point, they could simply step out from behind the table and just stroll across the finish line.

But Jake already knew her answer – especially after she had already saved him several times over during their break-in at the impound lot last night.

"She's not the type of person to leave people behind," he replied on her behalf as he rose to his feet, holding up his buckler with both hands behind his back. "And neither am I. Let's go."

"Wait – what?" Riley frowned as she lurched after him, holding her shield down low to protect their legs. "You don't have to do this. Foley's group is just up ahead. You can take the easy win."

"And Lincoln's group is right there," Jake pointedly glanced at the handful of survivors huddled beside the wall, squirming under the barrage of bolts slamming into their shields. "I'm probably not gonna make it through the rest of the tournament. At least let me go out with some pride."

She stared up at the determination lining his face, and nodded in solidarity.

Bracing their bucklers together with Jin and Hanzo, they ventured out from behind cover towards their friends, sidestepping back into the crossbowmen's field of view.

Almost instantly, their shields shook with a grisly greeting of bolt arrows, Riley's entire arm shuddering with the impact.

They held firm though, slowly making their way across the bloody shooting gallery as the firing squad sent volley after volley at their human targets.

The crowd's cheers erupted from the grandstands as the four latecomers reached the wall, overlapping their shields with the other underdogs still struggling to stay in the fight.

"Nice of you to finally join us," Dakota panted from the huddle as she gazed up at them with a glad smile, her buckler studded with spikes. The wooden panels were already starting to split at the seams. "Seriously though – thank fuck you made it."

"Did you expect anything less?" Hanzo shot her a wink as he and Jin took up a position by her side. He scanned the faces of the other survivors as they cautiously fanned out again, their hearts lifted with renewed vigor, "What are we all waiting for? Let's get the hell outta here!"

"*Yass!* It's about time!" Felix exclaimed from his crouch at Dakota's feet. He jerked a thumb over his shoulder at a fresh corpse slumped on the asphalt behind them, lying in a pool of his own blood. "Nobody's wanted to move ever since one of those arrow thingies bounced off my shield and hit that guy in the neck. I keep telling them that it's not my f–"

"Felix, do me a favor," Riley wanted to say *shut the fuck up*, but she had a slightly more reasonable request. "Switch spots with Dakota before we go. Her shield's about to break, and we've still got a lot of ground to cover."

"Well, I'm usually a bottom, but whatever," Felix reluctantly obliged as Lincoln, Georgia, Jin and Hanzo provided cover for their repositioning.

251

"Stop fucking complaining," Georgia muttered under her breath, her patience with the snarky man evidently wearing thin.

"Everybody ready?" Lincoln looked along the line, studying their faces as they nodded back at him. "Alright, we'll move on three. One, two – step!"

They strode forward in unison, with the bottom row of shields scraping along the asphalt.

Another volley of bolt arrows answered their advance, biting into the wall of wooden bucklers. The deadly projectiles somehow seemed smaller now though, as if their danger had diminished against the strength of survivors working together.

"One, two – step!"

"Keep your shield down," Riley reminded Jake, steering him forward with her free hand on his hip.

He was backpedaling bow-legged to compensate for his shield's height, unable to drop his grip any lower without exposing the back of his head.

Sidestepping across the arena had been far easier with just Jin and Hanzo beside them, but now that they were with a whole group, Jake was the chink in their armor waiting to be exploited by the medieval marksmen.

"One, two – step!"

They were making good progress, even enjoying a slight respite from the crossbowmen's relentless attacks, when the harsh sound of metal grating along the ground somewhere up ahead reached their ears.

A rash of gooseflesh budded up Riley's arms as she felt an ominous shift in the arena's atmosphere, and she cocked her head at the distinct lack of the white noise that had been blanketing the challenge from the beginning.

The crowd of spectators had stopped cheering.

Frowning, she peered through the cracks in between the shields.

Foley's group was already past the finish line.

The six marksmen at the rear of the arena had already laid down their crossbows to drag their table over to one side, and none of them were making a move to pick them back up again.

"Shit," Riley breathed, her mouth going dry with panic, "Were we supposed to cross the finish line together?"

CHAPTER 39

"The Shield Wall challenge is over," Miranda declared over the bullhorn, to the collective gasps of spectators and contenders alike. "Congratulations to those who will be moving on to the next round of the tournament."

Riley's group looked at each other in disbelief, the grip on their shields wavering.

"Do we keep moving?" Jake wondered as he frowned up at the woman on the platform.

Dagur raised one of his muscle-bound arms, preparing to signal his crew of armed men stationed along the sidelines, but he had his eyes trained on Miranda, waiting for her to give the command.

The grandstands shook as the sea of spectators rose to their feet, with harsh voices of dissent rising high above the noise of the rest of the clamoring crowd.

"Get your eyes checked, honey, this challenge isn't over yet!"

"They're still going, let them finish!"

"This is fucking bullshit, and you know it!!"

Miranda patiently squeezed the bullhorn's trigger again,

letting the speaker's whistling feedback wash over the angry mob, the jarring tone eventually lulling them all into a disgruntled hush.

Satisfied with their silence, she raised the mouthpiece to her lips.

"Those who are still in the arena have failed the challenge," she explained with a cold smile, casting her callous gaze over the remaining contestants as if they were nothing but pawns on the losing side of a forgotten chessboard. "By splintering off from the main group in their panic, they threw the entire shield wall into jeopardy. If this had been a real battle, the enemy would've rushed through the broken line and swept them all off the field. The true warriors stood their ground. These ones though... simply failed to hold the formation."

The sea of spectators glanced around among themselves, waiting for somebody else brave enough to offer an argument that they could all rally behind.

But either out of fear or a lack of ideas, the crowd was dead silent.

Riley's ears pricked up at the subtle rattles of metal on either side of the arena.

The guards leveled their menacing array of shotguns, assault rifles and sub-machine guns at the forlorn group of soon-to-be-eliminated contestants.

She swallowed.

They were utterly outmatched, with only a bunch of shitty wooden shields to fend off the approaching onslaught.

Riley was wracking her brain, trying to think of something – *anything* – that she could petition Miranda with, when a fervent murmur from nearby pierced her thoughts.

"Come on... come on..." Dakota was whispering to herself.

Riley's eyes lit up, and her sharp gaze darted beyond the barricades of the arena, scanning the boulevard for any signs of the Red Tigers.

Her desperate gawk traced over the derelict street corners, the abandoned strip mall's row of ruined storefronts, and the surrounding rooftops of ransacked restaurants and bars.

But there was nobody there.

We're on our own, she realized, her heart sinking to the pit of her stomach.

"They fought with heart, Valkyrie," a loud and baritone voice dared to speak up from within the walls of the arena, and everybody turned to see Foley standing with his arms stretched out wide as he made an appeal on their behalf. "And if that's not enough for you, then in your own words – *if this had been a real battle* – two shield walls would've been better than one. Surrounding the enemy in a pincer movement sounds like a good strategy to me. Don't count them out just yet. Let them keep going!"

The grandstands erupted with thunderous applause as the crowd roared their support.

Miranda tilted her head at the idea, appearing to reconsider as she weighed the words of the only other champion to have emerged victorious in past tournaments.

The cheers from the audience died down as they awaited the woman's decision with bated breath.

Riley flexed her gloved fingers, trying to ward off the nervous tension building in the suspense.

"Very well," Miranda finally conceded, before raising a finger against the crowd's delight as she added, "But only on one condition – they all cross the finish line before the ammunition runs dry."

Before the echoes of her curveball could even fade, the marksmen snatched up their crossbows again, hastily cocking back the strings.

"MOVE YOUR FUCKING LEGS, BITCH!!" Taylor screamed at the top of her lungs as the crowd whooped and hollered around her.

Icy adrenaline flooded Riley's veins.

"Get ready to move!" she shouted at the other survivors as they each braced their bucklers against the surrounding shields.

"On one!" Lincoln called out the count. "Step!!"

They strode forward together, walking straight into another volley of crossbow bolts.

"On one!!"

Riley shoved her shield forward and pawed along the asphalt with her free hand.

"On one!!"

A bolt arrow skittered across the ground, sliding harmlessly underneath the shield wall.

The shooters weren't even aiming anymore.

"On one!!"

"Keep your fucking shield down!!" Riley punched Jake in the hip as he left a gap the size of her head in between their bucklers.

"I can't help it!" he yelled back, struggling to keep up the pace with his bow-legged backpedaling.

"On one!!"

She was about to inspire him with an idle threat, when another crossbow bolt flew past her ear, and she ducked her head down, blindly driving her shield forward.

"On one!!"

"Come closer to us," Jin wrapped his free arm around Jake's torso, pulling him sideways.

"We need to close that gap," Hanzo agreed, motioning for Riley and the other survivors to compress.

"On –" Lincoln's count suddenly ceased, only to be replaced by a bellow of agony.

"Eww, what the fuck!?" Felix exclaimed as the line wavered mid-step.

"Oh shit!" Georgia screamed underneath Lincoln. "I'm sorry, I'm sorry, I'm sorry!!"

"Felix, where the hell are you g–" Dakota's shout ended with a pained snarl through clenched teeth.

"What's going on!?" Jake yelled, turning his whole upper body to one side, and his shield along with it, only to stifle a gag.

With Riley's head bowed towards the asphalt behind her buckler, she had no idea what was happening or who was left along the shield wall.

The only thing she knew for sure was that if they didn't cross the finish line soon – they were all going to die.

We have to keep going.

"ON ONE!!" Riley roared above the confusion.

She scraped her shield forward, and the rest followed.

"ON ONE!!"

Riley scuffed her knees across the sun-drenched asphalt, just as another bolt splintered her buckler with a wood-crunching *thock*.

"ON ONE!!"

Jake clumsily stomped on her free hand, and she resisted the urge to topple him over, forcing herself to bite back the pain.

"ON ONE!!"

A series of heavy wood-on-wood clatters sounded from less than a dozen yards away.

"THEY'RE ALMOST OUTTA AMMO – RUSH THEM!!" Jin shouted, and the shield wall broke off into pieces.

Nerves on fire, Riley surged to her feet alongside the rest of the bottom row, spinning Jake around as she pumped her legs into a headlong sprint.

Five of the crossbows had already been dropped on the table at the rear of the arena.

Her pupils dilated as the sixth shooter fumbled to reload his last bolt arrow.

With half of her group still straggling behind her, Riley knew that she couldn't carry them all across the finish line.

But she could carry herself.

Making a split second decision, she left them all behind, giving herself over to the raw adrenaline coursing through her veins.

Charging across the finish line with no intention of slowing down, she let out a ferocious war cry as she launched herself over the table, drawing back her shield in midair and bashing the last marksman across the face before he could let the final bolt fly.

Landing in a crumpled heap on the other side, Riley quickly scrambled upright, breathing hard and foaming at the mouth like a crazed animal as she wrestled the heavy crossbow from the fallen man's grip.

"Don't even fucking try it!!" she shouted at the first man to reach down for the weapon, holding his chest at point-blank range as she cradled the crossbow. She called over her shoulder, yelling out to the crowd, "They haven't run outta ammo yet – there's still one arrow left!!"

The audience roared with applause, giving her a standing ovation as the last of the contestants hobbled across the finish line.

"Congratulations," Miranda's icy tone came over the bullhorn, incensed by their unexpected triumph. "Dagur, clear the field."

Cracks of gunfire immediately flooded the arena, silencing the crowd's cheers in an instant as Dagur's crew sprayed lead at the slumped bodies strewn across the asphalt, ensuring that the corpses weren't just pretending to be corpses.

"I'll take that now," the guard standing over Riley pointedly glanced down at the crossbow in her hands. "It'd be a real shame if you did all that shit just to die here anyway, don't you think?"

"Fuck you," Riley seethed, reluctantly turning over the weapon.

She knew that a single shot from the crossbow wouldn't be enough to escape.

There's only one way I'm getting outta this alive, she thought to herself. Her gaze went from the boorish barbarians brutalizing the bodies in the middle of the arena, to the rest of the contenders exiting through the rear. *I have to win.*

CHAPTER 40

"I'm gonna fucking kill him!" Hanzo swore as he ripped out the set of brass knuckles that he had stashed in one of his socks. He shouted after Felix, "Get back here, you little bitch coward!"

The surviving contestants were all gathered in the space that stood in between the first and second arenas, catching their breath with anxious dread as they awaited the announcement for the next round.

"Oh my *gosh*, it's not like she *died*," Felix argued as he danced behind the other contenders, trying to put as much space in between himself and Hanzo as possible. "Don't you think you're overreacting a little?"

"Let him go – he panicked," Riley spoke up on Felix's behalf, against her own ill will towards the coward. She caught hold of Hanzo's elbow before he could give chase. "At least wait until we know what the next challenge is. We might still be able to use him."

"Yeah, fucking meat shield," Hanzo snorted with contempt.

He shrugged out of her hold, fists still clenched in anger as he begrudgingly eyed Felix off at a distance.

Dakota hissed in pain nearby as Jin snapped off the back half of a crossbow bolt, the medieval projectile having skewered through the thin flesh above her collarbone.

With a jaw-clenched grimace, she clasped Jin's hand before giving him a nod of resolve, and he gently pulled out the barb, threading the broken shaft the rest of the way through.

"I am *so* sorry," Georgia apologized profusely over the top of Dakota's shuddering snarl, the half-blonde half-brunette woman kneeling beside Lincoln.

"Not your fault," the dour man grunted, sitting slumped against the back wall of the first arena. He was holding half of his bruised face with one hand, the cracks of his fingers obscuring the bloody tip of a bolt arrow that had ricocheted off her shield and up into his eyeball. He kept his good eye's gaze fixed firmly on the ground, not daring to look around as he called out, "Jake? I'm gonna need you to do me a favor."

"Fuck, Lincoln..." Jake hesitated, already knowing what was going to be asked of him. He ran a hand through his hair as he stared down at the shaft protruding from the man's face. "I don't know if we should touch it."

Lincoln winced with disappointment.

Georgia clutched his free hand, interlacing her fingers with his.

"Whatever you need, I'm here," she spoke softly into his ear, before turning a sour eye towards Jake. "It's the least I can do for a friend."

"Never mind," Lincoln squared his jaw, his face lined with determination. "I'll do it myself."

He snarled three galvanizing breaths as he gripped the crossbow bolt in his fist.

Roaring in agony, he tore out the bolt from his own skull,

crushing Georgia's hand as blood and viscous white jelly spilled forth from his empty eye socket, the macabre mess erupting into an oozing dribble down his cheek.

His bellow was short-lived though, his breathing soon returning to normal as if he had merely ripped off a bandage, the battered bounty hunter both bruised and bleeding, but still unbroken.

The cruder members of the crowd whooped with excitement as Georgia tore a large strip from the hem of her shirt, the woman stifling an urge to gag as she wrapped the ripped fabric over Lincoln's horrible weeping wound and around his head.

Turning away from the grisly scene, Riley scanned the sea of spectators for Taylor and Barbara, soon spotting the two women shuffling towards a new pair of seats in the center of the set of grandstands.

"Get water," Taylor oddly mouthed back at Riley as they locked eyes, jabbing a finger towards Manny and his older brother.

The two vendors had parked their empty shopping carts opposite the clamoring crowd, occupying the sidewalk outside the abandoned strip mall.

They were idly shuffling their feet, checking over their shoulders as they waited impatiently for the rest of the water crew to come back with fresh carts brimming with more bottles to sell.

Get water? Riley furrowed her eyebrows in confusion.

There was no water to be had.

And she had no money to buy herself a bottle anyway.

She stared back up at Taylor, only to lose the girl behind the shifting tide of spectators still migrating towards new seats that would offer a better view of the second arena.

"The next challenge," Miranda's voice pierced Riley's thoughts as the cold woman mounted the staircase to the second raised platform. Only the mild rasps of her heels on metal could be heard as she purposely prolonged her ascent, savoring the crowd's silence. Reaching the top, she swept her sadistic gaze over the remaining contenders, her lips curling into a thin smile as she raised the bullhorn's mouthpiece to her lips again, "Is Rune Stones."

"Damn it," Dakota groaned as Jin finished patching up her shoulder with a makeshift bandage. "Why couldn't *that* have been the first one?"

Jake lifted his face up to the sun, heaving a forlorn sigh as the other contestants began distancing themselves away from each other.

"Okay," Riley frowned, watching as even the former members of her own shield wall shrank away from her. She asked the obvious question, "What the hell is *Rune Stones*?"

"I figured they'd wanna thin us out," Hanzo was the only one to offer her the semblance of an answer. He glanced around at the other participants still standing. There were roughly thirty of them left now. "Less than half of us are gonna make it through to the next round."

"The fates of Viking warriors were always uncertain," Miranda continued, relishing in the rabble's trembling unease as Dagur stepped forward with a wooden bucket, its contents veiled by a black cloth. "All too commonly, our forebears would return home from raids and war, only to find themselves swept up into an internal conflict between their own kin. Whether the cause was born from grudge or glory, riches or revenge – brother fought against brother, lover fought against lover, until the bitter end."

"Form a line!" Dagur rumbled, the thickset onyx ogre of a man rattling the covered contents of his bucket as he stalked among the remaining contestants. A red lightning bolt had been painted across the dome of his skull, zigzagging over one eyelid and running down to his jaw.

Foley was the first to step forward, followed closely by Tyson and Eddie, and like gravity, an orderly queue took shape behind them.

"Outta all the challenges we could've gotten," Jake began as Riley steered him towards the line, her gloved hand gripping his shoulder, "This one's a motherfucker."

What could be worse than being used for target practice? Riley wondered to herself, although standing at the halfway point in the line, she didn't have to give voice to her question.

She could watch and learn from the proceedings instead.

Foley reached into the bucket first, pulling out a chunk of blue epoxy resin, etched with some kind of Nordic symbol.

Tyson drew his lot next, also producing blue.

Eddie made an overly-dramatic display of rolling up his suit jacket's sleeve, demonstrating to the crowd that for once in his life, he wasn't trying to fool them.

His stone was red.

"That was a practice draw," he dismissed the result with a lazy hand-wave.

Dagur caught Eddie's wrist before he could toss the stone back into the bucket.

"Come on, surely we c—" Eddie's attempt to appeal was short-winded as Dagur crushed his wrist, grinning with grim satisfaction before throwing him out of the line-up. Eddie lurched over to his former cellmates, "This has to be a mistake. We're not *actually* fighting against each other, are we?"

"Looks like our deal's off," Foley shrugged, ignoring Tyson's sidelong snigger. The three men shuffled over to one side as the rest of the queue drew their stones. "There's always the other option though – you could try and make a run for it."

A low chorus of chortles went up from the crowd as Georgia drew blue, and Lincoln red.

Riley's ears pricked up despite the noise, straining to hear the rest of the conversation.

"*Make a run for it?*" Eddie echoed, glancing around at the guards stationed along the sidelines before looking from Foley to Tyson. "As exciting as that sounds, it doesn't have quite the same appeal as –"

"Too fucking bad, dickhead," Tyson front-kicked Eddie in the chest, silencing his protests. "I seriously doubt that you ever would've kept up your end of the deal anyway."

"Jin's with Lincoln," Jake's voice brought Riley back to the queue, craning his neck around to watch the ominous lottery. "We need to get on the red team."

"And if we're not?" Riley asked, watching as Hanzo drew blue.

Hanzo's eyes grew wide beside Jin, and the pair of former peacekeepers turned to stare at each other in stunned silence.

"That's why everybody hates Rune Stones," Jake gave a heavy sigh as he turned away from the crowd lining up for the bucket. He looked gravely back at Riley, "We have to kill the other team."

CHAPTER 41

Riley stared down at the blue stone in her hand.

It was a wonder how such a small thing could divide a whole group of people who – up until only a few minutes ago – had been depending on each other's strength in order to survive.

She held up the chunk of epoxy for the crowd, raising her eyebrows as some of the more unscrupulous spectators in the grandstands began placing their bets on the two teams, before she hurled the stone directly at Aksel's grinning face.

She missed her mark – but it hit the guard beside him well enough.

"What are you gonna do!?" Riley challenged the injured man, marching forward with her arms stretched out wide in defiance.

She had already been forced into an impossible predicament – either take part in killing her fellow survivors, or die by their hand.

It wouldn't make a difference whether she pissed off a guard or two in the process.

"Hey, calm down," Dakota sidled into Riley's war path, staring into her eyes. "You're not the only one who has friends on the other side."

Dakota had drawn blue, alongside Hanzo, while Jin had looked on from the side with a bleak expression.

Both Jake and Georgia were blinking back tears as Lincoln wished them good luck with the rest of the tournament.

"Fuck being calm," Riley spat, clenching her fists in rage. "How are you good with this!?"

"I'm not – *we're* not – but we don't have any other choice," Dakota replied, pointedly glancing around at all of the gun-toting guards just itching for a reason to pull the trigger. "It's kill or be killed, and I don't plan on dying today."

"Neither do I," Riley shot back.

Still wearing a bitter scowl, she sized up the competition as the contenders broke off into their assigned teams.

Two guards descended on the groups, tying blue and red ribbons around the left arm of each contestant.

"Look, all we can do is make sure their deaths won't be for nothing," Dakota offered a measure of consolation. She waited for Riley to make eye contact again, before dropping her voice to a whisper, "If we can make it through this challenge – and the next one – then we'll be in the best possible position to get our revenge."

"What are you talking about?" Riley furrowed her eyebrows, glancing up at Miranda on the raised platform.

The cold woman was watching with a thin smile as the few remaining contestants in the queue shuffled forward to reach into Dagur's wooden bucket.

"Radek personally congratulates whoever survives the tour-naments," Dakota answered, following Riley's gaze towards Miranda. "And since he's probably already dead, we'll just have to make do with whoever's second-in-charge."

"So we should focus on winning, just to get a *chance* to kill Miranda?" Riley cocked her head slightly. She rubbed the back of her neck, before dismissing the idea. "You realize that means we still have to kill Jin and Lincoln first, right? What about your people? Where the hell are they in all this?"

"Preparing," Dakota could only hope.

"No, that's not right," Felix complained loud enough for all to hear, dropping his stone back into the bucket. He was the last person in the line-up. Stepping back, he folded his arms with a shrug, "There's already sixteen people on the red team. I counted. That means I'm meant to be on the *blue* team with the rest of my bitches. One of you lunkheads somehow managed to fuck up putting an equal number of stones into the bucket, and now the teams aren't fair."

"Life's not fair," Dagur snorted in amusement, the big silverback gorilla grinning with grim satisfaction as he took a menacing step forward. "You get whatever the fuck you got."

With that, he tore the black cloth veil from the bucket and slammed it upside down on Felix's head, a single red rune stone clattering onto the asphalt at their feet.

The fifteen members of the blue team exchanged wary glances.

The red team outnumbered them by two.

"So they're just gonna run with it?" Riley narrowed her eyes with contempt as the rest of the guards sniggered from the sidelines.

"It's happened before," Dakota explained their indifference, even as Miranda began harping on about how opposing armies on any given battlefield had always varied greatly in both number and skill. "I wouldn't even be surprised if they did it on purpose this time."

"Suits me," Hanzo happily declared as he surged past the pair of women.

Cocking back his brass knuckles, he lunged towards Felix, who had only just removed the empty bucket from his head.

But before Hanzo could get within striking distance, Dagur stepped in between them, standing as solid as a concrete roadblock.

"Save it for the arena," the hulking henchman warned, towering over the two men.

"Like it'll make any difference," Hanzo scoffed, staring daggers at Felix. "He's dead, either way."

"You might be right," Dagur admitted, his brutish gaze zeroing in on his brass knuckles. "So let's make it interesting."

The muscle-bound monster seized Hanzo by the arm, holding him in place before throwing a full-bodied fist into his shoulder, sending him reeling to the asphalt.

"FUUUUUCK!!" Hanzo hollered as he cradled his incapacitated arm, his bellow of pain soon drowned out by the jeers of the crowd.

"Shit..." Riley muttered under her breath as all of the contestants were shoved into the second arena.

The challenge hadn't even started yet – and half of the teammates she knew were already nursing their own injuries.

CHAPTER 42

Riley, Jake, Dakota, Hanzo, Georgia, Foley and Tyson were directed towards a table lined with medieval weapons beside the arena's entrance, while Lincoln, Jin, Felix, Eddie and the rest of the red team were marched towards a similar table standing at the rear.

"Jin, wait up!" Hanzo's call seemed to fall on deaf ears, watching as his friend marched on ahead without a backwards glance.

"Let him go," Georgia said beside him, her eyes lingering on Lincoln. "We all know what we have to do to survive. It's probably easier if you don't talk to him again until... after."

Hanzo screwed up his face, doubting that they'd ever have another chance at a conversation again. Sighing dejectedly, his gaze turned downcast as he concentrated on removing the brass knuckles from his incapacitated arm, switching them over to the fist that could still throw a punch.

Riley studied the table strewn with primitive weapons – they were mostly swords and maces, along with a few spears, axes and pole-arms.

Flexing her gloved fingers, she realized that she wasn't

familiar with any of them.

Her options were dwindling fast as her teammates tested their chosen weapons, but she didn't want to rush her decision – knowing that the wrong choice would be her last choice.

Instead, she took a step back, allowing the others to pick their poison, while she clung to a thin hope that her confiscated combat knife was hidden somewhere among the blades and bludgeons.

"This one's mine," Jake declared half-heartedly, picking up a pole-arm halberd and testing its weight. "I can sit down in one of the corners and wave it at anybody who tries coming close."

"I think I might have to join you on the bench," Dakota prodded her bandaged shoulder, hissing sharply at the pain. She picked up a shield with her good arm, before glancing sidelong at Jake and his halberd, "You'd better do more than just wave that thing around though. Because if you get me killed, the last thing I'll do is hurl my dying body at you and pin you to the asphalt. I'll die happy knowing that your second-degree burns are getting charred up to third."

"I'm not gonna let that happen," Jake promised, gripping his pole-arm with both hands before thrusting and slicing through the air in demonstration. "Just because I have to sit in the shade doesn't mean I'm outta the fight."

"And what happens if one of your friends decides to attack?" Riley tested him, narrowing her eyes. "Could you kill them too? Think real hard, because Dakota's only got a shield. She's gonna be depending on you."

Jake swallowed as he considered the question.

"Our friends aren't the ones we'll need to worry about," Dakota spoke up on his behalf.

"Yeah, Lincoln and Jin won't be coming after us," Jake eagerly latched on to her answer. He stared over his shoulder across the arena, watching as the red team geared up. "But I have a feeling that Eddie and Felix are gonna be sticking to the sidelines, keeping an eye out for any easy targets."

For a moment, Riley flashed back to her first night in the marketplace, when Eddie had snuck up behind her and Taylor, the speculative scumbag set on scamming the pair of newcomers out of their food.

She had no doubt that he'd be among the first to prey on the weak and wounded.

"Let them come," Riley gave a small snort at the idea of catching Eddie on the prowl. "They won't find any easy targets here."

She scanned over the selection of weapons still available.

There was a giant sledgehammer, a spear, a pair of axes, and a wide variety of swords and maces.

"Has anybody seen a knife?" Riley asked the other survivors gathered around the table. "Or a dagger?"

If she was being forced to fight – then she would rather fight with what she knew.

"Here, take an axe," Foley advised, pressing the haft of a hatchet into her hand, before addressing the others who were also having trouble deciding. "They're the easiest to use. The maul's a bitch to wield. Spears take a bit of skill. And most of these swords look like antiques and display pieces – they barely have an edge – the only thing they'll be good for is cracking wooden handles and maybe a few bones." He tilted his head as those who had picked up a sword set them back down again. "I didn't say that'd be a bad thing. But if you're set on hacking and bashing, then you're better off with swinging a mace instead."

Hanzo heeded the suggestion, grabbing a mace in the grip of his brass-knuckled fist. With his preferred arm out of action – hanging limply by his side – he needed something extra to help offset the handicap.

Georgia selected the spear, despite lacking skill, opting for distance over her opponents.

Riley turned the axe in her grip.

It was small enough to hold comfortably with one hand.

The blade's sharpened edge whistled through the air as she took a practice chop.

The weapon wasn't what she had been hoping for, but she could work with it.

"You seem to know a lot about all this, Foley," Tyson observed as he picked up a mace. "What were you doing back before the world went to shit?"

"Might be the only reason why I'm still alive," Foley shrugged, the thrill-seeking veteran of past tournaments hefting the giant sledgehammer with both hands, turning the maul's bulky business end from side to side like a gigantic metronome. He locked eyes with Tyson, "Survive, and I'll tell you."

"Same goes for you too," Tyson replied before leaving to find some space to practice. "Got me all curious right before a fight..."

While the other fighters were busy familiarizing themselves with their chosen weapons, Riley sidled closer to Foley.

"I heard you mention something earlier," she began, bringing up the conversation that had been weighing on her mind, "What were you saying about *making a run for it*?"

"You were eavesdropping," Foley chuckled to himself,

before shooting a glance over at Eddie across the arena. He turned back to Riley, "That was just a desperate idea for a desperate man. Forget I ever mentioned it."

"There's a lot of lives on the line right now," she reminded him, subtly pointing with her axe head at the rest of their group, before tilting the blade towards the red team. "None of us have to kill each other if there's a chance that we can all escape."

"Alright," he conceded with a patient sigh, resting the end of his sledgehammer on the asphalt. He cracked his neck from side to side, disguising his pointed glances at the armed guards stationed around the arena. "See all these guys? Every last one of them is hoping that there's somebody in here who's crazy enough to try and escape, because it means that they can finally get in on the action. They might even give you a head start, but only to make for better sport."

"*Better sport?*" Riley echoed, furrowing her eyebrows.

"Escaping is another challenge – and you can start it off at any time," Foley explained, before waving his hand up the boulevard, gesturing towards a point lying somewhere beyond the third arena. "If you can reach the safe zone before Dagur's crew takes you out, it'll be the same thing as winning the tournament. You'll earn your position in Valhalla – guaranteed free pass to a room in the hotel. Radek said it himself in the first tournament, and The Valkyrie's held up the offer ever since."

"So why don't we all just try escaping instead?" Riley wondered, her gaze sliding sideways towards the abandoned strip mall. The nearest ruined storefront was only a short sprint away. "I mean, we've got weapons now. The guards can't kill everybody if we all rush them at the same time."

"Some people have already tried that – at another Rune Stones," Foley snorted at the coincidence. He turned his chin towards the rear of the arena, and his face darkened. "Somebody on the red team called a truce right before the fight started, and they brought up the same idea you just did. But when they gave the signal to run, only the reds left the arena, and they got slaughtered for it. The blues didn't have to do a thing, and they all went on to the next round." Foley stared into Riley's eyes, making sure that his next words would sink in, "Of all the people I've seen try to escape the arenas – nobody's ever made it to the safe zone alive."

Riley swallowed, and she turned away, flexing the slender muscles of her jaw as she weighed up her options.

Run and die, she thought to herself. *Or kill, and live.*

Whatever she chose, she knew that there was no way she could save everyone.

CHAPTER 43

"Alright, I want us all in a spearhead formation!" Foley's voice rang out loud and baritone as he took charge of the blue team's twelve able-bodied fighters. "Mace on my left. Mace on my right. Axes on the ends."

As instructed, two diagonal lines began forming up behind Foley, with Riley taking the last position on the right flank, giving her preferred arm ample space to swing her axe at any attackers.

"You've got my back," Georgia looked back over her shoulder at Riley. "I've got yours."

Riley nodded solemnly at the spear woman, before they both turned their attention towards their foes as the red team fanned out in a long line, their superior numbers spanning half the width of the arena.

The two teams stood staring at each other across the distance, anxiously waiting for Miranda's signal to start.

It didn't take long for each of the contenders to drop their gazes though, avoiding eye contact with the enemy as soon as they realized – they weren't so different from one another.

There was Lincoln, who had been beaten half to death, yet

the fire in his remaining eye was still blazing with spite for his tormentors.

There was Jin, who had been abandoned by his people at the time he needed them the most, now left to face off against two of his closest friends.

And then there were Felix and Eddie, who had simply pissed off the wrong people.

By the luck of the draw, Riley could have easily found herself standing shoulder to shoulder alongside any of them.

And now she was tasked with taking part in killing them all.

"Don't let the enemy get behind us," Foley continued reeling off his commands, almost as if he had recited the words a hundred times over. "If they break through one of our lines, call out *breach*. And as soon as you hear that word, pick a partner, and fight back to back over to the corner with the wounded."

They all glanced back at Jake and Dakota, who hadn't joined the triangular formation.

Instead, the pair of injured fighters had parked themselves in the shadiest corner offered by the arena's walls, with only a halberd and a shield to protect them from anybody who would see them as easy prey.

Hanzo was closer to the wounded than Riley and Georgia, standing in the center of the line on the left, clutching a mace in his brass-knuckled fist.

A hush fell over the crowd of murmuring spectators watching from the grandstands, and all eyes turned towards Miranda as she spoke inaudibly into a walkie.

As if in answer to the woman's radio call, the grinding whirr of a trailer-mounted diesel generator rose up from beside the third arena as the big engine rumbled to life, and along with it came the loathsome Viking music that grated against Riley's eardrums.

"As if this wasn't bad enough already," she clenched her teeth against the noise, trying to block out the infernal cacophony of discordant war drums, blaring horns and guttural chanting polluting the air.

The horrible song's jarring dissonance alone was enough to send her flying into a murderous rage.

Admittedly though, she supposed that's why they were playing it.

Riley blew a long breath as the red team began to advance.

"Stand your ground!" Foley shouted over his shoulder as he shook his giant sledgehammer at the enemy line. "Let them come to us. Let these little lambs deliver themselves to the fucking slaughter!!"

A fierce roar went up from the rest of the blue team, and their foes faltered – some stumbling a step, while others stopped marching forward altogether.

Chiefly among those hanging back from the crowd were Jin and Lincoln.

Lincoln held a spear in his hands, while Jin had chosen not to pick up a weapon at all.

Neither one of them was interested in taking part in the fight.

Nobody else seemed to share the same sense of sentimentality though.

Two men marching in the center of the red line raised their swords, shouting courageously as they led the attack, both of them aiming for Foley, intent on breaking the tip of the spear and seeing the rest of the formation shatter.

Anticipating the assault, Foley squatted down low and

raised his sledgehammer high, readying his swing.

The moment the pair of swordsmen came within striking distance, he swept his gigantic maul down at their knees.

The first attacker leapt over the arcing path of the hammer, only to catch a brutal overhand swing from Tyson's mace full in the face, making the man somersault backwards in midair.

The second swordsman was even less fortunate – the weight of Foley's sledgehammer snapped one of his legs in half, and he fell to the asphalt with a blood-curdling scream, before another mace stove in his skull, promptly putting him out of his misery.

"Let's just go around Foley!" Felix yelled as the red team split in half, approaching the triangular formation from either side instead.

Riley's grip around her hatchet tightened as she faced off against the encroaching enemies, sizing up a huge Pacific Islander woman wielding a halberd.

The pole-arm had twice the striking distance of Riley's axe, and from the sheer size of the red woman's arms, she'd have no trouble cutting down the entire blue team like a farmer's scythe cleaving through crops.

"Fuck," Riley breathed.

The grandstands yelled in excitement as the reds made their move, charging the line.

Icy adrenaline flooding her veins, Riley broke formation, running towards the Pacific Islander with a charge of her own, turning at the last second to ram her shoulder into the big woman's chest, winding her before she could even begin the reaping.

"RILEY!!" Georgia screamed over the hellish Viking music and the cheering crowd of spectators, the end of her spear stuck in the bowels of a mace-man's midsection.

She was struggling to pull her weapon free, while her impaled opponent roared with his spiked bludgeon held high, preparing to deliver a death blow, intent on taking her down with him.

Riley took two steps and swung, the blade of her axe hacking halfway through the man's forearm, his war cry climbing several octaves as his mace soared over the top of Georgia's head, flying into the back of the second line of blues.

"BREACH!!" Hanzo yelled as the woman beside him went down, blindsided by the mace.

The entire blue team broke into disarray as each member fumbled for a partner while still trying to hold their ground against their own opponents.

In all the confusion, Foley and his two mace-men wheeled around on the reds, bashing and bludgeoning those with their backs turned, as well as those who were retreating to regroup and face the forgotten threat.

Riley ripped her blade free from the red mace-man's mangled arm, chopping her bloody blade into the side of his neck before pulling Georgia from the melee.

"My spear!" she cried, glancing back at the haft of her weapon still skewered through the side of the slumped corpse.

"Forget it – it wasn't working for you anyway," Riley grunted as she hauled the unarmed woman back towards Jake and Dakota. "You'll have a better shot at surviving if you get *inside* their weapon range instead, then do whatever you can to disarm them. For now though, stay behind me."

Riley took up a position in front of their wounded friends, holding her hatchet at the ready as the rest of the blues fell back to the corner of the arena two by two.

"Looks like Foley's gonna win this challenge for us all by himself," Jake marveled as he watched the champion's sledgehammer bulldozing through the remaining members of the red team.

"No, not by himself," Dakota chuckled, pointedly glancing at Hanzo laughing aloud as he faced off against Felix, the skinny coward looking around feverishly, only to find himself abandoned and alone.

Seeing that all eyes were focused on the fight, Lincoln put a plan of his own into action.

Hefting the haft of his spear over his shoulder, he turned towards the guards stationed along the sidelines, and he hurled his javelin directly at Dagur, the hulking henchman standing at the base of Miranda's raised platform.

The spear hung in the air for what felt like an eternity, while blaring speakers swamped the arena with the sound of a Norse woman's wail warbling over war drums.

But Lincoln missed – his aim thrown off by his maimed eyesight.

Having caught his real enemy by surprise though, the battered bounty hunter bolted for the wall, rushing towards his tormentor.

Even with all of his injuries, Lincoln managed to vault over the arena's barricade, landing with a limp but still surging forward, before leaping like a wounded tiger with his pointed elbow flying directly at Dagur's face.

A roar of rifle rounds ripped through the air, contending with the crescendo of Viking drums as the bullets cut Lincoln down in mid-flight, killing him instantly.

"Fucking idiot," Dagur sniggered as he lowered his assault rifle, smiling to himself as he stomped on Lincoln's skull, making sure that he was truly dead.

Riley swallowed the urge to gag at the sound of the sickening *squelch*.

She knew that after all of Lincoln's suffering, a quick death was almost a mercy for the man.

That was probably why he had launched the suicide mission in the first place.

But still – he didn't have to die.

None of them had to die.

"INCOMING!!" Jake yelled, bringing Riley back to the arena.

Her pupils dilated at the sight of the huge Pacific Islander charging like a madwoman at what remained of the blue team, her bloodthirsty stare locked on Riley.

CHAPTER 44

The blue team's defending line didn't even stand a chance, the hulking Pacific Islander cleaving her halberd through three of their torsos with ease, as if they were just a row of overgrown weeds.

Riley's heart leapt up into her throat as the bloody axe blade sailed for her ribcage next, and her knees buckled on instinct just in time, ducking her head half an inch underneath the deadly swing.

Growling with battle-fuelled fury, the gigantic reaper turned her blade for a second strike, and Riley surged to her feet again.

But just as she cocked back her hatchet, the red woman jabbed Riley in the sternum with the butt of her halberd.

Winded, clutching her chest, Riley could only gasp for air as Georgia darted past, plunging her entire bodyweight into the burly woman, trying to wrestle the pole-arm out of her grip, only to be tossed aside like a scrap of food being saved for later.

Baying for blood, the red woman swung her massive axe at Riley again, but this time, Dakota's shield blocked the blow, the heavy blade crunching through thick wood.

With a primordial roar, the raging halberdier wrenched back her encumbered weapon, tearing the shield and its straps from Dakota's arm, before smashing the wooden buckler against the arena's wall, the shield exploding into a thousand splinters.

Jake aimed his own halberd low at the woman's feet, only for the huge Pacific Islander to step forward, catching the wooden haft with her shin and stomping her other foot down on the blade, snapping off the business end and leaving him with nothing but a broken stick.

Riley was still reeling from the blow to her chest, but she didn't have time to breathe.

This woman was going to kill them all.

Wheezing, Riley made a mad snatch at the red woman's halberd, catching the weapon halfway down the pole with her free hand.

She cocked back her hatchet again, preparing to strike, when her boots left the ground, the hulking reaper hoisting Riley in midair, spinning her around like a ragdoll on a stick, before slamming her upper back against the arena's wall, her neck whiplashing back and forth.

With the coppery taste of blood in her mouth, Riley collapsed onto the asphalt, dazed and rasping ragged breaths, only vaguely aware of her surroundings, barely able to see straight as her hatchet was torn from her slackened grip.

Streaks of movement flashed past her spinning vision, and she gaped up to see Georgia dancing around the lumbering giant, ducking and weaving inside the halberd's range as she swiftly sliced and slashed with Riley's axe.

Spurred on by the pain, the red woman roared with rage, and

285

she caught Georgia's wrist with startling speed, twisting her arm behind her back before wrapping her up into the crushing embrace of a bear hug.

Georgia let out a panicked scream, kicking at the air in vain while Jake swung his broken stick at the monstrous madwoman with a desperate series of impotent *thwacks*.

"Riley!" Dakota shouted over the top of the fiendish Viking music, the clamoring crowd of spectators, and Georgia's mounting wails of agony. "Use this!!"

Retching from the pain pounding up the base of her neck, Riley blinked hard as Dakota kicked the broken end of Jake's halberd towards her, the chunk of metal skittering across the asphalt.

The halberd's head was topped with a long spike, while the cleaving edge of an axe blade ran down the side.

Cold adrenaline coursing through her veins, Riley shook herself out of her stupor, seizing the makeshift weapon, and in one fluid motion, she rolled towards the red woman and plunged the spike through the top of her foot.

The hulking giant hollered in anguish as Riley twisted the blade in between flesh and tendons, making her drop Georgia to the ground as both women and their weapons came crashing down.

Ripping the spike free from the fallen reaper's foot, Riley scrambled over the pair of bodies, bringing the broken halberd's axe blade down on the red woman's throat, blood spattering across her face as she hacked twice more for good measure.

"WATCH OUT ON THE LEFT!!" Jake yelled over the crowd's thunderous applause.

Eyes going wide, still wheezing for breath, Riley's gaze

lurched left, only to see Hanzo chasing Felix across the arena, the shrieking coward trying to outrun him, while Foley and Tyson closed in from either side.

Dakota snarled spittle as she sprang to her feet, surging past Riley's right shoulder.

"Oof!" Eddie spluttered, his attempt at blindsiding Riley thwarted as the lithe woman spear-tackled him mid-swing.

Staggering around as he danced with Dakota, the callous opportunist held his sword aloft, still struggling to find his feet.

Using all of her lean strength, Dakota slammed his back into the arena's wall, when Eddie played her shoulder injury to his advantage, pressing his thumb into her bloody bandage, and gouging the wound above her collarbone.

She fell to her knees with an involuntary yowl of anguish, but that didn't stop her from delivering a savage hook to his crotch.

Eddie dry-heaved in pain, and his eyes flashed with rage as he lifted his sword again to bring it down on Dakota's skull.

CLACK!

Georgia met Eddie's swing with the hatchet's handle, his sword's blunt blade clashing against the solid wooden haft.

"Two against one hardly seems fair," Eddie complained, kicking Dakota onto her backside before squaring off against Georgia.

She was wheezing breathlessly, still recovering from the ribcage-crushing bear hug, but her jaw was set with determination all the same.

"Try three against one," Riley narrowed her eyes as she held the broken halberd's head low at her hip, sneaking in from the side to catch the prowling predator at his own game.

287

"And you weren't such a stickler for fairness when the teams were seventeen to fifteen in your favor."

"Oh please," Eddie slunk away from the three women, panting with a sour grimace as he cradled his crotch. "It was more like sixteen to fifteen, since Lincoln was utterly worthless. Getting stuck with your friends was barely an advantage to begin with."

"You son of a bitch," Georgia spat, gripping her axe with both hands and launching a full-bodied swing at the self-satisfied swindler.

Their weapons clashed again as Eddie blocked the blow.

Seizing the opportunity to strike, Riley raised her makeshift weapon, poising to plunge the halberd head's spike into his worthless neck, when an unseen hand caught her wrist from behind, twisting her weapon arm behind her back.

"Sorry," Jin grunted in Riley's ear before throwing her chest up against the arena's wall, wrenching hard on her wrist until she released her grip, the broken halberd's head clattering at their feet. "But if you wanna make it through to the next round with *my* friends, then you're gonna have to prove yourself worthy of standing by their side."

"Jin, what the hell are you doing!?" Dakota shouted up at him from the ground, still grimacing as she gingerly clutched her shoulder wound.

More *clacks* of wood on blunt metal sounded from behind as Georgia pushed on alone, going toe to toe with Eddie.

"I'm not dying without a fight," Jin replied, his voice calm and collected as he held Riley pinned up against the wall.

"You really think you can kill all of us?" Riley fumed, before throwing her free elbow back at his ribcage.

"No," he sidestepped to dodge the blow, before twisting her

288

caught wrist even harder. "But I can kill *you*. After all, you're the one who got us caught in the first place. We wouldn't even be in this tournament if you'd just taken Eddie to Valhalla like you were supposed to."

Doubled-over, wincing in his harsh grip, Riley stared over the top of the arena's wall.

Jin just wanted somebody to blame.

But instead of holding himself accountable for choosing to go along with the alternative plan, or Kentaro's people for abandoning him and his friends, he had decided that the fault of his fate lay solely with her.

Riley flexed the slender muscles of her jaw.

She wasn't the one who had gotten him captured.

She wasn't the one forcing them to fight in some twisted gladiatorial display.

And she certainly wasn't going to die for Jin's need of a scapegoat.

"You spineless piece of shit," Riley snarled, straining to shove herself off the wall.

Bent over at the waist, she searched the ground for his feet, before kicking back the heel of her hiking boot into his thigh.

The kick didn't faze him, but it was hard enough to break his hold on her wrist.

She whirled around to face him as he stumbled backwards into a fighting stance.

"Come on then," Jin dared her to attack, beckoning her with his fingers.

Not needing an invitation, Riley lunged forward with an open palm aimed at his throat.

But Jin dodged the hit, ducking underneath her arm with catlike agility before jabbing her across the jaw.

She staggered backwards, hands still raised, but stunned by the sudden sting.

"Protect your face!!" Taylor's voice rose above the clamoring crowd of spectators.

Riley seethed at having forgotten to follow her own advice.

Bringing her palms in closer to her cheekbones, she faced off against Jin again, when in the corner of her eye, she noticed the hulking body of the slain red woman lying on the asphalt behind him.

Riley knew that Jin was too quick for her to beat him in a fair fight, but if she could trip him up, then she'd have the advantage.

"You're good," she admitted, slowly side-stepping as she circled him into position.

"I'm not just good," he gave her a thin smile, turning on the spot to keep their shoulders lined up. "I'm better."

The arena's wall shook again as Eddie slammed Georgia against the barricade.

Jin's gaze flicked over towards the scuffling pair for a split second, and Riley seized advantage of his distraction, springing forward to thrust her knee into his groin.

But with a lightning-fast flurry of movement, Jin caught her knee with one hand, blocking the blow before jamming his other palm into her hip, almost as if he had been anticipating the attack. Then, simply turning on the balls of his feet, he shoved her off balance, sending her crashing backwards into Eddie before the pitiful excuse of a man could bash in Georgia's skull with the hilt of his sword.

Making a snap decision, Riley capitalized on the well-timed intrusion, latching on to Eddie's sword hand and digging her boot into the side of his ribcage, holding his arm outstretched and leaving him utterly defenseless.

"Wait!" Eddie cried, wanting to buy himself some time to conjure up a string of words that would somehow save him. Feebly trying to jerk his sword hand out of Riley's grasp, his eyes grew desperate as he realized that his glib tongue had finally run out of false promises. Instead, all he could yelp was, "Wait, wait, wait!!"

"No," Georgia panted plainly as she hefted her hatchet with both hands.

Staring down at the bloody axe blade in horror, Eddie hid his face behind his other arm, and Georgia went to work, hacking her hatchet sideways into his torso, blood spraying as she slashed the scam artist's black business suit into crimson shreds.

Riley extracted herself from the macabre mess, turning back around to face Jin again, only to catch a glimpse of his fist before he clocked her in the face, making her bandaged cheek flower with fresh blood.

She hissed in pain as her hand flew up on a reflex to protect her wound, shielding the gouged side of her face as she calculated her next move.

But Jin was too fast for her.

Disappearing into her momentary blind spot, his swift footsteps darted behind her, barely even giving her a moment to register what was happening before the crook of his arm wrapped around her neck, while his other hand clamped down on the base of her skull, locking her in a chokehold.

"Fuck," was the only word that Riley could manage to grunt before he cut off the air to her windpipe.

If he was blocking the blood flow to her brain, she would only have a few seconds before she slipped into unconsciousness.

Her hands instantly shot back to his arm around her throat, trying to pry it loose.

But his grip was solid, and it only made his bracing hand behind her head clamp down even harder.

Veins bulging from her forehead, Riley dropped down to her knees instead, using the sudden shift in angle to buy her some more time to escape.

His grip let up slightly, but he still had her locked in place.

"Let her go!!" Jake's voice pierced through the pounding in her ears as he charged towards them, exposing his burn wounds to the summer sun with no regard for himself as he swung what was left of his broken pole-arm at Jin.

But the frantic barrage of wooden *thwacks* still wouldn't break the hold.

Riley was losing both her strength and her sense fast, clawing at the man's wiry arm with her gloved fingertips.

"Don't," Jin warned as Georgia drew up beside them, blood and gore sliding off her hatchet's wet blade in crimson globs. He maneuvered Riley over to one side with ease, her knees scuffing across the sun-baked asphalt as they both stared up at her would-be savior. "If you swing that axe, I promise you – it's not gonna end well for either of you."

"Jin, what the fuck!?" Hanzo called from across the arena, finally taking notice of their fight.

"Is this really how you want us to remember you?" Dakota asked stiffly as she crept into the corner of Riley's blurring vision.

"No – this is how I want *her* to remember me," Jin replied, exhaling heavily, "I'm just making sure she does."

With that, he released his grip around Riley's neck, and

she keeled over to one side, hacking and wheezing as the atmosphere of the arena flooded her senses again – the sounds of the crowd's confusion, the murmurs of disgruntled guards, and the horrible Viking music that she found herself almost happy to hear.

"You lasted longer than I expected," Jin loomed over Riley as she fought to catch her breath. "You don't give up easy – I'll give you that much. But you need to watch your surroundings, or you're gonna end up getting good people killed trying to save you. If this had been a real fight, you'd be dead by now."

Riley clambered upright, her raw throat stinging with each breath as she doggedly squared off against him again.

"Wait – *if this had been a real fight?*" Georgia echoed with a confused frown, her hatchet wavering hesitantly in her grip. "You mean you weren't actually trying to kill her?"

"What would be the point?" Jin answered with a question of his own, not taking his eyes off Riley. He tilted his head slightly as he admitted, "I mean, I still have a grudge against you for not taking Eddie to Valhalla like you and your friends were supposed to. But I'd rather leave Dakota and Hanzo with all the support they can get for the next round... and that includes you."

Dakota hugged him then, and Riley dropped her guard.

The rest of the blue team gave them a moment, while sneers and shouts erupted from the grandstands.

"What the hell is this? I came here for a fight!"

"Is this how the Vikings won battles?"

"Just get it over with already!!"

Riley glared up at the loud-mouthed members of the crowd, knowing that every single one of them wouldn't have lasted more than a minute in the arena.

"So, what now?" she croaked, her raw voice barely audible above a whisper.

Jin was the last man standing on the red team.

Somebody would have to do it.

Dakota brushed her cheek angrily before turning away.

Jake and Georgia shared a glance of uncertainty.

And across the arena, Hanzo tossed his mace aside as he left Felix's bludgeoned body in his wake, holding his arms out wide in downright refusal to kill one of his friends.

Riley's gaze went over to Foley, Tyson, and another pair of surviving blues who could do the deed without being crushed by the weight of the guilt attached.

But Jin turned to Riley instead.

"End this," he implored her, his throat bobbing up and down as he swallowed his fate. He glanced sidelong at Dakota, who couldn't bear to watch. His voice dropped an octave, "End all this shit."

Summoning his resolve with a somber sniff, Jin marched towards the arena's barricade and climbed over the wall.

"Oh look, he's escaping," Aksel sniggered in amusement as he raised his pistol, along with Kuba and half a dozen other guards who were all too eager to join in on the fun.

Cracks of gunfire rang out over the top of the crowd's cheers and jeers according to their own wagers placed on the two teams.

Jin's body shook with every bullet as he slumped back against the wall, but Riley's stare was locked on Miranda now, her desire to survive the tournament growing with the sound of each gunshot as she vowed to carry out his last request.

CHAPTER 45

"Would somebody shut off that fucking noise!?" Riley shouted hoarsely at the raucous Viking music still grating against her eardrums.

Miranda stared down at her from the raised platform overlooking the arena, fixing the brazen gladiator with a scornful smile before lifting a walkie to her lips.

At her command, the infernal cacophony died, with only the rumble of the trailer-mounted diesel generator parked beside the third arena filling the ensuing silence.

"The Rune Stones challenge is over," Miranda stated the obvious over the bullhorn, the callous woman utterly unfazed by the contemptuous glares from the tournament's surviving contenders. "Congratulations to those moving on to the final round."

Out of the dozens of unwilling participants who had been marched out of the Valhalla Hotel's makeshift cell house that morning, only a handful of them still remained.

"I honestly didn't think I'd make it this far," Jake admitted to himself, his chest turned towards the sun to keep his second-degree burns from getting any worse. He glanced around at Riley and the others, "Thanks, guys. If it wasn't for all of you, I'd be dead by now."

"Save your *thanks* for the end," Dakota mumbled almost inaudibly, still staring at the spot beyond the wall where Jin had died.

The crowd clapped and whistled as the sea of spectators began their mass migration towards new seats, washing across the grandstands like a rolling tide, in search of a better view of the third arena.

"Blood tribute to The Valkyrie!" Foley declared above the noise of the crowd with a fresh corpse slung over his shoulder, gently laying the body on the ground a dozen yards away from Miranda's raised platform.

Miranda lingered in her descent, savoring the sight of the grisly gift as some of the other contestants began begrudgingly making their own offerings, perhaps convinced that honoring the woman would somehow make a difference for them in the next challenge.

"Blood tribute to The Valkyrie," Tyson echoed, pointing out his bludgeoned victims before setting down his blood-spattered mace.

Another man raised his hatchet to hack off the head of one of his kills, when he made the mistake of making eye contact with the deceased, and he dropped his axe, along with the contents of his stomach.

"Blood tribute to The Valkyrie," Georgia joined the ranks of the deluded devotees, tossing a severed hand taken from Eddie's corpse across the arena. She glanced sidelong at the others with a shrug, "I'll take all the luck I can get."

"You should've cut out his lying tongue instead," Jake snorted, eyeing Eddie's body with disdain.

"Hey, let me see that axe for a second," Riley reached for the hatchet in Georgia's hand.

"Don't tell me you're actually gonna do it," Dakota shook her head with a critical sigh.

"No, I've got a bigger prize in mind," Riley replied, turning towards Miranda with the axe clenched in her gloved fist, glistening gore still dripping from its blade. "I'm gonna give that bitch the blood tribute she deserves."

Stepping over the brutalized bodies of the tournament's unwilling participants, Riley filled her eyes with hatred as she marched towards Miranda, the sadistic woman simply gazing back at her with a cold cocksure grin.

She was the one responsible for all this needless death.

Even in Radek's absence, Miranda had chosen to perpetuate his twisted tournaments.

There was no telling how many people had died solely for her entertainment.

But with just one throw, Riley could ensure that nobody else would have to suffer.

"Hold on, what are you doing?" Hanzo sidled into her war path, his eyes darting towards the hatchet in her hand.

Riley didn't bother giving him an answer.

Because deep down, he already knew.

"Think about what'll happen if you try to attack her," Georgia cautioned as she caught up from behind. "They'll kill you – and probably the rest of us, too."

"It's better than us being forced to kill each other," Riley shot back with ice in her tone, keeping her stare locked on Miranda so that she wouldn't cut down either of them with the daggers in her eyes. "Lincoln had the right idea. *They're* the real enemies. Why the hell are we fighting among ourselves?"

"But it's over now – the fighting's done," Jake reasoned, wincing after the brief sprint with the summer sun glaring down on his scorched back. He turned towards the sun again as he added, "We don't know what the next round's gonna be, but there's still a chance that at least some of us can survive."

"And that sounds a hell of a lot better than whatever you're planning," Dakota agreed as she appeared beside Jake. She grabbed Riley by the forearm, staring into her eyes. "If the guards fire on us because you can't hold your shit together for one more round, then all those people who just died would've been for nothing. Jin's de–" her breath hitched for a moment, and she swallowed a sob. "Jin sacrificed himself so that the rest of us could make it through. Don't you fucking dare let that go to waste."

Riley's head was pounding.

The burning heat of the Nevada sun was beginning to take its toll.

The echoes of Viking war drums were still thundering in her skull.

And the burden of everyone's stares was almost too much to bear.

Even if they could survive the tournament, Dakota was still planning on killing Miranda.

Riley was just saving themselves the trouble of having to win the next challenge.

She clenched the hatchet even tighter, weighing up the choice that she held in her fist, before she finally relented, letting it slip from her grasp.

"I can't tell you how glad that just made me feel," Jake cut through the tension with a heavy sigh of relief. He raised his eyebrows at Riley with a wide grin, "I've seen the way you throw things. You can't throw for shit."

"Fuck you," Riley frowned back at him, but she was unable to stop herself from breaking out into a chuckle.

Dakota, Hanzo and Georgia soon joined in, letting the wave of shaky laughter wash over them in a cathartic release, taking the edge off everything that they had just endured.

As the remaining contenders made their way towards the rear of the arena, Riley caught a glimpse of Miranda in the corner of her eye.

The sound of their laughter so soon after the slaughter of their own friends was enough to chill the smile off the woman's face.

CHAPTER 46

The nine surviving contestants fanned out into the space that stood in between the second and third arenas, their faces a mixture of both guilt and gratitude as each of them pondered how they would have fared if they had drawn a red stone rather than blue.

"How are you holding up?" Riley asked Hanzo as she ripped off the blue ribbons that had been tied around their left arms.

"Pissed off," he grunted, grimacing as he tried to rotate the arm that Dagur had incapacitated just before the fight. He had a range of motion now, but it wasn't much. "Jin could've taken out *at least* two of those guards before they dropped him. But he didn't even put up a fight. What the hell was he thinking?"

Riley had no answer for him.

She had considered herself to be at least passably proficient in hand-to-hand combat, but Jin had been on another level – his lightning-fast reflexes and catlike agility allowing him to dodge her blows and mount counterattacks with ease – almost as if he had known her moves long before she even made them.

There was no doubt that he could have pounced on one of the guards, taken his weapon and squeezed off a few shots at the rest of Radek's men before they even got the chance to put him down.

"Maybe he just wanted to go out peacefully," Georgia offered an explanation.

"Don't get me wrong – I'm glad he found some peace before the end," Hanzo let out a pained sigh. "I just... I dunno. When it's time to go, you take as many enemies as you can down with you."

A memory of Grandma Eleanor flew through Riley's mind, remembering that in her final moments, the defiant old woman had conjured up a plan to drive Braxton Shepherd and his cultist raiders off of her property, and ended up burning down half the state of Nebraska.

"Well, I'm just glad that none of us had to do it," Jake interjected from the shade offered by the back wall of the second arena. "Otherwise, there would've only been eight of us for the next round."

"You got that right," Hanzo nodded darkly, still wearing the brass knuckles on his fist.

"What do you think the next challenge is gonna be?" Dakota wondered, gingerly prodding her shoulder wound as she peered into the third arena.

An elevated structure ran down the center of the arena, stretching lengthwise from one end to the other, while the top half was hidden behind overlapping sheets of blue tarp stirring slightly in the desert breeze.

A series of extension cables spiraled down the structure's support columns, spilling across the asphalt like the ribbons of a river delta, converging into a thick bundle of cords that ran towards the trailer-mounted diesel generator idling just outside the empty marketplace.

"Get some water!!" Taylor's voice rose above the sounds of the clamoring crowd, before Riley could even guess at what the final challenge would be.

She frowned up at the packed grandstands, scanning the sea of spectators for Taylor and Barbara. Unable to spot them in the crowd though, she glanced sidelong at Manny, his older brother, and the rest of the water crew.

They were standing at the mouth of the laneway that ran in between the plaza and the strip mall, and their shopping carts had been restocked to the brim with bottles of water.

Riley couldn't deny that she had worked up a thirst.

She couldn't even remember the last time she'd had a drink.

And it seemed to her that the vendors no longer had an interest in plying their wares to the crowd.

Before she even knew it, her legs were carrying her towards the water carts.

"I don't have anything to pay you with," Riley confessed, her face spattered with fresh blood and yet still turning out her pockets. "But I sure could use a drink."

"No problem!" Manny exclaimed happily, greeting her with a big smile as the other contestants eagerly began forming a line behind her. "All the water's already been paid for – it's free for everybody today!"

Riley returned his smile as she twisted off a bottle cap, gently touching her neck as she took small but grateful sips, her throat still raw from Jin's chokehold.

"Is this a tournament thing?" she asked in between swigs, glancing over at Miranda as the loathsome woman climbed the stairs to the final raised platform. "This is how they draw the crowds, right? Lure them all in with free water?"

"First time it's ever happened," Manny professed, happily shrugging at their stroke of luck. He kept making eye contact with Riley though, waiting for the other contenders to wander off with their bottles before beckoning for her to lean in closer. His voice dropped to a whisper, "I'm supposed to tell you that all the water's courtesy of Kentaro. Whenever you wanna go and thank him in person, all you have to do is bend down and tie your shoelaces."

But her bootlaces didn't need tying.

Riley furrowed her eyebrows, studying Manny's face for a moment as he quickly resumed his mask of innocence.

Wary of arousing any suspicion among the guards, she subtly scanned the surrounding area in between sips of water, searching for signs of Kentaro and the Red Tigers.

They've had a plan all along, the thought filled her with a reserved sense of relief as her sharp gaze swept over the nearby empty rooftops and street corners. *But where the hell are they?*

She was about to tell the others, when the whistling feedback of Miranda's bullhorn pierced her ears.

CHAPTER 47

"The Stamford Bridge is the final challenge of the tournament," Miranda announced over the bullhorn. "The berserker at the battle of Stamford Bridge was one of Viking legend. This unnamed warrior stood alone, single-handedly holding back the entire English army, fighting to a glorious death in order to buy time for his brethren to prepare for battle."

At a signal from Miranda, a pair of guards entered the third arena, and they began tearing down the blue tarps hanging over the sides of the elevated structure's framework.

The crowd of spectators hummed and murmured with intrigue while the contenders craned their necks, straining to get a better view of whatever awaited them.

Riley and the others had to climb up onto the arena's barricade beside the entrance in order to see properly.

"What is it?" Jake called from his seat in the shade.

"I'm not sure," Riley cocked her head to one side as she studied the cluttered walkway. It was lined with a labyrinth of spiked columns, pillars topped with slabs of concrete, and sharpened blades glinting in the sun. "It looks like some kinda... obstacle course?"

Dagur marched over to the trailer-mounted diesel generator still rumbling beside the arena, his brutish gaze lighting up as he began flipping switches.

The crowd and the contenders alike gasped in horror as the bridge whirred to life.

The spiked columns began spinning, their spiraling blades soon gyrating at deadly speeds.

Heavy chunks of concrete fell from the pillars, their rapid descent ending abruptly with sharp rattles, suspended in midair by thick metal chains that hoisted the payloads back up, only for them to drop down again.

A series of massive axe blades swung across the width of the walkway from each overhead beam, sailing from side to side like a row of gigantic pendulums.

And previously hidden underneath the bridge's decking, a plethora of motorized spears thrust upwards at random intervals, while the blurs of buzz saws ran across a network of tracks set in the floor.

"That's fucked," Hanzo was the first to say what they were all thinking.

"How is *anyone* meant to get across that?" Dakota stared in dread at the veritable death trap.

"Courage is easy to come by when you have warriors by your side," Miranda continued, sweeping her callous gaze over each of the remaining contenders. "But a true Viking accepts that their fate is their own. Your victory lies beyond fear. Walk this path, and you will find glory everlasting. Valhalla awaits!"

Dagur led the cheer among the guards while the crowd erupted into thunderous applause, despite not a single soul being envious of the contenders facing the challenge.

"Well, shit, who wants to go first?" Hanzo asked sarcastically, not expecting an answer.

"Yeah, I'll do it," Tyson volunteered himself with an eager grin. "All we have to do is dodge the shit. If you can time your run right, you're home free."

"Wait a second," Riley held up a steadying hand before the man could recklessly rush towards his death. She hopped off the arena's wall, beckoning for the others to join her in a huddle beside Jake. "I'm with Dakota – there's no way any of us are gonna make it through this one alive."

"It's that bad, huh?" Jake raised his eyebrows, not having seen the bridge for himself.

"So, what are you suggesting?" Foley wondered, arms folded across his chest.

"We make a run for it," Riley locked eyes with him. She was careful not to mention Kentaro and the Red Tigers. She had no idea what they were planning anyway, let alone whether she could trust half of the remaining contestants not to make a bargain with Miranda in exchange for a tip off. "Earlier, you said that as long as we can make it to the safe zone, it'd be the same thing as winning the tournament, right?"

"I did say that," Foley admitted with a dry chuckle, before shaking his head. "But if that's your plan – I think I'll take my chances in the arena."

"I used to compete professionally in courses like this all the time," Tyson revealed the reason behind his unexpected enthusiasm. "That's why I took the flight to Vegas in the first place. Me and a bunch of other athletes were supposed to run a course. The prize money was unbelievable. But just before it was meant to go down, the whole world went to shit." He waved a hand at the bridge, "This challenge was practically made for me – and I'm not gonna back away from what's probably my best shot at making it through to the finish line."

With that, Tyson, Foley and the other pair of survivors turned back towards the walkway of death, leaving Riley, Jake, Georgia, Dakota and Hanzo to themselves.

"I'm with you," Dakota didn't even hesitate to side with Riley. "Fuck that bridge."

"Count me in too," Hanzo shot them both a wink. "I'd rather take a bullet in the back than an axe to the face."

"Like I'm gonna abandon you guys now," Jake scoffed at the idea of splitting up with his friends. "My back's already ruined anyway – a couple of bullets wouldn't hurt. At the very least, I'll make for a good meat shield."

"Can I say something?" Georgia diverged from the group's consensus, biting the tip of her thumb as she glanced back at the bridge. "I think I might know another way that we can all pass the challenge."

CHAPTER 48

Riley stood on top of the arena's wall with the rest of the contestants, watching the whirring walkway from the best vantage point they had.

She glanced back at Jake, who was still sitting in his shady spot on the ground as he flashed her a thumbs-up.

"Come on baby, you got this!" Tyson jumped up and down at the entrance to the bridge, hyping himself up for the medieval obstacle course.

The former athlete had adamantly decided against letting Georgia go before him despite her insistence, wanting the glory of being the first to make it across the perilous path for himself.

"I can't hear you!" he cupped a hand to his ear, calling for the crowd to cheer him on even harder. "Do you wanna see me tear this bitch up or not!?"

The grandstands exploded with deafening applause, whistling and roaring their support.

Turning his focus back towards the task at hand, Tyson bounced on the balls of his feet, studying the first section of the treacherous bridge, spiked columns spinning and blades blurring across the walkway.

Then, taking two running steps, he leapt over a whirring buzz saw, twisting in midair to avoid the arc of a spiraling blade, before landing in a crouch beside one of the pillars.

A heavy block of concrete dropped down from the top of the pillar, and the chunk's chain suspension snapped taut, the load hovering menacingly above Tyson's head, mere inches from splitting his skull wide open.

"Shit!" Hanzo shouted vicariously, ducking his own head underneath an imaginary block.

Foley stared intently from his perch on the wall of the arena, studying the athlete's moves as he calculated a clear run through the obstacle course.

Tyson rubbed his hands together before tapping his fingertips against his thigh, keeping time with the motorized spears in the next section, their glinting metal barbs thrusting upwards in between the bridge's decking.

With a hop and a skip, he scrambled on top of one of the spinning spiked columns in the center of the walkway, jerking his feet up just in time before a spear could skewer through the bottom of his shoe.

Riley involuntarily crushed her empty bottle of water in the nerve-shredding suspense.

"Wow, he might actually make it," Georgia murmured as she clasped her hands underneath her chin, as rapt in his performance as the rest of the audience.

Tyson let himself spin around a few times on top of the rotating column, adjusting his crouch as he scanned the path ahead for the next safe point.

The crowd whooped and hollered as he leapt onto one of the massive axe blades swinging across the width of the walkway, holding on to the wooden haft with one hand as he wiped off beads of sweat from his forehead.

"Fuck this guy for making it look so easy," Dakota shook her head in disbelief.

Coiling his legs into a spring on top of the axe blade, timing his next jump just right, Tyson cleared another array of thrusting spearheads before rolling underneath a gyrating blade, stopping on a square where he could calculate his next move.

But his chosen perch sank slightly into the floor, and his gaze slid sideways at the sound of an ominous *clank* coming from inside one of the concrete-topped pillars.

Frozen in dread, his pupils dilated as a volley of bolt arrows flew towards him, rocketing into his ribcage and thigh.

Stabbed like a pincushion, Tyson keeled over to one side, robbed of breath as he tried to catch his balance.

The crowd erupted with cries of shock and dismay, jeering at the presence of a lethal trap hidden in an obstacle course that was already fraught with enough danger.

Not easily defeated though, Tyson spat blood across the deck, doggedly determined to push on, despite the spikes embedded into half of his body.

But just as he was struggling to his feet, the blur of a buzz saw ran through his steadying hand, slicing off his fingers.

His already-present state of shock nullified the pain as he lurched upright, staring down at the grisly remains of his four pulsating knuckles, when a spinning bludgeon from behind knocked him back to the floor again, delivering his neck directly into the path of a swinging axe blade.

Riley screwed her eyes shut and turned away just in time, but there was no mistaking the horrible sound of Tyson's head landing on the floor with a squelching *thunk.*

"I think I'm gonna be sick," Dakota scrambled down from the arena's wall, clutching her stomach as she made a beeline for the water carts.

Georgia was the first to blow chunks, her guttural retch setting off several members of the audience in a chain reaction, despite all the violent bloodshed that they had already witnessed.

"How far did he get?" Jake called up from his seat in the shade, having been spared the gruesome sight.

"Not far enough," Hanzo answered bitterly over his shoulder. "But that guy trained for shit like this. If *he* couldn't get through it, then I don't see how anybody else thinks they even stand a chance."

"It's not too late to back out," Riley elbowed Georgia as the woman spat out the bitter taste lingering in her mouth. "Just let me know when you're ready, and we'll go with Plan A. Dakota's already in position."

"No – it can be done," Georgia replied, to their surprise. Wiping her lips with the back of her hand, she dropped down into the arena with a nervous declaration, "I'm next."

"Atta girl!!" Foley led the applause as Georgia climbed up the ramp onto the bridge. "Watch out for the pressure plates and you'll be fine!"

"We're not actually gonna let her do this, are we?" Hanzo glanced sidelong at Riley.

She bit her bottom lip.

Riley knew that all she had to do was pretend to tie up her bootlaces, and Kentaro and the Red Tigers would launch their rescue plan – whatever the rescue plan was.

But Georgia had claimed that she knew a way for all of them

to pass the challenge.

If she was right, then they could avoid any unnecessary bloodshed.

"It's not up to us," Riley gave Hanzo the blunt truth, even as she kept her own doubts to herself, not wanting to shake the woman's uneasy resolve any more than it already was. "It's her choice to make."

Georgia glanced back over her shoulder, almost as if she could hear Riley's unspoken skepticism underneath her reluctant support. Taking a deep breath, she turned back to the bridge.

The crowd whooped and yelled encouragement and placed their bets as Georgia lingered at the entrance to the walkway of death.

Her knees were trembling as she gaped at the blurs of buzz saws and gyrating blades and colossal-sized axes swinging from side to side. Her ears were swamped with the whirrs of mechanical menaces thirsting for blood, the sharp rattles of chain suspensions snapping taut, and the grunting diesel generator rumbling above it all to power the bridge.

"Take your time, Georgia!" Dakota shouted from beside the water carts. "Don't rush it!"

Georgia shook out her hands to limber up, summoning her strength.

And then she jumped off the side of the walkway.

"Shit," Riley breathed, half-stooping to her bootlaces, when she caught sight of Georgia's backside underneath the bridge.

She was hanging from the walkway's underlying framework, rocking her feet back and forth to build up momentum, before swinging from beam to beam.

"You can do that!?" Hanzo spluttered in surprise, along with the rest of the crowd.

Riley and the remaining contenders standing on the wall dropped down to ground-level, staring open-mouthed as Georgia bypassed all of the death traps lining the obstacle course with ease.

There were still the bottom halves of the buzz saws and the motorized spear hafts to contend with, but without the clutter of everything else topside to distract her, she had no trouble avoiding them.

"Alright, this could work!" Riley called over her shoulder to Jake, who couldn't see anything from his spot in the shade. "We're gonna swing underneath the bridge instead."

"I'm good with that," he grinned back at her, "Keeps my back outta the sun, too!"

"What about us two?" Dakota nudged Hanzo as she rejoined them, pointedly glancing down at her shoulder wound with a grimace.

He tried to flex his bad arm, answering her with a bleak shake of his head.

"You could try doing it one-handed," Foley suggested, keeping his eyes trained on Georgia. "If either of you two try running the actual course with a busted wing, you wouldn't even make it half as far as Tyson did."

They both nodded in begrudging agreement, with Hanzo deciding that he no longer needed his brass knuckles as he stashed them away in one of his socks, before turning his attention back to the bridge.

Georgia was leaping from one support column to the next, skirting around a cluster of spear hafts plunging down from the bridge's decking at random intervals.

Clearing the snag, she sprang back towards the center of the walkway's underbelly, swinging from beam to beam again, on the home stretch, when she caught a low-hanging pole obstructing her path.

But the pole dipped suddenly underneath her weight, dropping her down by half a foot.

Her rhythm broken, Georgia dangled in midair for a moment, eyes on the finish line.

She turned her focus on readjusting her grip, failing to notice the subtle shift in the bridge's support columns on either side, the surface layer of each pillar drawing upwards, like long sleeves being rolled back.

Then all at once along the underbelly of the bridge, several spikes of sharpened steel shot out from each support column, with half a dozen blades spearing towards Georgia at breakneck speed, impaling her from both sides as she let out a scream of confused anguish.

And then the blades began turning.

As if skewering the wailing woman in place wasn't bad enough, small motors housed inside the columns to her left and right grunted as they churned against the resistance, and the gyrating blades soon cut their way through Georgia's maimed sinew, ripping free from her flesh only to spin back around, hacking her into gory pieces while her lifeless hands still clung to the pole.

"FUCK!!" Riley roared, turning on her heels and slamming her hand against the wall of the second arena as the rest of the crowd gasped in horror.

"What's going on?" Jake stared up at her, startled by her outburst. "She didn't make it?"

Riley glared down at him with fire in her eyes.

"We're doing this – back to Plan A," she spat, whirling around to see Miranda smirking down at the macabre display from her raised platform. "Right fucking now."

With that, Riley dropped to one knee, gloved fingers touching her bootlaces.

CHAPTER 49

"Glory only comes to those who walk the path," Miranda declared over the bullhorn, attempting to quell the crowd's dissent over the sight of Georgia's body lying in mangled pieces across the asphalt in the arena. "The berserker of Stamford Bridge didn't become a legend by hiding underneath it."

"What are you doing?" Jake cocked an eyebrow at Riley, watching with confusion as her gloved fingertips fumbled with her bootlaces.

"Come on… come on…" she muttered to herself, completely ignoring his question.

She glanced around at their surroundings, scanning the crowd lining the grandstands, the abandoned strip mall, the entrance to the marketplace, and the laneway that led to the Jade Mantis Hotel.

But there was no sign of the Red Tigers coming to their rescue.

What the hell? Riley mouthed at Manny.

He gulped under the weight of her stare, before looking away.

She was about to get up and extract an explanation from the kid, when a gravelly voice reached her ears.

"That's the signal!" Barbara hollered from the grandstands, her gaze zeroing in on Riley.

"RUN MOTHERFUCKERS!!" Taylor screamed at the top of her lungs as empty bottles began flying out from the crowd.

A cascade of plastic, metal and glass rained down on the arena, crashing and shattering, and the guards stationed along the sidelines threw up their arms and ducked for cover.

Icy adrenaline flooded Riley's veins.

This was their chance to escape.

Jerking Jake upright, she spun and sprinted towards the mouth of the laneway that ran in between the plaza and the strip mall, with the rest of the contestants hard on her heels.

Manny and the water crew abandoned their laden shopping carts in the chaos, having positioned them perfectly for Hanzo and Dakota to wrench to the ground as they flew past, leaving countless bottles of water rolling in every direction in their wake.

"They're escaping!" Kuba roared amid Miranda's threatening attempts to call for calm. "SHOOT THOSE *PUTA MADR*–"

But his bark was cut short by a heavy-handed blow to the stomach.

"You'll hit the generator, you fucking idiots!" Dagur bellowed as Kuba fell to his knees, wheezing for air. The muscle-bound monster began shoving guards towards the laneway instead. "MOVE, MOVE, MOVE!!"

Riley and the others bolted through the entrance to the empty marketplace, when a stacked tower of cardboard boxes came crashing down behind them.

Glancing back over her shoulder mid-run, Riley glimpsed

Heather crouching beside the entrance, along with Boomer, the brindle pitbull erupting in a series of startled barks.

"Head for the bar!" Heather waved frantically towards the rear wall of the plaza.

"Come with us!" Riley turned on a dime, doubling back for the fiery redhead, knowing that she'd need help getting across the square with her bad leg.

Hanzo was staring over his shoulder at their pursuers scrambling over the rolling bottles of water, not watching where he was running, when he slammed into Riley at full speed, sending them both crashing to the ground.

"Just fuck off already!!" Heather yelled at the sprawling pair, apparently having made her own arrangements. She wrestled Boomer over to a lean-to tent shelter beside the wall, before collapsing its support poles and taking cover underneath the crumpled canvas.

"Let go of my arm – fuck!" Hanzo shouted in pain as Riley tried to pull him to his feet by his busted wing.

He clambered upright behind her and they staggered into a sprint after the other escapees, tearing across the square towards a semicircle of barbecue grills that had been arranged around the entrance to the karaoke bar.

Cracks of gunfire rang around the plaza as the first of their pursuers hurtled over the barrier of debris, taking rushed pot-shots at the fleeing fugitives.

Riley and Hanzo caught up to the rest of the group just as one of the escaping contestants collapsed with a bullet in his back, face planting and skidding across the concrete.

Only a few yards away from the barricade of barbecue grills, another man went down beside Riley as a bullet burst through the back of his kneecap.

Her heart froze as one of his hands shot out to grab hold of her ankle, and she hit the ground hard.

Snarling as she pushed herself up off the concrete, Riley jerked her foot out of his grasp.

She was about to bolt for the safety of the barricade, when she felt the rush of a lead slug slicing through the air overhead, tearing directly across the path where she would have been running only moments ago, ricocheting off the lid of a barbecue grill instead.

"Come on!!" Riley shouted as she spun around to grab the wounded man's outstretched arm, owing him her life.

"Help me up!" he cried, desperation and dismay scrawled across his face, before another bullet ripped through the back of his skull, and he gazed up at her with empty bloodshot eyes.

Her mouth went dry as she stared back at him in horror.

"Move your fucking legs, bitch!" Dakota's yell from nearby broke the momentary trance.

Dropping his lifeless arm, Riley whirled back towards the barricade of barbecue grills, when she came face to face with the barrel of a sub-machine gun.

CHAPTER 50

Frozen in fear, Riley stared into the barrel of the sub-machine gun, even as a volley of hot lead bullwhipped from the marketplace's entrance behind her, hungry for flesh.

"GET DOWN!!" Batu roared, Kentaro's grave-faced body-guard reaching over the makeshift barricade of barbecue grills to shove Riley to the ground.

Snapping back to her senses the instant her knees scuffed the concrete, she dove underneath the grill's side burner and flung herself behind cover.

Behind the barricade were a dozen other lean rugged Asian thugs – armed with an array of weapons but standing as one – and the Red Tigers began raining hellfire on Radek's barbarian brutes, both sides blasting bloodthirsty bullets across the plaza.

"Come on, get inside!!" Dakota yelled from the entrance to the karaoke bar, the lithe woman hugging the floor as lead slugs ricocheted off the barbecue grills, bullet fragments flying in every direction.

Pulse pounding in her eardrums along with the deafening storm of gunfire thundering all around her, Riley scrambled on her hands and knees towards the open doorway.

She reached the threshold just as the bar's unlit neon sign exploded overhead, showering her back with shards of broken glass.

"Let's go, let's go!" Dakota urged as she shrank backwards down the flight of stairs.

Shaking off the glass crystals, Riley launched herself over the top of the staircase, sliding head first down the steps, banging her hips and knees and elbows over every stair all the way down to the bottom, where she landed in the foyer in a battered heap beside Dakota.

Despite the sharp pain of her throbbing bones, Riley felt like she could finally breathe again.

She glanced around to see Jake and Hanzo doubled-over and panting hard, along with a woman standing behind the coat room's counter cradling a pistol, craning her neck around the corner to see if there were any other survivors still coming down behind them.

"Don't tell me we're the only ones who made it," Jake huffed as the storm raged on outside. He had his hands on his knees, staring up at the rectangle of daylight outlining the entrance. "Where's Foley?"

"I saw two guys go down," Riley replied, rolling over onto her back as she caught her breath. "One of them might've been Foley – but I'm not sure."

"He was still watching the bridge when we tipped over the carts," Dakota answered, pushing herself upright to sit with her back against the wall. "I don't think he even moved when we started running."

"Crazy bastard actually wants to finish the tournament," Hanzo grunted, shaking his head. "Good luck to him." He

321

turned to the clerk behind the counter, "Hey, Dakota needs a proper bandage for her shoulder, and Jake needs a shitload of burn cream. Where's all the meds?"

"I'm afraid you won't have enough time for proper medical treatment," Kentaro's deep and resonant rumble entered the foyer just as the gunshots came to a lull in the plaza.

Dakota clambered to her feet, and both she and Hanzo silently bowed their heads, gazing down at the floor as a show of respect for their elder.

"What do you mean?" Jake was the first to ask.

"The tournament's not over yet," Kentaro replied cryptically, his gaze flicking up at the entrance as Dagur's crew hurled unintelligible slurs across the marketplace.

He smiled at their impotent threats, before gesturing for the four escapees to follow him through the doorway into the karaoke bar's main lounge.

Candle-lit lanterns lined ledges and tables, casting pale auras across the shadowy underground oasis.

"Clay!?" Jake exclaimed the moment he laid eyes on the other bounty hunter sitting by the bar, spinning an empty shot glass beside a green bottle of soju. "We didn't see you in the crowd – I thought something might've happened to you last night."

"Come on, you know me better than that," Clay grinned as he slid off the bar stool, clapping hands with Jake before going in for a hug. "It's good to s–"

Riley caught Clay's wrist before he could slap the second-degree burns on Jake's back.

"Shit, what the hell happened to you?" Clay gawked open-mouthed at the sight of his friend's scorched skin.

"Just be glad you didn't get caught," Jake attempted to

shake the traumatic experience from his mind, choosing to avoid delving into all of the details. "They got Lincoln too. He died in the tournament."

"Damn it!" Clay pounded the bar, scratching at his scalp in frustration before sitting down again. He stared up at the ceiling. "I'm sorry we bailed on you guys last night. But when those reinforcements showed up at the gate, we didn't really have much of a choice. Me and that redhead chick came straight back here to see what we could do to help break you guys out."

"Yeah, it looks like you've been *real* helpful," Riley lauded Clay sarcastically, glancing pointedly at his drink before narrowing her eyes at him. "Heather's out there right now, caught in the fucking crossfire, while you're down here catching a buzz."

"Trust me – she got the easy job," he raised his eyebrows in slight resentment at the accusation, before snatching up his bottle to pour himself another shot.

"How about you pour one for the rest of us?" Hanzo suggested, although it sounded more like a demand than a request. "I'd say we've earned a drink after all the shit we've just been through."

"For the friends who didn't make it," Dakota murmured quietly, extracting a nod of permission from Kentaro before sitting down on one of the bar stools.

"Allow me," the graying man offered, stepping behind the bar.

Riley rubbed the back of her neck as she watched him line up four glasses along the counter.

She found it contradictory that they had enough time to drink a toast for the dead, even though apparently they couldn't spare a moment to treat the wounded to keep them among the living.

Not wanting to argue with their savior though, she held her tongue.

"You'll need this for what lies ahead," Kentaro declared as he cracked open a bottle of water, eyeing each of them as he filled their glasses to the brim. "But we honor the dead only after the fighting is done – so that their ranks don't needlessly swell from something as simple as dulled senses."

Riley could drink to that.

Slaking their thirst, they held a silent memorial for the fallen instead.

To Lincoln, who had struck at their true enemy rather than turn on his fellow survivors.

To Jin, who had sacrificed himself to allow his friends to advance to the next challenge.

And to Georgia, who had surpassed all of their expectations in the tournament, even saving Riley's skin on more than one occasion.

"So, what's the plan?" Riley wondered as she set down her glass.

"We'll hold off Radek's men here – he'll fill you in on the rest," Kentaro nodded towards Clay. He locked eyes with Dakota, "You know the way." Then, drawing a pistol from underneath the bar and handing it over to Hanzo, he added, "And you know the risk."

Hanzo winced slightly as he took the handgun with his preferred arm despite the pain, gritting his teeth against the sharp twinge of overextending beyond his recovering range of motion, not wanting to show any signs of weakness in accepting his charge.

"Alright, let's do this," Clay downed his last shot, slamming his glass on the bar before leading the four escapees deeper into the Tiger's Den. Stumbling slightly, he added with a sigh of relief, "That's taken the edge off."

Riley's stare threatened to bore a hole into the back of his head.

Clay had drunk himself tipsy, in spite of Kentaro's insistence on staying sober until after the fighting was done.

From the sway in his step, she knew that he was going to be a liability.

Whatever the plan was, she hoped that he wouldn't have a major role to play in it.

But then again – they had made it this far without him.

They passed by the former karaoke bar's private function rooms, with their tinted glass doors lining both sides of the dimly-lit corridor.

The kitchen staff had hidden themselves among the makeshift barracks' bunk beds and storage racks, clutching knives and meat cleavers as they kept a wary eye on the movement in the hallway.

"So, you wanna tell us what we're doing?" Jake prompted before Clay could disappear around the next corner.

He paused at the end of the corridor, letting go of a heavy sigh before turning around.

"You guys have the best shot at ending this before anybody else dies," Clay replied, before relaying Kentaro's strategy. "Winners of the tournament get invited up to Radek's penthouse where he congratulates them personally. All you have to do is kill him, Miranda, and whoever else might stand in the way of Kentaro taking charge."

"Right, like that's so fucking easy," Riley snorted softly

before glancing back at Dakota, remembering their original plan. "I guess you and Kentaro had the same idea."

Dakota didn't return her smile.

Hanzo wasn't even paying attention, preoccupied by his own thoughts.

"Okay, but you said *winners of the tournament*," Jake echoed as he cocked his head with a frown, sensing that something was off. "That doesn't include you. So why the long face? Why were you just doing shots like you're the one who's about to put it all on the line?"

"Because," Clay began somberly, before plucking a candle-lit lantern from a niche in the wall, "There's only one way to get you guys topside again, without Dagur's crew catching you before you get to the safe zone... We're going through the basement level of the Jade Mantis."

"Fuck," Jake breathed, his mouth going dry in disbelief.

"Fuck, indeed," Dakota agreed, finally uttering the word that she had been holding on to as she took the lead. "Follow me."

"Didn't you say you locked up all the cannibals in the lower levels?" Riley remembered as they ventured down the next stretch of hallway. "How the hell is going through the hotel's basement even an option? We should be outside with the rest of your people – they could provide cover fire for us, and we'd all make it to the finish line without having to worry about getting eaten alive."

"Now you can see why Heather's out there," Clay grumbled aloud as he held up the lantern behind Dakota.

"We'd get minced before we even made it halfway across the plaza," Dakota knew, leading them past the open floor-to-ceiling mirror at the end of the hallway. "Batu and the others are just providing a distraction for us. Nobody outside the Red Tigers knows about the bar's emergency exit. By the time Dagur's crew realizes that we've escaped, we'll already be in the safe zone."

"Here," Hanzo tapped Riley on the shoulder, his voice echoing in the empty commercial kitchen space as he offered her the pistol. "If it makes you feel any better. I can't aim for shit with my left hand – but I can still do some damage with my knuckle dusters. Just make sure that you're looking out for everybody while we're in there, not just yourself."

Riley felt a wave of calm wash over her as she gripped the handgun.

She nodded her unspoken appreciation as she checked the safety lever in the dim light of the lantern, before finding a grip that she was familiar with, cupping the bottom of her right hand and the pistol's hilt with her left.

Their boots squeaked across the kitchen's rubber floor mats as Clay's glowing lantern shed light over the stainless steel bench tops and workstations.

"Anybody else got the sudden urge to use the bathroom?" Jake murmured as he picked up a meat mallet.

"Bathrooms are back in the hallway," Dakota jerked a thumb over her shoulder as she reached the door to the walk-in fridge. "You'd best do it now though. We haven't used this passage in months. I don't know what's waiting for us on the other side, but I'm willing to bet that if you shit yourself while we're in there, they'll smell it from a mile away and come flocking down on us like a swarm of flesh-hungry flies."

CHAPTER 51

"Alright, that's the last one," Jake reported as he tossed out the final piece of debris clogging up the kitchen's walk-in fridge, exhuming their escape route.

"This is a weird spot to put an emergency exit," Riley mused, pointing her pistol at the ground as she eyed the rectangular outline of a hidden doorway etched into the wall in between a pair of shelving racks.

"It was a fail-safe that got put in place a long time ago," Dakota explained as she entered the walk-in fridge, clutching a kitchen knife in her good hand. "Just in case any of the police on our payroll decided to switch sides and hit us with a surprise raid, we could all make a quick getaway with any contraband that they might've tried to pin us with."

"Cool – so are we gonna do this or what?" Clay wondered aloud, wary of losing his nerve as he held the candle-lit lantern aloft, scanning the indistinct exit for a door handle.

"You just worry about keeping that light up," Hanzo smirked sidelong at him before reaching for an obscure lever concealed behind one of the shelves.

Buried within the wall, the sound of a bolt rasping free of

its latch reverberated around the walk-in fridge with a heavy *clank.*

The hidden hatch swung open, and Riley jerked her gun up.

But all that was waiting for them on the other side was the back of an empty broom closet.

Shuffling in between shelves of cleaning chemicals, they made their way through the closet's front entrance to an old staff break room, with Clay's lantern casting its dim light over the basic amenities of a defunct fridge and microwave overlooking a cheap dining table.

Riley swept her pistol's barrel from one end of the room to the other, before dropping to one knee to check underneath the table.

They were the only ones in the room.

"I'm surprised those animals left this place in one piece," Dakota spoke softly, tracing her fingertip across the kitchen counter's fine coat of dust, before wiping it clean on an old valet uniform draped over the back of a chair.

"Keep your guard up," Riley trained her pistol on the exit as she reminded them all to stay vigilant.

They had just entered the cannibals' lair.

She knew that the man-eating savages could attack them at any moment.

"What's our game plan here?" Jake asked, eyeing the bathroom door warily as he addressed Dakota and Hanzo. "All of the hotel's lower levels got blocked off months ago – how are we supposed to get out?"

"The same way *they* got out two nights ago," Hanzo shrugged, making eye contact with Riley as he remembered her guess, "Through the vents."

"That's gonna be a fucking maze," Clay scoffed at the idea,

before glancing down at the lantern in his hand. "And if this candle burns out before we find an exit... we'll be crawling around in circles, lost in the dark, making a shitload of noise, just waiting to be eaten alive."

A spell of uneasy silence fell over the room as the macabre fate nestled in the back of their minds.

"Alright, so not the vents," Dakota decided promptly, sighing through her teeth. Her gaze wandered the walls in search of another suggestion, when her stare settled on the front door. "This leads out to the parking garage. If we can find the elevators, we could try getting inside one of the shafts and scale up to the lobby."

"Sounds good – but how are we gonna get the doors open?" Riley wondered dubiously, her eyes flicking from Dakota's kitchen knife to Jake's meat mallet.

She was certain that they wouldn't be able to pry open the doors without a proper tool.

Otherwise the cannibals would have done it already.

She took care to keep the skepticism out of her voice though.

Doubt was the last thing they needed in the darkness.

"You guys got anything heavy duty back there in the bar?" Clay glanced over his shoulder at the broom closet, with a sudden urge to return to safety.

It seemed that he had sobered up now, his liquid courage dissipating after learning that they were just improvising the escape plan.

"Weapon-wise, absolutely," Hanzo replied, before shaking his head, "Tool-wise, not so much."

"We could check the cars in the garage," Jake offered a solution as he wedged the back of a chair underneath the bathroom's door handle. "You can find just about anything in the trunk of a car in Vegas – and nobody was touching the underground garages until *after* the cannibals moved in here."

Riley rubbed the back of her neck as she turned the plan over in her mind.

She supposed that without any light to guide the cannibals down in the basement level, they might never have even gotten the opportunity to properly search for tools that would help them escape.

It also explained why the valet staff's break room had been left untouched.

This could work, she nodded to herself in silence.

Dakota stood by the exit, holding the handle of her kitchen knife underneath her chin as she made eye contact with each of them.

"Ready?" she whispered, clutching the door handle as the others drew up behind her.

Jake extracted a nod of resolve from Clay.

Hanzo flexed the brass knuckles on his fist.

"Hold on," Riley strode over to stand shoulder to shoulder beside Clay. "We all need to stick together in there. We don't want another Felix running off on his own," she glanced pointedly at Dakota's makeshift bandage above her collar-bone, the consequences of Felix's panic. Staring sidelong at Clay, she continued, "Stay close. Keep the light up high and in the middle. Take it slow if we have to. And make sure to call out anything that looks suspicious... Let's go."

Dakota cracked open the door, her blade shaking slightly in her hand as they shuffled out in a tight formation, the echoes of their footsteps almost deafening in the silence.

"Who the hell's Felix?" Clay whispered from the center of

the huddle.

Riley and Jake walked in lockstep on either side of the group, with Dakota taking the lead and Hanzo bringing up the rear.

But despite their close proximity to each other, nobody bothered to give him an answer.

They were too preoccupied – their heads on a swivel, warily scanning their surroundings.

The lantern cast its feeble glow over the dust-covered rows of abandoned vehicles lining the garage, shedding light on the cloudy windows of forgotten suburbans and station wagons, while the grimy shells of luxury sedans gave off dull sheens in the gleaming gloom.

Looming shadows leapt across the walls as they passed in between the concrete columns standing sentinel throughout the underground garage.

Riley's arms were flooded with gooseflesh as she kept her pistol pointed out to the side, straining her eyes at the few feet of space that stood in between each vehicle.

She had been staring for so long that she had forgotten to blink, but just as she finally gave herself permission to do so, and only for an instant, she thought that she caught a glimpse of a fleeting figure scampering out of the light.

"Did anybody else see that?" she whispered as an icy shiver ran up her spine.

"Don't fucking joke with me right now," Clay had his eyes locked on Dakota's backside, his arm already trembling with nervous tension as he held the lantern aloft.

"I saw something," Riley was sure of it. At least she thought she was. Gun rattling in her hands, she scanned the shifting shadows for the slinking silhouette as they continued their steady shamble, before murmuring over her shoulder,

"Hanzo, keep an eye on my side."

"You got it," he replied, walking backwards as he swept his gaze from left to right and back again.

Dusty taillights and tow bars of derelict trucks winked and glinted in the lantern's gloomy aura of lusterless light, and Riley began to wonder if the darkness was just playing tricks on her mind.

On either side of the garage, charred lips peeled back from slimy coal-like teeth, the sinister smiles of black phantoms slowly materializing into the cubic bulbs of a car's long-dead LED light strip, or a weathered rear window decal of a sports team's mascot.

"Almost there – it's just up ahead," Dakota kept her voice low as they approached the parking garage's elevator hall.

"Hey, there's a work truck over here," Jake whispered, pulling Clay by the arm as he steered the group off to the side. "Keep watch while I look for a crowbar."

But the moment that the words left his lips, the lantern's halo of light shrank at an alarming speed.

Riley's heart leapt up into her throat.

The darkness rushed towards them like a cloud of black smoke, threatening to engulf them within the depths of the void.

Her mind was racing, her thoughts filling with dread at the idea of the lantern's candle burning out, and she stumbled backwards from the edge of the rapidly receding light.

But Clay had simply set down the lantern before climbing up onto the bed of the work truck, and the dim light soon washed over the parking garage again as he held it aloft.

Glancing up at the ample amount of candlewick remaining behind the glass, Riley breathed a shallow sigh of relief as she returned to scanning their surroundings beside Dakota and Hanzo.

All three of them winced in unison at the reverberating metallic sounds of rustling and rummaging as Jake searched the truck's toolboxes for something that they could use.

"Best I can do," he announced after what felt like an eternity of echoes, proudly holding up a claw hammer.

"Alright, let's crack one of these bad boys open," Clay eagerly clambered back down, his lantern's aura of light contracting and expanding again as he quickly resumed his position in the center of the group.

They had just formed up again, when an ominous clatter resounded from somewhere deep in the pitch black bowels of the parking garage, the menacing noise bouncing off the concrete walls into obscurity.

"We're not alone," Riley knew, squinting into the shadows as she drove them all towards the elevator hall. "Let's move."

The darkness hadn't been playing tricks on her mind after all.

Her intuition had proven correct – much as she wished that it hadn't.

Jake broke formation the moment they reached the carpeted hallway, shoving the claw hammer's forked tongue into the crack of the first elevator's doors.

"Hey, if you just let us do our thing," Clay attempted to bargain with their stalkers lurking in the shadows, "We'll let you come up the shaft after us. Freedom for mercy – how's that sound?"

"Do you even know who you're talking to?" Dakota's tone dripped with loathing as she stared dauntlessly into the void. "Come any closer and we'll FUCKING END YOU!!"

The echoes of her challenge faded into the darkness.

And the pitter-patter of bare feet on concrete answered.

The threat hadn't discouraged the cannibals in the slightest.

If anything, they were emboldened now, drawn by the promise of fresh meat.

"I have a gun," Riley declared, as if the former humans couldn't see the metal of her pistol gleaming in the lantern's light. "Who wants to die first?"

Her mouth went dry then, belatedly realizing that she had no idea how many of them were hiding in the darkness – and how many bullets she had in the magazine.

Jake grunted and strained behind them, but the doors weren't budging.

"Stop for a second," Hanzo interrupted his efforts, retreating from their impromptu semicircular perimeter around the elevator to offer him a helping hand. "Get behind me and push on my elbow. Ready?"

They heaved simultaneously, digging their heels into the carpet as they thrust their combined weight into the small lever.

SNAP!!

The claw hammer's wooden handle shot off into the side of a parking ticket machine, while its metal head slid down the crack in between the elevator's doors, clattering onto the floor.

"Shit," Jake breathed in disbelief, "We're gonna need to find something bigger."

"We don't have the time," Dakota snarled back at him as she kept her eyes on the shifting shadows seeming to spread across the entire garage. "Just... find us an exit!"

"What about the garage's entrance?" Riley suggested,

squinting into the depths of darkness for an exit ramp.

"No-go," Hanzo shook his head somberly as he massaged his wrist. "Roller door's been locked, blocked and buried underneath a mound of trash from the outside. We only stopped piling it up after the door started bulging inwards."

"So where the fuck should we –"

Clay's question was cut short as he caught sight of a waiflike creature doddering out into the lantern's light, staring back at them with beady little eyes.

CHAPTER 52

"That's far enough!" Riley warned, holding her pistol at the half-starved urchin.

She scanned the shadows of the parking garage, searching for any other stalking silhouettes skulking beyond the circle of light emanating from Clay's lantern.

"Keep your eyes peeled," she whispered to the others, listening out for the faint pads of bare footsteps. "This one could just be a distraction."

"What the hell, Riley?" Jake exclaimed incredulously, placing a hand on her trigger arm as he sidled in front of her. "It's just a little kid."

She cocked an eyebrow at him before taking a closer look.

It was difficult to tell at first glance – the malnourished wretch was beanpole thin with sunken eyes.

But just because he was young enough to be considered a child didn't change the fact that he was one of the cannibals.

He was more animal than human now, his innocence long gone.

And besides, she had learned the hard way not to let her guard down around children, remembering when Dylan had betrayed her and the Seabrook sisters to the Lawson Family, getting their friends and countless others killed.

"He's one of *them*, Jake," Riley reminded him, jerking her arm out of his grip. "Kid or not – he's probably looking at us the same way we'd look at livestock walking into a slaughterhouse. He might not be the butcher, but he'll damn sure have a slice."

"I don't give a shit – I'm not gonna stand here and let you shoot some kid," Jake argued, turning his burnt back on her and purposely stepping into her line of fire before dropping to one knee, trying to appear less intimidating. Swallowing the severity in his voice, he mustered up a friendlier tone, "Hey, little buddy. What are you doing down here?"

The juvenile cannibal hesitated for a moment, his wide-eyed gaze sliding sideways towards a service corridor, its double doors chocked open by a scrap of wood.

"I... I'm looking for Momma," he answered timidly, his reedy voice as paper-thin as his gaunt face. "I've been looking all over for her, but she's not in any of our hiding spots. I thought, maybe with that light of yours... you could help me find her?"

Riley couldn't help but think to herself that maybe they had already found *Momma*, in the form of the hideous harpy that had ambushed them up on the fifth floor of the hotel only two nights ago, leaving her with a gouged cheek for a souvenir.

She hadn't even considered that those who had turned to cannibalism could have been capable of raising a child prior to the apocalypse, although arguably, her own mother had stooped to a similar station back at Lake Springworth, succumbing to the terms of the Nebraskan man-raping cult for the sake of her own survival.

Pushed to the limit, ordinary people were capable of doing anything.

"We've got our own problems, kid," Hanzo muttered under his breath as Jake continued the conversation with the waiflike child.

"We don't have time for this," Clay agreed, clenching his jaw at the futility of the exchange.

"Shut up," Dakota silenced them both, clenching her jaw against her own prejudice. "Let's see where this goes. He might be able to help us get outta here."

The thought held some merit.

If anybody knew an exit, it would be somebody who had somehow managed to survive inside the pitch black bowels of the hotel's basement, dedicating the past few months to exploring every inch of the gloomy labyrinth for an escape route.

Riley stayed frosty though, staring into the shifting shadows of the parking garage, knowing that every moment they were engaged in conversation was another moment for any potential ambushers to creep into position.

"Sam? That's a good name," Jake smiled as they all tuned back into the conversation. "I had a little brother about your age."

"Where is he now?" Sam glanced around the elevator hall eagerly, as if they had brought him with them. "Does he live down in the dark like the rest of us?"

"I hope not," Jake exhaled heavily, running a hand through his hair before shaking his head. "No, Tommy's in a better place now. Far away from all this..." He clapped his hands together for an abrupt change of topic, sending echoes through the murky depths of the parking garage, "Anyway, when's

339

the last time you had any food?"

"You mean like *real* food?" Sam asked with reserved excitement, his bloated stomach rumbling at the thought. "I can't even remember."

"Well, how about we make a deal?" Jake spread his hands as he offered a proposal, "If you can show us the way out, my friends up in the marketplace will –"

"Oh, you're from... outside?" Sam retreated half a step, like a deer preparing to bolt.

"They'll let you eat as much food as you want, any time you want," Jake bulldozed over the boy's anxiety, hoping to reach his stomach. "Then, after you're fed and rested, we'll come back here and help you find your mom. Sound good?"

At this point, they had no idea whether a way out even existed.

But it was worth a try.

Sam looked back over his shoulder, as if he could see something buried in the shadows that the rest of them couldn't.

Whatever he was staring at though – it made him wince in fear.

The boy swallowed in silence, his thin face twitching in the lantern's light as he fought an internal battle between dread and hunger.

His sunken eyes traced over each of them before sliding off to the side again.

"Bring the light," he finally whispered, and he made a mad dash towards the service corridor.

"Don't chase him – it might be a trap!" Riley shouted before the others could even think to follow on his heels. "Who knows what's waiting for us on the other side of those doors?

Let's keep trying these elevators. Maybe we can force one of them open with a crowbar."

"Hurry!" Sam urged despite her distrust, holding one of the service doors open as he beckoned them towards the corridor.

Torn with indecision, they all looked to Riley.

And that's when she saw them.

A dozen pairs of jet black eyes – maybe more – gleaming balefully in the darkness, their sinister onyx leers fixated on the five intruders in their midst.

CHAPTER 53

Riley stared back at the emaciated cannibals emerging from the black abyss of the parking garage, barely able to form words.

But she didn't have to.

They were all thinking the same thought.

Run.

Ice-cold instinct flooding her body, the gun barked in her hands like a starter pistol at a track meet, and they bolted towards the service doors just as the shadowy silhouettes sprang to light, the skeletal savages swarming the elevator hall in overwhelming numbers, eager to feast on their prey.

Riley squeezed off blind shots in her wake, unable to take aim while sprinting for her life, but the rabid wretches kept on coming, with nothing to lose and fresh meat to gain.

She surged into the service corridor barely an instant before the double doors swung shut behind her, with Hanzo and Clay bracing their backs against the cascade of cannibals crashing into the entrance.

Riley, Jake and Dakota threw themselves against the doors alongside Hanzo and Clay, digging their heels in to weather the storm.

But against a dozen deranged creatures driven mad with hunger, even their combined strength wasn't enough.

Clay had one foot braced against the wall, but he was still rocking forward every time the feral animals rammed into the doors.

Hanzo's shoes were losing their grip on the corridor's smooth vinyl floor – he was marching backwards just to stay in place.

Jake had his shoulder shoved up against the door, roaring in pain as the blisters across his burnt back began warping and stretching under the strain.

They were losing the battle.

The cannibals knew it too, growling and howling their ravenous revelry through the ever-expanding gap in between the doors.

"Looks like tonight's hunt came in fresh on a platter!"

"Young ones too – bet they're warm, tender, juicy!"

"They'll keep us fed for a month!"

"We'll have to keep them alive if we want the leftovers to last that long!"

Riley stifled a gag at the thought of being held captive by the cannibals, hacked up piece by piece in the pitch black bowels of the hotel basement, her forlorn subsistence prolonged only by the number of weeks it would take before her flesh began to rot.

Hot breath hissed through the crack in the double doors, and a gnarled hand forced its way into the breach, flailing around until it caught hold of Dakota's hair, the bony arm wrenching the woman's head sideways.

Snarling in raging agony, Dakota grabbed her attacker's

hand and tugged it deeper in through the gap, before shoving the blade of her kitchen knife into the fiend's forearm, slashing from elbow to wrist as the wraithlike wretch tried to pull away.

A shriek of anguish soon morphed into maniacal laughter as three more arms reached inside, thrashing about in search for the weapon.

"Warm, tender, juicy!" they screamed in frenzied unison, grabbing Dakota's thrusting knife hand as the doors began caving in. "Warm! Tender! Juicy!!"

Another ram against the doors almost sent Riley toppling over.

They couldn't hold on for much longer.

Thoughts of being eaten alive for weeks on end churned her stomach.

She glanced left and right at the others gritting their teeth, bracing the barricade with every ounce of strength they had left, but still losing ground inch by inch.

Riley screwed her eyes shut.

It was either abandon the doors now, or die a slow and agonizing death.

She picked the obvious choice.

Rasping two galvanizing breaths, Riley darted forward, plunging deeper into the corridor for distance before whirling back around, swinging up her pistol just as the first cannibal broke through.

CRACK!

Hot lead ripped through his throat, the half-starved wretch gurgling and clutching his windpipe with one hand, while the other was still outstretched and clawing for a victim, before a blow from Jake's meat mallet stove in his skull.

Two more cannibals crammed in through the breach on his heels, with one lunging for Clay's lantern, while the second savage dropped to the floor with her hands held high in surrender, gazing up at them with a look of salvation as she begged for mercy.

"Please, take me with —"

Drumming gunshots from the pistol drowned out the kneeling woman's desperate plea, and she hugged the floor as Riley squeezed off rapid-fire rounds into the clamoring crowd outside, cutting off their advance while Jake, Hanzo and Dakota strained to close the gap in between the doors again.

The corridor strobed with muzzle flashes, the murderous mob of monsters blazing and blackening with each shot fired into their repulsive ranks.

Meanwhile, the lantern's light swung violently across the walls as one of the gangly gargoyles tried to wrestle it from Clay's grip, intent on leaving them all blind in the darkness.

Heart racing at the thought, Riley lined up her sights on the bony brute, when a smudge of movement caught her eye, slithering in between the shifting shadows.

The second cannibal had ceased her surrender, seizing the opportunity to slink deeper into the corridor, her jet black gaze trained on the gun.

Pupils dilating in panic, Riley rushed her shot at the madman grappling with Clay.

Her bullet missed its mark, crunching into the door behind them instead.

But before she could line up another shot, the wild woman made her move, doubling over on all fours and charging towards Riley like a deranged chimpanzee.

"Help Clay!!" she shouted at the others as the grimy ghoul

tackled her to the ground.

Landing hard on her back, Riley thrust the barrel of her gun up into the harpy's hip and squeezed the trigger, blowing a hole through the sack of skin and bones.

Screeching like a banshee, the cold-blooded creature latched on to Riley's wrist and slammed it against the floor, again and again, trying to break her hold on the handgun.

Desperately fighting for control, Riley squeezed tight around the pistol's hilt, when her thumb accidentally hit the magazine release.

Her heart skipped a beat as the rest of her ammo slid out and skittered across the floor.

"Fuck," she breathed the first thing that came to mind, before remembering that there was still one round left in the chamber.

She would have to make it count.

The skeletal woman seethed with impatience, suddenly giving up on her frenzied attempts to smash the gun free.

She lurched over to the side instead, pinning Riley's fore-arm to the floor with her fangs bared, blood-tinged saliva slavering at the proximity of fresh meat.

Pulse pounding into overdrive, Riley went for the savage's throat with her other hand, gloved fingers clumsily scrabbling around her neck for purchase, before digging her thumb deep into the woman's windpipe.

Robbed of air and the chance to bite into a chunk of human flesh, the rabid wretch snarled and thrashed and clawed at Riley's throttling arm with both hands, before her eyes went wide as she realized her fatal mistake.

With her trigger hand finally free again, Riley jammed her gun up into the valley of the madwoman's protruding ribcage, and blasted the last bullet underneath her breastbone, shredding clean through the cannibal's beating heart.

CHAPTER 54

Shoving the convulsing cannibal's bag of bones aside, Riley clambered upright again to see Dakota seizing the other deranged degenerate from behind, deftly thrusting the blade of her kitchen knife through the base of his skull.

The man-eating mob's manic attempts to break through the double-doors had finally subsided, but Jake and Clay held the entrance steady all the same, while Hanzo propped up a corpse, unceremoniously forcing one of its gangly legs to thread through the door handles.

"That's not going anywhere," he declared proudly, dusting off his hands and stepping back to admire the morbid ingenuity of his makeshift brace.

It was quiet now.

Riley's ears rang in the silence of the corridor.

"What happened to the rest of them?" she asked warily as she retrieved her pistol's fallen magazine and rammed it home, thumbing the slide release.

"They're not in here – that's all that matters," Dakota shrugged as she surveyed the macabre scene. She turned her chin with a thin smile, "No point in chasing us now anyway.

They've got enough dead meat out there to hold them over for a while. Let them eat each other."

Riley could picture the pack of remaining cannibals on the other side of the doors, dragging away their dead as they disappeared back into the void of the parking garage, not letting a single morsel go to waste.

"Where's that kid gone?" Jake wondered aloud as he peered into the darkness ahead. "Sam, are you still in here?"

But only the echoes of his call answered from the dank depths of the service corridor.

Clay's candle-lit lantern trembled uncontrollably in his hand as the lingering adrenaline dissipated in shakes and jitters.

"Here, let me," Hanzo offered to take the lantern from him.

"Fuck off," Clay shot back, still catching his breath. "You just worry about watching our asses so they don't sneak up behind us again... Make sure you do your damn job this time."

"Hey, ease up," Jake placed a steadying hand on his shoulder. "We're not outta this yet."

"Dickhead," Hanzo muttered under his breath, drawing a chiding glare from Dakota.

"Shut up," Riley silenced them all as she turned their attention back towards the shadowy passage before them. "Let's see where this goes."

But before they had even taken the first step, the subtle sound of bare feet padded towards them.

"Sam?" Jake called out again.

No answer.

"You think they went around?" Clay gulped audibly, holding his lantern up higher to peer into the gloom.

"Shit, shit, shit," Dakota murmured to herself, glancing

back over her shoulder at the barred double doors.

They were cornered this time.

Nerves already on edge, they huddled together, preparing for a second assault.

Led into a another trap by another fucking kid, Riley reflected bitterly as she adopted a fighter's stance, turning at the torso with her left foot forward and right foot back, holding her pistol at the ready.

A lone figure emerged from the shadows.

"Is it over now?" Sam asked in a timid voice.

Breathing a collective sigh of relief, none of them bothered to give him an answer.

His wide eyes could see the grisly aftermath for himself.

He didn't shy away from it though – hardened to the sight of slaughter.

"Come on, it's this way," Sam beckoned them to follow him, the cannibalistic child eager to lead them all farther up the service corridor. "We have to be quick though."

"I'm still not sure if we can trust this kid," Riley whispered her misgivings as they reluctantly followed the half-starved waif. "If he knows the way out, then why the hell hasn't he left yet?"

"Because Momma said it's safer in here than it is out there," Sam picked up on her skepticism as they moved. "We only go outside to fetch water – and only after dark. Out there are all the snatchers, kidnappers, swindlers and killers."

"And in here are all the cannibals," Hanzo quipped, screwing up his face at the idea of the young man-eater taking the moral high ground.

"Hey, you guys wanna get outta here or not?" Jake hissed over his shoulder.

"Unless anybody's got a better idea," Dakota hoped for an alternative, searching their blank expressions before nodding towards Sam, "He's our guide."

Their boots scuffed and squeaked across the smooth vinyl floor in the ensuing silence, echoing into the shadowy depths of the corridor, contending with the collective sound of their nervous breathing, heavy in their own ears.

Every step forward seemed the same as the last, the lantern casting its dim light over the hallway's monotonous plain walls, overhead pipes and long-dead tubes of fluorescent lights, along with the occasional fire extinguisher that nobody would ever care to use.

And then the smell hit them.

Subtle at first, but growing sour by the second.

"What the hell is that smell?" Clay complained after the stench became unbearable.

"Death," Riley knew, all too familiar with the foul odor of decay and despair pervading their senses.

"We're almost there," Sam called back over his shoulder, evidently accustomed to the horrible reek.

They soon came across an intersection in the corridor, with the closed doors of a lone elevator directly ahead, a series of ruddy brown patches staining the floor on their left, and a dusty hallway lined with storage rooms on their right.

Sam led them left.

The floor's brown splotches began pooling together farther down the corridor, stretching wider until they culminated into a singular ruddy streak, ending at the feet of a pair of double doors.

"It stinks in here," Sam belatedly informed them, his hand poised to push open the entrance. "You guys might wanna cover your nose."

Riley yanked the front of her tank top up over her face, muzzling herself with one hand while she held her pistol in the other, ready for anything.

The doors swung open, and the loathsome stench surged towards them, the nauseating cocktail smacking them in the face with invisible slabs of rancid meat, pungent bulbs of rotten fruit, and the equivalent of a garbage dumpster that had been left to ferment in the heat of a thousand summers.

Both Jake and Clay struggled to stifle the urge to gag.

Dakota and Hanzo, on the other hand, had been around the stench of death before.

Just like Riley.

The dim light of the lantern cast its halo over the hotel's reeking laundry room, with dusty industrial-sized washing machines and dryers giving off dull sheens in the desolate gloom.

Their gazes pored over moldy piles of soiled linen littered across the floor, stained with strips of rotten flesh and gore.

In the center of the room stood a cluster of workbenches, the corners of each table fitted with fluffy pink handcuffs that were no longer pink or fluffy – undoubtedly where the five of them would have been destined if they hadn't fended off the attack.

And along the far wall stood the source of the sickening stench – a row of laundry carts brimming with the bones, tendons and ligaments of the cannibals' victims over the past year – the emanating cloud of corruption laden with festering rot, vile depravities, and the tormented screams of suffering.

Turning away from the diabolical carts of death, Riley stared up at a laundry chute and a pair of air vents in the ceiling, with mounds of linen piled high to reach each shaft's access point.

"Guess you were right about the vents," Hanzo followed her gaze as the realization dawned on them. "No wonder they got out the other night. They've got access to every damn floor from right here in the basement."

"This is the quickest way outside," Sam spoke over his shoulder as he clambered up a linen pile underneath one of the air vents.

"Alright, who's first after Sam?" Dakota asked as the others stood around sizing up the narrow opening in the ceiling.

"Not me," Hanzo snorted, shaking his head. "Fuck that. Somebody else can take point."

"Yeah, I think I'd rather go last," Riley agreed, still harboring her suspicions about the kid.

"Seriously?" Jake raised his eyebrows, his incredulous stare searching their faces before grasping the reason behind their apprehension. "You guys have trust issues you need to address. Not everybody's out to get you. Sam just saved our asses back there. Why the hell would he help us get outta the garage if he was planning on leading us into danger now?"

Unless his job was just to deliver us here, Riley answered him from the silence of her own thoughts, overcome with a sudden sense of dread as her gaze was magnetically drawn back to the restraints lining the workbenches.

"I think Riley should go last as well," Dakota took her up on the offer before admitting, "I'd feel a hell of a lot safer with the gun covering our rear."

"Screw it – I'll go first then," Jake volunteered himself with a huff, climbing up after Sam.

"I've got your back," Clay declared, carefully navigating his way up the pile of linen as he held the lantern aloft.

"You guys have to stay quiet now," Sam whispered from the mouth of the air duct. "If they think you're up in the vents, they'll come looking for us. And there are other ways to get into this room."

Riley rubbed the back of her neck as the others began climbing into the air vent, and she shook with an involuntary shiver as she wondered whether the ductwork was connected to the parking garage.

CHAPTER 55

It was impossible not to make any noise as they crawled through the ductwork, the surrounding sheet metal clanging and banging with every inch forward – and with six of them working their way through the ventilation shaft, the cacophony was almost deafening.

Riley could only hope that anybody within earshot of the ruckus would just assume that it was another group of cannibals heading out for the hunt.

If one of the former humans did try to follow them through the air vent though, she was confident that she could still twist around and fire off a few shots from her pistol, plugging up the narrow shaft with their pursuer's corpse.

But she had no idea how many bullets she had left.

That was why she had flipped on her safety lever.

She couldn't risk an accidental discharge – which was extremely likely from the way that they had been forced to crawl.

They had just enough height in the air duct to squirm forward flat on their stomachs, and very little wriggle room on either side.

She wondered how Jake was faring up ahead, knowing that he would have to take extra care not to let his scorched back scrape against the roof of the shaft.

The sound of a high-pitched whine pierced through the racket of clanging ductwork, ripping Riley from her thoughts.

Instinctively, she whipped her head around, hitting the ceiling with the back of her shoulder as she stared underneath her elbow and past her hip at the wall of darkness creeping up behind them, threatening to consume her.

The light of Clay's lantern barely reached Riley at the back of the group.

She could hardly see her own boots.

"Riley?" Hanzo whispered from up ahead, having picked up on her pause.

"I thought I heard something," she replied, squinting into the abyss.

She could feel gooseflesh budding up along her forearms.

Her thumb was tracing over the safety lever of her pistol, when the same high-pitched whine sounded again, but farther away this time.

"It's the support struts connecting the duct to the ceiling," Hanzo concluded as he continued the crawl. "I'm surprised this thing can even hold our weight."

Dakota shushed them both from farther up the shaft, reminding them that they were still neck-deep in enemy territory – or rather, above it.

An unbidden image of the air duct's support struts snapping free from the basement's ceiling flew into Riley's mind, bringing down the entire ventilation shaft and the six of them along with it, doomed to emerge one by one into the clutches of any cannibals drawn by the noise.

Biting her bottom lip, she pushed the thought aside, pouring all of her focus into keeping the silhouettes of Hanzo's shoes in front of her.

She had already lost track of the turns in the bleak network of rat tunnels, having passed by half a dozen other interconnecting air ducts branching off to the sides.

One wrong turn now – and she'd be crawling around lost in the labyrinth.

But despite the unnerving feeling of claustrophobia creeping in, she was breathing a lot easier than before. With every foot of distance that they put in between themselves and the foul fumes plaguing the laundry room, the killing floor's reek of human remains dissipated a little more, gradually giving over to the dank stale air of the ventilation shaft.

They were getting closer to the surface.

Riley found herself wondering how much time had passed since they had made their escape from the macabre tournament's final arena, and whether there was a time limit for them to reach the safe zone before they could consider themselves truly safe.

There was also Dagur's crew to contend with when they got topside again, but...

Her train of thought was derailed by another noise emanating from behind, distinctly different from both the clanging and banging of the surrounding sheet metal and the high-pitched whines of the groaning supports.

Riley strained her ears, frowning as she listened to the series of swift yet long and drawn-out squeaks, almost like the sound of a wet rag wiping down a mirror.

Whatever it was – it was getting closer.

Her eyes went wide in the darkness as she realized.

That's skin on metal.

"MOVE!!" Riley shouted, her voice reverberating around the rat tunnel.

"Fuck – are they behind us!?" Hanzo panicked as he picked up the pace, but his burst of speed only lasted for a moment before he was forced to slow down again. "Let's go, Dakota! Move your ass!!"

"I'm trying – it's my shoulder!" she grunted through the pain, unable to drag herself any faster.

The entire air duct shook dangerously as they all scrambled for safety, the clashing sheet metal thundering in their terror.

Riley's face was half a foot from the bottom of Hanzo's churning shoes, but she could hear the cannibals growing louder behind her, howling their taunts as they rapidly closed the distance.

"Did you really think we'd let you get away that easy?"

"You were dead the second you stepped into our house!"

"You crawled right into our trap – now you'll never see the sun again!"

Icy adrenaline coursing through her veins, Riley contorted herself around to take aim, holding her pistol down by her thigh as she trained her sights on the encroaching veil of darkness just beyond her boots.

She was trying to pinpoint the source of the maniacal monsters, when her ears pricked up at the sound of Jake hollering in agony somewhere up ahead.

And then the lantern's light disappeared completely.

Her heart sank to the pit of her stomach.

They were being attacked from both sides.

That fucking kid...

"Warm, tender, juicy!" the pack of primitive primates

chanted in raving unison, the crazed chorus flooding the narrow air duct. "Warm! Tender! Juicy!!"

Riley knew that Hanzo and Dakota were still in front of her.

But she was the first in line at the rear.

"You're gonna have to earn your meal!!" Riley roared over the echoes of their deranged chanting.

She flipped off the pistol's safety lever.

Aimed blindly in the pitch black.

And squeezed the trigger.

CRACK!

The deafening muzzle flash lit up the entire length of the ventilation shaft.

And in that ear-splitting instant, she locked eyes with one of the ravenous wretches, his gnarled hand outstretched, only a few inches from her feet.

The blood-curdling image burnt itself into her retina as the duct fell to darkness again.

Jerking her aim towards where his gaping jaws had been, she squeezed off three more rounds, strobing the air duct with sinister stop-motion snapshots of his death, while offering up fleeting frames of the skeletal savages swarming behind him.

Their snarls filled the harrowing emptiness as they struggled to squirm past the first cannibal's corpse.

Riley's eardrums were aching from the gunshots in the enclosed space, but she held her aim steady, intent on plugging up the hole behind her with another body.

Click.

Click. Click. Click.

Fuck.

She dropped her empty handgun, twisted around and

hauled ass.

Eyes adjusting to the gloom, her dilated pupils snapped on to something up ahead.

There was a faint glow emanating from the end of the tunnel.

But both Hanzo and Dakota were already gone.

She was alone now.

Riley commando-crawled towards the feeble source of light, arm over arm, kicking herself forward with the toes of her boots, crashing over the air duct's sheet metal while the bony brutes bayed for blood in her wake.

But just as she was inches away from reaching the light, she felt a rush of hot breath on her face, and a pair of freakishly strong hands grabbed her by the ankle, dragging her back into the darkness.

CHAPTER 56

Riley's heart leapt up into her throat as she was hauled away from the light, her gloved hands slipping along the walls and floor of the air duct's surrounding sheet metal as she scrabbled for something – anything – to hold on to.

The entire ventilation shaft rocked violently from side to side as she tried to twist and shake her leg free from the snag, but the wretched creature wouldn't let her go.

"If you don't stop struggling," the flesh-craving cannibal menaced behind her, "The first thing I'm gonna do is suck the eyeballs outta your skull!"

The swarm of savages sniggered in the darkness as they retreated back into the abyss with their prize.

Riley screwed her eyes shut – not that she could see any-thing anyway – remembering the laundry room's loathsome workbenches with handcuffs on each corner, undoubtedly where the feral fiends had feasted on all of their victims over the past year.

Not like this, she pleaded.

She had fought too hard and for too long to die a slow and horrifically agonizing death now.

But who could save her?

The rest of her group had been ambushed – they were probably already on their way to the same spine-chilling destination.

The Seabrook sisters might be willing to risk a rescue, but with Heather hobbled and Taylor too reckless for her own good, neither of them would make it very far – if at all.

I should've saved a bullet for myself, Riley began to despair.

But even if she'd had one, she would have used it against the cannibals by now.

Because she was a fighter.

She wasn't a victim.

She wasn't a quitter.

And she damn sure wasn't a piece of meat.

Riley snapped her eyelids open, glaring balefully at the black pit that had engulfed her.

She let out a guttural roar, raging against the darkness, drawing strength from the echoes of her own fury.

And in a fit of mad desperation, she slammed her elbows against the walls of the air duct, holding herself in place as she pulled her caught leg forward, before stomping down with her other boot.

She felt the ferocious strike glance off the bony brute's shoulder.

"I warned you not to struggle!" his ravenous temper boiled over. "That's it – I'll have your fucking eyes first!!"

But the threat didn't stop her.

If anything, it was yet another reason to keep going.

Riley blindly kicked out at her captor in the darkness, again and again and again, until her boot finally brushed against the fiend's forehead.

Drawing up her knee one more time, she bucked back with all of her berserk strength, her boot heel stomping on the skeletal savage's face hard enough to hear his malnourished skull *crack.*

"You fucking bitch!" he snarled in a slurred stupor.

But despite his outrage, Riley felt his grip around her leg slacken, and she shook herself free from his fingers before taking off back towards the feeble glow at the end of the tunnel.

Commando-crawling over the clanging sheet metal and out of the darkness of the void, she reached the aura of light, and in the same instant, she heard a familiar voice calling out to her.

"Riley – do you want me to come back!?" Hanzo's yell came from somewhere up ahead.

"Just keep moving!" she shouted, powering forward as she heard the swift *squeaks* of skin on metal closing in on her again.

Contorting herself around a corner in the air duct, Riley had to shut her eyes against a harsh blaze of daylight flooding the final stretch of the rat tunnel.

Almost there, she realized, blindly surging towards the exit with the cannibals bearing down on her heels.

But just as she could feel the heat of the surface warming her face again, she smashed the top of her head against something solid.

"What the *hell!?*" she cursed, squinting through her eye-lashes to see nothing but a dented wall.

There was no left turn.

No right turn.

And no way through.

She had crawled into a dead end.

"Hurry up and grab my hand!" Hanzo urged, somehow sounding like he was right beside her.

"Where are you!?" Riley shouted, desperately feeling around with her hands, only to hit out at the walls in vain.

"You have to flip over onto your back!" Sam's reedy voice floated down from above.

Banging her hips against the sides of the ductwork as she twisted around, Riley gazed up to see the shimmering outline of Hanzo's hand reaching down into a vertical shaft above her, his brass knuckles glinting in her dazzled eyesight.

"YOU'RE MINE!!" the wrath-filled wraith howled as he sped around the corner, swimming towards her with blood gushing down his forehead.

Without wasting another second, Riley latched on to Hanzo's hand, just as the flesh-starved fiend's filthy fingers thrust towards her ankle again.

Hanzo ripped Riley up out of the shaft just in time, raking her backside across the bottom rim of the vent's opening in his haste.

She yowled in pain, staggering a few steps before collapsing to one knee.

Her bleary vision swam with stars as her eyes readjusted to the blazing daylight.

"Dakota!" Riley called out to a pair of figures gathered around the blur of a body, "I need the knife!!"

The glittering blade skittered across the concrete towards her, and she snatched up the kitchen knife just as the ventilation shaft shook with her relentless pursuer rearing the back of his ugly emaciated head.

Spinning around in the vent, the feral former human

whirled towards them, his gaunt face covered in fresh crimson, the forked trail of his own blood foaming at the corners of his mouth as he moved to climb out after his prey.

Scrambling upright, Riley shoved Sam out of the way just as Hanzo clocked the cannibal across the chin with a devastating left hook, leaving him hanging halfway out of the vent in a slack-jawed daze.

"Suck on this, bitch," she snarled icily, shoving the kitchen knife into the grimy ghoul's gaping mouth before palm striking the handle, spearing the rest of the long blade through the back of his throat.

Unable to even gurgle his own death rattle, the cannibal's soon-to-be corpse collapsed, slumping back into the bottom of the shaft, his bony body blocking off the exit before the rest of the rabid wretches could spill out behind him.

CHAPTER 57

The ringing in Riley's eardrums began to subside as they rounded the side of the hotel, and she was able to pick up the sporadic gunshots and ricochets reverberating from the marketplace – the drawn-out fire fight between the Red Tigers and Radek's men still raging on.

"I thought it would've been over by now," Clay grunted as he cocked his head towards the noise. "How many bullets do you guys have?"

"More than we need," Hanzo replied through clenched teeth. "Every time our scavenger crews found a gun stash or we took in any new survivors, we added more ammo to the stockpile. We've been planning this for a long time."

Both men were straining underneath the weight of Jake's body hanging limp in between them, his slumped arms draped over their shoulders as his shoes dragged along the concrete.

Twisting around in the final stretch of the air duct had been his downfall – tearing and bursting the blisters of his burnt back in his rush to escape.

They had found him collapsed and unconscious at the foot of the exit.

He was still breathing, but his brain had switched itself off to break free from the agony.

Hanzo and Clay paused beside the debris-strewn entry ramp that led down into the hotel's nightmarish underground parking garage, taking a moment to readjust their grips on Jake's arms, since they couldn't hold him up by the torso without doing any more damage.

"How far is it to the safe zone?" Riley wondered, her voice thick and soft and heavy in her own ears, still impaired from the gunshots within the confines of the air duct.

"Keep it down!" Dakota hissed, quickly clapping a hand over Riley's mouth. "Dagur's crew might be hanging around back here, trying to find another way into the Tiger's Den."

"Don't tell me there was another exit we could've taken," Clay fumed at the possibility.

"There isn't," Dakota answered as she peered around the side of the building, searching for any signs of Radek's barbarian brutes. "But they don't know that."

"I can check for you guys – they're not looking for me," Sam volunteered himself, the waiflike child tottering out from behind cover before anybody could stop him.

He swept his wide-eyed gaze across the front of the Jade Mantis Hotel, shaking his head, before stealing across the laneway towards the rear wall of the plaza, edging slowly over to the corner to scout the path ahead.

Looking back over his shoulder, he gave them the all-clear.

Creeping forward carefully, Riley checked the front of the hotel for herself, before sidling up beside Sam to stare around the corner.

The alley was a straight shot towards The Strip, with high concrete walls bordering both sides of the laneway.

A green tarp had been laid out in the middle of the six-lane boulevard, its edges stirring lazily in the late afternoon breeze, marking the finish line of the tournament.

Dagur's men in the marketplace wouldn't even see the four escapees coming until they were already standing in the safe zone.

"This is as far as I can go," Clay declared, clucking his tongue with a sidelong glance at Jake, before extracting himself from the burden of his body. "If they catch me helping you guys out – I'll be the first in line for the next tournament."

"Don't worry," Hanzo began, grunting as he shouldered the additional weight, "After we're done with Radek and Miranda, there won't be another tournament ever again."

"Make sure you take Sam with you," Riley urged Clay as she picked up the slack, draping Jake's free arm around her shoulders. She looked down at the half-starved urchin, the child a piteous sight now that they were in the light of day. "I was wrong about you, kid. You really pulled through for us. Look for a woman named Barbara, Heather or Taylor, and tell them Riley sent you. They'll get you something to eat, and we'll see you in a little while to help you find your mom."

Sam nodded meekly, salivating at the thought of finally eating some real food again.

"I'll cover his meals," Clay promised as he led the boy away. "Good luck, guys."

"Alright, let's do this," Dakota exhaled as she ventured down the narrow laneway.

Riley and Hanzo followed her lead, dragging Jake in between them.

Despite their salvation lying less than a hundred yards away, Riley began to feel cold fingers of dread tracing up her spine, and she glanced back over her shoulder to make sure that they weren't being followed.

With her pistol and Dakota's knife lost in the air duct, and Jake's meat mallet unaccounted for, the only weapon that they had left was Hanzo's brass knuckles.

Dakota was wounded.

Jake was unconscious.

And after the day they'd just had, they were all on the verge of breaking point.

Riley could only hope that there were no more hidden surprises along the way.

CHAPTER 58

"I can't believe that crazy son of a bitch actually made it," Hanzo whispered in the alley, staring at something up ahead.

Riley frowned for a moment, before the object of his attention came into view.

Foley was sitting with his back towards them, perched on the corner of a low brick wall near the mouth of the laneway, soaking up the afternoon sun as he savored yet another victory in the deadly arenas.

He was pawing at a fresh bandage around his arm, when his ears pricked up at the scrape of their footsteps behind him, and he spun around, his gray eyes lighting up in surprise to see the survivors of the tournament's escape challenge.

Quickly averting his gaze though, as if he hadn't seen them at all, Foley stared off to the side as he furtively dropped one hand to his knee, subtly beckoning them closer with his fingers.

Based on his body language, Riley knew that somebody else was prowling the boulevard, guarding the green tarp that marked the safe zone.

But there was no point in turning back now.

This was their best chance to reach the canvas and clear the target on their backs.

Exchanging a sidelong nod with Hanzo, Riley slid out from underneath Jake's limp arm, edging along the concrete wall towards the corner, with Dakota shadowing her footsteps.

The closer they came to the canvas though, the harder it was for Riley to resist the urge to burst into a headlong sprint, ducking under any flying bullets as she dove onto the green tarp.

But in order to do that, she would have to leave her friends behind.

And she wasn't going to abandon them now.

They were only a few yards away from the sidewalk, when Foley's fingers suddenly stretched out, signaling for them to *stop!*

Heavy boots scuffed the pavement as the hidden sentry began patrolling the area.

Riley flexed her gloved fingers as the footsteps grew louder, approaching the laneway.

"What a day, huh?" Foley tried to distract the guard. "Are you guys gonna be hanging around out here all night?"

"Until The Valkyrie says otherwise," the familiar brassy growl of Kuba sounded from around the corner.

"Seems a bit pointless to me," Foley shrugged with a feigned yawn, before slowly curling one finger towards the street. "I mean, you already know where the last contenders are hiding. You should just storm into that bar and get it over with already."

Riley glanced back over her shoulder at the others.

She and Dakota could sneak along the wall stealthily enough.

But they wouldn't be able to stop Jake's shoes from dragging along the ground.

Not without hauling him out of the alley by his hands and feet, putting them all at risk.

"You're so invincible in those arenas – why don't you do it for us?" Kuba dared Foley, his tone dripping with sarcasm. "No? Little *puta* can't dodge bullets, huh? Shut the fuck up."

Ignoring Foley's gesture to keep going, Riley held up her hand with a plan of her own.

As quietly as she could, she lowered herself to the ground, coiling into a sprinter's pose, intent on catching Kuba by surprise.

She drew three galvanizing breaths, her gloved fingertips barely touching the concrete as cold adrenaline flooded her body.

"Nice try, bitch!" Kuba barked as he suddenly leapt out from behind the wall, jerking up the barrel of his shotgun. "Looks like your luck ran out this time."

Riley froze.

He was holding her at point blank range.

If she charged him now, all she would be bolting towards was a gaping hole in her chest.

And if she sprang sideways, then Dakota would be next in line for the blast of buckshot.

Riley flexed the slender muscles of her jaw.

There was no good option no matter what she chose.

Forcing herself against the tension of her muscles, she rocked back on her heels and slowly rose to her feet, holding up her hands in surrender.

"Hey, Aksel!" Kuba called over his shoulder, his scarred face grinning back at Riley, refusing to take his eyes off the prize. "Get word back to The Valkyrie. Tell her the tournament's officially over!"

BADOOM!!

The shotgun's blast thundered into the alley.

Riley's heart stopped as time slowed down to a standstill.

Did he just fucking shoot me!?

She staggered backwards in slow motion, instinctively shielding her face, sacrificing her forearms to be shredded in the shower of lead pellets, clinging to the thin hope that the projectiles would slow down before they hit her skull.

But if the shotgun's barrel had been aiming at her chest, then there was nothing to stop the buckshot from rocketing right through her rib cage.

Hanging for an eternity in the dreadful moment, Riley braced herself for the searing pain.

"RUN!!" Foley roared, breaking through her petrified pause.

Time sped up again as Dakota shouldered past, hauling Jake in between her and Hanzo.

Frowning with confused relief, Riley dropped her arms to see Foley wrestling with Kuba for control of the shotgun.

"Aksel, get your ass over here!!" Kuba bellowed in the struggle, before rearing back his neck to hit Foley with a brutal headbutt.

Foley's skull snapped backwards, his eyes blinking up at the sky in surprise.

Riley surged forward then, ramming her shoulder into the brawny Latino at full speed, throwing him off balance.

Not wasting a moment, she seized hold of the shotgun with both hands, using the barrel for leverage as she thrust her knee up into his groin, making him dry heave in anguish.

Cracks of gunfire sounded from farther down the boulevard as Aksel came running.

"Let's go, Riley!!" Dakota shouted from the green canvas.

Shoving Kuba reeling into the street, Riley ducked her head down into her chest and sprinted towards the safe zone, the shotgun clattering to the sidewalk in her wake as Aksel's lead hornets ripped through the air.

Heart hammering in her eardrums with every step, Riley doubled over and dove for the canvas, skidding across the green tarp until she slid to a stop at her friends' feet.

"Hey, she made it – we all made it!" Hanzo yelled, pivoting himself into the path of the pistol's barrel as Aksel came rushing towards them.

"Like I give a shit," the rangy balding man panted balefully as he stopped to train his sights on them. "We lost some good people after that little stunt you pulled," he pointedly cocked an ear towards the occasional rifle report resounding from the marketplace. His eyes lit up with a spiteful grin, "Now, whether your bodies are found on or off the canvas, who else is gonna know that you actually made it?"

Riley glanced around.

The grandstands overlooking the three arenas were empty now, the crowd having disappeared after the chaos of the final challenge.

Miranda was nowhere to be seen either.

If Aksel decided to kill all five of the tournament's winners, there would be no witnesses.

"They're in the safe zone now," Foley backed them up from the sidewalk, leveling Kuba's shotgun at Aksel. "They're the first ones to ever pass the escape challenge. You can take it from me – both Radek and The Valkyrie are gonna be fucking furious if you pull that trigger one more time."

Riley clambered to her feet, breathing hard.

Dakota grunted in pain as she slipped Jake's arm from around her wounded shoulder, and Hanzo laid him down gently on the canvas.

All eyes were on Aksel now.

"Put that fucking gun down," the guard menaced, turning his pistol on Foley instead.

"Sure thing," Foley shrugged his indifference, turning the shotgun's barrel aside before cocking the breech and ejecting the shells across the sidewalk. A mocking smile played at the corners of his mouth as he tossed the empty firearm at Kuba. "Little *puta* can have his gun back now."

But Kuba barely even registered the taunt.

He was curled up in the fetal position, rolling from side to side in the street, still groaning as he gingerly held his smashed groin.

Riley stifled a smirk.

She had gotten him good.

But her smile dropped the instant Aksel pointed his pistol at her again.

"You still haven't answered my quest—"

"Valkyrie here," Miranda cut him off, her voice crackling over a walkie clipped to his belt. "Say that again – you caught the runaways?"

Aksel soured at the interruption, glowering at the four gathered on the canvas.

He rattled his pistol at them, showing them just how close they were to certain death, before lowering the gun with a heavy sigh, deciding that he would rather not risk Miranda's wrath, especially not after the torture he had seen the sadistic woman inflicting on Jake.

"I have them here, Valkyrie," Aksel reported as he thumbed the switch on his walkie, his gaze tracing over Jake's burnt back. "They made it to the end. Do I just let them go?"

Riley glanced sidelong at the others with a reserved sense of relief, wondering if they would be allowed to walk away so easily.

"No," Miranda snapped back over the radio, her voice as cold and sharp as a blade of ice. "Bring them to me."

CHAPTER 59

The elevator ride up to the top floor of the Valhalla Hotel was stifling to say the least.

Walking the length of The Strip with Jake's limp body slumped in between them had taken its toll on Riley, Hanzo and Foley. They had kept Dakota out of the rotation due to her wounded shoulder, but after the day they'd just had, they were all running on fumes now.

Despite her aching muscles though, Riley's physical fatigue wasn't at the forefront of her mind.

Her primary concern was the cold barrel of Kuba's shotgun shoved squarely in the center of her spine.

The puffy-eyed man hadn't uttered a single word since the end of his excruciating throes on the asphalt outside the plaza, but it seemed to Riley that he was holding somewhat of a grudge.

DING!

The elevator doors opened, leading out into a carpeted hallway illuminated by the foreign glow of ceiling lights.

Aksel and Kuba marched them out into the corridor, the elevator sliding shut in their wake as they approached the security checkpoint occupying the middle of the hallway.

"The Valkyrie's been expecting you," one of the guards spoke through a tinny speaker. "Weapons, please."

"Fuck off," Aksel sneered at the request. "Do you really expect us to walk this mob in there without our guns?"

"That's the only way you're getting in," the man behind the reinforced window replied. "Leave the winners with us if you want – you can go back downstairs. We'll just tell Radek that you were too pussy to walk them in yourselves."

Growling his resentment, Kuba shoved Riley aside, before hobbling forward to drop his shotgun into the counter's security tray.

"You've grown some balls since yesterday," Aksel grunted as he placed his pistol inside.

The woman behind the counter averted her gaze as she buzzed them through, and a door without a handle popped open beside the booth, allowing them access to the other half of the hallway.

Dakota shot a sidelong glance at Riley as they passed through the checkpoint, her head subtly jerking back towards the pair of disarmed men.

Foley caught the movement as he helped Hanzo carry Jake.

"Takes away from the immersive experience," he winked back with half an explanation. "They didn't have guns back then."

"What the hell does that mean?" Hanzo cocked an eyebrow in confusion.

"You'll see," Riley knew as they reached the door at the end of the hallway.

She turned the handle open and threw the door out wide, taking the lead as the others shuffled in through the entrance.

Dakota and Hanzo stared around like they had just stepped into a portal to another era.

The Valhalla Hotel's penthouse suite had been remodeled into a large medieval hall. Any trace of modern interior architecture had been hidden behind rough-hewn layers of recycled timber. Thick animal furs sprawled across the floorboards, painted wooden shields lined the walls, and a collection of Scandinavian flags hung from the rafters of an artificial cathedral ceiling.

And despite the oppressive heat blanketing the big room, a shallow fire pit burned brightly in the center of the floor. The bonfire cast its hellish hue over a large dining table, flanked by sideboards and weapon racks brimming with gleaming blades and bludgeons, completing the Viking-themed decor.

Riley had already seen it all, but her stare was similarly spellbound by another sight – one that she had never expected to see.

Laid out across the dining table was a mouth-watering feast.

But it wasn't the canned soup, jerky and peanuts that she had grown accustomed to.

There were succulent char-grilled cuts of steak, chunks of roast pumpkin, scalloped potatoes, buttered mushrooms, herbed flatbread, and wedges of cheese and boiled eggs nestled in between rich red tomatoes and crisp leafy greens.

The sound of her own stomach rumbling snapped Riley out of her salivating stasis, and she wiped her mouth with the back of her hand.

She had been running on pure adrenaline for so long, she hadn't even realized how hungry she was until just now – the last meal that she had eaten was yesterday's lunch with

Heather, Barbara and Kentaro.

"Congratulations," Miranda's impassive voice cut through the room's enticing atmosphere like a knife, the sharp-faced woman sweeping past a curtain drawn over the bedroom's doorway. Her callous eyes narrowed with a hint of contempt as she recognized Riley standing among the tournament's winners. She tilted her head in reluctant civility, "Your performance today has earned each of you a place in Valhalla. Our cooks have prepared a feast in your honor. Join me, in celebration of your victory."

Riley followed her gaze towards the dining table, but her legs wavered at the invitation.

This has to be a trick, she suspected, in spite of the hearty feast's wafting aromas beckoning her closer.

"You heard The Valkyrie – move!" Aksel growled behind them, shoving Dakota forward.

The lithe woman staggered a few steps before catching her balance, and she whirled around to face him.

"Touch me again, and I'll cut your fucking throat," Dakota warned, glaring dauntlessly up at the man's tattooed tear streaks running down both cheeks. Her stare lingered on him until he blinked, and she glanced around the room. "Where's Radek?"

"He'll join us when he's ready," Miranda replied tersely, glancing back over her shoulder through the bedroom's partially-transparent curtain before walking towards the head of the table. Aksel and Kuba moved to join her, but she froze them in place with an icy glare.

Riley craned her neck, hoping to catch a glimpse of Radek in the bedroom – if he was indeed still alive – but she couldn't see anything beyond the doorway's veil.

"Come on, let's set Jake down over here," Hanzo jerked his head towards one of the animal furs stretched out across the floor.

Miranda's gaze traced over Jake's second-degree burns, scornfully smirking at her handiwork as Hanzo and Foley laid him down gently.

Approaching the feast with caution, Riley joined her friends as they gathered around the foot of the table, succumbing to the temptation of a full stomach, and the comfort of a steak knife in her hand.

"Where'd all this food come from?" Riley wondered as she followed Foley's lead, loading up her wooden plate with anything that he reached for first.

He snorted as he realized that she was using him as a guinea pig, but he nodded his understanding as he passed her the potatoes, being the only one among them who had eaten a meal in the penthouse and survived.

"People will trade anything for fuel," Miranda answered in between small mouthfuls, a cold smile playing at her lips. "Their skills. Their morals. Their resources. And occasionally, food. We have an extensive network of farming communities that rely on our diesel deliveries to keep their machinery running. And in return, they keep us fed."

"Meanwhile, the rest of us make do with whatever we can find," Dakota grumbled bitterly as she stared down at her plate, robbed of her appetite as she thought of all the other people outside the Valhalla forced to subsist on wild lizards and snakes.

"Perks of power, I guess," Hanzo supposed around a mouthful of mushrooms. He scarfed it down before lowering his voice, leaning across the table towards Dakota, "This might be the last decent meal we ever have. Better enjoy it while we can."

"You're winners of the tournament," Foley reminded them as Dakota picked up her fork. "You can eat like this whenever you want."

"Is that true?" Riley looked to Miranda for confirmation.

"Every word," she replied, studying them from the other end of the table. "Valhalla is your home now. And our people never go hungry."

Riley gave a small snort at the contradiction as she glanced over at Aksel and Kuba standing by the door.

They sure seemed hungry to her.

"What about everybody else?" Dakota asked, her gaze going over to Jake as he lay twitching in his sleep. "Some of us have family and friends out there."

"They're welcome to join us too," Miranda shrugged with an insincere tone of generosity. "Provided that they can prove themselves in one of the tournaments, of course," she imposed the costly condition, before setting aside her cutlery. "I'm sure you can understand that we can't just let everybody in here, otherwise we'd be stretched thin feeding a horde of useless mouths. But we're always on the lookout for strong and resourceful people like yourselves to bolster our ranks."

"Hold on – you want us to join you?" Hanzo screwed up his face at the idea, even as flecks of boiled egg fell from his lips. "I thought this was just a free meal."

"It's not that bad around here," Foley chimed in as he leaned back in his chair. "I mean, after a while, it all gets a bit boring, that's why you see me in the tournaments all the time. But apart from a belly full of good food, you get hot showers, housekeeping on demand, movie nights, access to the gym... you can even have a new name and identity if you want. A couple of months in here, and all the people out there you used to know won't even recognize you anymore."

Riley had heard enough.

She clenched her steak knife, locking eyes with Dakota as Hanzo finished his mouthful.

Between the three of them, they could take out Aksel, Kuba and Miranda with ease, especially since the guards had disarmed themselves of any proper weapons on their way in.

Foley would just have to catch on and realize that the hotel was about to get a whole lot less boring.

But before any of them could make a move, Foley kicked back his chair, abruptly climbing out of his seat.

"You know, people can change a lot over the course of a few months," he continued as he carried his wooden plate up the length of the dining table, picking at some of the untouched dishes. "For me, I shaved off most of my beard... grew my hair out... giving up the bottle was a big one. So by the time I started joining the tournaments, nobody even knew who I was. And after my first win, I told everybody that they could call me by my last name – Foley. Drake Foley." He shot them all a wink, "But you can call me Radek."

CHAPTER 60

"What the fuck!?" Hanzo exclaimed as he turned his head between Riley and Dakota, all three of them caught by surprise. "How the hell did we miss that?"

"I've only ever seen Radek from a distance," Dakota muttered, staring down at the table in disbelief as she searched her memories for a better explanation.

"If you're in charge, why would you even wanna join those tournaments?" Riley stared along the length of the dining table at the man formerly known as Foley. "I mean, you were out there in the arenas risking your life with the rest of us. It doesn't make any sense."

"I already told you – it gets boring around here after a while," Radek shrugged, savoring the shock on their faces. He drew a necklace from under his shirt, revealing an upside down hammer pendant identical to those worn by Aksel and Kuba, and all of his other followers. "Besides, what's the point of having all this power if you can't have any fun?"

With that, he grabbed Miranda by the throat and hauled her up out of her seat, throttling the woman with one hand while she held up a steak knife to his windpipe, the blade's serrated edge drawing a trickle of blood through the stubble of his beard.

They stared at each other with bloodlust blazing in their bestial eyes before Radek released her with a grin, taking his seat at the head of the table while Miranda caught her breath, massaging her raw throat as she ogled at him with depraved desire.

"I just wanna apologize for pointing my gun at you earlier, sir," Aksel was the first to break the uneasy silence in the room, bowing his head beside the door. "I didn't know."

Kuba nodded in dumbfounded agreement with his gaze downcast, as if he was searching for an apology of his own written somewhere on the floorboards.

"You were just doing your jobs," Radek dismissed their justifiable ignorance with a wave of his hand, before turning to Miranda, "But have you done yours?"

She nodded curtly, drawing the walkie clipped to the belt on her hip.

"Send them in," Miranda ordered as she thumbed the switch.

Riley cocked an eyebrow at the command, and she whipped her head around as the penthouse's door swung open.

"Let go of me, you dumb bitch, I can walk myself in," Taylor Seabrook was the first to enter the room with her hands cuffed behind her back. Her bruised face lit up the instant she locked eyes with Riley, "You're alive! Yes!! We couldn't stick around to watch until the end – those fuckers came after us as soon as the bullets started flying in the plaza."

Riley clenched her steak knife, when a shrill shriek rang out through the room.

"Jake!? Jake!!" Mrs Roscoe screamed, rushing towards her

son's body on the floor, collapsing by his side to lament over his scorched back.

"Ugh, Mom?" he finally stirred as her wails softened into confused and horrified whimpers. "What's going on?"

His pupils dilated in terror at the sight of the blazing bonfire in the center of the room, and he scrambled backwards to the nearest corner on traumatized instinct.

"I told you not to stay out too late," Mrs Roscoe bowed her head beside the animal fur that Jake had been lying on, too weak to struggle to her feet and go after him with her hands shackled behind her back. "You should've been home... You should've been home..." she sobbed, tears rolling down the fragile woman's cheeks. "My boy... My beautiful baby boy... Oh, Tommy..."

"Tommy's gone now, Mom – it's me, Jake," he fought back tears of his own as he gazed around the room, gathering his bearings. "What the hell is she doing up here?"

"It's my fault," Barbara Greene shouldered the burden of responsibility as she lingered beside the doorway. "I spotted her wandering up the boulevard just as the chaos broke out, and I couldn't leave her to get lost in the crowd."

Riley's heart panged with pity as she remembered that Mrs Roscoe suffered from severe memory loss due to her condition, but she couldn't imagine which fate would be worse – roaming the streets lost and alone, or being handcuffed and surrounded in a room full of strangers.

"That's all of the pris–" one of the checkpoint guards stopped mid-sentence as the hallway's security door buzzed open behind her. "Scratch that. Looks like we have a few more."

She bowed her head and backed out of the room as Dagur

marched through the entrance with four more captives in tow.

"Wow, this place is a shithole," Heather Seabrook laughed aloud the moment she limped into the Viking-themed abode. Her striking green gaze flicked between Taylor and Riley for a moment, flecked with fleeting fear, before hardening again to settle on Radek sitting at the head of the dining table. "You've got all this power, and no air-con," she glanced pointedly at the bonfire in the center of the room despite the sweltering heat. "Here I was, thinking you guys were a bunch of sadistic psychos – now I see that you're all just fucking stupid."

Radek grinned at the accusation, and Kuba kicked out the back of her knee.

With her hands cuffed behind her back, all Heather could do was fall face first onto the floor to keep her bad leg from flaring up again.

"You cocksucker!!" Taylor spat angrily at Kuba, before Aksel threw the impetuous girl down beside her sister.

"I should've known the lauded champion was you all along, Radek," Kentaro recognized the man as soon as he stepped into the room, his hands similarly shackled behind his back, but still walking with all the grace of a distinguished Oriental gentleman swelled with a sense of pride. "I never cared to watch any of your twisted tournaments, but there's no mistaking the malevolence hiding behind your treacherous eyes."

"Wait, isn't that Foley?" Jake frowned with belated confusion, still catching up.

"You know something, Kentaro?" Radek ignored the puzzled stares as he rose to his feet. "Out of all the dinosaurs who were in charge of this city before I did what had to be done – you were always my favorite. You made compromise

387

after compromise to keep the peace until I was sure you were broken. That's why I let you and your people live for so long. After all, somebody had to keep the workforce from killing each other. But I thought we would've had an understanding by this point. Why ruin a good thing now?"

"Is it too much for an old man to want revenge?" Kentaro kept his composure, as if he was reeling off a speech that he had prepared for this very moment. "I've been planning your death from the day of your massacre. Slaughtering everybody who placed their trust in you, and then calling yourself leader... I thought it only right to convince you to place your trust in me in turn. And like a fish to the hook, you mistook my pacifism for submission. But every compromise I made was a maneuver, positioning all of my people in place while you indulged in the illusion of peace. Even now, you think you have the upper hand over me – but perhaps all of this has been a ploy to see your face one last time before you die."

"Perhaps," Radek laughed at the idea, before walking over to one of the weapon racks. "Or perhaps you should get on the fucking floor."

"Eating with the enemy now, huh?" Batu's face appeared in the doorway next as Kentaro was kicked to his knees, the rigid bodyguard souring at the sight of Dakota and Hanzo still sitting at the feast-laden dining table.

"We were just waiting for the right opp–"

"Why isn't he wearing handcuffs?" Dakota cut across Hanzo's attempt at an explanation, zeroing in on Clay's unbound hands as he entered behind Batu.

"This one's our latest recruit," Dagur reported with a rumble, the big silverback gorilla clutching Clay's shoulder as he shut the door behind them. "He showed us a hidden entrance into the bar. It took some work clearing a path into the garage behind the building, and most of my men in the raid, but these two are the last ones left."

He glanced pointedly at Kentaro and Batu, stark shadows of the Red Tigers' resistance.

"Clay, you sold us out, you piece of shit," Riley seethed, narrowing her eyes at the back-stabbing bounty hunter. "You wouldn't have lasted for a fucking minute in that hotel's basement without us."

"Yeah, well, maybe I didn't wanna end up living like those animals," Clay argued, still scarred after their encounter with the cannibals. He turned his gaze between Barbara and Jake. "You guys know how hard it is to find new people nowadays. And with Lincoln dead and Jake one of the new champions, it's gonna get a whole lot harder now. Without that bounty money rolling in like it used to, how long's it gonna be before I have to start selling my soul for scraps? Fuck that. I'd rather eat with the big dogs up here. Just look at the food on that table and tell me that you wouldn't have done the exact same thing."

"There goes your *hero status*," Heather snorted at him over her shoulder, remembering their conversation in the ransacked Italian restaurant. "Let's not forget who was siphoning diesel outta all those vehicles at the impound lot last night."

"Oh, fuck off," Clay sneered at her attempt to discredit him in front of his new friends. "Don't pretend like you weren't right there with me."

"Stealing diesel is an offense punishable by death," Miranda smirked as their latest recruit's face turned ashen.

"Wait, what? No!" Clay protested, staring sidelong at Dagur. "I'm one of you guys now. You said. We had a deal!"

But with a one-armed shove, the stone-hearted hulking henchman sent Clay reeling into Aksel and Kuba, who threw him to the floor in turn.

Both Jake and Barbara averted their gazes as the double-dealing snake's pleas for mercy fell on deaf ears.

"That's what you get, dickhead," Hanzo sniggered, the whole room nodding in agreement.

"ENOUGH!!" Radek barked, having endured all of their taunts and petty squabbles for long enough. Everybody fell silent as he drew a maul from one of the weapon racks, testing the weight of the weapon's bulky business end. "You, you, and you," he singled out Batu, Barbara and Mrs Roscoe, "On your knees with the others."

Both Batu and Barbara fell to the floor on either side of Kentaro without an argument, already resigned to their fate.

"Wait – what's my mom got to do with any of this!?" Jake scrambled to his feet as Aksel hauled the fragile woman towards the kneeling Seabrook sisters.

"You can thank Kentaro for this," Radek replied cryptically as he hefted his sledgehammer's gigantic head over one shoulder like a reaper's scythe. He cast his gaze over Riley, Dakota, Hanzo and Jake, before beckoning Clay to his feet, earning Miranda's displeasure. "I intend on sparing all of you, but after what happened today in the plaza, I'm finding it hard to place my trust in new people. So you're gonna have to prove yourselves first."

"Haven't we already done that?" Riley snarled, pointedly glancing around at the other winners of the tournament. "Don't tell me there's another fucking challenge."

"You all know who I am now," the man formerly known as Foley shrugged. "Not many do. And I'd like to keep it that way. That's why I can't let any of you leave this room without being sure of your intentions. So I'm offering you a choice. You can all die here – or you can live, and join me."

"And what do we have to do?" Hanzo crossed his arms skeptically, waiting for the catch.

"I want you to pledge your loyalty to me – and I want it in blood," Radek swept his hand towards Mrs Roscoe, Heather, Taylor, Barbara, Kentaro and Batu. "Each of you must take a life to save yours. Kill them. Or die with them."

"But there's six prisoners, and only five of us," Clay clarified the numbers as he gladly distanced himself from the condemned. "If we only have to kill one each to save ourselves, what happens to the other one?"

"What *other one?*" Radek asked, feigning surprise before lunging towards the line of captives, lifting his massive maul to deal a devastating death blow.

CHAPTER 61

Batu's dead gaze stared into the flickering flames of the blazing bonfire burning in the center of the room, his eyes glassing over into a thousand-yard stare.

The rough-hewn walls of the Viking-themed penthouse reverberated with Mrs Roscoe's terrified screams at the sight of blood.

Heather and Taylor winced at the sound of the woman's ear-piercing shrieks, but they didn't turn away from the body, both sisters already numb to such displays of brutality.

Stifling a gag, Barbara screwed her eyes shut, edging sideways on her knees away from the corpse as the contents of Kentaro's cracked skull oozed forth across the floorboards, chunks of the man's shattered bone and brain matter spilling out into a sickening soup.

Riley, Dakota and Hanzo were on their feet in a flash, their chairs crashing to the floor behind them as they snatched up their steak knives.

"Bold, but stupid," Radek warned as he whirled around to face them, having anticipated their reaction.

Riley wavered for a moment.

She had seen how dangerous the man was with a sledge-hammer during the tournament.

The steak knife shook slightly in her hand as she calculated the distance from her blade to Radek's neck.

She had a lot of ground to cover, and every inch of his maul's swinging range was an invitation towards death.

Dakota and Hanzo were standing in a similar stasis, sizing up the others in the room.

Aksel, Kuba and Miranda would be easy enough to handle, but Dagur – even unarmed – was still a significant threat, the big muscle-bound monster just itching for an opportunity to put his giant paws to work.

"I just did you all a favor," Radek took their hesitation as submission. "What could Kentaro have possibly offered anybody besides using you all to fulfill an old man's revenge?"

"No more fucking tournaments, for a start," Hanzo growled in contempt.

"Kentaro was our leader," Dakota hissed through gritted teeth as her gaze filled with the sight of the man's body. "All he wanted to do was keep everybody else safe and fed."

"But I already do that – even for the people outside these walls," Radek twirled the handle of his maul, globs of gore sliding off the hammer's head. "When's the last time you've been attacked out on the street? I bet you can't even remember. That's because any criminals are sent straight to the tournaments. The construction and removal of the arenas provides jobs for people to get paid for their labor. Whatever they choose to spend their money on is up to them, but I'm pretty sure there's food in that marketplace you've got out there. See? Safe and fed." He turned his stare from Dakota to Hanzo, "You wanna get rid of those tournaments? Then you can say goodbye to your little community's economy, and it won't be long before everybody's back to stealing and killing without consequences."

"Not if we kill you first," Riley countered, remembering that the cannibals in the Jade Mantis Hotel had been normal people once too, back before they had been captured and stripped of everything that they had owned. "Nobody would have a reason to steal and kill if you just fucking fed them."

"You really haven't thought this through, have you?" Miranda regarded the three of them with her smug smile. "All the food you see in this room came from *our* network of suppliers. We reach them using *our* routes, *our* guns, *our* vehicles, and we trade with *our* diesel. You remove *us* from the equation, and this entire ecosystem collapses, followed by yours."

Riley felt her resolve beginning to fade as the realization settled in.

Radek and his people were holding all of the cards.

Putting an end to his tyranny meant chopping off the hand that was feeding them.

They couldn't have one without the other.

Maybe Kentaro had thought of another way to sustain the colony's community without the overbearing boot on all of their necks, but whatever his grand plan was had just been spilled all over the floor.

"It is what it is," Radek shrugged as they all came to grips with the hard truth. "You think we're horrible people – but in reality, we're just taking care of our own." He extracted nods of agreement from Dagur, Aksel and Kuba before continuing, "It's no different to any time throughout history when there wasn't enough to go around for everybody. *Us against them*, and only the strong survive. But when everybody's just out for themselves, nobody wins in the long term. I saw this city starting to fall apart over a lack of resources, and I knew exactly what people needed to regain some form of civilization again. It's the only structure that makes any sense in this society full of savages – the Viking way of life. Warriors can eat like kings. Merchants are free to trade their way up. And anybody who wants to be a servant can make do with the scraps. Whoever you wanna be is up to you."

"Why not just let us all go?" Heather spoke up from the row of kneeling prisoners. "We never asked to be here. And I'm pretty sure we're not the only ones. You could kick all of us out right now, and you'd still be the king of your little Viking paradise or whatever this fucking hotel's called.

"Because people are a resource too," Miranda answered, casting her scornful stare over the remaining captives like they were nothing more than commodities. "Workers, soldiers, entertainment, examples to keep everybody else in line, and in your case, subjects to be used in testing the loyalty of our latest rec–"

A metallic *clink* cut her off.

All eyes in the room turned to Jake, who had been using their distraction in the conversation to quietly sneak over to one of the weapon racks, plucking out a sword.

"I'm not your fucking soldier," he spat with iron in his voice.

"We'll see about that," Radek held up a pragmatic hand to steady his men. "Put that sword back though – you used a halberd in the arena." He turned to Riley, Dakota and Hanzo next, nodding at each in turn, "Axe, shield, mace. It's time for all of you to make a decision. You can sever your ties to

395

the past and join me, and live like royalty, or you can take a gamble."

Try to kill him and all of his people without dying, Riley silently filled in the blanks.

She carried her steak knife over to the nearest weapon rack, not discarding the blade until she had a hatchet in her hands.

Testing the weight of the axe, Riley knew that even if they succeeded in killing Radek and his men, she would still be sentencing everybody else in the city to a slow death.

Eventually, they'd run out of fuel.

Eventually, they'd run out of things to eat.

Eventually, they'd all turn on each other.

She flexed the slender muscles of her jaw as she processed the real choice.

Kill her friends, or risk her life only to ultimately starve to death with them.

CHAPTER 62

"Should we really be giving them weapons?" Aksel shifted his weight as he watched Riley, Jake, Hanzo and Dakota approach the row of captives with a hatchet, a halberd, a mace, and a painted shield with a sharp spike protruding from the center.

"I'd rather see if they're loyal now, than find out a year later," Radek answered, pointedly glancing down at Kentaro's corpse. Holding his sledgehammer at the ready, he raised his eyebrows at the rangy guard, "What's the matter – you scared?"

Aksel scoffed and shook his head at the thought, but his hand still went to his holster, reaching for the pistol that was no longer there.

Riley stood staring down at Batu, Barbara, Taylor, Heather and Mrs Roscoe.

There was no way that she was going to turn her axe's blade on her friends.

For all she knew, this was just the first round of Radek's twisted loyalty test.

But she was still drawing blanks on coming up with a plan to get them out of it.

You can't expect to save everyone, Riley, Heather's words echoed in her thoughts, even as the fiery redhead was gazing up at her. *Sometimes, we've gotta save ourselves.*

"I wasn't in the tournament," Clay reminded them all as he lingered beside one of the weapon racks. "What should I choose?"

"Pick whatever you want," Radek didn't even bother to look over his shoulder, his gray eyes laser-focused on Riley and the others. "Just make a decision, before I change my mind about giving you a choice."

Quickly plucking a spear from the rack, the treacherous bounty hunter hurried over to the line of prisoners marked for execution, stopping in front of Heather.

"I figured you'd pick me," she stared up at him with a cynical smile. "But are you sure you wouldn't feel more comfortable with stabbing me in the back instead?"

"Ha!" Taylor laughed aloud, scowling beside her sister before she spelled it out for him, "She means you're a fucking traitor."

"Hanzo," Batu called him over from the other end of the line, shadows shrouding the grave-faced man's eyes despite his thousand-yard stare gazing into the blazing bonfire's flames. "You and your friends still have a chance to survive. But the rest of us are dead either way. Do me a favor and make it quick."

"You wouldn't mind if I have a death stick first to help see me off?" Barbara gazed across the room at Miranda, who simply smirked back without an answer.

Not waiting for permission, Dakota dropped her shield and knelt beside the gravelly-voiced woman, finding the box in her breast pocket before lighting up a cigarette for her.

"Thanks, honey," Barbara winked back at her with a puff of smoke. She took a grim glance at Kentaro's body lying beside her, before looking up at the dining table, "I hope it spoils the food."

Riley locked eyes with Jake.

There were only two left.

Taylor and Mrs Roscoe.

"Pick one, bitch," Kuba menaced, still missing the brass in his voice as he stalked behind the Seabrook sisters to stare back at Riley. Drawing her stolen combat knife from his belt, his scarred face cracked into a grin, "Or I'm gonna enjoy slicing you up from slit to scalp."

Riley narrowed her eyes at him as she clenched the handle of her hatchet.

She stepped forward.

"What the fuck, Riley!?" Taylor bristled the moment she was chosen.

Riley flicked her on the forehead, silently hoping that the girl would remember what they had discussed on their first night outside the marketplace.

Protect your face.

But Taylor simply scowled back up at her with a blank stare of betrayal.

Fuck.

"Look, I get it," Heather's gaze turned downcast with a dismal twist of her lips. "If you don't kill us, none of you would make it outta this hotel alive. You'd be lucky to even make it outta this room..." She let out a long sigh before she stared up at Riley, and a shadow crossed her face, "But just promise me one thing. I don't care how long it takes – kill all these fucking guys."

Dagur sniggered at the unlikelihood.

But he was the only one laughing.

"I'm not doing it," Jake finally shook his head, turning his scorched back on Mrs Roscoe to face Radek and Miranda. "I don't give a shit what you do to me anymore. Beat me. Burn me. Bash my skull in. I'm not killing my fucking mom."

"Then you can die with her," Miranda shrugged indifferently, smiling back at all the rage and anger contorting his face.

Radek hummed his disappointment, before lifting his sledgehammer.

"Wait!" Clay cried, holding up an imploring hand, pleading them both for more time. "Jake, I had no idea that *this* was gonna happen, but you don't have to die. Your mom... she doesn't have that much longer left to live anyway. Just look at how bad her condition has gotten. I get that you don't wanna do it, but you know it'd be a mercy for her – and for you. They'll let you live. Come on, make the smart choice."

"He's right, Jake," Mrs Roscoe's voice was as soft as a whisper, but her mind was as clear as ever. "I want this. And I want you to live, for me. I'll see you again one day, and I'll have Tommy to keep me company until then. We'll be waiting for you – for a long time, I hope. Thanks for taking care of me. But now it's time to let me go... You're the best son a mother could've ever asked for."

"Mom!?" Jake dropped his halberd, tears brimming in his eyes as he fell to his knees, not wanting to waste a single second of her moment of clarity. "Mom, I love –"

"NO!!" Clay shouted suddenly, kicking Jake to the floor, saving his friend from the deadly arc of Radek's swing. Having failed to convince Jake in time, Clay thrust his spear into

Mrs Roscoe's chest, piercing her through the heart before beseeching Radek and Miranda again, "Let him kill Heather instead! He'll do it!!"

Jake stared in stunned silence as his skewered mother slumped sideways onto the floor.

She gave him one last smile before the life left her eyes.

Roaring in outrage, Jake sprang to his feet and charged headlong into Clay, both former bounty hunters crashing on top of Heather, making her erupt with a guttural scream as a bolt of sharp pain shot up her bad leg.

"Taylor!!" Riley yelled, seizing her chance in all of the chaos.

The girl's gaze snapped away from her sister and locked on to Riley's hatchet as it cut through the air towards her forehead, and she ducked underneath the blade at the last possible instant, the axe sinking sideways into Kuba standing behind her, hacking through his midsection – just underneath his ribcage – bursting open his beefy belly with an explosion of bowels and blood.

"KILL THEM!" Radek bellowed furiously, cocking back his sledgehammer. "KILL THEM ALL!!"

CHAPTER 63

Still holding the hatchet, Riley stumbled over Taylor's legs as Kuba staggered backwards in surprise, slumping against the penthouse's door and sliding down with the axe blade embedded deep in his guts.

She was struggling to wrench her hatchet free, when the shadow of Radek's gigantic maul loomed over her, its silhouette painted across the wall rapidly receding as he swung down.

An icy bolt of adrenaline rushed through Riley's veins, and she flung herself sideways, ripping the stubborn axe blade free from Kuba's stomach with a sickening *squelch*.

The force of Radek's brutal blow shattered the dying man's thighbone, and with a croak of agony, Kuba abandoned his futile attempt to hold his entrails from spilling out.

Spurred back to life with new purpose, Batu leapt to his feet, headbutting Dagur in the chin, while Hanzo charged towards Aksel, whose hands shot up to catch the swing of his mace, both men violently wrestling for control over the bludgeon.

"Booth, we have a situation!" Miranda yelled into her walkie, rushing over to the nearest weapon rack with Dakota hard on her heels. "Get your fucking asses in here!!"

Still on the floor, Taylor spun around, kicking out with both of her feet in a frenzied effort to knock Jake and Clay off the top of her sister, while Heather screamed in pain underneath the weight of their scuffle.

"Dakota, behind you!" Barbara shouted a warning as Radek turned his attention towards the shield-bearing woman.

Whirling around, Dakota hoisted her wooden buckler in the air just in time, absorbing the blow from Radek's sledgehammer with a resounding *crack!*

Riley dashed across the room to her rescue, when she spotted Miranda pulling a short sword from the weapon rack. Veering off course, she hacked her hatchet at the woman's neck.

But Miranda blocked the blow with the flat of her blade, turning the axe aside to take a stab at Riley, forcing her to backpedal for distance.

"None of you have what it takes to be a champion," Miranda seethed as she pressed the attack, advancing with her free arm behind her back.

"Who said any of us wanted to be one?" Riley snarled, gripping her hatchet with both hands for a savage sideways slash at the woman's sword arm.

But Miranda parried the blow with ease, batting away the axe like it was nothing more than a mere annoyance.

"You wouldn't have survived that second arena if I was in there," the loathsome woman hissed, smacking Riley's bandaged cheek with the flat of her blade just to prove her point.

Miranda was too skilled with the sword.

For all Riley knew, the woman had spent every day up in this room practicing in the sweltering heat, honing her prowess.

If Riley wanted to win this battle, she would have to get creative.

"I doubt the shit outta that," Riley spat back, despite her cheek's bandage leaking blood. "You haven't had to fight for your life in a long time. I bet all this comfort and security has made you weak. Meanwhile, I've been living on the edge of death every fucking day."

With that, she lifted her hatchet for an overhead swing.

But Miranda blocked the blow yet again.

Just as Riley had predicted.

Seizing hold of the woman's sword arm, Riley sprang forward, swinging her boot out to hook her ankle behind Miranda's back leg just as their shoulders bashed together. Following through on her own momentum, Riley shoved the woman off balance, tripping her over and sending her reeling backwards into the dining table.

Miranda grunted in pain as platters of food leapt up at the impact, and she latched on to Riley's axe hand with her other arm.

Growling and snarling like a pair of feral beasts, the depths of their savagery surfaced as each woman struggled for superiority, both weapons rendered useless in the deadlock.

A thunderous *crash* against splintering wood somewhere behind Riley – too close for comfort – told her that Dakota was just barely fending off Radek's relentless assault.

She had to finish off Miranda quickly.

But the pinned woman was already drawing up her knees, trying to kick Riley off.

Riley strained to pull her weapon free, but no matter how hard she tried, she couldn't rip her axe hand out of Miranda's vise-like grip.

And with every passing moment, she was losing her leverage.

In a fit of mad desperation, Riley let her hatchet's handle slip down through her fingers, until the axe's blade was just above her fist. Then, flicking her wrist, she began bashing the butt of the handle into Miranda's face, each strike intensifying in force as the woman's grip began to falter against the unchecked knocks to her nose, cheeks and chin.

And then finally, Riley struck one of her eyeballs, and whether by instinct or idiocy, Miranda let go of her axe hand to shield her face.

Riley seized advantage of her momentary lapse in judgment, and with a vicious downward thrust, she drove the bottom of her hatchet into Miranda's mouth, smashing the front teeth out of the woman's cold cocksure grin.

"*Blood tribute to The Valkyrie,*" Riley growled, mocking the motto of all of Miranda's mindless minions, before raising the axe again and lopping off her sword hand. She caught hold of the woman's other arm as it flailed about in agony, pinning it to the table before she hacked that hand off as well, literally disarming her, before pulling Miranda upright to snarl in her ear, "I can't remember all the details of the *blood eagle*, but I'm pretty sure you're not allowed to scream if you wanna make it to Valhalla."

With that, Riley shoved the maimed woman headfirst into the blazing bonfire.

She screamed.

Long and loud and bone-chillingly horrible.

She screamed.

Riley took a second to scan her surroundings as Miranda's

shrieks faded in the flames.

Batu and Dagur were exchanging brutal blow for blow, both men seeming to enjoy the devastating duel, even as blood streamed down their faces, as if pain was the only feeling that either of them had left, with the handcuffed Red Tiger trading kicks and knee thrusts for the big silverback gorilla's heavy-handed hooks.

The guards from the security checkpoint were pounding against the penthouse's door, trying to force their way inside while Barbara braced her back against the entrance, the lit cigarette still lolling from her lips as she stole fleeting puffs of smoke in between every impact.

Sitting beside Barbara's feet, Heather searched and scrabbled for Kuba's stolen combat knife and the keys to their handcuffs, her arms still shackled behind her back as her fingers fumbled blindly over his disemboweled corpse.

Only a few feet away, Taylor was holding one of Clay's hands down, while Jake beat his former friend senseless in a vengeful rage over his dead mother.

"Riley, Dakota!" Hanzo shouted through clenched teeth as Aksel hit him with a cheap shot, gaining the upper hand over him, dangerously close to wrestling the mace out of his grip. "Help her!!"

Riley was about to rush over to Hanzo's aid, when she heard the other half of his plea.

CRASH!!

She whipped her head around to see Dakota falling among the wreckage of one of the weapon racks, with dozens of blades and bludgeons clattering to the floor all around her.

Dakota held up what remained of her splintered shield against Radek's sledgehammer, groaning as she spent the last ounce of her strength to hold off one final swing of his ruthless attack.

"Hey, motherfucker!!" Riley called for his attention, his distracted swing glancing off the remnants of Dakota's shield as he whirled around. She jerked her head towards Miranda's body smoldering in the bonfire, "Did I pass the loyalty test?"

Radek's gaze burned red with rage, his blood boiling into a berserker's frenzy.

Roaring his wrath, he took an underhand swing at Riley's chin.

She sidestepped the strike, the huge hammer's head whooshing past her cheek.

Without a pause, Radek turned his gigantic maul in midair, slashing sideways next.

Pulse pounding in her ears, Riley ducked underneath the deadly arc, weaving in closer with her hatchet to take a chop at one of his thighs before hacking at his hip in quick succession.

But both cuts were too shallow to slow him down.

In fact, it seemed that the flesh wounds only served to enrage him even further.

Winding up for another chop, Riley aimed for one of his elbows, knowing that he needed both arms to wield his weapon.

But Radek anticipated the attack, blocking the blow with the long handle of his sledgehammer.

She cocked back her axe for another swing, when one of his hands suddenly shot out, seizing her by the throat and lifting her up into the air, her boots kicking in protest before he hurled her like a ragdoll over the dining table.

Riley crashed to the floor on the other side, dashing the back of her head against the floorboards with the coppery taste of blood in her mouth.

She was clambering to her feet again, when in the corner of her eye, Radek leapt up onto the table, bellowing an animalistic howl, his long braided hair swinging wildly like an unhinged Neanderthal, before raising his sledgehammer high and launching towards her with a brutal death blow.

Riley tripped over her own feet as she scrambled out of the way, the massive maul crashing down through the floorboards in her wake with enough force to shake the entire room.

Radek grunted as he tried to wrench his weapon free from the floor.

Seizing the opportunity, Riley shot upright, hacking at the side of his neck.

But her axe blade came in at an angle, slashing the back of his shoulder instead.

Snarling spittle, she reared back and went in for another swing, when Radek jerked his maul up out of the floorboards in an explosion of splinters.

He whirled around with an unprecedented burst of strength and speed, and their weapons clashed with enough force to snap her hatchet in half and send the axe head flying across the room.

Riley's pupils dilated as she glanced down at the broken haft in her hand.

Her only option now was to bludgeon him to death.

Tightening her grip around the handle, she smashed his face with the splintered end, hitting him hard across the cheek.

But with his mind buried deep within his berserker rage, Radek barely even felt a thing.

Grabbing Riley by the throat again, he lifted her up into the air before slamming her down on top of the dining table, dragging her headfirst up its length while she madly thrashed and thwacked at his sinewy arm with her broken hatchet's handle, to no effect.

It was almost as if Radek was completely immune to her attacks.

With her free hand, Riley scrabbled madly for a knife or a plate or *something* that she could use while platters of food crashed to the floor on either side.

The backwards slide stopped abruptly at the head of the table, and Radek wrenched the snapped axe handle out of Riley's grasp, cracking her across the forehead with the makeshift bludgeon before tossing it aside with a clatter.

Riley blinked through her daze to see him hoisting his maul again, poising to cave in her skull with one final swing.

Stunned, but too stubborn to surrender, Riley rolled up her legs and double-kicked him in the chest, sending him stumbling backwards as she tumbled out onto the floor, sprawling over his chair on her way down.

Untangling herself from the fallen chair, she keeled over onto her back, panting hard as she tried to sit up again.

But before she could even rise, a shadow flashed down over her eyes, and within the same instant, a solid bar rammed lengthways against her throat, yanking her backwards and smashing the base of her skull onto the floorboards.

Radek's knees swam in her peripheral vision as he choked her with the handle of his sledgehammer.

Squirming underneath the immense weight laid across her windpipe, Riley struggled to push back against the bar to break free of the hold, her legs thrashing wildly with her neck pinned to the floor.

"I made it so fucking easy for all of you," Radek growled as he throttled her. "All you had to do was kill somebody who was gonna die anyway."

Riley's strength was fading fast.

Still holding the suffocating bar with one hand, she reached towards the fallen chair with her other arm, but her gloved fingertips could barely brush against the chair's top rail before she started seeing stars, her oxygen-deprived gaze beginning to blur.

A streak of red clouded her vision as her muscles involuntarily gave way, the blood vessels of her eyes bursting under the asphyxiation, her entire body shutting down.

Riley's mind flooded with a burst of memories as she was filled with a strange sense of inner warmth.

Eating peanut butter and jelly sandwiches with her father after school.

The sight of her mother wrapping her arms around Grandma Eleanor.

Keith Bowman's colorful string of curses at the sight of his bullet-riddled truck.

She was dying.

All of her happy memories spun together, culminating into a single bright light.

Riley Armstrong floated towards the center of its dazzling radiance, when she heard Heather's voice interrupting her ascension, with a strange phrase from only a few days ago.

"You look like you could use a bath," came the woman's husky tone.

A hot gush against Riley's face sent her descending down into darkness again.

She blinked herself back into the mortal realm to see Heather shoving Radek aside, with Kuba's stolen combat knife protruding from the base of his neck as the fiery redhead kicked the sledgehammer off Riley's throat.

Riley gasped for air, but only for a moment, retching at the realization that Heather had bathed her face with Radek's blood, the hot gush drizzling down into her mouth.

"I was going for his skull," Heather casually rued the aim of her lifesaving stab, her hands still cuffed behind her back. "Looks like I slashed his spinal cord instead."

Radek was lying on his side only a few feet away, growling and groaning and thrashing his head around.

But that was all that he could do.

CHAPTER 64

Riley lurched to her hands and knees, sucking in sweet lungfuls of air as she crawled towards the paralyzed berserker.

"You said *only the strong survive*," she could barely manage a whisper as she loomed over Radek, her throat stinging raw after almost being choked to death. "Looks like my team's stronger than yours."

Together on the floor, they gazed around the room.

Batu and Dagur had battled their way over to a weapon rack, both of their chins and chests coated with their own blood as they tore a pair of swords from the medieval array of blades and bludgeons.

Dagur held the advantage over the chained prisoner, the thickset onyx ogre of a man viciously thrusting his sword through Batu's midsection, making him fall to his knees.

But on his way down, even while wielding the weapon behind his back, Batu drove his own sword through the top of Dagur's foot, before flicking his blade upwards, impaling the hulking henchman's chin as the muscle-bound monster went down, the two men roaring their victory until their voices faded in one last primal attempt to determine who won the fight before they both bled out.

Hollering in tear-streaked rage, Jake swung his halberd down into Clay's chest before finally collapsing beside his dead mother, his scorched back glistening red in the light of the bonfire as he sobbed in grief and pain and sorrow.

Taylor struggled to her feet the moment she spotted Hanzo on the floor, with Aksel finally wrestling the mace free from his grip.

He savagely kicked the downed man in the face, before looking around the room for his allies, soon realizing that the battle was already lost.

The rangy guard ran for the door, aiming a rushed sideswipe at Taylor – who ducked underneath the mace's swing – on his way past.

Aksel drove his shoulder into Barbara next, bowling her over and kicking Kuba's corpse to one side, before ripping the door open, letting the checkpoint guards storm in.

"Shit!" Heather ducked for cover behind the dining table. "Everybody, get down!!"

Radek laughed aloud as Taylor, Hanzo and Barbara scrambled for safety.

But Jake wouldn't leave his mother's side.

And Dakota wasn't moving at all.

Riley glowered back at the guards from her crouch beside Radek.

They were both armed with real weapons – each one holding a pistol.

"What the hell are you waiting for!?" Aksel growled, shaking his mace towards Taylor as she took cover behind a sideboard. "Shoot these fucking traitors!!"

But they simply stood in the doorway, staring around at the

veritable bloodbath.

Miranda's corpse was crackling in the bonfire.

Dagur had fallen silent, slumped beside Batu.

And Radek couldn't lift a finger to save his life.

CRACK!

Aksel's skull snapped backwards, and his body flopped onto the floor, his head lolling to one side with a bullet hole in between his eyes.

"*Desk jockeys*, huh?" the gunman growled bitterly, lowering his pistol as he entered the Viking-themed penthouse. Stopping in between Aksel and Kuba's corpses, he locked eyes with Radek across the room, "Fuck you and your fetish for the Dark Ages. You're done. We quit. We don't work for you anymore."

Backing up her partner, the other checkpoint guard fished into the collar of her shirt, producing a necklace with the same upside down hammer pendant worn by all of Radek's minions, and she snapped off the clasp before tossing it into the bonfire, as a symbolic declaration of freedom.

"That's what happens when you force loyalty on people," Riley whispered hoarsely into Radek's ear as his whole world crumbled around him. "Nobody wants to be a fucking servant."

Ripping her combat knife from the back of his neck, she slammed the blade down through his temple, putting a bloody end to his Viking way of life.

CHAPTER 65

"Who the hell are you guys?" Taylor demanded, even as one of the checkpoint guards unlocked her handcuffs.

"Disgruntled employees," the man snorted at his own joke. "Well, ex-employees, now."

"Everybody was sick of being treated like second-class citizens," the woman offered a better explanation. "So when word got out that most of Dagur's crew got wiped out in the plaza, and since the convoy that went after those diesel thieves still hasn't come back yet, the hotel's workers started a rebellion. It's all over the radio chatter. Miranda's call for help set it off. Anybody who was still loyal to Radek is either hightailing it outta here, or they're already dead."

"How come we didn't hear anything?" Riley wondered, glancing down at the remains of Miranda's body burning in the bonfire as if in answer to her own question, before remembering that Aksel had also been wearing a walkie.

"I dunno what to tell you," the first guard shrugged as he helped Heather out of her handcuffs. "Maybe they dialed down the volume for the dinner that you guys were supposed to be having."

Studying the skepticism lining their faces, the second guard surrendered her weapon, laying her handgun down on the floor, with her partner soon following suit.

"That's good enough for me," Barbara decided, bending down to pick up the discarded pair of pistols. She jerked her head over towards the dining table, "Help yourselves to some food."

"I kinda don't trust your judgment when it comes to people, Barbs," Heather leveled her accusation with a wry smile as the pair of guards hungrily descended on the feast. "Weren't you the one who said that us girls just don't have it in us to eat at the same table – sharing the same food – with somebody we're about to stab in the back? Look at how that turned out."

She pointedly glanced down at Radek, prodding at his lifeless head with her good foot.

"Fuck, Heather," Riley couldn't help but snicker, her own face freshly painted with the man's blood.

"So, what happens now?" Dakota groaned as she stirred back to her senses, extracting herself from the mess of fallen weapons.

"I have no idea," Barbara admitted, staring around at all of the death in the room. "I thought you'd know better than me. My involvement in any of the plans always stopped at the point of Kentaro taking over. But now, with him and Batu gone... your guess is as good as mine."

"Batu's gone?" Hanzo echoed as he clambered to his feet, gazing across the room at Batu's bloody corpse lying beside Dagur's. He heaved a heavy sigh as he looked over at Dakota, "We're the last ones left."

"There's gonna be a power vacuum if somebody doesn't take charge," Riley reckoned, with the remainder of Radek's men on the run and the Red Tigers all but gone. "If you don't decide on somebody to take the lead now, somebody else is gonna decide for you."

"I don't think we're cut out for it," Dakota confessed, bowing her head at the sight of Kentaro's corpse. "We wouldn't even know where to start."

"Yeah, we're better as soldiers," Hanzo nodded in agreement. He sniffed and turned his gaze towards the ceiling as he added, "And now that all the fighting's done, I'd prefer to just honor the dead."

"What about Barbs, then?" Taylor suggested, frowning in encouragement even as the leathery woman shook her head. "Why not? Everybody knows you. Everybody likes you. Motherfucker, I like you, and I don't like anybody."

"I dunno – I think I'd feel better about it if Lincoln was still around," Barbara tightened her lips, turning away from being thrust with the sudden responsibility. "Maybe one of you girls would be better suited for all this. Or Jake – he's a strapping young man – choose him."

Jake shook his head, his breath still hitching in silent sobs as he cradled his dead mother, not even daring to glance over at Clay's corpse in the aftermath of his blind wrath, only now realizing that his friend had just wanted to save Jake's life.

"Like we told you outside that sheriff's office – we're just passing through," Riley replied on behalf of herself and the Seabrook sisters, rejecting the offer. "The city's all yours. We'll be taking one of those armored trucks off your hands though."

"Take me with you," Jake mumbled, blinking back his tears as he pleaded Riley. "I don't wanna stay here anymore."

"I think the person who doesn't want power is the best

suited for it," one of the checkpoint guards interjected as he looked up at Barbara from a platter of steak, the cold meat's juice dribbling down his chin. "Maybe we can help with bearing some of the burden. You know everybody out there. We know everybody in here. Believe me – nobody wants another Radek in charge."

Barbara's fingers trembled as she reached for the box of cigarettes in her breast pocket.

She lit up one of her death sticks, taking a long and shaky draw.

"That was the deal, right?" she stared at Riley through the plume of smoke, "An armored truck and a full tank of diesel."

Riley glanced sidelong at Heather, and they both nodded.

"I'll give it to you," Barbara promised, before her gaze turned downcast. "But first, I'm gonna need some good people like yourselves to help me run this shit show – for a little while, at least."

Riley stepped towards the head of the table, laying down her combat knife and peeling the gloves off her hands as she considered the proposal.

She had no idea how Barbara intended on keeping the colony going, especially without Radek's network of suppliers.

But the community of survivors in the marketplace had been getting by just fine.

Under Barbara's leadership, the Valhalla Hotel could become a safe haven for any survivors struggling to stay alive on the road, and a stronghold against any raiders who came cruising into town.

And Riley's chances of getting back to California in one piece would certainly improve if she and the Seabrook sisters lingered long enough to recruit a few more allies to join them.

"Alright, I trust you," Riley finally gave Barbara an answer, admitting the words that she never thought she'd hear herself speak again. "Besides, I've got something that I need to take care of before we can leave." She held Jake's blank stare for a moment before turning her gaze between Heather and Taylor, "There's this kid named Sam back at the Jade Mantis. We promised we'd help him find out what happened to his mom."

* * *

Riley's story will continue.

Flip the page and follow me to find out when the next book gets published!

Find out what happens next!

Thank you so much for reading Cutthroats of The Fall. I hope you enjoyed the story.

Join my newsletter here to receive an email when the next book gets published!
www.steveheuzinkveld.com/newsletter

I'd also like to invite you to my Book Fans Facebook Group. Chat with me, have a character named after you, talk with other fans, and win exclusive prizes and giveaways.
Join the fun!
www.facebook.com/groups/SteveHeuzinkveldVIPFans

Here's a QR code so you don't have to type out any links:

ACKNOWLEDGMENTS

As always, first and foremost, I want to thank my beautiful wife, Hariezoy, for supporting me and encouraging me every single day, and for giving me the freedom to burn the midnight oil to hit the keyboard every night until the sun comes up.

I'd like to thank Robert Call and Richard Badgley for their expert insight into describing the interior of an armored truck. It's unsurprisingly difficult to find any publicly available information on the topic, and I've probably looked up armored truck interiors so many times that I've ended up on some kind of watch list!

A big salute goes to all of my fellow authors who keep in semi-regular contact – ranging from daily to twice a year. When you're in a field without coworkers, it's nice to have a support network that you can lean on and celebrate the little wins with in between book launches so that we're always excited to keep on doing what we love.

I also want to give a massive shout-out to Andrada Vasia Nane, Tamara Louise, Jordy Bartel, Lisa Eu, Paul Slater, Rachel Jones, Leslie Schneider Beard and Martine West. Thank you so much for sharing my books across social media in the various reading communities and convincing other readers to embark on the same thrilling adventure. I screenshot your posts and use them for motivation – they honestly make my day!

And last but not least, thank you. As an independently-published author, this is very often a one-man show, and after the hours upon hours I've invested into this project, it means the world to me that you've taken the time to meet the characters living in my head.

Be sure to follow me on Amazon to receive a notification when my next book releases!

www.amazon.com/Steve-Heuzinkveld/e/B09FZFK2XW

P.S. I love hearing from my fans - feel free to contact me any time!

-Steve

author@SteveHeuzinkveld.com

www.SteveHeuzinkveld.com